69 SHADES OF KINK

BIG BOOK OF EXPLICIT DIRTY EROTICA SHORT STORIES

KELLIE GRANIER

plicit Press
Erotica Fiction

CHAPTER 1

A FRUITY AFFAIR
(PLAYTIME...)

ZOE GIGGLES as she raises her legs and settles her feet into the silk covering their bed. Ethan, her hotter than should be legal Canadian husband is already soaking the rubber fruit they had purchased for the purpose of some creative pleasure in bed. The grapes, strawberries, pears, bananas, guavas, and large mango are all perfect in color and size. They are made of the firm rubber used in the making of penis replicas, and so they seem the perfect play-mates for this afternoon of pussy plundering. Curiosity had always been an integral part of Ethan and Zoe's sex life.

The pillows propped up behind her mean that Zoe has a good view of her cunt. She can see clearly what her husband is going to do to her. He has already removed a few of the purple grapes from the warm water they soak in, to give the rubber a slightly softer edge. The grapes aren't big enough for her pussy to need any additional lubrication, but to send them into her dry would probably be a little uncom-fortable. The three orbs are held tight in the palm of one hand and Ethan moves towards his wife's pussy with his tongue. He licks her clit and then drives his tongue into her vagina so that he can encourage its natural lubrication.

Pulling on her clitoris with his lips has her moaning and pushing herself into his mouth. It's clear that she is aroused now, but the question is whether the inside of her cunt is ready for some play. Ethan sends a finger into her and waits a minute, almost as if he is trying to read her temperature. The heat is inviting. But this isn't about his cock. At least not yet! He moves his finger around inside her for a while, until her cunt starts to produce enough liquid to make the next step acceptable. They exchange a look between them that words cannot articulate. There have been a lot of firsts that have passed between them. This was another one. Their arousal is laced with apprehension and some anxiety, but the possibilities are so exciting that going ahead is the only option.

Ethan removes his finger from inside Zoe and immediately a rubbery grape is inserted. He goes on and inserts the other two, and then gently pushes them all the way up inside her. Happy that they are far enough up her vagina he proceeds to give her cunt a generous lick. He sucks on it in a mock attempt to extract the grapes now. Zoe responds by pushing them towards his mouth using the forces within. Ethan pulls on her pussy, arousing her all the more. It takes just a few determined sucks and the first of the grapes pops into his mouth. The second and third follow shortly thereafter... Instead of removing them from his mouth though, he uses his powerful tongue to push them right back from whence they came. They repeat this several times until Zoe has her first orgasm.

Pleased with the achievement, Ethan looks for an indication from his wife as to whether he should proceed. She twists herself towards him and takes his cock into her mouth as he removes the grapes from his. He bends forward and gives her cunt a few gentle licks, careful not to lick too much of the natural lubrication off of it. He takes one of the rubber strawberries, warm from the bowl. He thrusts his cock deep into her mouth as he carefully lets the fruit fill up the entrance to her pussy. The strawberry slides into Zoe easily, even at the bulging base of it, and Ethan is careful about not letting the entire unusual shape disappear into his wife. He just keeps fucking her gently with it while she sucks progressively harder on his dick.

The strawberry gets wetter and wetter with its movement in and out of Zoe, and Ethan licks up some of the excesses occasionally. The fruit is pinched tightly between his fingers now as it slips all the way inside her, along with some of his thumb and index. Her vagina has become a lot more giving and so the movement in and out of it is almost effortless. Zoe slaps herself on the inside of her thighs as she takes Ethan's cock completely into her mouth and sucks harder still on it. Her pussy has made a steady progression towards a second orgasm and, reaching it, she moves her head off the sheets and into Ethan's dick so that his balls rest on her lips for the totality of her consumption of his cock. He continues fucking her with the strawberry until she has swallowed his first load and he has pulled out and licked up her second.

With his first orgasm out of the way, he has a new patience. This is going to be needed for the next elevation in their experimentation. He pulls a guava from the bowl and examines it. It is a rather large fruit in comparison to the grapes and strawberry, but its girth isn't too much unlike a rather large cock. Not Ethan's of course, his dick modest by all standards, but not impossible.

The surface of the fruit is perfect, with no leafy or

thorny bits. So he settles it on her cunt and then covers the base of it with his palm. Removing his cock from her mouth, he adjusts himself so that he is half next to her and half on top of her, their faces aligned. He starts to kiss her as he moves his hand in small circles over the guava, pushing down on it at the same time. Zoe grabs the sheets between her fingers and squeezes down hard despite the gentleness with which her husband progresses with his vaginal invasion.

The circles remain constant even as the pressure increases. Ethan lifts his mouth from Zoe's occasionally to check the progress of the guava in her *guava*. Halfway to full entry he lets up the pressure and returns to kissing his wife. He continues with the circles though and lets them widen despite the tight squeeze. Zoe's cunt gets ever the hungrier for the fruit and suddenly, and without notice, her hand is on Ethan's and she pushes down hard on it while lifting herself off the bed. The fruit lodges quite firmly in her cunt, completely enveloped by the pussy that now has her man's palm flat on its surface. He gives her a surprised look and she shies away. He pulls her face to his with his mouth and nose and kisses her to indicate how impressed he is.

He moves down to examine the area and finds that Zoe's pussy has completely closed over the guava, trapping it inside. This isn't altogether involuntary as she is controlling all the muscles in her vagina to move the fruit up and down against her walls. Ethan adds three of his fingers to this mix, one at a time though until the hot mess inside her is one huge pleasure party. Without giving it too much thought he reaches for the banana, large and long. He can't remove his fingers from her cunt, the feeling of the inside of it sending shard after shard of pleasure to his cock. He places the banana next to Zoe and reaches for the jar of body butter. She helps open it and the smell of citrus fills the room. Ethan's free hand dips the banana into the jar and then positions it on her asshole. They make the needed adjustments so that he is between her legs and her legs are resting on his neck.

The banana enters her ass with a little more difficulty than the guava had done in her cunt. But with determined and repetitive thrusting it is soon a quarter of the way inside her. As the contents of her cunt mix to become a third orgasm, the banana slides halfway into her tight butt. The loud screaming that accompanies her third orgasm is enough of a sign for Ethan to let her have the rest of the banana, and all eight inches of it lodge deep inside her as she has a massive fucking orgasm. He fucks her ass with the firm fruit while removing his fingers from her fanny and then letting her eject the guava herself. The sight has him adjust again so that his cock is in her mouth, the banana locked in her ass by the bed as he drops her completely on the sheets and licks gently on her clit.

Once she has come down from her cloud Ethan pulls his cock from her mouth. He knows it will be a while before he can cum again and so there is no pressure for this to happen between her lips. He turns his woman over and works her gently with the banana. Her ass gets more and more elastic with each deep entry, each penetrative stroke. Zoe reaches for the bowl without looking and feels around in the warm water. She pulls out the mango and giggles loudly. Ethan looks up and watches as she takes a generous amount of butter from the jar and coats the top of the fucking huge mango. He watches as she moves it underneath herself and lifts her ass into the banana fucking her. He listens as she moans loudly, forcing the smallest part of the fruit into her cunt from below. He fucks her harder with the banana, as though it had the same nerve endings as his dick, while he lets his imagination inform him of what is going on just out of sight.

A loud groan escapes Zoe as the mango settles inside her. Ethan has to see and so he removes the banana gently and turns her to her side. He is behind her but has a clear view of her cunt. No mango in sight. He can't believe it. He has her on her back and lifts her legs towards her breasts. Backward and forward he moves them until sure enough, out births the mango. He takes it in his hand, and after giving his wife's cunt a few kisses, reinserts it, slowly, gently. He is rock hard at the sight. With the mango back inside her he returns her to her side, and instead of the rubber banana inserts his own meat stick into her ass. He reaches for her pussy and blocks the entrance with his palm as he fucks her ass hard.

It takes a half an hour of solid fucking for him to reach the beginnings of an orgasm. As he gets closer and closer, he raises Zoe's leg and moves it up and down while she pushes on the contents of her cunt from within. By the time Ethan is ejaculating masses of cum into her ass, the mango is exiting her pussy and his fingers are ripping the punani to shreds, bringing her to what feels like a million simultaneous orgasms. They collapse into the silk and can't move for a while... Then Ethan remembers the pears!

CHAPTER 2

A HARD-EARNED BUTTON

THE WEDDING HAD BEEN BEAUTIFUL. Not all the pomp and circumstance that ends up sucking all of the joy out of it for most couples. Just a perfect day on the beach with a handful of friends and family, and although it had been beautifully simplistic, it was nevertheless exhausting. "The dresses, flowers, and oh my God, the parents! I have no clue how brides deal with the stress of a big wedding, this kicked my ass," Tori exclaimed. She flopped onto the bed, completely oblivious to the grandiosity of the hotel room. The manner in which Nick removed his cumbersome tie said he agreed. She stepped out of her flowing gown and into the shower, leaving it puddled on the floor. Nick entered the spacious enclosure behind her, taking his new wife into his arms, and together they let the warm water wash the day's stress away. Nick massaged her shoulders feeling the knotted muscles release against his masterful touch before Tori stepped out and wrapped her weary body in a soft thirsty towel. Too sleepy to unpack Tori opted to lie down and rest while Nick finished his shower. When he came out, he found his love sound asleep, her wet curls draped across the soft white pillowcase. Pausing a moment to adore the angelic view he kissed her forehead and covered her naked body before snuggling in beside her.

Awakened by the spying of a tropical sunrise Tori stood at the uncovered French doors admiring a view so marvelous even a postcard couldn't challenge it. Lost in its beauty and serenity she didn't sense Nick approach from behind and was slightly startled as he wrapped his arms around her waist and kissed her neck. "Morning love," he said. She leaned back into his embrace enraptured in the perfect morning greeting as she pressed her naked body against his. "Sorry I crashed on you last night" she replied. She had nothing to apologize for, her needs were his reason for living, yet he teased, "How about you make it up to me?" lightly brushing her perfect ass with his growing erection. "Maybe later" she returned his banter, turning quickly away from him as she exaggerated her sexy walk across the room, tossing her disheveled locks. He laughed as he pursued her, scooping her up and tossing her onto the bed. Looking into one another's eyes, they shared a lover's giggle as their stare became more serious. He pressed against her, his strength overpowering her. As she gasped, his tongue slipped into her mouth in a violent kiss. Breathless, she turned away exposing her neck to his animal magnetism. He raked his teeth across her throat as he raised her arms above her head. He flashed that knock-out smile that had always gotten him anything he wanted. Her body filled with anticipation as warm moisture grew between her legs. The playful struggle became a writhing beneath him. So aroused by her own resistance, the eroticism of being dominated by him increased her need to have him inside her. Using his knee to spread her legs she complied with the man that possessed her. His erection tentatively pressed against her opening, the creamy moisture he'd created urging him to enter. She shifted her hips upward; her body's need for him was her only motivation as she wrapped her legs around his waist. He slid his engorged dick all around her silken folds, concentrating on her sensitive nub. Waves of passion crashed within her. He felt her desperation to be fucked immediately and chuckled. "Patience love" he teased. Completely owned by the pleasure that only this man could provide her she whimpered. Convinced he would make her wait, she was caught off guard when he thrust his entire length inside her until he was completely sheathed by her pussy. He filled her completely, his every movement deliciously drawing her closer to climax. Her tight walls encased him so firmly she could actually feel his load moving within him. Nothing had ever aroused her so. His rocking became faster and harder, burying his gifted cock so deep inside her. The sensation became almost unbearably pleasurable. Neither one is able to fight it any longer their bodies united in release.

Her pussy clamping down in reward of his skill and pouring her satisfaction all over him as he pumped her full of his.

I love him so much, Tori thought, squeezing the blood from Nick's hand as she nervously waited to board the plane. She was terrified of flying, so naturally, Nick's wedding gift to her was a honeymoon in Hawaii. He, of course, was as cool as a cucumber flipping through the latest edition of Car & Driver while she fidgeted with the sequins on her "bride" t-shirt. "You'll be fine, love" he comforted, wrapping her loose blond curl around his finger. Nauseated beyond human comprehension, she just nodded, all the while planning on spending the entire flight throwing back cocktails. Tori was pacing the concourse when the announcement was made: "Flight 1031 non-stop to Honolulu now boarding" causing Nick to take her hand and lead her on their journey to paradise.

Jill, Tori's maid of honor, had been right, the "bride and groom" t-shirts she'd given them got the newlyweds an instant upgrade to first-class even though Nick refused to wear his. This flight might not be bad at all, she thought until she felt the thrust of the engines upon take off. She needed a drink, and she needed to update her Facebook status, she told him in a tone more serious than even Nick could believe. The flight attendant giggled overhearing Tori's distress call and assured her that as soon as they reached altitude she would bring her a cocktail and allow her to turn her cell back on. Tori felt a bit embarrassed but was consoled by her small talk. Before she knew it she was sipping champagne and had her seatbelt unbuckled. While Tori was wrapped up in social networking, Nick snuck away to the restroom. Her tweeting was interrupted by a text message - "cum 2 the lavatory" it read.

Grinning like a Cheshire cat, she sauntered down the aisle and softly rapped on the door.

Nick opened the door and salaciously pulled her in. She literally laughed out loud covering her cackle with her hand as she noticed everyone in earshot staring as she tripped through the door. Tori knew he was up to no good, but was astounded to find him buck-naked in the claustrophobic bathroom. "Mile high club," he said wiggling his perfectly rounded little ass as if he had to try to seduce her. She pulled off her snug black tee and shimmied out of her mini skirt revealing a completely sheer bra and matching thong the precise shade of her eyes, Caribbean blue. Leaving on her black pumps Tori stalked her lover, his eyes regaling the delicate bounce of her breasts as she approached. As he sat on the edge of the seat flaunting his full erection, she lifted her flawless leg positioning her spikey heel against his chest, and shoved him back before straddling him. He could feel the heat radiating from her moist flower as it opened against his thigh. Her nipples, so hard, battled the silken barrier inhibiting her lover's contact until Nick opened the menacing brassiere and raised her soft mound to suckle. Although Nick initiated their escapade, Tori relished the opportunity to be the aggressor. "Baby lay back and let me fuck you," she purred as she stood and turned her back to him squirming out of her panties before lowering her throbbing pussy onto his cock. He was substantially thick and filled her petite frame completely. She began to rock her hips against his, driving his shaft to its ultimate depth, his pubis softly caressing her clit with every stroke. Her growing need turned her movements furious until she was slamming her aching cunt upon him demanding its sweet release. Finally, her quivering walls milked his ejaculation covering him in velvety delight. "That was incredible love," he professed lifting her hair and blowing a sated breath against her fevered neck. Tori giggled and mussed Nick's as they shared the smile that only lovers share before getting dressed and leaving the makeshift love nest. Holding hands and laughing they took the walk of shame back to their seats to a chorus of catcalls both real and imagined.

Tori swore that her fear of flying was cured by a single injection of testosterone and vowed to have one every time she flew. Needless to say, the happy couple enjoyed the rest of their flight savoring a succulent meal above the Neptunian abyss before paradise was visible through their window seat. Once they landed, the flight attendant winked and discreetly slipped something into Tori's hand. Once she disappeared from sight Tori opened her hand to find a dainty heart-shaped button reading "mile-high club," she snickered and proudly pinned it to her shirt.

CHAPTER 3

A LITTLE KINK IS A GOOD THING

ANY COUPLE WILL TELL you that things can get a little stale at times. It is because of this that things have to be spiced up from time to time. Beth and Tony have been married for nearly twenty-five years. Things are still as fresh in the way of sex as they were the night they were married. It has been a perpetual changing up of things that have allowed the couple to remain fresh.

One time both of them had the chance to be off on the same day. They decided to head to the park for a picnic. It was a beautiful day and they were determined to spend it together and get the most out of the day. Beth had taken great care as to pack a lunch that they both would like. This was the first chance that their schedules allowed them to spend time together. Tony knew that something had to be done before their relationship was destroyed. This was the purpose of the picnic. No work, no computers, nothing - just a couple spending the day together being a married couple.

. . .

They found a place that they could sit and get a perfect view of the lake. It was nice to just sit there and enjoy the ducks that were swimming across the lake as well as seeing other people just like them all living their life and being in love with one another. Tony leaned over and asked Beth if she was in the mood to do something naughty. Beth was up for almost anything that Tony had in mind.

Beth whispered back to her husband, "What if me and you were to have sex right here right now, in front of all these people? Come on it'll be fun! The thrill of knowing all these people are watching you screw me silly and the fact that the cops could come and arrest us, the thought alone is making me all wet in just thinking about it. What do you say? " Beth pulled her skirt up a little to expose her panties. There was a wet spot that had formed. Beth then took her panties and pulled them aside to expose her shaved cunt. Tony could tell that she was wet.

"Come on big man you know you want to eat my pussy, your lips are wet from the thought of you diving between my legs right here and eating me out like the dirty whore I am."

Beth began to finger her cunt, making sure to pull out and lick her fingers and tasting her pure essence that was oozing from her loins. Finally, Tony had to act on the urge. He went over and laid her on her back while he dove between her legs and began to take in all of her juices. She was so wet by the time that he got there that some of her juices had flowed down her cunt and had made a wet spot on the grass underneath her. Tony took time as to explore every crease and fold of his wife's slit. He drove his tongue as deep into her as he could, he wanted to make sure that he got every ounce of her juices that he could. Beth grabbed his head and drove her cunt into his face. Tony had been with his wife enough to know that the next thing to happen was that she was going to remove her top and have her husband use and abuse her D cup breasts. Sure enough about a minute after he was driven into her muff, Beth removed her top and began to twist and pull on her nipples. Tony continued to soak in the sweet nectar that was pouring from his wife's sweet cunt. Tony headed up into the position that he was able to slide in and out of his wife with his cock. It was not his length but his girth that allowed him the chance to be able to drive any woman into a frenzy by the sensation of him rubbing the inside walls of her cunt. Tony was careful to make sure that he was giving his wife the pleasure that she needed so badly from a man.

There was a bit of excitement that was going through him as he saw that there were a number of people in and around where they were located. Tony to a degree hoped that they would get caught as he saw this as being a very hot thing to have happen. Tony kept going in and out causing his wife to let out little moans with each thrust that he gave his wife. The sensation of this was getting both of them to the point that they were about to get to the point of no return. Finally, Tony was not able to withstand any longer and had to unleash his cum deep into his wife. Finally, his wife loses with her own earth-shattering orgasm. Both of them looked around and saw that there were a few people that were standing around watching. Tony was almost proud of himself as to what he had just done in public with his own wife.

· · ·

This was the secret that these two had for keeping their relationship fresh. Many couples would never know the joy that Tony and his wife experienced.

CHAPTER 4

A STEP TOO FAR

DIANE WAS an achiever at work and it showed. Consistently at the top of the sales rankings, she dominated the division and her mixture of assertiveness and charm had marked her out for bigger things. Of course, there were frustrations, but it was a good life, with good rewards.

In her family life she was content too, although Sam, her husband was a little too passive for her. He was an accountant. In one way, Sam was a brilliant partner but in another, his lack of assertiveness disappointed her and she couldn't think what about that annoyed her. Most women she knew would kill for a partner like Sam and that thought usually made her smile. A combination of factors had upset her today and she was not handling it well. A big deal had fallen through and that had pissed her off greatly. There was a sales conference tomorrow and she had ducked out 90 minutes early, to get her bags packed and get mentally in the zone.

. . .

As she walked through the door, the house was untidy and although the kids were at their grandparents for the week, Sam hadn't tidied. It was no good, she had to admit to herself, she was really angry.

"Sam", she rasped, what have you been doing all day?" He came from the kitchen, dirty and sweaty, and just looked at her. The look should have told her that she should be careful, but she wasn't looking for it and it passed her by. By this time, her blood was up. "I've had a terrible day and you've done nothing here, the kids are away and I thought that you would respect me a little more than to leave me this fucking mess to come home to."

Sam then did something that surprised her, he lost his temper. It was so unlike him and she almost reeled back. "How dare you! First of all, I cleared the garden and I was just coming in for a shower, and then I was going to tidy up. Secondly, I am not your servant, and don't address me as one. And thirdly, who made you boss in this house?"

Her blood was boiling after that tirade, but not with anger. Something else had replaced it, a burning sensation. His bronzed sweaty, dirty body and the way he had treated her like a naughty girl, made her remember why she was so turned on by him in her youth. His passion and manliness awoke a naughty side in her. "Why don't you tell me who is boss then?"

· · ·

The truth was Sam was angry at her as often he was the lightning rod of her discontent. During these times, he struggled to make his voice heard. Clearly, things were different today. Her look was that of a woman who wanted to be tamed and after a day in the soil he was feeling up to the task.

"I am the boss in this house and don't you forget it" The words came out without thinking and her responsive face robbed them of their silliness.

"Oh yeah?" she replied, "Show me." He was on her in an instant dragging her to the sofa, furiously, wildly kissing her. Diane was lost as his dirty hands ruined her designer suit as they felt for her tits. Her nipples were stiff and her pussy was wet, as he started talking dirty to her. "You're a stuck-up bitch, you know that don't you?" She suddenly felt his hard cock through his jeans and she was waiting for what would happen next. Suddenly he was marching her to the dining table and she found herself face down and he was pulling up her skirt. "You're not only a stuck-up bitch but you're a dirty bitch too." Her ass was in plain view as her thong exposing her ass cheeks and she was really aroused.

Suddenly his hand came down with a smack and she gasped as he spanked her. "Who is the boss here, dirty bitch?" he asked. Her excitement was intense and she knew that she wanted his punishment again. "I am," she said, and turning round she knew that he was excited by her refusal to buckle first time. He waited a few seconds and spanked her even harder this time. Her ass was stinging and her pussy was soaking by this time.

. . .

He asked her again, "Who is the boss here, dirty bitch?" and again she answered that she was. This brought about a thorough and incredibly sexy spanking that turned her almost into a wild woman. Smack followed smack as her ass turned red as she yelped and moaned.

As suddenly as it had started, he stopped and taking her panties in his hand, he pulled them down and ordered her to open her legs. It was a fantastic experience and she felt the wetness over herself. She was ordered to kneel and she complied, and she greedily watched him slowly taking off his jeans. He ordered her to pull down his shorts and she did what she was told and when he grabbed the back of her head, she greedily took his cock in her mouth. His thrusting was gentle at first and she greedily licked his pre-cum from the head and she held his ass as he thrust in her harder and harder. At that moment, she was desperate for him to come in her mouth but Sam had other ideas. He withdrew and forced her down on all fours and pulling back her hair, he entered her pussy, and then the real torture began. He began to thrust inside her and spank her ass, occasionally stopping to make her beg for more. His language got dirtier, "Beg me bitch, beg me to fuck your cunt." It drove her insane and she obeyed. "Please fuck my cunt," she begged him. They were both on the edge of a sexual madness by now and he took her to the bedroom and dragged her to the side of her bed. Opening her legs, he began to lick her clit while finger fucking her, and it drove her wild.

His command was absolute, "You cannot come till I tell you, do you understand dirty bitch?" It drove her demented, almost insane. Her whole body was shaking and she was conscious of herself begging him almost in a disembodied voice to let her come. "Please let me come." He stopped licking her and just said, "Tell me who is your master of your cunt, the boss of your whole filthy dirty bitch body?" With that, he licked her clit with a fury that almost took her breath away, and through muted gasps of air she just about managed, "You are my master please let me come." Suddenly she was aware that he was rubbing her asshole, fingering her soaking wet pussy, and powerfully licking her clit, and she could hold herself no longer. Her muscles contracted and a rolling tremor exploded through her body again and again. The orgasm hit her like a train and his tongue would not stop licking her making her buck in the air. She wailed, "Oh Fuck" again and again and she eventually realized he was not licking her anymore. Her body was sweaty and limp but she was ravenous with a need to have him fuck her and fuck her hard.

He stood up and spreading her legs even wider, thrust his cock deep inside her and she moaned at the deep satisfying pleasure of it. His excitement at making her beg for permission to come had made this a trial, as he had to focus all his energy on not coming too quickly. His thrusts were slow and steady but her wetness pleased him and he loved her moans as he ground his cock inside her. He started talking to her again. "Did you remember who is boss now, dirty bitch?" She nodded, now incapable of speech. He loved it and it quickened the pace of his thrusting and she began to wail again as the base of his cock began to rub her clit. All she could get out was, "Please fuck me harder," and he could only go one way. He began to really fuck her, only stopping to rip open her blouse and place his hands on her shoulders, pinning her to the bed. He fucked her with everything he had and when she came again he could not stop himself. He unloaded what felt like a pint of come in her and again and again, his cock throbbed as her contractions gripped it. They fell apart and kissed each other furiously for what seemed like hours than almost at the same time fell asleep in each other's arms, the house untidy and now completely forgotten.

CHAPTER 5

AGAINST THE BRICKS

JOHANNA LIKED FRIDAYS. On Fridays she would go to Oasis with her boyfriend, Tim, to have a couple of drinks and to celebrate the fact they have both survived through the whole week. Besides, Oasis was one of her favorite bars and by 6 pm it was usually packed with people.

In short, in here she always had a good time.

It was around 7 pm and she was already a bit drunk. Tim was laughing at something he saw on his phone when a tall blonde girl walked by their table and upon seeing Tim, shouted, "Hey! Timmy! Remember me?"

Timmy frowned at Johanna and turned around in confusion which was soon replaced by a warm smile.

. . .

"Katherine! Long time, no see! How are you?"

"Good! It was ages since I last saw you. I almost didn't recognize you!" They hugged and Tim offered her a seat.

"So, what have you been doing for the last six years?"

Katherine was Tim's old friend from college. Johanna immediately didn't like her. She was too smooth and too polished and she smiled too much. She talked and talked, about the old times and old friends, barely paying attention to anything else but Tim.

Johanna tried to be nice. She really did. But when Katherine put her hand on Tim's thigh, plain for her to see, Johanna decided she had enough.

"Excuse me. I need another drink. Be right back," she rose quickly from the table and started to make her way towards the bar. When she got there, she gestured at the bartender and said:

"Vodka, straight up," and swallowed down the alcohol in one go.

Johanna was furious and the alcohol burned her throat just right. She wanted to go back there and smack Katherine in the face, take her by her blond, tacky hair and kick her out into the street. But she was better than that and after another two shots, she went back there, calm and composed.

A good-looking lawyer started to flirt with her and offered her a drink. She hesitated for a moment. She didn't talk to men in bars while her boyfriend was sitting thirty feet away. She wasn't like that. She always did the right thing. And most certainly she never flirted back with lawyers named Brad, she also never whispered sweet nonsense in a seductive tone, counting that her boyfriend would see it all and get jealous.

But if Tim could sit there and flirt with Katherine, she could do the same with the lawyer.So she sat and laughed and enjoyed her expensive drink, throwing occasional glances at Tim and Katherine. They were still there, completely oblivious to everything else.

"How about we get out of there, hmm?" offered Johanna, leaning closer to Brad. A content smile stretched his face. He put down his drink and took her by the wrist.

"Ladies first."

They started moving towards the exit. Johanna made sure that Tim saw her. She walked right by the table and, without saying anything; she looked at him in a challenging manner. Tim's expression was blank, but he didn't move. Before Johanna could do anything else, she and Brad were already outside.

"My place or yours?"

Johanna measured him from head to toe and made a quick decision. "Neither. Follow me."

She took his hand and guided him to the back alley on the left of the club. It was a dark corner that led to a back-yard. She didn't really know why she just went with it like it was nothing. But she still saw Katherine's hand on Tim's thigh and it makes her blood boil.

"Here?" asked Brad, looking around, a bit hesitant.

"What? Afraid you're going to destroy your suit?" Johanna teased him, leaning against a wall.

In a second, Brad's lips were on hers and his hands pinned her to the bricks. He thrust his tongue inside her mouth violently and sucked on a bottom lip. Kissing him was so different to kissing Tom and Johanna felt strange.

Suddenly, she was kissing the air.

. . .

Brad was brutally yanked from her and she heard a loud crack. Then Brad screamed when someone kicked him, hard. Then she saw Tim, furious and reeling, in front of her.

"Get the fuck out of there!" Tim took Brad by the shirt and threw him on the ground.

When Brad was gone, Johanna and Tim were intently staring at each other for a second, both breathing heavily.

And then they were all over each other.

Tim sank his teeth into her skin and threw her against the wall. Johanna winced in pain as she hit the bricks with her head but she was too busy clawing at his clothes to even notice. She yanked his jacket and almost ripped his shirt apart with her teeth. He threw her sweater on the floor and opened her shirt to bare her breasts. With a growl, he rolled up her skirt, lifted her, and pushed her against the wall. He spread her legs and Johanna threw them around his hips so that she was literally hovering in the air, suspended only by the strength of Tim's arms.

When Tim shoved two fingers inside her, Johanna wailed.

"Yeah, you like it, don't you?" Tim fingered her roughly, scissoring her, making her more wet and needy by the second. "You like to do it in a dirty alley, like a slut?"

. . .

Johanna could only moan in agreement and grind against his bulging erection.

"You want me to fuck you here?" He bit her nipple and released his cock, all ready and slick for her. He placed her hand on his pulsing hardness. "I will fuck you so hard you will forget who you are. I will make you scream."

"God yes," and then he entered her with one thrust, bucking his hips violently, showing her into the wall with an almost brutal force. "Fuck yes!"

He started pushing in and out of her like a machine, as fast and as brutally as he could. He palmed her exposed ass and kissed her lips, biting so hard Johanna tasted blood.

"Fuck, don't stop!"

"Look at you, just loving it, taking me like this." He sped his thrusts even more. "I want you to scream my name; I want everyone to hear you moan like a shameless bitch." He plunged deep inside her, hitting the spot time after time, mouthing a string of profanities as she thrashed against him, craving release.

. . .

Tim reached around her and slipped a finger inside her, moving it in sync with the movements of his hips. "Yes, like this," he bared his teeth and licked her ear, and continued to fuck her without mercy until she thought she could take no more. "Come for me."

And she did, her orgasm hit her with so much force she almost blacked out. Tim continued to thrust inside her, not slowing down, until his movements became erratic. Johanna felt a wave of heat erupt inside her as he came with a loud shout.

She sagged against him, completely boneless. Tim adjusted his shirt and hugged her close to him. Then he raised her chin and kissed her, so gently and delicately Johanna thought she would melt.

"Don't ever make me jealous again," he whispered against her lips.

"Don't ever make me make you jealous," Johanna countered, leaning into his strong, safe embrace.

"You could have just come to the table and kicked Katherine out." "I know," she smiled. "But I like it when you're jealous."

"Oh yeah? How much?" he cocked his eyebrow.

. . .

"Let me show you how much," she said with a purr and she pinned him against the wall.

CHAPTER 6

ALISON'S SURPRISE

ANOTHER EVENING on her own walking in the woods and another evening of frustration with her husband sat in front of the TV watching sports. It was hopeless and the offer from a colleague of NSA sex was looking ever more appealing. All she wanted was the attention more than the sex, just to feel she was desired. It wasn't as if she had let herself go, she was slim and she even had been chatted up by a young kid at work.

So another frustrating evening walking in the woods with the light dimming. It was now September and soon she wouldn't have this activity to look forward to. The crisp, brisk walk to clear her mind and keep her in shape was a godsend and Alison loved it. The fact that autumn would soon change to winter was depressing her enormously tonight. She was about to turn to go home when a noise ahead alerted her to someone else ahead. It was a groaning sound and it sounded like someone in pain.

· · ·

With a natural caution, she walked ahead to a clearing and was amazed at what she saw in the twilight. It was a couple fucking. She couldn't call it making love; it was a dynamic statement of lust. The couple were in a '69' with the girl on top. She was licking her partner's cock in a teasing gesture and stroking his balls. The moaning was his although this was muted as the girl was really grinding her ass in his face. It took Alison a moment to creep nearer and had she not been so frustrated she would have crept away. Tonight however she might as well get some enjoyment from sex even though it was second-hand.

Her view was unrestricted as the couple carried on apparently oblivious to her. The teasing of the man's cock continued and the girl was talking to him and Alison strained to hear.

"You think that just because you know how to use this big hard cock, you can treat me like a whore don't you?" The man, who Alison guessed was substantially younger than his partner groaned, and it was clear that in this sexual encounter, the woman was in charge. "Do you want to stick it in my hot wet cunt?" Again there was a groan from underneath her. "You have to lick it harder first. Lick my clit, you bastard." Alison could see him relishing his task, licking her clit and finger fucking her, to his partner's delight. Her moans triggered Alison's own sexual responses and her nipples were growing harder as the woman was responding to the expert attention of her lover.

They changed positions and to Alison's delight, the girl was still teasing him and then straddled him, rubbing her wetness on his cock but not letting him penetrate her or even touch her. His groans got louder and she slapped his face and told him to "Shut the fuck up". She reached for his cock and grabbed it and made him stick it deep inside her. In an instant, she began to ride his cock, and all the time she pinned down his hands and made it clear to him she was in charge. "You are a little fuck just because you have a big cock. You think you're god's gift, don't you? You know that you are my fuck toy, don't you? You're just like a good vibrator you bastard, now fuck me." Expertly, she rode his dick and kept working him harder and harder. Her wetness covered his cock and Alison was entranced by the girl's ass rhythmically fucking him. She longed to walk over and take his cock in her mouth and watch as the girl talked to him like he was her sex toy, "You dirty bastard fuck my cunt, you little prick." Alison gently moaned and all she could think of were these lovers locked in their fuck frenzy and her heart ached with jealousy. By now she was on fire and her hand lifted her skirt and felt the dampness of her panties. She was so aroused, and the moaning and filthy talk from the couple fucking each other was almost unbearable and she began to touch herself. It was through her panties at first but soon she was rubbing her clit that was soaking wet. Her fingers began to explore her pussy and as she watched the couple's filthy fucking she was working herself into a frenzy.

Her fingers were furiously working her clit and the more frantic the couple in front of her fucked the more she worked on her sexual frustrations. Her husband, her work colleagues all popped into her head as she unleashed her desires and her fingers were soaked in her silky wetness.

· · ·

The girl now got off her partner and began to work her cunt into his face again as she furiously began to jerk off her lover, and her urgency was obvious. "Lick my cunt you bastard lick it hard, harder. " Her ass gyrated as her excitement grew, and she pumped harder and harder on his cock occasionally licking or sucking the tip drawing a long low groan from his lover. Alison was watching the girl panting now and it was obvious that her lover was orally fucking her to a climax. As that was going on the boy's back was arching and she grabbed his cock and opened her mouth and swallowed the come that shot from his cock as his low moans announced his orgasm.

Alison was beside herself as the woman began to orgasm and her moans filled the clearing. She furiously worked her hand over her throbbing clit and had to bite her lip to stop herself from screaming. Meanwhile, the couple was reaching the end and she urged her lover on savagely, "Lick my cunt harder you bastard, harder", she demanded. Then with a shuddering moan, she came, and as she did so, she rubbed her pussy into the man's face to complete his sexual humiliation. The shock of it drove Alison bonkers and her orgasm was one of the most intense of her life. The feeling was so emotional she felt like crying as she felt her wetness soaking her panties.

Resting on the tree, Alison closed her eyes and drifted off into a daydream of sexual fantasy, remembering how the woman had used her lover but that they both played the game so sexily, so beautifully. Her eyes were watering and she had to mentally shake herself to regain her composure.

Opening her eyes she saw with a shock the couple in front of her, and both looked at her curiously before advancing on her. The woman just kissed her and she was followed by her partner. He gently inserted his tongue in her mouth quickly and withdrew it then whispered, "Don't be shy next time, come and join the party."

They started off, hand in hand, at which point Alison asked, "Are you here tomorrow?" The lovers turned, nodded, and blew her a kiss. Alison's heart began racing again and she knew that she would be back.

CHAPTER 7

AN APARTMENT WITH
A VIEW

CHERI AND GREG HARRIS had just fulfilled their dream of finding a place that they could call home, that was also within their budget. They discovered that they had an opportunity of a lifetime; there was an opening at a place where they really wanted to live. Cheri was crazy about the place because of the balcony that overlooked the city. The view was amazing. Cheri was able to sit on the balcony nude.

There was little chance that anyone would see her unless she was at the edge of the balcony. They were newlyweds. This was a perfect situation for them. One day Greg decided to come home early and surprise his wife. Cheri was a caterer who worked from home. Greg came in with a dozen roses. Greg always wanted to show how much he loved Cheri.

She was taken aback by the sweet gesture. She was even more surprised when he suggested that they go into the bedroom and screw their brains out. She had a better idea;

she went into the kitchen and told Greg to wait in the living room. Cheri came out a little while later with a bikini made from whipped cream with cherries over her nipples and her cunt. Cheri had made a sign that she attached to her stomach that simply said: "Eat Me." Greg did not have to be told twice. He immediately went over to Cheri and began to lick at one of the nipples of Cheri. He wanted the cherry that she was so desperately withholding from him. Greg was going to have to fight to get Cheri's cherry. The licking quickly turned into a little more than gentle biting as Greg finally got down to her nipple. Her nipple rings made nipple play a lot more enjoyable for both of them.

"Greg I have an awesome idea. Why don't we have sex on the balcony, we have never done that and I think it will be something that could be adventurous. This could be a great time to try something new."

Greg thought about it for only a second. Cheri led Greg out onto the balcony and closed the storm door behind him. She had the only key and she was not about to just give it to Greg, she took the key and slid it up inside her cunt. There was only one rule: Greg had to use only his mouth to get the key out. Cheri knew that this was going to lead to a wild session of cunnilingus. The sensation of a tongue sliding in and out of her wet hole was just magical to her.

Greg went down onto her wet cunt and began to explore with his tongue the outer edges of her slit as well as the inside. Greg found the string that the key was attached to and tried to move it into a position that he could get a better grip on it with his teeth. Finally, he was able to move it into position. The entire time Cheri was being driven into a frenzy as all of her sensitive spots were being hit with his tongue. By this time that she was dripping wet and was more than ready for him to mount her. Cheri walked over to the edge of the balcony and bent over. This allowed her top half to hang over the ledge of the balcony while her lower half was in perfect alignment with him. Greg walked over and began to finger her wet hole from behind. This was driving Cheri even more over the edge. Another thing that was driving her to the point of no return was that she was being watched from a man below her on the street. The thought of being screwed while being watched had her wet and horny more than anything. Greg went and drove the full length of his member deep into her. The sensation of this took her by surprise a little bit but she quickly recovered and became more adjusted to the pounding that she was about to receive. The in and out action was causing her tits to swing freely in the air and as the motions continued her tits began to hit the balcony. She noticed that the man was apparently getting very erect, as he had to adjust himself to be more comfortable. Greg continued and became more comfortable.

Greg was an old-fashioned type of guy and usually thought that there were only a couple of positions that were acceptable for a man and a woman to have sex in. Greg got over this in a hurry. He was about to have his first orgasm in the outdoors while having sex. It was a sensation that he never thought he would have even thought about having. Cheri had opened his eyes to a completely new world of sex and for that.

. . .

Just as he was about to pop, Greg pulled out of his wife's hole and turned her around to where he had a perfect shot at her tits. This was the perfect ending for an almost perfect sexual experience. He had a feeling that he was going to love the new place that Cheri and he were living in.

CHAPTER 8

BEAUTIFUL NIGHT

THE WAFTING aroma of coffee and caramel permeated the frosted door out into the snow-covered street, inviting her in. She kicked the snow off her black leather boots as she pushed open the heavy door and stepped inside. It was quaint, trendy yet homey. The clientele were quite eclectic, mostly fellow students she presumed, but there was an elderly couple sharing pie, a group of children reading in the corner, and at center stage, literally, was a woman singing an Eagles tune and playing guitar. She took off her coat, putting her hat in its pocket and hanging it amongst the others who had also escaped the blizzard. Her chilled skin beneath the silky platinum blouse made her seating choice easy as she settled into the oversized chair aside from a roaring fireplace. She removed the laptop from its case sitting it atop the distressed wooden side table as the barista took her order. She shook out her blue-black hair still damp and flattened by the snowstorm as he walked her way. "May I share your plug?" he asked. Her confused posture prompting him to gesture to the outlet attached to the table lamp. She chuckled slightly as she understood saying, "of course."

She gave the handsome stranger a good look over as he fumbled with his briefcase removing his computer and chucking his wet coat onto the back of his chair. His long dark hair was pulled back into a ponytail, his face was chiseled with a perfectly groomed beard, and eyes were shockingly dark. Their eyes met for a split second sending an odd chill down her spine as he smiled at her revealing dimples too adorable to accompany such mischievous eyes. "Beautiful night, isn't it?" he asked. "Beautiful?" she questioned. "Well it's beautiful from where I sit," he said once again teasing her with that naughty smile. He found her blush charming, whether it is from the glow of the fireplace or his flirting, though he hoped it was the latter. "I'm Blake," he said, extending his hand to her. "Angelia," the name rolled off of her tongue like poetry he thought as her small hand slid into his. "Wonderful to share this beautiful evening with you Angelia," he replied. His voice was so intriguing, as deep and rich as the latte she sipped. Their conversation was somewhat sporadic as both gave half of their attention to whatever filled their computer screens until a little girl sat down on the carpet in front of the fireplace and between their chairs. She was playing with a baby doll, feeding it a bottle when she suddenly sneezed. Angelia blessed her, and without looking up from his screen he said, "Au nom de pe're, le fills, et de sacr'e spectre." Her eyes shot immediately to him clueless to what the words meant, but desperate to know.

. . .

As if he felt the weight of her gaze upon him, he spoke, "in the name of the father, the son, and the holy ghost" again without shifting his face from his work. Her heart pounded; it was so beautiful, and pure, yet at the same time she found it unbelievably sexy. The hopeless romantic in her fell in love with him that very instant. She didn't know what to say, but she had to say something. "That was breathtaking," she spoke barely above a whisper. He lifted his hypnotic gaze to hers without uttering a word. "What you said to that girl, it touched my heart," she continued. He began regaling stories of studying French and Latin abroad, but it wasn't the beauty of the language that beguiled her, it was the beauty of the man. Before she could hear another word she interrupted, "I'm new to the city but I've noticed there is a constant chatter, a mind-numbing buzz that is totally meaningless yet still has the ability to rob one of solace. You're not like that. I must know a man of such depth." Her confession both stunned and delighted him. "You're a poet," he said. "I write, yes," she acknowledged. "A passion we share," he replied as he flashed a smile. "Want to get out of here?" she blatantly asked. "Music to my ears, angel," he replied flashing that smile that couldn't get them out quick enough for her.

With her hand in his, the angry blizzard became a winter wonderland. His presence was so commanding, not in an obnoxious manner, but in a way that made her feel protected and cherished. He couldn't keep his eyes off her. The way the holiday lights played upon her face bathed her in an angelic glow. His need grew with each step until he pulled her into his arms mid-stride causing her to fall into him. They shared an intimate gaze as he stroked her face with the back of his hand before pulling her into a magical kiss. It was soft and gentle at first, his soft full lips introducing themselves to hers. She ran her tongue over his bottom lip before getting totally lost in the most passionate kiss she'd ever experienced. She had never been reckless or even impulsive but she had to do this, she had to experience this man. He could teach her, broaden her horizons she thought, and she just plain wanted him. Oblivious to the temperature they shared many kisses on the walk to his place. His pace slowed as she awaited another kiss, he instead nodded toward the staircase that entered his building and asked, "Yes?" "Yes," she declared without hesitation.

Angelia's heart was racing as they stepped into the building's freight elevator. Sensing her nervousness Blake backed her aggressively into the corner devouring any apprehension with his kiss. She wrapped her arms around his neck as he pressed his body to hers, the evidence of his desire grinding against her stomach. As the doors parted they stepped into a loft that any New Yorker would kill for. Spacious with straightforward minimalist decor, yet it had his warmth. The outside wall was all windows and the ceiling arched forming a cathedral-style skylight at its peak. "Wow it's beautiful!" she exclaimed as she twirled breathing in the ambiance. "May I?" he asked as he removed her coat. "Of course," she replied as she wrapped her bare arms around herself, chilled by the coolness of the vast space's concrete interior. Blake of course noticed her dimpled skin and started a fire. He took her hand and led her to the weathered leather sofa directly in front of the fireplace. As they settled into its buttery softness he draped her legs across his lap, unzipping her boots and tossing them to the floor, and massaged her feet as they thawed. "Mmm, that feels nice," she cooed as she scooted closer to him, her deep gray wool skirt rising as she moved revealing the black lace trim on her thigh-high stocking. Completely aware of her exposure she was delighted to find his stygian eyes undressing her. "Now that's nice," he said as his hands followed his eyes rolling the sheer fabric down her leg. Her panties moistened as his masterful hand stroked her inner thigh, her body trembling in reply. He raised his eyes to the golden glow of hers and unbuttoned the flimsy blouse not even remotely concealing her erect nipples. As her shirt fell away, it revealed a black lace bra with tiny bows at each strap like a fantastic gift that he couldn't wait to open. He lightly bit her neck, trailing his kiss down her décolleté'. As she lowered her gaze to watch him enjoy her, the satin strap slipped down her delicate shoulder displaying her abundant cleavage to his hot kiss. His beard tickled as he caressed her breasts with his face while reaching around to open her bra. As her breasts bounced free he took her hardened peak into his mouth circling her rosy nipple. He slid his tongue down her abdomen licking her navel as she raised her hips pleading to get out of her skirt. "What angel, do you want me to make love to you?" he teased. "Yes!" she cried, the hot need pulsing in her pussy. "And I will," he promised, adding "later" further tormenting her.

He lifted her hungered body from the sofa and forcefully, yet controlled he tossed her onto the bed. She shimmied out of the suddenly itchy skirt revealing a matching black lace panty. It lay perfectly against her porcelain skin and he had to touch the intricate fabric before ripping them from her body. He felt her soft mound through the satin fabric pressing his finger against its center, his gloved touch lightly fingering her clit indirectly as Angelia begged him to take her.

He lowered his face to the obstructive fabric pressed a kiss to the soaked material and inhaled her arousal. That was it, she could take no more. "Fuck me, dammit!" she demanded. He laughed as he slid the panties down her perfect legs revealing the love that awaited him, a flawless black powder puff sitting atop a pussy he couldn't wait to taste. He lightly stroked her as shivers racked her body. "Blake please," she purred. "One more thing first, angel, if I may." He pulled long strands of ribbon from the bureau. "Raise your arms, my sexy angel," he commanded. She complied. He wrapped the ribbon around her wrists and secured it to the bedposts. She writhed about testing their solidity and found she was now his to do with as he pleased. That thought turned her on unbelievably. He stood for a moment simply looking at her naked body sprawled out awaiting him. He undressed before crawling into bed. His body was even more gorgeous than she'd envisioned. His upper body was lean and cut with no hair until right above his massive erection. His ass was small and tight, the kind you could cup with her hand, and damn they looked fine in a pair of Levi's. He positioned himself between her legs, parting her moist lips with his tongue. She lost her breath momentarily at his tender touch. As her hips settled against the bed, he opened her wide and plunged his tongue into her depth. Her restrained twisting beneath him made tasting her even more delicious. She bucked her hips pleading for more and more was exactly what she was going to get he thought. He buried his face in her throbbing cunt, licking and sucking her swollen nub until her body lunged with the last wave of ecstasy it could hold before surrendering and feeding her lover her sweet release. "Oh my God Blake, that was incredible," she said breathlessly. "I've only begun to pleasure you, my angel," he whispered.

Blake lay next to Angelia, her body still wild with orgasm. He began trailing the lightest touch all over her body. The charge already coursing through her intensified. The sensation was a cocktail of ticklish and arousal, and she was intoxicated by his skillful caress. Her satiety quickly turned to famish as the hunger to have him inside her became unbearable. His cock hardened again as he enjoyed the movement of her breasts as she flailed in her lust for him. He straddled her, aligning his erection with her opening, rubbing and teasing it just a bit before shoving his full length into her aching cunt. She screamed as his girth more than filled her. He fucked her at a magical angle that caressed her clit as his balls spanked her ass with each and every stroke.

He pulled out until only his head penetrated her and then slammed his dick into her pussy again, training it to hold onto his shaft. He kept her at the cusp of climax until her pussy begged for release. "God baby, you know how to fuck," she confessed as he allowed her the first ripple of orgasm. The moment he felt it he fucked her like a wild animal, his huge cock slamming the bottom of her tight little hole as her entire body quaked with a feral orgasm. Her walls clamped around him sucking his dick and taking him over the edge as he poured his hot load into her, his breathless body falling against her. He rolled over and untied his angel. Her coal-black hair spilled over the white pillowcase like midnight meeting dawn as he snuggled up behind her, their naked bodies melding into one they watched the raging snowstorm as Angelia asked, "Isn't this a beautiful night?" Blake replied, "Sure is from where I'm sitting."

CHAPTER 9

BEYOND THE BREAKERS

TAKING her man to work is one of the duties that come with their schedules. They have one car, and as a lifeguard, Nathan often needs to be at work long before Pamela, a PA. So she has the responsibility of getting up with him on such days and getting him to the beach before sunrise. They have settled nicely into this routine, and it isn't too much of a mission getting up and getting out of the house on mornings such as this one. They're pulling into the empty parking lot at the beach just a little before 4:30 AM, and by the time the sun starts to glimmer orange in the distance, a little before 5, they've already finished their coffee in the life-guard station and are hand in hand on the beach, playing with the sand between their toes.

Pamela is in her man's boxers and a tank top, not entirely unacceptable given the early start, and Nathan is already in his red Speedos. A brief scan of the area reveals that they are still alone and so Nathan grabs Pam in his arms and spins her around in the tiny waves breaking around her ankles now, the tide coming in. His cock starts to harden as soon as their lips join. This isn't very helpful since the tiny Speedo cannot contain his twelve-inch tool. But it's too late to pull back the cock that shoots straight up out of the red and pushes against Pamela's pussy, snug on it as she coils her legs around his waist. Nathan continues to kiss her as he walks into the water instead of away, realizing suddenly that his hard-on is going nowhere now and so will need to be taken care of.

Only once Nathan is waist-deep in the water and the cold ocean touches her ass does Pamela register just how deep in he's carried her. It's too late for her to protest as a wave rolls over them and her shorts are wet, along with half of her top. She gives herself to the moment, the cold shaking a good few giggles from her. Nathan is pleased, kissing her again as he lets her drop her feet to the sand. Their embrace is close, tight in an attempt to warm up a bit despite their acute awareness of the cold and the impossibility of anything but. There is no way for them to escape the water and its temperature. They can only escape into each other.

Even with his lips on Pamela's Nathan is aware of their surroundings. They're not so far from the shore for his intended quickie to go by unnoticed by a pair of eyes that happened to glance upon them. So he has to make it really quick without making it conspicuous. He moves Pamela's arms up so that they hang around his neck. Reaching down under the water he adjusts the Speedo so that his dick and his left leg are both extending out of the same circle. His cock has gone limp now in the lower temperatures of its new playground, but there is no way that Nathan is going to let this go. He knows what awaits him just underneath the loose boxers that do a very bad job suddenly of keeping Pamela's pussy warm.

Finding her clit under the shorts Nathan gives it a light pull. He listens out for her response, and as soon as he feels the bean flesh out between his fingertips he gives it a firmer squeeze. He starts to pull down on it, dragging it towards the ocean floor. Pamela gets more and more into it and so he lets his other hand join in, and proceeds to milk her clit beneath the rising waters. They both bob around and lose their balance occasionally, but Nathan plants himself firmly in the shifting sands and finds the rhythm of the ocean. Pamela holds on to him, trusting that this is his territory. Soon they're working with the ebb and flow, Pamela's cunt steadying on towards a high tide of its very own.

Again Nathan is tugging on her clit with the fingers of one hand, the other required to pull on his thick limp cock. The blood starts to make its way into his meat and pretty soon he is pulling on a solid scepter again, his cock so long, so thick that its head is way past the surface of the water.

He takes them in just a little deeper. Nathan knows this beach, he knows how it works. He finds just the right spot for them in the sand, a solid rock somewhere below so they don't move around as much. This provides him with the stability required to make a good job of stroking his cock without neglecting his pussy preparation.

Pamela moves in closer to him as he fills her cunt with the first finger. A second finger follows quickly. She holds onto him tightly as he moves things around inside her, pushing, stirring, tugging, pulling, and then pushing again. His fingers seem to think that whatever they are looking for is deep inside her cunt, and they are determined to find it. Nathan fingers her hard, but not fast. He moves inside her with a force that makes the perfect substitution for what, in different circumstances, would have been rapid fingering for the purpose of wetting Pamela's punani. His deep digging, once it becomes familiar, starts to have this effect though, and soon his fingers are diving in and out of a slippery, sticky pond.

It would be way too risky for them to bring their covering below their asses. So Nathan sends his cock under the boxers, under one of the legs. His fingers are still inside her and they need to make the necessary room. He removes them slowly and then takes his cock in hand. He finds Pamela's cunt and pulls her onto him. His cock settles inside her in one long, languid move and she again latches tightly onto him as he makes a passionate connection with her mouth. Nathan exercises every ounce of discipline that he has not to start ramming in and out of Pamela's love nest just as soon as his cock is completely enveloped by the vagina.

Slowly Nathan pulls some cock from her; Pamela digging her heels into the sand at the same time so that her cunt follows his cock. His natural movement is to then thrust back into her, but since Pamela is now straightening up again, her pussy purrs away from him. This happens for a few more strokes and then Nathan pulls her close, holding her in place so that he can get started with the business of fucking her. This is going to be a slow session, but not a long one. So the owner of the cock needs to be in as much control of the proceedings as is possible. Nathan is not accustomed to the snail's pace but the cunt he is digging into makes the pace worth it. He gets all inside her and despite the inclination still to thrust wildly, he reminds himself of the lack of balance, and the man walking his dog on the beach.

Finally, his entire body joins his cock in the snail race. There is a sudden calm as every part of him catches on to the pace of this strange fucking that is nothing like their usual high-intensity sessions. They are now quite literally at the mercy of the elements and so Nathan positions them so that the current pushes him into Pamela and the returning rip moves him around inside her.

This new strategy works and he is soon fucking her in longer, lulling strokes, the swirls around them adding a definite twist that works. Pamela cannot bring herself to open her eyes. Her entire focus is on this new fantastic style of fucking that she hopes is as easily applied in their bed back on dry land.

The only temperature now is fucking hot as the entire focus becomes the slow-moving, far-reaching, and deep digging cock inside Pamela's fire-hot fanny. Nathan dicks her pussy with powerful, deep thrusts, achingly slow as the beach starts to fill and he needs to make it look like they're simply having a conversation that requires them to stand so intimately close to each other.

He lets the water pull Pamela from him a little, creating a massive cunt-drag for the power of the pull. She bobs around away from him for a while, her cunt still firmly attached to his cock. The urge to pull her back and just fuck the shit out of her almost consumes him but he just has to throw his eyes in the direction of the beach and he is reigned in. There is a very present acceptance that he is in the hands of the ocean.

The dragging on his dick created by the movement around him is way past satisfactory. The water is clear enough for him to see the smiley faces on his boxers. He lifts the leg of the shorts so that he can see just below the surface as his cock moves around in Pamela. Actually what he is seeing is her pussy moving around over his cock. She moves less and less now as Nathan takes them closer to orgasm.

His fucking gets progressively harder but remains steady in its pace. Hard and slow, hard and slow he fucks Pamela, drilling through her in lengthy thrusts that make him wish the world would just disappear. For Pamela, nothing exists except Nathan and his dick.

It's now officially morning, the sun falling generously on their backs and all around them. Some of the other early morning beachcombers start to threaten the skirts of the waves, a couple of them already ankle-deep. There is nothing for it now but to make for a climax. Pamela leans back as though she is about to float away from Nathan face-up. This creates the illusion that she is further away from him than she is. It is her head that is to the shore so that Nathan faces the beach. He starts to walk towards her, which is actually faster stroking his cock into her cunt.

Every step is a stroke, bringing them both closer and closer to climax. The shore gets dangerously close, the water threatening to run just below the belt on the next outflow. Nathan pulls Pamela back to him and gives her the deepest hardest strokes he can manage, wanting her to cum first. Instead, he shoots a large load into her and she gives him a deep kiss. A few moves of her waist and she too has a massive orgasm just as the water moves back way below their butts. Fortunately no clothing had been removed and so they simply disengage and swim back to shore.

CHAPTER 10

BLAME IT ON THE NEIGHBORS

WE FOUND our apartment purely by chance one hot summer's day when my hubby and I noticed an ad in the real estate shopper one night. "500 square feet, 2 bedrooms, and a spectacular view of the city" the ad proclaimed. We called and arranged an appointment to see it and instantly fell in love, again, only this time with the apartment.

We had only been married for a little more than 3 months and still were having trouble finding time to do anything but have sex in our "spare time". Finding that apartment had been a dream come true and we had just settled in. The balcony off the living room did indeed have a spectacular view of the entire city. We immediately furnished the balcony with a patio table and chairs and began eating our meals in grandeur.

One early evening we had just sat down to eat out dinner, spaghetti, and meatballs when Bob put his finger to his lips motioning for me to be quiet. I listened carefully only to hear the sounds of gasping and moaning coming from the deck directly above us. We had met the couple on the elevator shortly after moving in and they both seemed like nice people. They had only been married a short while as well and we had often heard the sounds of thumping and loud moaning coming from above us. Neither Bob nor I needed any encouragement to have another wet round of sex, but knowing that the couple above us were going at it like bunnies on Viagra, we always found it hot as hell and ended up making a bit of noise of our own.

I sat there chewing on a piece of meatball listening to the activity above us. Bob looked at me with a twinkle in his eye that I knew meant more than a second helping of spaghetti. I reached underneath the table and found his cock stiff and swollen and unzipped his fly immediately. His swollen cock felt like solid steel and I pumped it slowly. One thing about living on the 21st floor, you don't really have to worry about anyone watching you.

"Oh God," I heard from down below on the deck, "God it feels so big tonight Hun." I looked at Bob, glanced with my eyes towards the deck, and smiled. Bob stood up, moved over beside my chair, and stuck his stiff cock straight in my face without a word. I didn't need to be told what to do and my mouth was on his cockhead faster than you could say, Rotelli. My hand couldn't help but slip down to my own lap and up underneath my sundress. My naked pussy was almost drenched from hearing the neighbors and having Bob's cock in my mouth at the same time. I never wore underwear, which somehow always seemed to make me hornier, not that I needed any help with that either.

. . .

I sucked hard and furious on Bob's dangling trouser snake. It tasted like pasta mingled with the sauce in my mouth. In fact, I took a bit of sauce and parmesan, smeared it on his quivering cock head, and lovingly ate it off. I looked up at him with that dangerous and exotic look I knew turned him on immensely. He knew once my green eyes turned a shade darker he was in for some hot, wild sex.

"How about I go grab the comforter off of the sofa?" I whispered with a sexy growl to my new hubby.

"Sure baby, and then get ready because I am going to fuck the ever-living cum out of you when you return," he said in a naughty and growling tone.

I quickly ran inside and grabbed it when I came back out onto the balcony I heard from the deck above us, "Yes, yes, yes fuck my wet cunt like you've never fucked it before!" followed by a long and sexy moan.

I looked up at Bob who was all-out stroking his stiffened meat by now and chuckled. I walked over to my gregarious groom and began to kiss him passionately no holds barred kind of passion and zeal. I grabbed him behind the neck and pulled him down onto the comforter with me. I couldn't wait for him to thrust his stiff meat inside of me under the night sky.

. . .

When we lay back on the comforter, I saw a familiar twinkle in Bob's eyes. I knew that twinkle all too well. Before he fucked me he wanted to tickle my whiskers with his if you catch my drift. Bob always had been one to opt for dessert first. I laid back, peered up at the moon and stars, and got ready to experience heaven in between my legs. My hubby was the best there is at eating cunt. I had never had anyone come close to his expertise and terrific tongue tricks.

His mouth felt like velvet kisses as he brushed his tongue delicately across my luscious and swollen labia. My lips were always so eager for a hot tongue or finger between them. Their reaction was very erotic to watch. The more they were stimulated the wider they spread and the longer they got. I had always toyed with them as a young woman, pulling on them and twisting them in between my fingers

I could have an orgasm just by pulling on them, which made Bob's tongue almost a dream come true. His mouth would suck them into it and he'd clamp down on them with his lips and pull. And while he did, the tip of his tongue would flick up and down along the sensitive swollen flesh. They turned into rubbery lust in his mouth, something he was always more than willing to do as well. When it came to eating my cunt, Bob was a master. I always got so hot that Bob would finish eating my pussy and have a coating of my cum all over his handsome face.

As the sounds from the balcony increased so did my hubby's and my intensity. He ate me right to the point of orgasm and then flipped me over for some hot doggie-style fucking. I loved it when Bob rammed his stiff member in me from behind. The feel of his slapping gonads against my ivory flesh made me a ball of sexual nerves set on fire. I couldn't get enough of him inside of me. The more he thrust inside, the deeper I wanted him inside my needy folds. I was hungry, more like I was starving for my husband's girth. He blew me away with his animal lust. It was raw and wanton and I loved every second of it. He had never once failed to amaze me when it came to lovemaking. As the couple below us neared their mutual orgasms, my lover and I neared ours with extreme intensity. The slapping of my hubby's balls became more vehement. His groans became deeper and more growl-like. My moans neared the scream level as I pushed my cunt out as far as possible to meet his pounding thrusts inside of me. We heard this on the deck above us and that is all it took to send us into combustive orgasms:

"Fuck yes baby I am about to c-c-cuuuuummmmmmm" as the woman above us screamed out in a sexual sound that would make a dead man shoot-off.

That's when I knew hubby was about to unload tons of seed inside of me. His balls were as tight as a tennis ball. They slapped against me with a force to be reckoned with. He groped my waist like an animal, as he groaned loudly not once but three times and unleashed wads inside of me. I could feel him flood my inner folds like never before. It was one of the best orgasms I ever remember my husband having. That was all it took to send me into ecstasy.

I felt the orgasm creep through my body straight to my tiptoes as I screamed out in equal animal lust and pleasure. It was like the four of us cumming in unison. Our cries of pleasure seemed as though they might be heard 5 miles away. It infiltrated the area around our balcony and theirs. I have always wondered if they heard us fucking as loudly as we heard them. If so, I am sure theirs were as intense as ours were.

Hubby and I collapsed back onto our comforter and giggled quietly. I looked at Bob and said, "Sure now you want to be quiet!" He answered with, "Blame it on the neighbor's baby doll. What can I say? A man's gotta do what a man gotta do." I playfully punched his bicep and he reached for me lovingly and gave me a passionate kiss and warm embrace. I kissed him back with absolute love and affection. I loved the guy like a crazy lady, and yes, I do blame the neighbors!

CHAPTER 11

BOARDROOM SURPRISE

THE TINY BOARDROOM smells of expensive wood. But while the dark mahogany of the table is impressive, sexy Shawna has another type of wood on her mind. The privacy of the tiny boardroom just off her husband's office is perfect for him because he can get twenty minutes of uninterrupted sleep, and perfect for her because she can play out her plan without any disturbances. The knee-length charcoal skirt and white shirt make her look like a secretary or personal assistant, and the expensive Armani Clive her sleeping hubby is wearing makes them look like they both belong exactly where they are. Their looks, and the fact that Shawna isn't wearing any panties, play into a cliché that is about to make the morning fucking awesome.

For a minute Clive is sure that he is dreaming, his wife's perfume full in his nostrils as she moves her neck over his face. Her familiar lips on his force his eyes open just long enough for him to make the confirmation. A finger on his mouth silences him before he takes up too much time asking the obvious. Shawna gives him a little breathing room by loosening his tie, and then works her way under the desk and between his legs. Her fingers move over his bulging cock as it swells under his trousers, and Clive moves to his belt in order to give her the scope she needs to play. A quick glance at the door and he sees that the knob is in the locked position. She's thought of everything.

What cannot happen is for Clive to be in any way disheveled once they're done. She also needs to leave the building looking like she just came to pick up her husband's checkbook. With his pants undone, his zipper pulled down, his cock is brought out into the open. He opens his legs so that his wife can get between them without making too much contact with his pants. Her elbows rest comfortably on the leather and her hands take firm hold of his dick. He watches as her fingers move up and down his shaft, knowing full well that in a minute his cock is going to be satisfied with nothing else but the inside of her cunt.

She pulls his dick towards her mouth and gets the tip between her lips. Her position doesn't allow her to move too far down his shaft but the parts of his cock that are in her mouth are enough for her to send pleasure through Clive's entire shaft. He watches her move on his dick with her lips while her fingers manually manipulate the rest of his penis. The magic firing into him from her fingers has him almost wrap his legs around her, but then he remembers his pants.

He wheels back the chair so that she can get up from under the table. Her one hand continues its work on his cock while she gets to her feet and manages to lift her leg high enough for her heel to rest on the table. Clive wheels a little closer to her again and lifts her skirt. No panties make for easy access to her pussy. He doesn't wet the finger that he drives into her cunt. Instead, he settles it deep inside her and coats it in the wetness of Shawna's vagina. Her cunt is moist enough for the finger to exit very well lubricated. It makes a few more entries before Clive adds a few more fingers.

He fingers her cunt as she brings him close to orgasm with one hand. He flows with the movements of her hand on his cock until again their location and his Italian pants a recalled. Clive reluctantly stops her by using his free hand to remove hers from his dick. He decides to make her pussy the focus for a while. One hand holds onto her thigh, holding her steady while the fingers of the other move into her deep and hard. Shawna finds a hold on the table and leans back so that her pussy pushes forwards, Clive gaining even more ground as his fingers completely disappear into the wife's hot honey pot.

He pulls her to him, his chair gliding to her, and licks her cunt. He sends his tongue into her vagina and keeps it in the flames for as long as he can, moving it around fast and far, enjoying the taste of her arousal. Clive sucks on her punani as hard as he sends his tongue into her, his cock now salivating at the prospect of this pussy. His fingers replace his tongue for a bit to make sure that the stretch has been satisfactorily achieved. He gives his dick a few strokes and takes the stray precum between his fingers. He transfers his juice to her cunt and digs into it a little more to maximize the coating. With all his fingers having inspected the inside of her, Clive is ready to take Shawna to all the places his fingers have been promising.

By the time he is on his feet, she is turned around and bent over the table. He lifts her skirt and rubs her naked ass before bending to give it a lick. His tongue settles on her asshole and he wets it as much as he can before sending his finger into it. Clive enjoys fingering her asshole because it's so fucking tight. It takes a while to warm up the hole but the time and effort is so worth it.

She really has a beautiful hole. Clive loses himself in licking and rimming and then fingering and tonguing the tight asshole. Shawna breathes heavily her enjoyment of his efforts. It isn't long before he has three fingers moving easily in and out of her ass all at once.

Clive runs the length of his cock along the inside of her butt. Shawna can't help but push her ass into him. His head is on the entrance quickly and Clive stands there, allowing Shawna to feed herself his cock. She eases back, and then forward, and then back onto the cock again. It isn't long before the length of his log is disappearing into her. Once she has managed half of his shaft Clive takes the reigns and starts to fuck her ass hard. He has had the forethought to fasten his belt so that his pants don't fall to the ground and crease. He shoots his dick into her as it protrudes through the zipper of his pants. Her pleasure is signaled by husky, low breaths.

He finds the inside of her cunt with his fingers just as soon as he has got his entire dick into her ass. His fingers move deep into her as he fucks her as deep as he can without touching his shirt to her. The care taken not to fuck up their looks is sending all the attention to their groins so that all the sensations transmitted through them are amplified. Clive is clever enough about the pace of his fucking and fingering so that the only sweat that is shared between them is coming from the inside of Shawna's pussy. He has them well on their way to heaven, his cock a swollen mass in her ass, his fingers massive fillers in her fanny. The neatness with which he is achieving the fucking hot mess between her thighs gives incredible insights into why her man is such a successful CEO. His method is incredible. And this method translates effortlessly to everything he does.

The moisture in her cunt makes it impossible for him to

resist it any longer, and after a careful exit from her ass, he explodes into her cunt. His thick dick forces her vagina to make a massive adjustment, and just as it settles, he is fucking the hole hard. His meat is fucking her so hard that his cock is practically pushing her onto the table. She holds onto the wood and pushes herself back, needing all of her man inside her. Clive digs well into her depths and sends stroke after piercing stroke into every part of her cunt at once. She pushes even harder onto him as her pussy starts to vibrate violently in anticipation of a massive eruption.

He pulls her further back so that her back is flat now and sends his cock deep into her. The strength of his thrusts is unbelievable, Shawna having to steady both herself and the table now as Clive threatens to shoot them into the wall. For all her effort though it takes him just a dozen or so thrusts before the table is in fact lodged against the wall. The upside of this is that now he can fuck her hard, knowing that her perfect pussy is going nowhere. His cock now takes its pounding to the next level and Shawna's tiny cunt is completely obliterated.

Clive fills her with his load. There is just no holding back. He thrusts into her all the while his serpent spits fire into her depths. He keeps thrusting, his cock still rock hard. She hasn't cum yet so he has no intention of letting up until she does. There is no loss of power in his penis as he continues digging into her dripping cunt. He cannot leave her without finishing what they started. He loves the sound of her orgasm. He loves the feeling of having satisfied this woman that loved him enough to say *I do*! So despite the fact that he has reached the end of his own climax, he has enough in the reserve to deal quite adequately with his wife.

His cock stays hard for ten minutes after he ejaculates.

This is all the time he needs to pull an ecstatic moan from Shawna as she has her orgasm. This is the moan he loves. He lets it linger. He lets it linger very long before he finally pulls his cock from her. Once he has his meat on the outside of her, he reaches for her bag and pulls out the wipes he knows he'll find there. She turns to him and parts her legs at his suggestion. Relaxing back onto the table, she lets him clean her up, his gentleness arousing her again so that he uses his fingers to bring a final climax from her depths. He has her cleaned soon after, a single wipe making sure that his own cock doesn't mess his trousers. Shawna uses her tongue to clean the remainder of his cock, and then her mouth to pull a second orgasm from his flaccid cock, before he returns it to his pants. Clive is ready for the rest of his day, and Shawna exits the building with a stride that gives away the satisfaction between her legs.

CHAPTER 12

BOOK WORM

RENEE RUBBED HER DRY, tired eyes, and then stopped abruptly as she remembered she might smear her heavy black eyeliner and mascara. She blinked several times trying to return moisture to her rich, brown eyes that she was sure must look bloodshot and glazed.

Looking back down at the thick book spread open on the table in front of her; Renee noted the page number with astonishment: page three hundred and seventy-eight. She hadn't realized she had been buried in that old tome for so long.

Renee stood up from the hard, uncomfortable chair she had been glued to and stretched her arms high over her head. The blood rushed to her extremities, and it made her toes tingle inside her tightly laced black leather boots.

The library was empty at this late hour. Even the head librarian, Renee's loathed boss, had left for the night, asking Renee to turn out the lights and lock the building up when-ever she decided to leave. The room was deathly quiet, and the only light still on was the one directly above the table at which she had been reading.

Renee looked around at the ceiling-high shelves of books upon books. She loved working at the library and helping connect other readers with exactly what they were searching for in a good read. Nothing was as satisfying to Renee as flipping through the yellow-edged gopages of an old book that smelled like a forgotten attic, being the first person to open up a new novel fresh out of the publisher's box, or carefully arranging the books on a shelf in alphabetical order. Well, almost nothing.

Renee twirled a section of her long, straight, brown hair around her ringed finger. She propped her butt on the edge of the table and crossed her ankles. She had just had a deliciously evil thought, and her twirl became faster and more determined as she decided to act on the idea forming in her mind.

Renee pulled her battered old cell phone out of the pocket of her short, black skirt that was covered in metal studs and straps. She dialed the first number in her phone's history, and a man's voice answered almost immediately.

"Hi, Renee."

"Hello, lover," Renee answered in a deep, sultry tone. "What are you doing right now?" "Well," the man answered, "I was thinking about getting something to eat. Got the late-night appetite."

Renee smiled at the way she chose to interpret his words. "Hey, that sounds awesome, mind if I join you?" She twirled away at that lock of hair, eyes darting back and forth.

"Not at all. Where do you want to meet?"

"Well, why don't you just come over here to the library and pick me up, Paul? I'm here late researching, and... Someone slashed my tires," Renee improvised. She cringed. Perhaps that was a little extreme.

"What the fuck?" Paul said, the volume of his voice rising. "Who would do that?" Renee sighed. "I don't know who did it, just come get me."

"You don't seem too worried about it," Paul commented.

"Oh, I needed new tires anyway," she lied. "Just get over here. I'll be inside."

Renee ended the call without waiting for Paul's response. She tossed the phone down on the table with a clatter and looked around the large, empty library. The phone began to ring, and she knew from the distinct song that it played that it was her boyfriend calling back.

Renee resisted the urge to answer it, and instead, she let it move itself a few inches across the table's slick surface from the vibrations. Sex was even better sometimes when someone was pissed off. The room went quiet again. The old analog clock on the wall ticked away the seconds.

Renee pushed up from her seat on the table's edge and paced around the room, twirling her hair nervously. She and Paul lived only a few-minute drive from the library, so she knew he would get there pretty quickly. She was glad because the more she thought about the idea of getting her brains screwed out in this sacred public institution, the more impatient and turned on she was becoming.

Finally, Renee saw the headlights reflecting through the library's front windows as Paul pulled into the parking lot. She heard the car door slam, then the library door open.

Paul's footsteps echoed in the dark front part of the library, and he called out, "Hello?

Renee? Where are you? I'm starving."

Renee had taken off her shirt and bra already. She was standing in the next room in nothing but her black leather combat boots and short Gothic skirt, and she was twirling her panties on her finger. Her other hand rested on her jutted hip.

Paul froze in the doorway and said, "What the fuck?" He looked around in utter confusion.

"What's the matter, Honey, you never seen a naked woman before?" Renee giggled. "You are fucking crazy. Put on some damn clothes," Paul replied, not able to keep from admiring the tattoos on his girlfriend's chest and arms.

"Make me," Renee dared him. She marched toward him and dropped the panties she was holding. "Just make me."

Renee kissed Paul passionately, her lips engulfing his. She nibbled on his lower lip, knowing just how to make his blood start rushing from one head to the other. She bit down harder, then harder, and he pushed her away.

A fire burned in Paul's eyes. He studied his girlfriend's face, her seductive brown eyes, and pouty purple lips. His eyes moved down to the smooth skin of her neck, shoulders, and small, perfect breasts. He could not resist her pull.

"It's like that, huh?" Paul said, wiping a tiny droplet of blood from his lip.

Renee gave him a sardonic smile and reached up to tug on his long, curly brown ponytail. Paul's head jerked back from her yank, and he suddenly grabbed her around the thighs and tossed her up onto his shoulder. He moved quickly across the room, her skirt bouncing up with his gait and showing off the round bottom that was right next to his face.

Paul dropped Renee down onto the table, her legs dangling and her ass bending the pages of the book she had left out. He tore his shirt over his head and pressed the huge bulge in his jeans between Renee's legs. She spread them farther apart to accommodate the size of his pelvis and thighs, then wrapped her long, tattooed legs around his waist and squeezed.

The two lovers kissed again, long and hard, and Renee tasted the salty, metallic flavor of the blood she had drawn. Paul grabbed her arms and wrenched them behind her, making her small, round tits stand erect against his chest.

Renee struggled to break her arms free, but Paul was much stronger than she was. The solid lump in his pants rubbed against her clit, making it as hard as her nipples. She threw her head back, tickling her back with her long hair. As soon as Paul let up his strong grasp of her wrists, she began to undo his pants.

Reaching into the fly of his jeans, Renee grabbed the thick base of Paul's dick and moved her hand up and down. She pumped the shaft deftly with her soft, delicate hand and felt it grow harder with her touch. Ripping the pages of the book as she slid down the edge of the table, Renee knelt on the floor and looked up at the enormous cock above her.

Paul tangled his fingers in Renee's hair as she slowly sucked his penis down into the back of her throat. Moving her tongue slowly around the crease between his head and shaft, she tasted the salty precursor leak into her mouth. She began to suck harder, pushing Paul's cock in and out.

Renee looked up at Paul with wide, dark eyes as she sucked on him. Her eyeliner had finally smeared, making sexy dark circles around her eyes. Her long eyelashes batted as she worked her tongue, and he melted into her mouth.

Renee swallowed the warm, salty load that had shot into her throat. She stood up from the floor, picking up the tattered book that had landed there with her, and wiped off her mouth.

"Well, I..." Renee started.

Paul grabbed the book out of her hand and lifted her up slightly. He nearly ran a few long paces, and then rammed her into the bookshelf just hard enough to startle her. Books rained down on them, one hitting Paul on the head, but he ignored it entirely to look into Renee's brown eyes.

Paul was so turned on; his penis had barely missed a beat. It stood hard and throbbing again already, and he rubbed the head firmly against Renee's clit. He slid it down to her hole, then back up to the clit, then down to the hole. He teased her with it, and her body ached for it to go inside her.

Still pinned against the bookshelf, Renee wrapped her legs around Paul's waist again.

Her pussy was so wet, his dick just slid inside like silk. She rocked the shelf as he pounded into her, and more books fell with each thrust. The sound of the pages ruffling, the books thudding on the floor, and the shelf creaking from the strain seemed to make some kind of music.

Renee's arm flailed as she grew closer to explosion. She knocked a row of books over like dominoes. Paul wrapped his arms around her and carried her, still riding his cock, across the room.

Although the library now used computers for everything, the old card catalog remained behind for nostalgia and reference when the computers were all in use. The drawers were just the right height for Paul to lay Renee's torso on top of them while he still stood with his penis inside her.

Renee stretched her arms out, and Paul thought she looked like a cat doing so. His hands felt amazing massaging her perky tits, and he thrust harder and harder, shaking the whole card catalog. As she neared orgasm, Renee accidentally kicked her leg out, knocking the adjacent set of drawers askew. That set of drawers fell into the next, creating a chain reaction of destruction.

Index cards flew overhead as Renee doubled over with the sensation of dissolving into the air. Her whole being seemed to pulse with the sexual energy that was being released. Her legs jerked, and her toes curled inside her combat boots.

The array of cards was scattered everywhere around Renee and Paul. She laughed almost hysterically, her laughter making the muscles of her vagina contract against Paul's cock. It was going to take forever to get the cards back in alphabetical order.

CHAPTER 13

BREAKFAST TEMPTATION

THE SMELL of the fresh coffee fills the entire kitchen. Lennox is already halfway through the business section of the Saturday papers when Amanda finally creeps downstairs. Their greetings are non-verbal, affectionate glances as Amanda starts to fiddle with the beginnings of breakfast. Opening the fridge, she is met with a stiff breeze that reminds her that under her light silk robe she is still naked from the night before. Suddenly she is wondering if Lennox himself has anything more than his boxers on under his own robe. She closes the fridge and makes her way to the table where he sits absorbed in market indicators and an interesting story about a controversial CEO appointment that has filled half a page.

She places her hands on his shoulders and kisses the back of his neck. He giggles, wanting to know what she needs. Biting into the side of his neck now, she reaches far enough around him to land both her hands on his cock. Silk boxers cover the tool. She gives his dick a few good squeezes, moving her lips over his neck, then onto his ear before settling kisses on the side of his face. Lennox clears his throat, wanting to know what was happening with breakfast. From experience, he knows though that there is about to be massive preparation before the meal that involved everything *but* bacon and eggs. His cock responds in keen anticipation, lengthening and stiffening all at once.

She pulls his face so that she can kiss his mouth as she moves around to get onto the table and thereby bring a complete end to her husband's paper reading. Before it is crumpled completely under her ass Lennox throws it to the floor and pulls off his glasses so that he can join in on the game that Amanda has planned for them. She sits on the table in front of him and then lifts one leg at a time onto his shoulders. Slowly she pulls on the belt of her robe, releasing it completely. The robe gives way to either side of her and right before Lennox's eyes, within reach of his mouth if he leaned forward a little, is Amanda's pretty little pussy. He smiles, lifting her legs off his shoulders and pushing them forward so that Amanda is forced onto her back. He pulls her to him again so that this time her knees bend over his shoulders, and he can just about manage to get one hand between her legs from underneath.

Lennox runs a finger along the inside of Amanda's vagina. She loves the immediate intensity. The finger moves up and down the length of the slit to her fanny, pushing into it as it moves north, and then south. His finger finds her entrance and is inside her quickly. Even Amanda hadn't thought he would be so swift about penetrating. But she can't complain. She knows how he loves playing around in her cunt. He reaches forward, his finger forced a little deeper as he tries to get to something behind her. Her legs are pulled apart again and she slides back on the table until her feet can rest on its surface. Her head has knocked the sugar over but somehow this is suddenly inconsequential.

The smell of maple syrup fuses with the coffee aroma already heavy in the room. The syrup is thick and cold on her cunt as Lenox drizzles it generously over the entrance where his finger just was. Amanda is adjusted again towards him just enough for her feet to remain on the table with her knees bent, and for him to reach her cunt comfortably without getting off the chair he is sitting on. His finger is in her hole again, coating the inside of her cunt generously in syrup. He has a steady flow pouring directly onto the hole now as he moves his finger deep into her to get as much syrup on the inside of her cunt as possible. Lennox is *obsessed* with maple syrup, and eats it with *everything*.

After licking the excess from his finger, he places Amanda's legs back onto his shoulders. Her cunt is so close to him now he can smell the inside of it. He drops his head between her legs and laps up the streams of golden goo on the outside of his wife's sticky pussy. Then he sends his tongue into her vagina and starts to clean up the mess that he made. He gets into her pussy quite deep, the thick muscle protruding from his mouth a formidable tool. Amanda braces herself on the sides of the table and tenses her legs on his neck, half squeezing them together. Lennox continues with his cleanup, knowing that he has her already in the grip of his expert mouth. He gives her fleshy clit a few kisses, nibbling on it for a bit before sucking hard on her vagina so that he pulls his maple deposit towards his mouth.

The powerful suction that he creates pulls her vaginal walls towards each other. Her cunt seems to tighten as the liquids inside it make a dash for the exit. It takes several hard sucks for the stream of liquid leaving her pussy and falling into Lennox's mouth to become a steady one. After he has sucked and licked until no more fluid is forthcoming, he lifts off her and examines the pussy. He dips his finger in to check if he missed any spots. It takes him a few long digs, a slow and steady search before he is happy that the inside of her pussy is syrup-free.

Lennox is a strange man. He enjoys a good fuck, as does any bloke. He likes to cum, a lot. But these are all secondary, simple byproducts of his primary indulgence: *pussy play*! Of all the things he enjoys, he absolutely loves playing with a pussy between his fingers. So it isn't that he has now taken over Amanda's game. She is simply giving him his favorite toy to play with, knowing that his playing is always tantamount to her pleasure. He gives her punani a long quizzical look and then scans the immediate surrounds. She has awoken his cookie monster and now she will have to suffer through whatever this demon wants to do to her tender, pink bits. She can't wait.

The large, firm, seedless red grapes are the closest thing to him, Lennox not yet ready to stand up off the chair that has become his comfortable place. He pulls the fruit bowl to himself and takes a grape between his fingers without giving the rest of the bowl too much of a look. He'll come to the other fruit once he's explored the possibilities of these grapes. Again, he can't resist the maple syrup, and lightly drizzles some over Amanda's pussy, and also on the grape. A finger does the work of soaking the inside of the cunt. There is no sense of urgency as Lennox reaches deep into his wife and then dances around slowly inside her, determined not to miss a spot. He really is every bit a pussy perfectionist. Then the grape is positioned on the entrance to her. In the tips of his fingers, Lennox moves it around on the slit that opens into Amanda's hot vagina. He takes his time about pushing the fruit into her, careful not to rupture it. He wants it inside her first.

The grape makes it into the hole, but no sooner has it

disappeared inside Amanda's pussy than its juices are running out. Unable to contain her excitement, the walls of her fanny close tightly over the grape and send its dark liquid streaming out. This is licked up quickly by Lennox, who has no problem with a little grape juice with his breakfast. It takes several grapes for Amanda to become acquainted with the sensation and as soon as she does, Lennox is able to get seven large grapes inside her before he himself squeezes her legs together so that the grapes inside her pop and he gets a decent drink from the vaginal vine he's created. His tongue does the dirty work of clearing her pussy off the drained orbs.

Bananas have always gone well with maple and Lennox can't resist biting into the large one he's just skinned and coated. He turns it so the bitten part is between his fingers and eases the domed tip into Amanda. She takes deep, very loud breaths and wills her pussy to comply. One squeeze and the banana will become a delicious mash inside her too soon. The fruit is a healthy, firm texture and makes it all the way inside her, even the bitten-off bit. It slips out partially a few times for all the goo inside her but retains its shape so that it is easily reinserted. Lennox pushes it so far into her that his entire index follows behind it. Again, he pushes her legs together for a minute, ensuring that the banana is completely fused with the contents of her pussy. Then he opens her up and waits for it to start its escape. Every bit that peeps from her pussy is bitten off until he has consumed the entire fruit.

Looking down at his shorts, he sees that his cock is straining to become the sausage at this breakfast table. There'll be plenty time for additional play later so he pulls his dick free and then slides his wife over the table towards him so that she drops off it and onto his lap, where her pussy is met immediately by penis. His cock is so hard that it shoots into her without his help.

She wraps her punani over the rod and braces herself on the legs of the chair. Lennox is immobile, so Amanda moves herself up and down on his dick, her strong legs making each movement a powerful one. He reaches around her and holds on to the table as she starts to ride his dick with real gusto.

Amanda moves her pussy up and down, backwards and forwards, and around and around on his cock. Lennox pushes his feet into the floor, unable even to attempt to thrust as his wife assumes full control of his joystick. Her body is so tightly wrapped around his that there is the sense between them that the wooden chair might shatter underneath them. But this does little to deter them as Amanda rides her stallion. She had a whole lot more planned, but they have the whole day for that. Lennox's dick inside her now is sufficient. Pushing down hard onto his cock now, she gives every one of her pussy muscles a final squeeze. Lennox manages one solid upward thrust without lifting his ass. They lock in a beautiful climax before relaxing their death grip on the extremely tolerant chair.

CHAPTER 14

BREAKING IN THE NEW CAR THE RIGHT WAY

KATRINA and her husband had been looking for a new car for a while. Then they came across a car lot that was having one of their usual sales. They decided to go ahead and look at the selection. They got out of their car and were bombarded by a swarm of sales. Hank was not as forceful as Katrina was; she walked up to the sales clerk and told him what it was that they were looking for. Hank was shy and wanted to let the sales clerk do all of the talking. After a few minutes, the two gave their approval and they were on their way to owning a new car. The keys were handed over and Katrina and Hank were on their way.

Katrina was in a playful mood and rubbed Hank's leg, then began to rub her clit through her tight pants. The fabric did not do a good job of hiding that Katrina was getting wet.

Hank finally said, "Sweetie, you know what would make this perfect? If we broke this car in the same way that we broke in the old one. You remember when we parked on the side of the street and got into the back seat and we screwed our brains out for an hour before we finally both came? I think that this time we add a little spice to it and do it in the parking lot of a mall. What do you think? We could have wild sex in the parking lot while everyone walks back and forth unless they look in or hear you screaming. "

Katrina liked the sound of this proposition. Katrina was willing to try this risky sexual exploit to bring the spark back into her marriage. On the way home, they pulled into a parking lot of the mall and parked they tried to not be right up near the mall but still in an area that would allow them the chance of being seen. Katrina got into the back seat and began to unbutton her top. She was wanting her husband to see her getting the spirit of things. Hank was watching in the review mirror the striptease. Hank loved the sight of his wife's naked tits. Her nipples were just the right size and were not too large or small. Ever since her breasts implant surgery, they also seemed a lot firmer and allowed him to get a better grip on them when he was sucking on her nipples. Katrina reached into her jeans pocket, pulled her cigarette lighter out, and began to tease placing the flame near her nipples. This was a practice that got both her and Hank worked up. Katrina was very much into nipple play and was not afraid to get a little risky at times in her playing around. Hank soon joined her in the back seat and already had stripped down to his tighty-whities. The sight of him and his impressive bulge caused Katrina to suddenly want to discard of her pants as well. Hank was able to see quickly that Katrina was more than ready to get going as her panties were soaked all the way through. Katrina took her panties and handed them to Hank for him to sniff to help him get in the mood to pound her. Hank took his rigid member out and placed it against the opening of Katrina's wet and ever-so-ready cunt. The motion and sensation of Hank sliding in was almost enough on it's own to drive Katrina over the edge into the land of orgasm and sexual satisfaction.

Hank sliding in and out was getting her even wetter than she already was. Katrina had been sexually active for a number of years but this was her first time doing it in the backseat of a car. She was glad that if this was going to her first time that it was with her husband. Hank continued to pump in and out of Katrina driving her to the point that she was about to pop. She was getting louder and louder in her moans and screams. She was begging Hank to fuck her like a cheap whore. The sound of this was getting her husband even more worked up. He was a big fan of dirty talk. After it was all said and done, only a few people had actually stopped and looked in to see what was going on. These few really enjoyed the show as much as Hank and Katrina enjoyed putting it on.

CHAPTER 15

CHANGE IT UP

STELLA ARRIVED home later than usual that night. She came in the front door and tossed her keys onto the telephone stand in the foyer. Entering the dining room, she was surprised to see that it was dark except for the candles lit on the table and around the room. The table was set with their good china and silver.

Her husband, Rick, was nowhere in sight, but a delicious aroma was coming from the kitchen. She went to the kitchen to find Rick presiding over various pots and pans on the stove. He looked up and spotted her. A big smile lit his handsome face.

"Hi, baby," he said coming over to her and placing a tender kiss on her lips. Stella enjoyed the kiss and then pulled back a little. "What's all this?" she asked.

Rick's blue eyes crinkled when he smiled. They were one of the things Stella loved most about him. "Well, I know how hard you've been working lately and I thought you needed some pampering. I made your favorite dinner and I have some other things in mind."

Stella's dark eyebrows raised a little. "Oh? What kind of things?" Rick kissed her nose playfully. "You'll just have to wait to find out." "All right, then," Stella conceded.

Taking Stella's hand, Rick led her back into the dining room and pulled a chair out for her. Stella smiled as she took her seat. Rick poured some wine into a glass and handed it to her.

"Thank you," she said and took a sip.

"I'll be right back with dinner," Rick said and went back to the kitchen. Soon he was serving her chicken cacciatore, which was her favorite dish.

"It smells wonderful," Stella said appreciatively. Rick was a good cook and made the cacciatore just the way she liked it. She took a bite and let the flavor flood her mouth. "Mmmm,"

"Good?" Rick asked. "Delicious."

"That's what I was going for."

Their dinner was relaxing and filled with laughter and good food. When they'd finished, Rick came and took Stella's hand.

"Come with me," he said. "It's time for some more pampering." "All right," Stella said wondering what was in store for her.

Rick led her to their bedroom and said, "Undress, baby. You need to have a nice hot bath and get rid of all that office tension. I'll get it ready."

Stella laughed. "Really?" "Really."

Rick left her and went into their private bathroom. She began undressing as she heard water being drawn into their large garden tub. A wonderful scent began floating out of the bathroom to tease her senses. Rick returned just as she became completely naked. As always, the sight of her beautiful, slim body made his breath catch in his chest.

Her small, beautifully formed breasts made his hands itch to touch them and his mouth water with the thought of sucking on her nipples. He came to her, enfolded her in his embrace, and kissed her neck. Stella shivered in his arms in response.

Rick cupped her heart-shaped face and softly kissed her full lips. "Go ahead and get in.

It's nice and hot."

Stella gave him another brief kiss and then went into the bathroom. More candles gave the bathroom an exotic air and she slipped into the tub and rested her head back against it. The hot water began to relax her and she closed her eyes. Movement to her right caught her attention and she opened her eyes to see her naked husband kneeling on the floor by the tub.

Her dark eyes reflected her surprise as he dipped a soft washcloth into the soapy water and began washing her.

"What are you doing?" she asked with a smile.

Rick ran the cloth over her shoulders and then lifted one of her arms and washed it. "Pampering you. Remember? Now, just lay back and enjoy."

"Ok. I'm just not used to this," she said and lay back again.

Rick went back to washing her, paying attention to each area of her body. Stella gasped a little when the washcloth hit her nipples and especially when she felt it slide over her pussy. She would have been lying if she said it wasn't turning her on. Rick even washed her toes, which tickled her. He ran the cloth back up over her legs and between them.

He found rubbing the cloth over her pussy and not

being able to touch it was highly arousing. After a few minutes, he got rid of the cloth and began massaging Stella's sleek body. He teased her ears, her nipples, and then cupped her pussy before sliding a finger along her slit.

By this time, Stella was getting hot and bothered and when Rick hit her clit, she moaned and spread her legs wider. Rick stroked her clit and then inserted a finger inside her cunt. Stella shifted again and whimpered as hot sensations skittered along her nerves.

Rick moved his finger slowly, not intending to make her cum yet, but to make her horny as hell. It was working. Stella moved her hips, seeking relief.

"Oh, that feels so good, baby," she said.

He kissed her, touching her tongue with his and teasing her more with his hand. Then he took his hand away and smiled at her.

She moaned in protest. "Rick, I need, you know..."

"I know," he said with a nod. "I have something special for you." "Special? What is it?"

Rick picked up a mini-rabbit clitoris vibrator from the floor and showed it to her. "This." "What is it?" Stella asked eying the device.

"It's a little vibrator and it's supposed to do incredible things," Rick answered with a sensual smile. "Are you game to try it or are you chicken?" he teased.

Stella's chin went up at his challenge and then she smiled. "Let's give it a whirl." Her bravado couldn't completely mask her nervousness. They'd never used a toy before or had sex in the tub, but she was enjoying the new experience and figured why stop now?

Rick submerged the vibrator and slowly slid it along the outside of Stella's pussy. Her lips curved in a smile at the tickling sensations it created. Rick stroked her clit with his finger a little and then replaced it with the vibrator.

Stella's eyes went wide as the vibrator shimmied against her clit and she spread her legs wider as pleasure began stealing its way along her limbs. She grabbed onto Rick's other forearm which rested over the edge of the tub.

Rick laughed softly at her reaction. "Feel good?"

"Oh, yeah." She let out a groan and then said, "I never tried one before. I l-like it."

Stella's breath grew quicker as the vibrator pulsed against her pleasure center. The vibration was faster than anything she'd ever felt and it drove her relentlessly toward a climax.

She felt it looming, growing ever closer. She held on to Rick as the feelings intensified and then she came.

Her cries of pleasure were loud and echoed off the walls as a powerful orgasm shook her. Rick grinned as he watched his wife enjoy the bliss. His groin grew tight as he thought about the way her cunt always clenched when she came. Water sloshed as Stella's hips moved and her legs tensed. Then she began sagging as the spasms began to fade.

Rick took away the vibrator and turned it off. "So you liked it, I take it," he said with a

grin.

Stella laughed with him. "Definitely. That was amazing and felt different."

"Good. This water is getting cold. Let's get you out of that tub," Rick said and stood up. He helped her out of the tub and insisted on drying her off. Then he took her into the

bedroom and had her sit on the side of the bed. Without

speaking, he took hold of his cock and began stroking it. Stella was surprised because Rick had never done this before. She was fascinated as she watched him harden before her eyes.

Her gaze traveled over Rick's well-toned body. During their eight-year marriage, Rick had always kept in good physical condition and Stella found him as sexy now as she did when they'd first gotten married. As of late, their sex life had gotten a little predictable so these new things Rick was doing were welcome and novel to her.

Rick's excitement was enhanced by the fact that Stella was really enjoying the show.

He'd been a little nervous about doing it, but he found that he needn't have been. Her lips were parted and her eyes were riveted on what he was doing. When he got to a certain point, he stepped over to their dresser and pulled a can of whipped cream out from behind the TV there.

Stella laughed when he started putting it on his dick and then licked her lips. "That looks delicious," she said. "Bring it here."

Rick did as she said and stood before her. Stella took a lick of the whipped cream and closed her eyes as she let the sweet treat melt on her tongue. When her eyes opened, she began licking Rick's cock, the sugary cream giving it a different flavor. She dove in with gusto, licking and sucking and Rick wondered why they'd never tried this before. Stella always gave a good head, but this was something different altogether.

Soon the whipped cream was gone and Stella enjoyed Rick's own taste again. He was incredibly hard and suddenly she couldn't wait to feel his cock jammed inside her. Rick seemed to be on the same wavelength and gently pulled away from her, but that's where the gentleness ended. He scooped her up and tossed her on the bed.

Stella exclaimed in surprise and then laughed.

"Ok, you sexy bitch; on your knees," he ordered her.

"Yes, sir," Stella said, secretly thrilled with this more forceful side of Rick.

Quickly she rose up on her knees and presented her ass to him. Rick loved her ass and squeezed it and slapped it. Stella thought this was fun and giggled; something she hadn't done in a long time. Rick slapped her again and it turned Stella on even more.

"I'm gonna fuck that sweet pussy of yours, honey," he told her. Stella nodded. "Yeah, fuck it, baby. I want you so bad."

Taking hold of his dick, Rick parted her pussy lips and slid into her entrance. She was warm, wet, and tight. Rick filled her slowly, letting her adjust to the invited invasion. Stella moaned and moved back against him, taking him in completely.

"Oh, god, that feels so good," she said.

"You're telling me," Rick responded.

He started moving, slowly pulling out and pushing in. It felt exquisite. Stella's cunt gave just the right amount as he applied smooth strokes to it. He was caught up in how sensual she was as she moaned and moved with him. Their tempo grew faster and they groaned and talked to one another, saying all kinds of dirty things.

. . .

Rick slipped his hand around to the top of Stella's pussy and found her clit. Even as he slammed into her from behind, he began stimulating her swollen bud. Stella was lost in powerful sensations. Spasms of pleasure began deep inside of her and she felt as if she were going to shatter. She whimpered louder as climax neared.

Just when she thought she couldn't bear it anymore, she shot over the edge and intense joy flowed through her body as she came in an orgasm so strong that she saw brilliant lights and lost all sense of time and space. Rick felt Stella tense and almost convulse as she came and couldn't wait any longer. His own climax shook him to the core as he pounded at her. Cum shot from him and he gripped her tightly as his body jerked in bliss. Neither one could speak. The only sounds they made were growls and moans of mutual ecstasy.

Ever so slowly, they came down from those highs, drifting down through layers of passion. Stella sagged onto the bed with Rick on top of her. His weight felt good and she put a hand behind her and stroked his hip. Rick reached down to hold her hand. They stayed that way for long moments, just enjoying being there together.

Then Stella said, "Baby that was...I'm not sure what to call it. You sure do know how to pamper me."

Rick chuckled in her ear. "I'm glad you enjoyed it. I don't really have words for it,
either."

He slowly moved off her and lay beside her. "I love you, babe. I just wanted to do
something special for you."

Turning to face him, Stella said, "It was definitely special. I really liked doing things in the tub and the little vibrator. Maybe we can do some more stuff like that?"

"I have all kinds of things in store for you and feel free to do some of your own," Rick responded.

"Ok." Stella snuggled close to him.

They began drifting off, each of their imaginations at work coming up with new ideas to put more pizzazz in their love life.

CHAPTER 16

CHEATER

I USED to think working in an office would end me. I contemplated quitting on a daily basis. Nothing about it excited me and everything about it bored me.

Yet just when I had prepared myself – my resignation papers in hand – she walked into my place of work. I managed to catch a glimpse of her before she disappeared between a set of cubicles. At first, I only blinked, frozen in place by surprise, my cock pulsing. But the way she moved, the sway of her hips, her elegant and smooth, black hair, made me follow her. Something drew me to her – her thighs and the lingering fragrance of her perfume as I chased her, made me sweat. I caught sight of her again as she moved behind a bend leading to a water cooler. I quickened my pace. I longed to hear her voice, even if just to hear her say "Hi". But her moans were what I really wanted to hear.

In my haste to reach the corner, I bumped into her, and spilled the glass of water she was now carrying all over her blouse.

"I'm sorry," I said. Her wet skin and the elegant curve of her hand as she gently touched her glistening neck made me shiver. I licked my lips on impulse. The look of surprise upon her face was replaced by something else as she looked into my eyes and saw just how attractive I thought she looked. I wanted to fuck her and she smiled because she knew. I struggled with keeping my gaze from her drenched skin.

Her scent made me want to lick the water off her, the low lights making her all the more inviting. Her smile broadened.

"It's just water," she said. "But you'll make it up to me somehow," she told me, her tone playful. "Perhaps you can pour me another and bring it to my desk?"

I nodded and promised to do it after she had told me where she worked and promised me a tour of her desk. That smile never left her lips and she turned. I watched her go, my anticipation growing to unreal heights as she subtly touched her own tight ass, wiping her wet hand over her jeans. She knew I was watching her, enjoying the sight. She caressed herself slowly, her movements playing out in tantalizing slow motion. I forgot where I was. My hand found its way to my crotch. I blinked only as she disappeared behind the first cubicle. I quickly grabbed a cup and filled it with water from the cooler.

I found her sitting at her desk, her legs crossed, her red blouse unbuttoned enough for my imagination to flourish. With a smile and a buzz in my head, I handed her the cup. Our fingers touched, hands halting for a moment in mutual pleasure. She stood up, looked into my eyes, and, breathing out said, "Grab me."

I knew exactly where she wanted my hand, where I wanted it.

The heat between her legs, her breath upon my lips and her moan, made my eyes flash with images of her ass up and her face down. She knew I was on the edge as she unzipped my pants with gusto, pulled it out, got on her knees, and filled her mouth with it. I almost came, when we heard someone walking towards her cubicle. We made ourselves decent and acted as though we were just talking. Two colleagues talking and exchanging ideas. Our eyes, however, told of different ideas than what our mouths were saying. "Come to my place after work, I'll meet you on the parking lot," she said.

I was reluctant. I do have a wife at home, you see. I explained this to her and she begged me to come anyway. She didn't have to ask twice.

When we came to her home, she bid me to wait on the couch. I sat for ten minutes, my cock in hand, hard as can be. Truth be told, it had been hard the whole day at the thought of her. When she came back, dressed in latex and a whip in hand, I nearly burst. All she had on were her latex boots, a corset, and collar. She grabbed my hair and pulled my head between her legs. The taste of her made me want to forget that there's a world around me. That I have to go home after this, to a wife. When she pushed herself against me and began to move her hips in slow, circular motions, it made it easy to forget. I slurped all that came out, swallowed it, and licked everything. I licked her clit, her thighs, put my tongue inside her, I even bit her. But she didn't like that. Oh no, she cracked that fucking whip of hers and grabbed my cock. I could almost take her seriously if only her hands weren't so damn soft. She wanted to be in charge, but I wasn't up for such a game. I stood up, grabbed her by the hair, and pulled her down on the couch. She protested but knew the more she moved, the more her hair would hurt. With my free hand, I pushed down her lower back until her ass was all the way up. I spit on her asshole, twice for good measure. A clean-shaven asshole is a thing of beauty, my friends, truly. I could feel it pulsing as I rubbed my dick on it, the saliva making the sensation all the more satisfying. I felt she wanted to arch her back up, but my handheld her tight until my whole, thick dick was in her ass. I don't have the longest cock in the world, but to see the thickness of it as it spreads a woman's asshole is something to cherish. If art imitates life, then this was the pinnacle of it; my hard cock spreading its way like my determination to fuck through life and its challenges. She moaned into the couch as I fucked her in slow, ramming thrusts. I removed my hand from her back and got my dick out.

She knew the tables have turned and obeyed without question. "Spread that ass for me, slut," I said.

I could see her enjoying every second of it as I rammed it back into her. I pressed her down with my weight, pushed on her back again, and grabbed hold of her neck from behind. The arch of her made my balls fill up like a grenade with the pin removed, timed, and explosive. She looked me in the eye as I slammed myself in her ass until her moans became a wordless sensation of cumming. With her in a grip of half-paralysis, I slowly put my dick in her mouth.

"Good girl," I said. She licked it clean, then gagged on it while I fingered her pussy and fondled her ass. The softness of it nearly melted between my fingers and made gentle waves each time I slapped it. The sound of it was intoxicating. I got her on her feet and sat down. Her knees on the couch, she went slowly, taking it all in, but it was too slow for me. I hugged her hips and pushed her down and myself up into her. Her tits went along as I helped her bounce on top of me. I set free those white pearls of hers and put her whole breast in my mouth. I sucked and licked and fucking slurped.

"Fill me up with your cum, daddy, please!" she said between breaths. And that word, that fucking word, made me instantly fill her up. I felt it drip down my balls while she continued to bounce on top of me, holding *my* neck for a change. Her bounces became controlled as she found the spot and fucked herself crazy with my still stiff cock. She gasped for air as fucked her until we both stopped and just sat there.

My cum mixed with her juice and dripped down my balls. We were wet, satisfied, and enjoying when the guilt kicked in. I fucked her five times that night, and each time I filled her up, it only made it harder for me to think of going back home.

CHAPTER 17

COMING HOME TO DISCOVER A SEXY SURPRISE

MELISSA WAS ALWAYS LOOKING for ways to surprise her fiancé. She always wanted to make every moment that they had together special. After they said their vows, Melissa began planning the ways she could keep her new husband interested in sex. One of her friends gave her an idea. She suggested that Melissa dress up as her favorite female superhero and have another costume that was her husband's favorite.

The plan was to act out a scene that would involve the two having wild unbridled sex. This idea sounded like it would be fun for her and her husband to act out. She decided to give it a try. Melissa rented a Wonder Woman costume and got a Spiderman costume for her husband. She never did understand the attraction that he had to Spiderman but she went and bought the costume.

When Jack got home, he saw a note on the counter that was laying on top of the Spiderman costume. The note said to put it on and to make his way to the bedroom. Jack did as he was told. Melissa surprised Jack and fought with him a little. The idea was for them to have a play fight. Jack would lose and be tied up by Melissa. After a few minutes of this, Jack was overcome and placed onto the bed.

Ropes were tied to him to keep him from escaping. It was now time for the fun part of the plan to be put into motion and for Jack to learn the real meaning of being careful and aware of his surroundings. Melissa got onto the bed and stood over her husband in a way that he could see that she was not wearing any panties under the Wonder Women outfit. This was meant as a way to tease Jack. The idea was for him to be denied sex until he was forced to beg her to let him have his way with her.

Jack could see that her cunt was dripping wet and she even went to the point to make sure that some of her juices leaked onto his face. Jack was getting worked up and very hard at the thought that his wife's bare pussy was right there and that he was not able to do anything about it. This was making Melissa even hornier as she watched the reaction of her husband. He was desperate and said that he would do anything just for one taste. Melissa loved the way that this was going and decided to take it as far as she could.

As part of the act, Melissa said that the only way she would agree was to see who it was that was under the mask the entire time. Jack as Spiderman made the concession and said that he would give her what she wanted if he could just lick her clit for a few minutes. Melissa removed the mask and took a peek at under the mask. She loved the way that this was going. Then she yanked it off his head and laughed at him. This was so real that Jack almost forgot that this was all an act. Melissa lowered her cunt down over his face and parted her lips a little to let some of the wetness that had been trapped the chance to drip out onto his face right at his mouth. Jack took the opportunity to lick up every drop of the moistness that was on his lips and to savor it. Melissa lowered her cunt down onto his face and allowed him to take in all he wanted of her. While he was doing this, Melissa took the opportunity to lower his tights. Jack had a seven-inch pole that was throbbing and dying to be inside of something tight, wet, and warm. Melissa gave him the option that he could have her ass or her pussy. He had to guess the correct answer to the question that she was going to answer. The response was going to determine if he fucked her ass, her pussy, or simply just got a blowjob. Jack was desperate and would do anything he had to in an effort to get the wetness of her cunt to be wrapped around his cock.

Jack was able to answer the question correctly and sure enough, he got his wish as he was going to be able to pene- trate the most precious of regions. Melissa lowered herself into position and allowed him to slide inside of her wet slit. Both Jack and Melissa were in heaven. Melissa was riding her husband and still was in control of the motions that were being used in the sexual experience. The speed and depth of Jack's fucking of Melissa was being controlled by her. Jack had to learn though that sometimes the woman being on top was the best Jack tried to adjust his hips to where he was going in and out with a regular rhythm. The problem was that Melissa controlled the pace; he was not able to get into a position that was good enough to be able to match Melissa. When it was over, Jack shot a large load of his superhero seed up inside of his wife.

This was going to be a fun marriage as Melissa had a million more ideas to use.

CHAPTER 18

(CUFF 'N CUM)

"AND WHAT WERE YOU THINKING, *Mrs. Paton?*" Rob asked at the sight of his absolutely gorgeous wife in handcuffs, her wrist attached to the basement piping.

"Just shut up and get me out of these things Rob." Linda is flushed with embarrassment. She was dressed in nothing but her husband's dirty t-shirt and handcuffs. She wishes she hadn't played with the damn things and just focused on the laundry she had come down to do.

There is a look of mischief in Rob's eyes. Linda knows this look. A hand disappears behind his back and then reappears. But instead of the keys, Rob dangles a second pair of cuffs. Linda throws him a *'don't you dare'* look. Her husband holds her gaze as he bends down and feels in the pile of dirty laundry that stands between himself and his wife, naked except for his old police-college volleyball t-shirt. He pulls out a striped grey shirt, also his, and approaches his wife menacingly with the shirt and the cuffs. Linda's laugh is a nervous one.

Rob pulls her to him and kisses her on her mouth briefly before moving in behind her. In what feels like one movement he blindfolds her with the soft, grey cotton. She laughs even louder now, more of a nervous edge to it. Rob turns her laughter into panting as he settles wafts of warm air on her neck. He bites into the tenderness between her earlobe and her shoulder and she moves both away from him, and towards him. He grabs her hips under the t-shirt barely covering her ass and the cold cuffs brush against her thigh, sending sharp shivers up her spine and onto her neck where they fuse with the warm air from Rob's mouth. Linda's entire body shudders and she grabs firmly onto the pipes.

His teeth are on her ass, biting into the firm round cheeks as he parts her legs. Rob places his entire head between Linda's legs and finds her pussy with his tongue. The taste receptors on his tongue let him know that his wife has been dripping considerably already, her wetness coating the surface as he works it over her cunt. He pauses to bite into her inner thigh before finding her pussy again, his powerful tongue digging into her vagina. Rob bites down on the flesh of both Linda's legs as he makes his way to her ankles. He has them shackled together in an instant.

With her legs limited to the width of the cuffs on her ankles, there is no room between her legs for Rob's head. His hands grope the inside of Linda's legs knowing the limits he's imposed and lets his fingers squeeze firmly on her thighs before he lets them find her clit. He pinches the moist bulb between his fingers and his wife moans. He pinches the soft pink to the same rhythm that the engorged flesh beats, a rather rapid tempo. Linda is extremely turned on by his game.

Finally freeing his cock Rob stands up. He pulls his wife down so that she forms a perfect parallel with the floor. He sends his ten-inch bone into her mouth and fucks her strawberry lips as Linda wraps them tightly around his thick, solid dick. Both Rob's hands hold her head in place as he keeps sending the full measure of himself into the back of her throat, repeatedly.

Linda manages some serious sucking despite her entire oral capabilities being overwhelmed and overtaken by Rob's rod. The warm wetness brings him to a steady pre-cum, Linda's pussy-juice streaming down her leg.

Rob pulls his cock from Linda and drops to his knees. He pulls on her clit again, now a slippery orb. He uses the thumb and index on both hands to milk her as he would a cow, pulling firmly on the clit, which seems to extend with each tug. Her gasping is hoarse and raspy, sounds that have always turned him on immensely, and so he keeps tugging such that she keeps gasping. Linda stumbles a few times, her legs too close together for her to get any sort of solid footing. Rob catches her each time by cupping her cunt in both hands.

Linda's wet cunt receives Rob's fingers easily. He slips his index and middle fingers into her together and uses the thick appendages to fuck her hot cunt hard. His other hand holds her up at the waist as he stabs her juicy cunt repeatedly, savagely, with his fingers. Her gasping is now soft screaming as her pussy starts to collapse in on itself, the walls coming down in the direction of an orgasm. Rob pulls his fingers from the slimy cove, licks them of Linda's flow, and then shoots them straight back into her, stirring her pussy to an almost climax again and again. Every time she seems like she might blow he pulls his fingers from her, and dips them in his mouth until her cunt catches its breath before re-fingering her.

Suddenly both his hands are on her hips. His mouth is on hers. There is hardly time to process the kiss when Rob sends his cock into Linda with the force required by the cunt he has caused to flood. The entry is almost effortless, the vagina craving every inch of the cock it has received completely. Then Rob's hands are on her ass, pushing her towards him as he shoots his cock so deep into her that the end of each of his hard thrusts has him on his tiptoes. Linda's bound legs mean that her pussy squeezes tightly on the cock darting in and out of her despite the overwhelming wetness of its walls.

After wetting his fingers in his mouth, Rob lets them find Linda's asshole. He fingers the tight hole while pulling her cheeks apart at the same time. She tries to bend so that he can send more of his fingers into her ass without losing any of his cock in her cunt. All she manages however is to raise her ass slightly. This is all that is needed, thanks to Rob's long fingers, and his long, thick cock. Both her holes are now fucked, her hands and feet bound so that she has no more control over what is happening to her cunt.

Rob pulls his rod from inside Linda and makes his way behind her. He forces her to arch over, finds the gap between her thighs, and sends his cock into her pussy from the rear. She exhales loudly, relieved and not that his cock isn't in her ass. Rob has a considerably thick cock, and with so little control over proceedings, there really is nothing she can do to ease the entry into her tight rear end. But he's inside her cunt again, pounding savagely, and so she relaxes into his fucking. Over and over, he sends his cock into her cunt from the back, a firm hand on her spine to keep her from straightening up.

His fingers find her hair, pull hard on the rich locks, her back arching backward. Harder and harder, he fucks her, rougher than he's done in a while. Something about the vulnerability of her position has him super aroused. Rob pulls on Linda's hair hard, sending his cock into her as hard.

She yelps, and then groans, bringing on a series of super savage thrusts, Rob's cock again lodging so deep inside his wife that he ends up on the tip of his toes, Linda jolting forward. Her free hand is against the wall now so that Rob's cock doesn't send her head bashing into it. Her cunt rains pussy-poison down her thighs.

The slippery wet hole manages a firm hold on Rob's fuck-stick throughout. The absence of real friction is negligible as Linda's pussy cushions the dick inside it tightly. Even though her orgasm, Rob doesn't lose his position, sending ten thick inches in and out of her, her panting becoming gasping, panting again and then screaming. She holds tightly to the pipes, plants her toes into the floorboards and maintains her position while Rob pulls her through her very loud orgasm. Her shaking is uncontrollable for the duration of her orgasm.

Rob wets his finger in her cunt-juice and then circles the finger on her asshole. He drops a thick blob of hot saliva on the hole for good measure, dips his cock in the saliva, and then pushes it into the little hole. Linda can't move away from the cock and so she takes a deep breath and pushes onto it. Five inches of her man's thickness are inside her. Rob pulls back a few inches and then rams his entire cock inside her. She pants loudly, heavy raspy breathing sending Rob into a sort of delirium. He fucks her asshole hard.

His fingers find her cunt to console her. He can't bring himself to slow down, or be any gentler. Her ass is hot, tight, and has taken his entire dick inside itself. He loves the feeling of the hole and knows that he will come to one mother of a fucking orgasm in the compact space. He sends as much finger into her cunt and starts to bring her towards another orgasm, her dripping pussy indicating that he is on the right track. She's panting again, and then gasping. Rob's fingers bring her pussy closer and closer to eruption, her ass bringing his cock to the same place. Rob bends his knees slightly and brings her onto him so that he can find more of her cunt with his thick fingers.

Four fingers are in Linda's cunt now as Rob gets closer and closer to shooting his load. Both his indexes and both his middle fingers penetrate the vagina and pull it apart as his cock does some serious damage to her ass. Linda's back arches so that her neck tilts all the way back in search of Rob's face. She wants his mouth on her mouth. Instead, he bites into her back, and then into the side of her arms. This is not about romance. It's about fucking. Rob is fucking her ass with little thought of anything but his own climax.

He's close now, so close. He settles his dick deep inside Linda and starts to gyrate violently, stirring the inside of her ass with his cock. He thrusts deep and hard, completely penetrating her with the conviction of someone who knows exactly how to extract from her ass what his cock needs. Linda knows her husband. She knows that the beating, pulsating and throbbing of his cock means that at any second she is about to be warmed from the inside with the contents of his rod. She knows this feeling, and she anticipates it keenly.

Linda's cunt gives way again and she starts the violent throws of her second orgasm. His fingers pull, push and dig as rivers flow from her cunt. The warm contents almost completely coat his hands. Rob can't hold out a minute more and thrusts deeply into Linda just as jets of cum start to shoot from the tip of his cock. Her climax is so complete that she is unaware of his. It's the same now for him as he shoots massive amounts of fiery hot jizz into Linda. Rob's hands are no longer in his wife, gripping her hips instead so that he can keep her firmly attached to his cock. It takes a good minute for his dick to be drained of all its contents.

The first cuffs to be undone are the ones on her ankles. Rob parts her legs so that he can lick up the product of her pussy that has run quite far down her legs. He takes her pussy into his mouth as he fumbles with the set of cuffs that attached his wife to the pipes in the first place. Linda removes the blindfold herself and then watches Rob on his knees, between her legs, eating out her pussy. She runs her fingers through his hair and then touches her ass gently for a bit. Rob's cock is really too large for her tiny asshole. But he loves it and so she lets him have it. They fumble for a bit before collapsing on the pile of dirty laundry, Rob doing the same damage to her pussy now that he has just finished doing to her asshole...

CHAPTER 19

DANGER AND TROUBLE ON THE TRAIL

IT WAS A BEAUTIFUL AUTUMN DAY. A brisk breeze whipped the fallen leaves scattered across the ground up into the air. Red, orange, yellow, and brown twirled on the waves of wind that blew through the countryside.

Liz was saddling up her Tennessee Walker for a ride down a wooded trail. She wanted to ride every opportunity that came up before the trees were bare spindles, the sky gray, and the weather miserably cold. Her horse Danger knew it was almost the time of year for him to retire to the barn and await the handful of days nice enough for Liz to ride in the winter.

Liz buckled the last strap, pulling the saddle tight around Danger's belly. Leading him lightly by his reins, she walked him out of the old barn.

Danger whinnied and pawed at the ground with his front hooves as they stepped into the cool breeze. He was the color of the deepest reddish-orange hued leaves, with a shiny black mane and tail. Liz ran her hands down his sleek coat, stroking his neck and chest.

"You ready for an adventure?" Liz asked Danger as she brushed a strand of her blonde hair out of her face.

Danger snorted his approval. Liz pulled her hair back into a ponytail to keep the wind from blowing it around her face.

"Now hold on just a minute there,"

Liz spun around to see her boyfriend strolling toward the barn. "Jacob," Liz exclaimed. "Did you get finished early?"

Jacob nodded as he put his arms to rest on the top wooden slat of the fence. He was in well-worn Wrangler denim and red flannel.

"Yep," he said, reaching out to touch Danger's muzzle, "the tractor quit running on me.

Going to talk to Tony about fixing it tomorrow." "You think it's a simple fix?" Liz asked.

"Probably," Jacob replied. "But I don't know much about fixin' tractors. I just know how to drive them."

"Well at least you get the afternoon free," Liz pointed out. "Maybe you could saddle up Trouble and join me for a ride."

Liz put one foot in the stirrup as she prepared to mount Danger, but in one swift motion, Jacob had ducked under the bottom rung of the fence and grabbed her around the waist. She squealed, startled, but Jacob kissed her long and hard to silence her.

Jacob pulled his lips off Liz's, breaking the suction but still holding her tight. Liz laughed, "So that's what you want to do on your day off?"

"You bet," Jacob said with a grin.

"Well," Liz replied, "you're going to have to catch me first!"

Liz swung her leg over Danger's back and had already

spurred him into action by the time her butt hit the leather saddle. Danger broke into an immediate gallop, kicking up dust and dead leaves.

Liz's laughter disappeared into the wind.

Jacob barely missed a beat. He ran to where Trouble, a strong black stallion with a white star on his forehead, was grazing nearby. He almost startled the horse as he leaped onto the bareback and hit his heels on the horse's side.

"Come on, Trouble!" Jacob yelled, and he let out a whoop like an Indian war cry as he galloped after Liz.

Liz had gotten a good head start, but Jacob was the more experienced rider. He tore after Danger and his rider. The wind blew back his brown hair and the pounding of the hooves drowned out any other sound.

Liz kept glancing over her shoulder as Jacob covered the ground between them. She laughed excitedly, her adrenaline pumping like Danger's strong legs. The horse and rider transitioned smoothly onto the dirt path that began at the tree line and disappeared into the forest.

Jacob followed his prey onto the trail. His firm, muscular rear end bounced hard against the horse's back, and he kept a tight but gentle grip on Trouble's long black mane to keep himself from flying off in mid-gallop. He ducked to miss low-hanging branches as he gained on Liz.

After a short while, Liz came to the part of the trail where it began climbing a steep hill. She decided not to try taking at full speed since she was not as skilled on a horse as her boyfriend was.

"Whoa, Danger," Liz called out, and she was already dismounting before he came to a full stop. Her feet hit the ground running, and she tore into the underbrush as she ran off the trail.

Liz heard Trouble's gait slow as he came upon Danger at the base of the hill. She was nearly breathless as she tried running without making much noise. Despite her efforts, Jacob saw her and sprinted through the trees, completely oblivious to the branches and vines that caught at his skin as he ran past.

Jacob closed in on Liz. As she attempted a last burst of speed, he tackled her carefully, and the two tumbled laughing through the crunchy fallen leaves on the forest floor.

As their roll came to a halt, Jacob had landed on top. He pinned Liz's arms to the ground on either side of her head. Her long blonde hair was a tangled mess full of leaf matter and knots tied by the wind of the ride. Her enormous smile crinkled the skin by her eyes and scrunched her perky freckled nose.

"I caught you," Jacob laughed, wild-eyed. He was breathing heavily, and beads of sweat rolled down his fore-head and sinewy neck.

"I guess you did, Cowboy. Now what?" Liz responded with a challenging tone.

Jacob didn't waste any time. He grabbed Liz's buttoned-up flannel shirt and bra and bunched them up to her chin. Her breasts fell out, and he grabbed them in his strong, calloused hands.

Jacob kissed Liz, pressing his face into hers so hard she could barely catch her breath. Her chest heaved with the effort, and her hands fumbled with the buttons of Jacob's work shirt. Most of them undone, she spread his shirt open and shuddered as her breasts touched his warm, wet skin. Her nipples tickled his chest.

Jacob sat up and unbuttoned Liz's jeans. He discovered she wasn't wearing any panties today. He jerked the pants down to her knees and put his hands on her hipbones. He touched her stomach and moved his hands down to the neat little patch of short curls that peeked out from between her legs.

Jacob leaned back down and kissed Liz on the neck and shoulders. She closed her eyes and emitted little sighs as each kiss became more pleasurable than the last. Jacob began massaging her clit, surprisingly gentle for such rough, work-worn hands.

Liz pressed her pelvis harder against his hand, and he slipped a large finger into the moist hole that opened with desire. She rubbed her hands down his chest and sides, sending ripples of chills across his skin. She rubbed him down again, this time letting her fingernails slide lightly down. Jacob shivered.

"Harder," Jacob suggested, and this time Liz dug her fingernails in deep, leaving bright red lines behind. He groaned softly.

Jacob unbuttoned his pants deftly with one hand and yanked the zipper undone. He slid his pants just far enough down over his butt to let his throbbing cock and tight balls flop out of the confines. He crawled up a bit, letting his package hangover Liz's face.

Liz lifted her head and took him into her mouth. She licked around the tip and up the base, timidly sucking on the first half of the large penis before her. Anxious, Jacob thrust his hips, driving his cock deeper into Liz's throat.

Liz would have choked if there were room for her throat to contract, but there wasn't, so her reflex just tightened her throat on the swollen head. Jacob moaned with pleasure and began rhythmically swaying his hips forward and back as she sucked.

Jacob jerked his penis out of her mouth, making a pop as the suction broke. Liz's mouth hovered open for a second with the surprise of suddenly being empty. He moved back down and, taking his dick in his hand, he began to stroke Liz from the clit down into her crevice.

"Put it in," Liz begged, going crazy with anticipation.

Jacob rammed his rock-hard cock into her pussy, and she let out a little scream at the rough sensation.

"Oh, yeah," Liz called out as Jacob moved in and out of her, thrusting hard enough to hit her cervix with each pump. He was so deep inside of her that she felt like her eyes were bulging out of their sockets each time he drove it in.

Jacob grabbed Liz by the wrists and held her arms down. She struggled against him in her throes of ecstasy, but he held fast, his muscles flexed. Liz watched his ab muscles contract and release as he plunged up and down into her.

They were both dripping sweat, and it intermingled until neither knew who was sweating more. Panting, Liz began to find herself getting close to the release.

"Harder," she commanded, and Jacob gripped her shoulders as leverage to propel himself deeper and harder into her. The impact sent vibrations of pleasure throughout her body, and she began to feel that telltale unfolding of nerves in her center. Her vaginal muscles began contracting on the huge, throbbing penis that was pounding against her cervix, and she felt like she was spinning, sinking, and curling all at once.

A voice that sounded far away and not her own at all escaped Liz's mouth, startling her.

As she rode her orgasm through to the end, she felt

Jacob's cock grow larger in the final moments before his imminent ejaculation.

She was still recovering from the intensity of her own climax when Jacob suddenly ripped his member out of her vagina and blew his load. The creamy whiteness spewed from the tip onto her tits. It dripped down onto her heaving, flat stomach. Jacob's shoulders hunched over as he squeezed his dick, getting every last tingle of orgasm out of his body.

With his penis still in his hand, Jacob started at the sound of rustling in the bushes nearby. Liz lifted her head and looked in the direction he had turned.

Danger and Trouble had come to find their riders, confused to be left alone on the trail. The two horses stared at the couple in various states of undress on the forest floor, chewing their bits and wiggling their ears.

The couple laughed deliriously at the ridiculous scene. Jacob kissed Liz through his smile as they began putting themselves back together.

CHAPTER 20

DRIPPING WET

MY HUSBAND and I have been married for about a year now so I guess you could say we are newlyweds. The spark and passion between us still existed though, and we were always looking for new and exciting ways to spice up our love life. The spontaneity between us was one of the best aspects about our relationship, and it always had been. Both of us had always been eager to try new and creative things to make each other feel wonderful when it came to love and sex. We had an amazingly hot and romantic relationship. Love and lust could be mingled in my opinion. Who says you can't combine the two? I think you can and if you do, you might be surprised at the intensely erotic outcome.

CHAPTER 21

RISQUÉ RENTAL

FOR THE PAST year since we tied the knot, hubby and I had tried numerous sexual adventures to spice things up or shall I say keep them burning. I had racked my brain all week trying to come up with a sexual tryst that would not only spark things up, but also possibly cause a three-alarm fire to rage inside of our amorous bodies. After searching online and flipping through all of my Cosmo magazines I had finally settled on something I thought would blow my husband's sexual mind! My husband and I had toyed around with public sex a bit, but we had never had it all-out. It was something we had been dying to experiment with. I think I had finally found a way we could. This way would be so smoking hot it would be a miracle if we weren't arrested before we were through. That means it was the perfect choice so I got on the phone and arranged the place.

As we drove down the street towards our sexually deviant destination, my hubby and I exchanged capricious glances. We knew what we were about to embark upon was a sexual experience that would put the N in the word naughty. I couldn't help but squirm a bit on the passenger side of our SUV. I could hardly contain the fires of passion that raged inside of me. My juices were flowing and there was no stopping them. I don't know which was more eager, my mind or my pussy.

My husband pulled into the parking lot of the Spa spot. My lips were watering at the thought and not my mouth either. I could feel the familiar wetness on my thongs right were my lips lay, as my lips kissed the silky fabric between my legs my mind was whisked away to the sexual thrill that awaited us inside the spa.

We went inside and rented the hot tub of our choice, and then headed down the hall towards our erotic destination. The walk seemed to take a month since we were both on fire. Not just our bodies were melting but our minds were caught in a seductive net of intrigue. My mind swirled with anticipation. The thought of publically embracing and then my husband's delicious cock slipping inside my hungry folds was more than I could bear and his fingers twirling one nipple at a time making my inner flesh seethe with raging desire.

We finally made it to our hot tub and we waited for the attendant to say her proverbial banter, and then we looked at each other like two teenagers about to "do it" for the first time. I felt my cheeks turn a rosy pink as my husband looked at me with his smoldering hazel eyes. His eyes alone could turn me on and make me wet and needy for his starving mouth and touch. His eyes also teased me as if to ask, "Okay who's first? Who will start this incredibly exciting adventure we have embarked on?"

I decided it would be me. My hubby loved it when I demanded attention and sexual energy from him. Nothing made him more turned on or got him rigid faster than my demands for his arms and his lustful passion. If I wanted to unleash the animal within him, all that I had to do was simply demand he give me what I wanted and was so hungry for. I slipped into the hot tub and I was immediately engulfed by the waves of incredible heat flowing over my body. I playfully removed my bikini bottoms and threw them over my shoulders and onto the cement. I looked at my husband with mischief in my eyes. He peered into the heated pool and licked his lips while lingering on my folds baring all.

I loved how he truly seemed excited to see me naked under the water once again as if he never tired of my pussy and all she offered him. He stepped into the hot tub with me and surprisingly engulfed me with his kiss. I was pleasingly taken aback and loved the taste of need on his lips. As he kissed me feverishly, he reached under the water and grasped my pussy lips between his fingers. He played with my pubic hair pulling it up and down seductively. I grabbed his face and kissed him back as our tongues transferred the heat from our groins. Even though I had made love to him many times each time felt more like the first time and I grew hungrier for him with each touch and each blending of our flesh.

He knew just how to entice my folds. He played gently with my lips under the jetting water. He has always loved my luscious pink labia and he twisted each one, one at a time slowly between his thumb and third finger. My pussy danced upon his fingers practically making me stand straight up out of the water and plunge down on top of his fist. I greedily groped for his swollen cock in his swim shorts and pulled it out of the hole. It was rock hard and I could feel the smell of sex on it. I could taste his hard-on as I stroked him and ran my fingertips around the swollen ridge. The intensity between us grew to a smoldering level. We were seconds from his cock ambushing my pussy under the water. The need suddenly became a demand!

Then we heard footsteps and the door open up behind us. We tried to pull apart and act natural but it was achingly apparent we were turned on way beyond a controllable level. The attendant tried to pretend she didn't notice, but our sexual passion was far too obvious and I am certain she felt and smelled our desire in the air. We couldn't wait for her to leave. The anticipation was torture.

Once the door closed behind her, we attacked each other with a desire that was a raging wildfire. The thirst was unquenchable. Our kisses became vehement and more demanding. He lifted me to his lap and I plunged hard down onto his waiting need. He sunk deep into my chasm. My folds enveloped every inch of him. My lips wrapped snugly around his girth as if they might never let go. I felt them cling to him like a wet suit to the flesh. The ripples of water tickled my hard nipples as he drew them to his mouth one at a time. As he nursed my nipples, sparks shot through my entire body like an electric current. He suckled them hungrily and ravaged my flesh like a starving animal.

Our bodies moved with the rhythm of the jets. As the jets shot warm liquid so did my pussy upon his steel meat. One orgasmic wave after another spiraled throughout my body and then I felt his girth get as hot as fire and as hard as stone. My lips gripped tighter. My body became rigid and under his control. I bounced on him knowing any moment someone could walk through the door, but I didn't care as I had yet another orgasm all over his wet lap. The harder we screwed the more insatiable it became. He groaned as quietly as possible his cock became catatonic and hard inside my folds.

We embraced, as our bodies became one wet urgent

demand that wouldn't stop. We gritted our teeth to keep from screaming out as one more wave of orgasm pierced our bodies until they collapsed into the jets completely relaxed and spent. It felt like a whirlpool had pulled us underneath its erotic tug. The experience was invigorating just like the hot tub itself even more so. The water and jets only added to the seduction and to the tidal wave of pleasure my husband and I shared sexually and intimately.

The thought of being caught as I plunged onto his cock was exhilarating and made me cum harder than I ever thought I could. The warmth of the water combined with the essence of our attraction was more than any woman could hope for. It made me feel like I was all woman inside and out. When a man makes you appreciate being the woman you are there's nothing more erotic in my book. When you feel as though you are the object of all he desires lustfully and you are all he truly ever needs in his heart that is the ultimate turn-on of all turn-ons.

CHAPTER 22

ELECTRIC MAN

HANK SANDERS ENTERED the back gate of the address where he'd been instructed to go by his boss. A master electrician, he was in high demand during the hot summer season to fix air conditioning units. This was such a call.

He went through the back gate that opened onto the concrete patio of a large in-ground pool. The shimmering blue water called to him and he would have liked to have jumped in.

However, he had a job to do and he started towards the back door. The house owner had instructed that the repairman should come to the back.

He knocked on the door and it was soon opened by a blonde woman wearing a sheer white robe. She had nothing on underneath, much to Hank's delight.

"Uh, hi. I'm here to fix the A/C unit. I'm Hank," he said. Her full breasts drew his eyes and he practically salivated at the sight.

"Hi, Hank. Nice to meet you," she said as she openly gave her husband the once over.

Roni liked what she saw. Hank was fairly tall with broad shoulders and a strong chest. It was hard to tell about the rest of him due to the uniform he was wearing, but Roni knew that underneath it were hard abs and powerful thighs. She knew he had a big cock, too, and intended to help herself to it.

"Thanks," Hank said. "If you point me in the direction of the unit, I'll get right on it." "Sure thing," Roni said.

She scooted out past him and led him towards the pool. The sheer robe didn't do anything to hide her shapely ass and Hank enjoyed following her. As she started shedding the robe, Hank once again thought about what a good idea it was that they'd installed a privacy fence.

Roni tossed the robe to the side and stood naked in front of Hank. "Would you like to go for a swim with me?" she asked.

Hank said, "Oh, I'd love to but the boss wouldn't like that."

"You wouldn't want me to complain to your boss that you didn't follow directions, would you?" Roni asked with a coy look.

Hank pretended to be reluctant. "Well, I guess not. I need the job. I don't have a suit though."

"You don't need one. I don't have one, see?"

"I sure do. Ok, I'll just get out of these," Hank said.

"Hurry. My unit is overheating and I need you to cool it down," Roni teased.

Hank quickly shed his uniform and Roni jumped in the pool with a squeal. Hank jumped in after her, swimming smoothly through the water. He caught up with her easily and grabbed one of her legs, stopping her progress.

Roni laughed and tried to kick him off but he was stronger and held on. He pulled her around to face him and wrapped his arms around her. Roni thoroughly enjoyed their bodies sliding against each other in the water. They were near the side of the pool and Hank easily lifted her up and sat her on the side of the pool. He stood between her legs and they kissed.

They nipped and sucked each other's lips and melded their mouths together so that their tongues could play.

Roni loved the feeling of Hank's chest rubbing against her pussy. He didn't shave his chest and the hair there created a pleasant friction against the sensitive skin of her privates. Hank worked his way down from her mouth to her neck, biting and sucking as he went. Then he came to her ample breasts and their dusky nipples. They were erect and looked delicious.

Hank took one in his mouth and licked and sucked it, drawing small moans from Roni. He gave the other one the same treatment and then started stroking her pussy. Roni moaned and leaned back on her palms so he had greater access. Hank brought more water up from the pool and spread it across her pussy.

He lowered himself into the water further and brought his face even with her pussy. It was so pretty and Hank kissed it. He licked the whole length of her slit, enjoying the way she tasted. He settled on her clit and Roni jerked as his warm tongue began flitting back and forth over it. Hank had a very talented tongue and knew just what she liked and where to lick.

Hank inserted two fingers inside of her cunt and began stroking her G-spot. He moved in short quick strokes as he continued to lick her clit. Roni's nerves were stretched to the limit as Hank rapidly brought her to orgasm.

"Oh, fuck, baby! That feels so good. Oh, shit! I love the way you make me cum!" she shouted as her orgasm flowed through her in intense spasms.

Hank moaned against her pussy, trying to keep the feeling alive as long as possible.

When she relaxed a little, he withdrew his fingers and pulled her back into the water with him. Roni wrapped her legs around Hank and felt him place his hard cock at the entrance to her cunt. She then started bobbing up and down in the water, moaning and gripping his shoulders tight.

Hank guided her hips as he thrust upwards to meet her on the way down. Roni's blue eyes locked on Hank's dark ones as they moved together. Hank's cock filled her every time he thrust inside and the sensation was exquisite. Her clit rubbed against Hank's groin and it sent pleasure tingling along her limbs and inside her cunt.

Hank could tell that she was going to cum by the way her pussy tightened around his cock and the way she gripped his shoulders.

"You gonna cum for me, baby? Is that sweet little pussy of yours gonna cum?" he asked. "Uh huh. Oh yeah, Hank. My pussy is gonna cum for you. Just for you, honey," Roni said.

Hank said, "Good. I want you to cum all over my cock."

She loved it when Hank talked dirty to her. It made her even hornier. "Oh, god, I'm almost there, Hank. I'm so close," Roni whimpered.

Hank pumped harder and the combined friction sent Roni soaring over the edge. Her pussy tightened around Hank's dick and she cried out her pleasure. Hank let her enjoy her climax and then withdrew from her. He laid her back in the water and spread her legs while he held her up. He began rubbing her pussy rapidly, centering on her clit.

Roni grabbed the back of her thighs to keep her head above the water. Hank was merciless as he drove her towards another orgasm. Roni was excited by the determined look on his face as he stroked her clit. It felt fantastic and Roni moaned and whimpered. Those whimpers grew into loud, high-pitched groans as she came again.

It was so intense and Hank kept it going for her. Her body jerked with the pleasure of it and she couldn't speak for a few moments.

"Oh! Oh! Shit, shit, shit!" she cried.

Hank slowed his movements and then kissed her pussy gently.

Roni righted herself and then said, "Your turn, Mr. Electrician. Come over here to the shallow end."

"Yes, ma'am," Hank said. He was amused when Roni took his dick and led him by it.

She got down on her knees and worked his cock making it harder again. It was such a nice cock and she loved the way it felt in her hand. Then she took him deep inside her mouth until he went down her throat a little. Hank groaned and ran his hand through her wet hair. Roni wanted him to cum; she wanted to watch him cum. She created strong suction when she pulled back and Hank moaned loudly.

"Suck it, baby," he said. His voice was hoarse with need. "Faster, Roni. I need to cum so bad."

Roni moaned and complied, her head moving rapidly and swirling her tongue around the head as well. She played with his balls and then grasped the base of his dick hard and sucked faster. Hank gasped and groaned. His hips began to thrust as she became more urgent about her intentions.

His cock pulsed in her hands. Hank knew the throbbing meant that he was going to cum and told Roni.

She stopped sucking him and began jerking him off hard. She wanted to see him cum. "Come on, baby, cum for me. I want to see that big, beautiful cock squirt all over the place," she said.

"Here it comes, Roni. Here it comes!"

Hank threw back his head as hot cum spurted from his dick. His groin tightened and he cried out hoarsely as the orgasm crashed through him.

"Fuck, fuck, fuck!" he shouted as he came.

"Yeah, baby, yeah!" Roni said as she watched him climax.

As his release abated, Hank grabbed Roni and hauled her against him. "How's your unit now?" he asked her.

Roni kissed him and said, "It's working fantastic now. Thank you for servicing it." "Any time, babe. Any time."

They swam a little more and then went inside, both happy with the service call that day.

CHAPTER 23

EXPOSED

LUNCHTIME: another solitary stroll around the park before heading back to the insurance office where Celia had worked for the past six years. *At least I'll be getting some fresh air,* she thought, *rather than another soul-destroying lunch nibbling vending machine sandwiches in the staff common room.* It was safe to say that Celia was fed up. At thirty-eight, she shouldn't have been feeling like this. She and Cal hadn't wanted to have children, and had set out on their married journey together with the sole purpose of enjoying life; traveling, and spending quality time together with their double income. But their jobs had become more and more demanding. They were both too tired at the weekend for any kind of hedonistic adventures. Over the past eight years, they had fallen into a routine of long office hours and evenings spent slumped in front of the TV with a takeaway between them. Sex, well, that was now saved for special occasions when they both felt obligated.

. . .

"Do you wanna, you know?" Cal asked the week before on their wedding anniversary, giving her shoulders an affectionate squeeze.

"Um, yeah, sure..." Celia trailed off, trying to avert his gaze. "I'll just go and brush my teeth."

When it was over, and Celia had faked yet another orgasm so as not to hurt her husband's feelings, they had put their pajamas back on and kissed each other good night.

It wasn't that they didn't love each other; they had known each other since college and had become the best of friends as well as lovers. Cal's endearing shyness and propensity to blush at anything had made him utterly adorable to Celia. It was just that they had grown so familiar with the habitual routines that dominated their lives.Their mortgage had to be paid. They had to work as much as they could. *It just wasn't meant to be like this.* Celia had thought that morning after their anniversary. She finally admitted to herself that things needed to change.

Celia confided in her best friend, Julie, who seemed to be an expert in relationships. She was always having romantic trysts and dramatic affairs, luxuriating on the memories of the hot, steamy sex she'd been having.

"The only hot thing about our bedroom is the electric blanket in the wintertime," said Celia, dryly.

"Why don't you try something different?" suggested Julie, "Like sex in public?"

"In PUBLIC!" cried Celia. "We'll get arrested!"

"Not if you're careful about it, choose somewhere you know you won't get caught. Honestly, Dave and I did it in the back of my car in a parking lot the other night. Man, it was good. There's something about the danger and risk that makes it so hot!"

Celia could see her friend daydreaming again and envied her.

"Alright, I'll give it a go. But I'm embarrassed to even talk to Cal about it!"

Julie had known Cal and Celia since they were both in college so she took it upon herself to broach the subject with Cal.

"You need to spice things up with Celia, she loves you but she's desperate for something more - some excitement!"

Cal immediately blushed a deep beetroot color. "Er, ahem, well, yes I suppose we have been having a few problems recently." But he hadn't realized she'd been so unhappy. Julie, for all her bluntness, had been right. He needed to let Celia know she was still sexy, still wanted, and still beautiful.

Celia sat on the bench and let the light rain dampen her hair. She resolved to talk to Cal tonight about spicing up their sex life. Suddenly, there he was, sitting beside her. "I called the office to see where you were and they told me you'd gone for a walk, I figured you'd be here."

"Cal! You surprised me!" Celia was genuinely happy to see her husband. Perhaps now was the time to talk. They both started to speak at the same time.

"Ca, Cel..." both of them laughed. The look in each

other's eyes told them what they were both thinking - they'd known each other for that long.

"I want to make love to you." Cal said softly, cupping his wife's face in his hands. "Right, here, right now."

"Here? Are you serious?" But already Celia could feel herself getting wet. Cal took her elbow and pulled her up, wrapping one strong arm around her waist and leading her away from the benches.

"I've found a clearing we can use; our chances of being spotted are slim."

"Slim? Is that good enough?" Celia said through a sly grin. She could feel him hardening against her as he pushed her forwards - passing another couple as they scurried to escape the rain. He led her through a gap in the hedges, her stocking catching on a low branch and ripping a hole.

"Don't worry," he said, pulling her through the wet undergrowth. "They're coming off anyway."

Was this the man who Celia had known all these years? The shy, awkward college graduate had worn his virginity like a dead weight around his neck. They made it into the clearing, and Celia was now completely at his mercy, willing and wanting. "Take off your coat," he ordered. She did as she was told, letting it fall at her feet. He moved towards her and pulled her head back, kissing her hard and deep on the mouth. His other hand pulled at the buttons on her blouse, letting it fly open. He stood back to admire her and she let the cool rain dampen on her now hot skin, out in the open air, just feet away from onlookers. He moved in again with his mouth, onto her breasts and took her nipple in his lips, making them harden instantly, Celia let out a groan. "Can we do it? Please? I want you inside me."

"Wait," he whispered. His mouth moved down, hungrily, tearing at her already ripped stockings. Still standing, she parted her legs slightly and grabbed the back of his head as his tongue found her clitoris, and two of his fingers circled her opening, which was now fully moist and dripping. Celia let her husband lap her up. She suddenly felt totally exposed out in the clearing with her ripped clothing, the moisture in the air building a hot sweat on her brow that trickled between her breasts. She heard a rustle, and then footsteps.

"Cal, we've been spotted," she panted, panic set in but at the same time, she could feel her orgasm building, riding on the excitement of the exposure.

But Cal was elsewhere. Celia came into his mouth, unable to silence the excitement that came out of her. The footsteps could be heard, quickening into the distance. Whoever had seen them had decided to leave them to it.

"My turn," Cal said, breathless - his usual soft brown eyes were now boring into Celia, his pupils dilated with an intensity that almost frightened her.

Were these the same eyes that had looked at her so tenderly on their wedding day? "By that tree," he said. She stepped backwards. "Turn around; I want to fuck you from behind." After all these years of labored sex, facing one another beneath the familiar duvet, having him enter from behind felt like a completely different experience. What had she been missing all these years? Celia turned, bending forwards and presenting herself to him in all her naked glory. She gripped the tree, which was wet and cold, and dug her nails into the bark, waiting for the moment when he would slam into her.

She held her breath. Nothing.

"Cal?" She turned her head to find him undoing his tie.

"You need to be tied up," he moved around the tree and bound her hands together with his necktie.

"Cal, hurry up!" Celia urged.

"Alright, here it comes." Cal gripped her behind and parted her, slamming himself inside and pumping hard and fast. Celia felt the bark and the tight knots he had made chaffing on her wrists- relishing both the pain and the urgent pleasure that was once again building inside her.

Her husband's cock rammed and teased that delicious, secret space inside of Celia: the space that only her husband could reach.

CHAPTER 24

FISTING FANNY

LUTHER'S HANDS glide over his wife's body, the warm oil on his palms making his movement effortless. Her nakedness in the dim light makes his cock so hard that the sarong around his waist is forced undone by a massive erection. The light fabric hangs briefly on his fifteen-inch boner before he shakes it to the floor. Stacy is face-down on the massage table, soft moans escaping her as her husband's large, expert hands work into every part of her, relaxing her completely. This is going to be essential if they are to successfully explore the fetish they stumbled across by accident in their search for a little spice...

On her back on the massage table, the warmth from the leather moves gently through her body from below. The heat from above comes from her husband's hands moving over her breasts and then down onto her thighs. He doesn't part her legs too much since the thin table won't allow for this without having to hang Stacy's legs uncomfortably over the sides. And for what they have planned, she needs to be very comfortable. He feels around her clit and then rubs on it. Then he fingers for her hole and, finding it, sends his thick finger into her willing vagina. He digs deep into her pussy while fondling her breasts. He works the single finger around in her cunt and scoops out the contents of her pussy while a few fingers on the other hand move around in her mouth, stretching her lips wide.

Keeping his fingers in her mouth, he removes the wet appendage from her cunt. He replaces it with his thumb, and while digging his thick thumb into her cunt, his middle finger finds her asshole. The long finger in her ass goes all the way inside. There is no need for Stacy to lift off the bed because of Luther's large hands. He simply covers the surface of her vagina with his palm and lets his fingers travel where he wants them to. His finger curves inside his woman's ass and then he proceeds to dig deep in and pull slightly out over and over again. His thumb fucks her cunt so hard that she has several mini orgasms. During these climaxes, he is able to stretch her asshole a little more by adding another two fingers. She moans softly at this invasion. His cock drips at the sounds escaping his beautiful wife.

He pours a little oil on the surface of her cunt and after easing his fingers out of her ass, sends the index into her pussy. He lets his middle finger join it after a few minutes of fingering. Adding more oil, he gets up to four fingers. The scoop intensifies now as he again proceeds to dig out the contents of her cunt. He continues to rain oil over her cunt and her body while she moves some of it to her breasts and touches herself. She pulls hard on her nipple and squeezes her breasts hard as Luther digs into her pussy with four massive fingers that fold over each other so that the full side-by-side length of them doesn't overwhelm her.

Again, he pulls the fingers from her fanny and lets the oiled members find her asshole. The insertion is deliberately slow as Luther expands Stacy's rear, one finger at a time. He gets up to the four fingers, but still, they are crossed over each other so that the stretch isn't too much for her. He uses his fingers skillfully to expand the tight circle, the stretch a beautiful one. Luther watches Stacy's face, her eyes closed as her hands move over herself and his fingers lodge ever deeper in her ass. Her vagina is perfectly placed for an attack, but he wants to give it a final fingering before bringing out the big guns.

With his fingers still in her ass, he takes his other hand and plays an imaginary piano on her pussy. Then the first of his fingers is inside her. He sinks it into her and makes sure that while he pushes it down he pushes the other four in her ass up. When the fingers in her ass can't go any further, he keeps them in place, able now to focus on filling her punani. He adds a second finger and digs deep with the two while maintaining his upward thrust in her ass. With three fingers in her cunt, he starts to wriggle the four in her ass and mimics this action in her fanny. Stacy is overtaken by the sensation that a million serpents dance around in all her holes and is oblivious to the addition of the fourth finger in her pussy, or even to the fact that these fingers have been stretched apart, turning her cunt into a gaping void.

The dildo that they've purchased for this occasion is no thicker than three of Luther's fingers, but still, almost double the girth of his cock. So when he removes his fingers and replaces them with the tool, Stacy's vagina feels incredibly stuffed. Sticking the massive dildo into her is an exercise that moves him to nibbling on her clit as he pushes the toy into her. His mouth is right next to her hole and his eyes watch the dildo move up and down so near to him that he can smell the rubber. He sucks on her clit a little longer and then moves himself off of her until he has a more complete view once more. He digs into her with the dildo using the power in both his hands, both of hers moving over her breasts again, pulling them away from her body and then pushing them back into it.

He holds the dildo in place in her pussy and pulls a set of Thai balls from their bag of goodies. The balls are half the girth of the dildo and so the fit into her ass is not an uncomfortable one. The twelve balls are inserted into her one at a time until the last one disappears into her ass. All that is left outside of her is the string that holds all twelve together, interspersed by varying distances of up to an inch but no more. With all of them packed into her snug rear end, Luther resumes his dildo assault and fucks her pussy hard, both hands back on the tool that now plows aggressively into her pussy.

He brings her close to orgasm, watching her closed eyes. She is delirious for the pleasure he is giving her. He continues to fuck her with the dildo, waiting for the beginnings of her climax. He positions his other hand on the string that will bring the balls from her ass, but does nothing but take it between his fingers firmly. As the telltale screams of orgasm escape her Luther hits the back of her cunt hard with the dildo, ramming it into her repeatedly while extracting one ball at a time from her ass. He times it perfectly and by the time he is done pulling the last ball from her, she is a lump of post-orgasmic bliss on the massage table.

Stacy holds the dildo in place in her cunt as soon as she lands from heaven and lets Luther turn her onto her stomach. Her legs close tightly to keep the large boner inside her and her hands find the sides of the table, and then rest finally under her forehead. The balls make another complete entry and are then pulled from her faster than before. They are inside her a further two times, each time ripped quicker from her asshole. Then he sends his fingers into her, first two, then three, and then four. He adds an enthusiastic thumb to her ass after coating his hand with oil from the wrist down, and after some brief resistance, he has his entire fist in her ass. This sends an immediate *fuck* instruction to his cock and he can keep his fist inside her for less than a minute before removing it and climbing onto her, hoping the massage table can take their combined weight.

The table proves most sturdy and he is soon fucking her ass while she fucks her cunt with the dildo. He reaches for it and frees her hand by taking control of her cunt action as well, sending her further into a daze as she is almost immediately having another orgasm. He pounds her ass hard, fucking her cunt as hard. Then he removes the dildo slowly, drops it to the floor, and digs into her pussy with his fingers. His cock is on fire in her ass as it once again closes itself tightly over his boner. His cock remains in her ass all the while his fingers milk her cunt until eventually he too shoots a load inside her. They take a moment to recover before Luther is once again standing beside the table and Stacy is on her back on top of it.

After taking a moment to prepare his hands he coats her cunt with generous amounts of oil that runs onto the table. The reason for the leather finish is suddenly clear. Luther brings all his fingers together into a cone shape and gently inserts the entire shape into Stacy. She receives the entire cone easily. Her cunt seems ready for anything. Inside her completely he forms the cone into a fist and then pulls it from her fanny slowly until his hand is outside her again. His fingers become a cone again and again he is inside her. After forming a very large fist with his fingers, he slowly removes it, a second time. Luther stretches her cunt repeatedly, removing and reinserting fist until she has her loudest orgasm yet.

He manages to oil up her ass without removing his fist from her cunt and is soon stretching this tighter hole open with the same cone formation. He has to be very patient with her ass, especially given that she is on her back, but eventually, his fist is inside her. He has double plugged her now with his fists and Stacy is left gasping. The ease of movement inside her is surprising, especially since they had both prepared themselves for considerably more effort. But Luther fists both ass and cunt at the same time and she is in absolute ecstasy. Both her holes have given way to his massive globes and it is just his cock left wanting.

Pulling a final massive explosion from her is almost effortless. Stacy literally sprays the contents of her cunt high into the air as Luther removes the fist he has lodged there. As she squirts through her pussy, he removes the fist in her ass as well. With her holes now vacant and her satisfaction complete, she takes his cock in hand and starts to pull on the hard rod. Luther goes off for a minute to sort his hands out and returns to the table, mounts and dicks her immediately, and fucks her selfishly until he shoots gallons of jizz into her now worn out cunt. He keeps his cock inside her as he slumps down in a heap and they lay there for a minute in a tangled mess.

CHAPTER 25

FROZEN

IT WAS A PRETTY WINTER MORNING; the world was white and serene. Olivia liked days like this. She felt as if time stood still and all her problems ceased to exist. Here, surrounded by eternal silence, it felt like they were the only living people on the planet.

She took a deep breath of cold air. Together with their friends, Christa and Mark, they've been walking in the woods for over an hour. Olivia felt tired. She turned around to see her husband. She saw that he was leaning against a tree, breathing heavily.

"Come on, get a move on. Or I'll leave you here for the wolves," said Olivia with a warm smile and gestured at him. Jack rolled his eyes.

"Remind me not to listen to you next time and stay indoors. I hate walking in the winter." "You love it. Now get up and be a man."

Jack stood up reluctantly and soon enough, they caught up with Christa and Mark. But as they continued walking, Emily felt John's hand trailing down slowly from her back to palm her ass.

"John. What are you doing?"

He huffed, leaning closer, and whispered to her ear, "I thought you wanted me to be a man." With the other hand, he opened her winter coat from behind. "Well, let me show you how manly I can be." He kissed her behind the ear. She shivered. John took off her scarf to have a better access to her neck, massaging her breast with the other hand.

"John..." Emily tried to protest but then he spun her around and silenced her with a kiss. She latched onto him, urging him to come closer. Suddenly, she felt clothed in too many layers.

John backed her against a tree and continued to kiss her. Emily had to really try and not to moan when he caressed her breasts again. "They're going to see, John," she glanced quickly to her left – Christa and Mark were pretty far away but they only had to turn around to see what they were doing.

"So?" He stepped between her legs so that they were inches apart. Emily could feel his hardness pressing to her. He lifted her sweater and sneaked a hand into her jeans. Oh, God. When he slipped a finger inside her, she whimpered.

"Emily, are you coming?" shouted Christa from afar, making Emily jump. Jack didn't even react; he just continued to stroke her gently. She glanced at the road; they were out of sight.

"Jack needs a moment... he's really... tired!" she shouted back, hoping her voice was really steady and normal, because now John crooked two fingers inside her. "We'll... be right with you!"

"Yeah! Don't... worry! We'll catch up... in a moment!"

She finished with a weak moan and titled her head back. Oh, now she didn't really care about Christa and Mark. She just surrendered and gave into the moment. The one thing she still found hard to believe was that they were doing it here, in the open. John wasn't much of a spontaneous husband, but apparently, today was different.

Her arousal was slicking hot around his palm. "Oh God, don't stop!" she wailed, moving her hips onto his fingers, urging him deeper. His fingers spread her wide and it felt amazing. She was so wet she was almost dripping onto the snow.

Suddenly, John stopped. "What are you..." but she didn't get a chance to finish – John yanked her jeans down in one smooth movement, and then he almost tore her pants off.

He dropped to his knees and Emily shuddered. She knew what was coming next. Jack drew a line with a tongue on the inside of her thigh, fingers following the wet, hot trail. He opened his mouth against her arching skin and lifted his face, angling his mouth to her entrance, lapping at her wetness. When he finally licked her, she almost blacked out. Her tongue was inside her, probing, teasing, and sucking. John wasn't being gentle when he pressed to the sensitive bundle of nerves and Emily arched up, moving her hips in unconscious sync with the movements of his tongue. John was sinfully good at this. She tugged at his hair, watching the movements of his head, pleasure starting to quickly overwhelm her.

"If you keep doing this..." Emily whispered.

In response, he just licked her and licked her until she was lost. She came, arching into his mouth, as he kept sucking her sensitive flesh. He coaxed every last drop out of her, licking her clean, before releasing her. Emily felt as though her feet would give up. She pulled him flush against her and kissed him, tasting herself on John's tongue. She wanted him inside her and she knew he wanted the same thing.

Without saying anything else, she reached to undo his belt, his hardness clearly visible through his jeans. John stepped out of his trousers and threw them somewhere into the snow. He wasn't wearing briefs. A wave of heat ran through her when she realized he was probably planning to do this all along.

"You..."

"Oh yes," he smiled mischievously. "I was."

Emily moaned when she felt him, hard and leaking, against her naked thigh. Her hand closer around his length and she couldn't wait for the moment he would enter her. She could feel the heat emanating from his body, melting the air around them.

"God, you're so gorgeous, you know that?" said John, his voice husky, overwhelmed with desire. He started kissing her all over, hands roaming over her body.

"Shut up and fuck me already," replied Emily, too impatient to wait any longer. He complied; his strong arms lifted her up and she clang to him when he lowered her onto his cock, his green eyes watching her intensely. She panted, trying to catch her breath, filling the air with muffled moans as he pushed into her all the way, until they were joined into one.

John didn't hesitate. With a grunt, he grabbed her hips and drove into her, as hard and as fast as he could, pulling her back to meet his thrusts. She yelped, still sensitive from her last orgasm, but she loved to be so stretched, so full, she loved when John was in control. She clenched her inner muscles around him, feeling him withdraw almost completely, and then he plunged back into her, snapping his hips. His mouth found hers again, devouring her in a hungry kiss, swallowing her screams.

The silence was filled by their ragged breathing and the smell of sex was hanging in the air. Emily felt pressure building inside her again, this tingling in her nerves. John changes the angle of his thrusts and then he hit that spot, sending a sudden jolt of pleasure through her. Emily stiffened, feeling her whole body tingle in consuming pleasure of her orgasm as John worked his hips in a maddening rhythm. He sucked the skin on her throat, marking her with his teeth. He continued thrusting into her, and she was so spent she could only hang onto him as he plunged into her again and again, heavy and unrelenting.

Finally, he tensed up and released a low groan from the back of his throat, and Emily felt hotness spill deep inside her. John collapsed into the snow, taking Emily with him. They laid flat on the ground, too exhausted to move.

"Wow," this was all Emily could say as the pleasure started ebbing away.

"Yeah."

"So..." she smiled seductively, tracing patterns on his chest. "You think Christa and Mark will do without us for another ten minutes?"

"Are you saying what I think you're saying?" "Oh yes, I am,"

CHAPTER 26

GOING DOWN IN AN ELEVATOR

LAURA GRANGER LOVED HER JOB. She worked her ass off to get this job. . It had been a long road for her and now she had finally become an executive with Lancaster Media. Laura had become the marketing manager with a corner office overlooking the Memphis skyline. Laura called her husband to give him the great news about the promotion. Her husband, Brad, wanted to come by and take her out to lunch to celebrate her promotion. Laura agreed to meet him at the restaurant when she was able to get away.

Laura loved her husband and would do anything for him. Laura had a couple more meetings that she had to attend before she was able to slip out. Eventually, she was able to make it to the restaurant. It had been a long time since they had been able to have lunch together. . Brad had a small gift that he had picked up on his way to meeting Laura. She walked in and immediately spotted him and headed over.

Brad had supported her the entire time she was going through the process of trying to get her promotion.

Laura took a seat and looked at the menu. "Laura

Sweetie, I have already ordered lunch for you. I am so proud of you and you deserve this promotion. I want you to feel that you are the most special girl in the world." Brad took the bracelet that he had bought and gave it to Laura. Laura read the inscription that was engraved on it and knew then and there just how much that her husband actually loved her. He had an inscription that was special to her put on the bracelet and that way it would be with her at all times they were away from one another.

Brad and Laura enjoyed every bite of the lunch that they had ordered. After lunch, Laura had a ton of meetings and told Brad that she would more than likely be working late tonight. Brad was disappointed then he got an idea. He leaned over and whispered into her ear. She had a look of shock on her face.

Laura and Brad made their way to the parking garage. The plan was to have sex in the parking garage. When they got there, Laura came up with a new plan and told Brad to follow her. They made their way to the elevator of the building. As soon as they were both in the elevator, Laura began to unbutton her top Soon, her top was fully open, exposing her blue lace bra that she was wearing. Laura gave a little tease to him by pulling the strap down for a second to expose her breast then pulling it back up in a hurry. Laura did it again except that this time she lowered both sides and allowed her breasts to fall free.

· · ·

Laura gave Brad a seductive look and motioned for him to come over to her. Brad went over to the other side of the elevator and was right against her. He could feel her bare breast pressing against his shirt. Laura reached up and began to unbutton Brad's shirt to expose his chest. She then pressed her heaving bosom against his bare chest. Brad reached up and began to fondle the flesh mounds that were against his skin. Brad reached up under the skirt and pulled Laura's panties to the side. He began to finger her now dripping wet hole of Laura let out a moan to show her approval of the. Laura pulled Brad closer and whispered into his ear. "You know what would be hot? If you were to take your cock and fuck me in the elevator. That would be fucking awesome. And I would be so worked up at the thought that these doors could open at any time and we could be caught having wild sex in the elevator." Brad took his cue and began to undo his pants, he was not about to miss an opportunity to fuck her regardless of where it was. He would do her in the middle of a church if the opportunity presented itself to him. Brad slid his member into his wife and began to glide back and forth in and out of her wet hole. He was getting more and hornier at the thought that the more likely it was they would be caught. Part of him wanted to just stop and leave before something happened, while the other part was hoping that something did happen and that they were caught screwing in the elevator. Brad could sense the excitement that was flowing through his wife as her cunt was grasping onto the member that had invaded her and was not wanting to let go no matter what. The motions that he was using became more and more controlled and eventually, they were s in a pattern that when Laura thrust forward, he was driving in and when she pulled back, he was withdrawing.

. . .

This continued until finally, Brad was at the point that he could not hold back any longer. He had a mind- blowing orgasm. Laura grabbed her husband's hips and thrust them as close to her as she could. She wanted every drop of his seed to go into her wet, throbbing hole. Laura let out a loud moan that had to have been heard all the way through the building as Brad released into her filling her insides. This had been one of the best days in her life. Laura had finally got the promotion that she had been working for and then got pounded in the elevator by her loving husband. . One thing was for sure even if she did work overtime; she was going to be one happy Marketing Manager for Lancaster media.

CHAPTER 27

GOING UP!

THE ELEVATOR DOORS have hardly closed and Lamar is on his wife. Oversleeping this morning because of watching the late game meant that he missed out on his usual morning deposit in Kelly's pussy bank. So now, the coincidence of stumbling into an elevator with nobody in it but his wife in a knee-length pencil skirt and no panties cannot possibly be ignored. He manages to lock the elevator for the top floor and as soon as it starts to move, he lifts her skirt, exposing her clean-shaven cunt.

The slow-moving lift will take eight minutes to get to the top floor. So there isn't time for foreplay or theatrics. Lamar's finger is inside Kelly already, his other hand unzipping his pants and pulling out his cock. He fingers Kelly while she wets her palm and strokes his cock and balls. His cock is hard almost as quickly as she gets wet. Lamar goes for her cunt just as soon as his finger lets her know he can, Kelly bracing herself on the lift's railings for her husband and his lengthy ebony python. The serpent slithers into her in one powerful thrust.

Immediately Lamar is fucking her hard. His speed is

determined by the rock music coming from the speakers somewhere in the elevator. They both know and love the tune playing. As hard as Lamar is fucking her, Kelly is using every part of her pussy to fuck him right back. With each stroke he checks the red light on the screen above the door, the numbers flashing by a little too fast for his liking. He pushes himself harder, deeper into Kelly, whose pussy is a delicious mix of fire and fluid. She loves his thick rubbery dick, rock hard and not. If her cunt isn't chewing it, her mouth wants to. She pulls her skirt further up so that she can see him moving in and out of her. He looks down, motivated by the view.

Watching his cock in her pussy the whole scene seems to slow down. She watches as each inch leaves her pussy, sticky and wet, the length of Lamar increasing steadily outside her pink place. Then, just when she thinks that every bit of the massive dick is about to exit, he shoots the entire tool into her in a very quick stroke. There is no time to try to account for the inches filling her, her cunt stretched all the way back into itself. Again, the slow exit allows her to make estimations as to the number of inches she's just had inside her, and again her estimations are confirmed by a swift ramming of the thick black dick all the way up into her vagina. Kelly loves her husband, and her. But they both know that had they not had such mind-blowing sex on that first date, chances are there wouldn't have been a second. And there definitely wouldn't have been a wedding.

There are less than twenty floors to the roof now. Less than five minutes left in the elevator. Lamar lengthens his strokes, for the benefit of Kelly. The longer he drags on her pussy the more she can process the sensation of his cock and reach climax. Fifteen inches in and fifteen inches out he pulls and pushes. They both can't take their eyes off this action, even the wild movements of Lamar's ass and waist not distracting Kelly from where his cock is destroying her pussy rather completely. It's getting more and more likely that she'll cum before they reach the roof. This is all she can think of now. It's impossible for her to think of anything else. Lamar's fucking makes thoughts of anything else unlikely.

Short, fast stabs replace his long lingering thrusts and he grabs Kelly's waist. Pulling her towards himself while she holds tightly to the rails, Lamar sends his cock into her fast and hard. Every inch of him is inside her and he pulls very little out on each thrust. He just releases an inch or two to allow for a hard stab back into her cunt. She starts to yell out, a series of profanities that belie the soft rock coming from the sound system now. The elevator will be at the roof at any minute now, and Lamar's cock is determined that it will not abort the mission. With barely four floors to go, he pulls the loudest, wildest orgasm from his wife. So intense is the climax that her cunt sprays its contents on her thigh and then onto the floor of the carriage even through the thick cock inside it.

Resigning himself to a quick wank once he gets to the first bathroom he can find, Lamar withdraws from Kelly's exhausted and very satisfied cunt. But instead of her pulling down her skirt, she hits the *stop* button, locking the lift in place, pulls her skirt higher up, and turns to offer her perfect ass to her husband. With his huge cock and her tiny ass, it won't be five minutes from penetration to climax. He goes for the opportunity, pleased that Kelly is willing to give him so quickly what he usually has to beg for, and what usually takes him half an hour to prepare. Kelly takes his cock into her mouth, wetting it as best as she can before turning back around and lifting her one leg high onto the rail. She pushes her ass out towards Lamar who dresses it in several loads of spit from his mouth.

There really isn't any time to waste. He sends his index into her hole and uses it to coat the inside of the hole with the spit resting on the outside. Once this is done, he adds his middle finger, then the ring, maximizing the stretch. He uses all the force he can muster to move the thick fingers all together in and out, then around and around in her ass. Kelly's ass is wrapped tight around the fingers, no sign of letting up. So Lamar drops a few more warm bombs from his mouth and further coats it, inside and out. Then, with a swift removal of the fingers, he sends his cock in deep and hard, thrusting immediately so as not to give too much time for processing. Instead, Kelly immediately starts adjusting. There's something about her man fucking her tight ass that is acceptable.

Knowing that he enjoys her, she starts to relax. She also appreciates the complete orgasm he gave her, and can't help herself from returning the favor. She pushes onto him as he pushes into her, and before long way more than half of Lamar is inside her. He has a perfect view of his cock moving to and fro, to and fro inside the hot space. His cock gets thicker and thicker as the squeeze gets tighter briefly and then relaxes. With each relaxing, he sends a little more into her, which results again in a tightening. The tightening is such a beautiful feeling on his cock that he fucks her hard without moving, enough for her to relax again, repeating the cycle.

It's Lamar now who can think of nothing but his own orgasm. It's been just minutes but it feels like hours. He can't even look at where his cock is digging into his wife, his focus now entirely on the sensation. Eyes closed, Lamar drills completely into Kelly now, Kelly very generous about feeding him herself completely. He has no idea how much of his dick is inside her, and neither does she. All he knows is that his climax is close, and all Kelly knows is that her fingers on her pussy are about to bring her to another one as well. She digs into herself as Lamar throws his full weight into her.

The speaker on the side panes starts to crackle and an invisible man asks if everything is okay in the elevator. Somebody must have contacted maintenance when the lift didn't move. Of all the lifts in the building, why did they need to ride this one so badly? Lamar and Kelly pause, then burst into laughter. They haven't been caught out, but it feels like it. The pause has Lamar's cock retreat from his climax, something that frustrates him visibly. Kelly catches the look on his face and decides to do something about it quickly. They've already come this far. She looks at the flashing light, then at the speaker, the voice coming through it now crackling frantically.

She gives her husband a cheeky look and then pushes him off her ass gently. Turning to face him, she gently pushes his cock down and between her thighs, directly below her cunt. Then she settles herself onto the thick meat, Lamar pushing it into her as well. They know now that time is really not on their side so the thrusting begins instantaneously. Hard fucking has replaced all other activity and Kelly herself is riding Lamar, on her tiptoes with herself braced on the railings. She feeds her cunt to him from her position, taking him so far into her that Lamar feels like she's sucked his balls into her cunt.

He moves into her and joins his lips to hers. He sucks on her tongue as soon as she puts it in his mouth. They kiss through the giggles escaping both of them at the sound of the maintenance crew on the speakers. They could break through the doors at any minute. But they would have to first get to the roof, at least an eight-minute trip. It's all the time they need. Lamar is now absolutely annihilating Kelly's cunt, bringing her to her climax quickly. He won't leave her vagina before coming to his own too. She knows this and so she pushes even harder onto him. Lamar is in the farthest reaches of Kelly's pussy and his thrusting is a deep stirring. He's closer now to an orgasm than the maintenance people could possibly be to the roof.

Kelly can't move anymore, her cunt completely drained. Lamar needs to get himself over to the other side, and she can only give him full permission to use her pussy for this purpose. He shoots deep into her repeatedly, each stroke deeper and harder than the one before. The progression of intensity brings her in and out of her orgasmic euphoria, waning between reality and fantasy. His cock is as far into her as her vagina will allow and so he replaces lengthy strokes with deep circles. The circles become wide and firm, his climax making its appearance. The completeness with which he fills her cunt is so surprising that even when he has stopped shooting, even when he has removed his cock from inside her, his seed drips out of her vagina and on to the floor. They are both very grateful for the wet wipes in the elevator used to wipe the rail for those prone to excessive hygiene. They unlock the lift and exit on different floors...

CHAPTER 28

GOLDEN GIRL

I KNOW WHAT THEY SAY: never, ever, ever date your boss. But I just couldn't help it! His name was Jake Kim. He was Korean by birth, and Canadian by nationality. He had this adorable twinkle in his eye, kind of a goofy smile, and this really quite a beautiful face with high set cheekbones and flawless skin. By the shoulders on the guy, you could tell he worked out. Beneath that sharp suit, I knew there was a packed, lean body and washboard stomach. I wanted the job badly. It meant I wanted to be close to Jake.

The morning of my interview started badly. My hairdryer decided to blow up so I left the house with damp hair. By the time I'd gotten to the building where my interview was taking place, it had dried into this frizzy mess. Then, I'd stumbled into the boardroom scattering my portfolio all over the floor.

"You looked kind of wild and so, so sexy," Jake tells me when we reminisce and recall the day we first met. I'm *so* glad my broken hairdryer has this effect on men.

In case you're wondering, I got the job because I'm a hot copywriter, not just because Jake wanted to date me. He could have done that even if I hadn't got the job. I always stress this to my friends who tease me about the 'advantages' I had over the other candidates. Three years on and I'm now a partner of the company with Jake by my side. Our working relationship is equal, honest, and open, and utilizes both our talents. Our *sex life* on the other hand is wild, filthy, and steamy and also utilizes both of our talents!

The first time we made out was on the third day of my new job. My head was full of accounts, ideas, new systems, and an aching desire to see Jake Kim naked. "Have you been up to the 20th floor to meet the design team yet?" He asked after lunch.

"Er, no, not yet."

"Ok, I'll take you up there now. Let's take the elevator." We'd been making eye contact all day. Great, alone in the elevator with him! As soon as we stepped in there, he pushed me against the wall.

"Are you thinking what I'm thinking?" He said to me, those dazzling bright eyes looking into mine, mischievously.

"Hell, yes," I said, in a hoarse whisper. That's when he took my head in his wide hands and kissed me full on the mouth, his tongue searching mine and its tip making a slow caress around my lips. Suddenly the doors sprang open onto the 20th floor, opening into a bright boardroom, thankfully deserted. The design team was not back from lunch yet and we giggled, embarrassed, and flushed. "You know, I totally respect your talent for this job and our professional relationship." He told me. "But can I see you *personally* at work, too?"

"Does this mean we're dating?"

"Yes! Of course! I mean, I hope so, if that's what you want?" "I do. How about dinner this Friday?"

"Dinner this Friday. Deal" He replied.

We started to date in secret because we didn't want the whole office gossiping. He'd call me up just to talk dirty, and I'd try and keep a straight face.

"Is that Miss Golden?"

"Yes, this is she," I'd say, business monotone.

"I'd like you to come to my office with the Johnson account please, take out my cock and hold in that sweet hand of yours."

"Yes, Mr. Kim, certainly. Is there anything else I can help you with?"

"When you're doing that, I'd like to lick each of your nipples with the tip of my tongue."

"Alright, I'll do that right away. Would you like me to help you with the last part? Perhaps work a little harder on the part two?" I was dripping by this point. "Sure, make sure you're not wearing any underwear."

"Certainly, right away Mr. Kim." Click, brr...

My friends were worried for me. "He's got all this power over you," they told me, "If you dump him he can fire you."

"Not without an unfair dismissal case. "

Besides, I was excelling at my new job, winning new accounts, writing dazzling advertising bids, and, according to the CEO, producing "some of the finest work this company has ever produced".

I remember Jake looking at me proudly when the CEO had congratulated me. He called me up to his office for a 'private meeting' that afternoon. That was when our fucking became more risky, more hot.

"Get into my office now, Miss Golden, I'm going to give you exactly what you deserve for all the hard work you've put in this last month."

"Right away, Mr. Kim."

Jake's assistant, Sam, buzzed me through. "Must be an important meeting," he said, clueless. "He's canceled his whole afternoon for you."

"Yes, Mr. Kim wants to go over the strategy for the next year." I said, straight- faced.

"Just call if you need anything," Sam said. "Thanks, I will!" I called over my shoulder.

When I stepped into Jake's office, he was sat behind his desk, a great big goofy grin on his face. "I bought you these, to congratulate you," he leaned down and produced an enormous bunch of red roses. "Also, I wanted to tell you that I'm in love with you,"

I didn't know what to say. "I'm in love with you too!" My heart started beating hard in my chest with love and passion for this gorgeous, successful, sexy man who was in love with *me*.

"And now I am going to fuck you like you've never

been fucked before." He said. From his back pocket, he produced two pairs of those ridiculous fluffy handcuffs. "Mind if I do?" I laughed in agreement. He handcuffed each hand to the big leather chair, so that I was completely at his mercy. "Now I'm going to undress you and make you come, but you have to be quiet." I nodded eagerly. Jake undid my blouse slowly, kissing the inside of my neck with that sweet mouth of his, nibbling my ear and sending shivers between my legs. He took each nipple in his hands and squeezed them until they were hard, biting down and making me cry out. "Shhhh," he said into my ear, and he put two fingers into my mouth to quiet me. His mouth moved down to my stomach, and I parted my legs for him. He ran a hand gently up my leg, unrolling each of my stockings. I groaned. Jake sent small, light kisses up the inside of my thigh and finally found my open, wet sex- his tongue making small circles on my clitoris and then finding its way inside. I wanted to ram his head in further and hold him there, but my hand were locked- I was aching and quivering for him. He drank me further, hungrily until I came hard into his mouth- my blouse undone and every-thing open.

"Can I fuck you?" he said, looking into my eyes.

"Oh god yes," I said. He unlocked me and lifted me up onto his hips. He laid me down onto his desk and opened my legs wide, gazing right at me. He took off his pants and shirt and stood there, naked, with his huge erection waiting for me. He bent down and circled my opening with the tip of his tongue, teasing and tantalizing me.

"I want to be inside there," he told me, and I couldn't open myself up more for him. Then, he finally leaned in over me and pushed himself inside, holding each of my palms to the desk so I couldn't move.

"God you're so tight," he said, as he thrust into me, slowly. Just then, the phone rang.

"Answer it," I told him, daringly. He clicked the accept button and put one hand over my mouth while he continued to grind away. I could feel another orgasm building.

"CEO here," came a familiar voice. "Have you got our Golden girl with you?" He said. I looked at Jake, panicked.

"I sure have," Jake said, not betraying anything.

"Tell her she just got promoted, gotta run, pass on the message and tell her I'll be down with the details," said the CEO, clicking off. Just then, I came hard, every muscle giving way to the ecstasy of my big achievement.

CHAPTER 29

HOSTAGE SITUATION

RAY'S BREATHING was slightly rapid as he sat handcuffed on the chair. He'd gotten a note that said that his wife had been kidnapped and that he should come to the Addison Inn for further instructions. He'd come to the indicated room and been ushered in by an unknown person. They had been behind the door and he'd been instructed to not turn around.

He'd been made to sit on the chair and put on the blindfold that lay on the bed beside it.

Complying without question, Ray now sat sweating slightly as he waited for whatever would happen next.

"Mr. Erikson, you've done well so far," said the voice.

He couldn't tell if it was male or female because they had altered their voice electronically.

"Where's my wife? Is she ok?" he demanded. "If you've hurt her, you'll pay." He was shocked when the captor straddled his lap.

"I don't think you're in any position to be making demands, Mr. Erikson," they said.

The scent of perfume came to his nostrils then and he

realized that his captor was a woman. She pushed his suit jacket off his shoulders as far as she could and then started unbuttoning his shirt. Soft lips brushed his and Ray shied away.

"I don't know what you're playing at, but I'm a very happily married man and I'm not a cheater, so you can just forget it," he said harshly.

"We'll see about that," she said.

She parted his shirt and yanked it out of the waistband of his pants. She ran her hands over his well-muscled chest and leaned forward. After flicking her tongue over one of his nipples, the woman bit it lightly and then sucked on it.

Sudden realization dawned on him; this was something that Mandy always did to him because she knew that it drove him crazy.

"Mandy?" he asked. "Is that you?"

The electronic chuckle he heard clued him in that this was his wife. "Figured it out, did you?"

Her weight disappeared from his lap and Ray heard the rustling of clothes. Then she was back on his lap and slipping the blindfold off him. He focused on her beautiful brown eyes, which were laughing. Anger and relief warred within him. Then he noticed that she was completely naked. Ray could tell that Mandy was having a hard time not laughing. Her lips were pursed and her chin quivered.

The humor of the situation finally got to him and Ray started chuckling, which then turned into full-blown laughter. Mandy laughed with him and soon both of them had tears in their eyes from the laughter.

When their mirth subsided, Ray said, "You really got me. I was really scared."

Mandy caressed his face. "I'm sorry, baby. It was just a joke. I really thought you'd figure it out because we stayed here a couple of times and like to eat here. I didn't think you'd take it seriously."

"Well, I did," Ray answered.

Mandy kissed him then, touching his lips with her tongue. Ray opened willingly to her and twined his tongue with hers. Her breasts grazed his chest and Ray's crotch began to feel tingly. Mandy played with his nipples and fiery desire began to spread through Ray. She undid his zipper and belt and pulled his pants down.

"Lift up that sexy ass of yours," she said.

Ray did so and Mandy slid them down to his ankles. She got rid of his shoes and socks and threw all the garments to the side. She saw that Ray's cock was starting to harden.

"Oh, boy. It looks like someone is getting excited," she said.

Ray nodded as he looked at her lithe form. Her breasts swung slightly as she moved and he longed to suck her nipples. He wanted to cup her soft pussy.

"Get rid of these handcuffs," Ray said.

Mandy shook her head. "Oh, no. I have some things in store for you and they don't include your hands."

Ray moaned as Mandy took his cock in her hand and began stroking it. She saw his hungry gaze fall on her breasts.

"Do you like what you see?" she said.

"You know I do," Ray responded. "I want to suck your tits, honey."

Mandy let his cock go, straddled Ray's hips again, and then stood up a little so that her breasts were on level with his mouth. She grabbed her left breast and rubbed the nipple against his lips. Ray licked it and then sucked on it.

Mandy ran a hand along the back of Ray's neck as little frissons of heat snaked from her breasts to her cunt. When Ray was done with that one, she gave him her other breast while she stroked his cock.

He was hardening rapidly and throbbed in her hand. Ray released her tit and kissed the valley between them. Mandy backed off, still stroking his cock. It was now nice and hard and she rubbed it against her clit as she sat on Ray's lap.

"Oh, god, baby, that feels so good," Ray said as she kept doing it.

Mandy was so horny and her clit was very sensitive. The sensation of the head of his cock gliding over it was intense. She did it just a little harder and faster and she was ready to cum.

"Honey?" she said, "I'm gonna cum for you."

Ray wished that his hands were free so that he could hold his dick for her, but he was fascinated by what she was doing.

"Do it, Mandy. Make that pretty little pussy cum for me," he said.

Mandy felt the pleasure spasms start and threw her head back. She moaned as she climaxed and her thighs shook as it reached the peak. Her moans grew loud and her hips thrust as she was held in its grip. It began to subside and she brought her gaze back to Ray's. His eyes were smoldering with passion and it excited her all over again to see him looking at her that way.

She knew she was wet and she wanted Ray inside and figured that he wasn't going to object. She got off his lap, turned around, and scooted back, poising herself over his dick. Then she guided him inside, going down as far as she could. Ray bit her back and then soothed the sting away with his tongue.

"You feel so good inside me," Mandy said. "I want to fuck your cock, baby. Do you want me to fuck it?"

"Oh, yeah. Fuck it, Mandy," Ray said.

Mandy moved up and down slowly at first, rubbing her clit the whole time. She loved the double sensations and she enjoyed touching herself. It was one of the things Ray loved about her. It turned him on to watch her masturbate and it turned her on, too.

Ray was in heaven to feel her hot pussy stroking up and down on his cock. He loved the way she rode him. Mandy began bouncing up and down on him, faster and faster. She needed to cum, needed the release again, and meant to have it. She rubbed her clit harder and faster as she moved and sent herself into a powerful orgasm.

Ray felt her cumming and growled out, "Yeah, baby, come on my cock. That's it!"

Mandy rode out the orgasm and then slowed down as it faded. She changed positions so she was now facing Ray. They kissed long and passionately as Mandy put Ray's cock back inside her cunt and sat down again.

"I'm gonna make that big cock cum," Mandy told him as she held his gaze. Ray nodded. "I need it, babe. I'm so horny."

"Good. I'm glad I make you feel that way."

She started moving and Ray gasped at how intense feelings she created. Her pussy was so wet and slid up and down his shaft with ease. Her strong thighs lifted her and brought her down and with each stroke, Ray drew closer to climaxing. Mandy added a circular motion and Ray groaned as the pleasure grew stronger.

"Mandy, I'm going to cum. Keep doing that. It's incredible."

Mandy responded by going even faster and she felt another orgasm building inside her. It broke over her gently, rolling inside her as a gentle wave laps the shoreline.

Ray knew that when his dick began pulsing that he was right on the brink. His climax was so powerful that he shouted. Mandy swiftly pulled him out of her and kept working his cock as hot spurts of cum shot from his dick. It covered her hand and was slippery and warm. She kept stroking Ray's cock until she felt his body relax.

She leaned forward and kissed his cheek. His rapid breath brushed her cheek. She smiled and looked into his eyes. "How was that?"

Ray laughed. "How was it? Fucking amazing. That's how it was." "That's what I was going for," she answered and moved away. "Can you take off the handcuffs now?" he asked.

"Do you promise to be a good boy?" Mandy asked.

Ray's gaze raked over her. "I'll show you just how good I am." Mandy laughed. "I'm looking forward to that."

Mandy left him to go into the bathroom and Ray let his head fall back. He laughed and pondered how much fun his wife was and how lucky he was to be married to her. He'd be her hostage any time she wanted him to be.

CHAPTER 30

"HYPNOTIC"

THE SHADOWS of the alley beckoned to her. It was perfect. Public enough to excite her, private enough to limit most of the danger of being caught. She doubted the school where she taught junior high social studies would look fondly on her being arrested for public lewdness, or whatever the charge was for having sex in public.

"Rafael," twenty-six-year-old Angeline DeChardin tugged on her boyfriend's hand. He stopped and looked down at her, dark chocolate brown eyes turning nearly as black as his hair as he read her face. They'd been dating for just nine months, sleeping together for just as long, and shared most of each other's kinks, including this one. It was actually how they'd come to be together.

Rafael had been roommates with JD Perez for three years when JD had announced that one of his old high school girlfriends was moving to the city for a teaching job and needed a place to crash. According to JD, they'd broken up after graduation but had remained friends. It had been love at first sight for Rafael. Long dark red hair that hung in a straight sheet down to a trim waist. Ultramarine eyes that sparkled with intelligence and humor. Then, two weeks later, JD had mentioned Angeline's exhibitionist streak, and Rafael had put aside his reservations about dating a friend's ex and asked JD if he'd mind. That weekend, he'd taken her to the club where one of his friends worked the door. Before the night was over, they'd fucked in the women's bathroom.

Since then, they'd had sex in various places, including the dance floor of a club, in the stacks at the local library, in his car and she'd even given him head under the table in a restaurant. Up until recently, the weather had been cold enough that they hadn't done anything outside. This night, however, had been warm enough for both to forgo their coats.

"Are you up for it?" Angeline grinned, knowing full well what the answer would be. Rafael was always up for their games.

He smiled in response and let her lead him into the alley. Once there, he waited. She'd been the initiator so she was in charge. Angeline grabbed the front of his shirt and shoved him back against the wall, setting his heart pounding. When she dropped to her knees, his blood raced south. He was hard before she finished unzipping his pants. He moaned as her fingers wrapped around him, the sound turning into a hiss of near pain as she moved her hand, the dry friction nearly painful.

"Do you want my mouth?" Angeline looked up at him through her lashes, knowing full well the effect she was having on him. "Want me to lick you like a lollipop, suck you into my hot, wet mouth?"

"Fuck, yes," Rafael's hands tightened into fists. He groaned as she wrapped her lips around the head of his cock, sliding down until her nose touched the dark curls at the base. She bobbed her head a few times, thoroughly wetting the thick shaft before releasing him with an obscene pop. Her hand immediately closed around him again and began stroking, slow and steady with just the right amount of pressure.

"Is that what you wanted?" Angeline could feel the heat uncoiling in her belly as she spoke. Her free hand crept under her skirt, down to her aching pussy. Her breath caught as she rubbed over her the soaking crotch of her panties and pantyhose. "Or do you want something else? Maybe you want my cunt? I'm so wet and hot. My pussy's throbbing. Do you want to fill me? Stretch my pussy until it fits you like a glove? Pound into me so hard I'll scream, not caring that someone could hear?"

"Yes," the word tore out of him, raw with need.

"Then take me," challenge dripped from those three words.

Rafael's hands closed around her shoulders and he yanked her to her feet. He spun them around, pushing her back against the wall hard enough to drive the air from her lungs. He growled as he reached beneath her skirt.

"I hope you're not too attached to these."

He didn't wait for a response, his eager hands making short work of her pantyhose. His fingers brushed against her lower lips as he slid his fingers under the elastic of her panties. One quick tug and she felt cool air against her very overheated core. Rafael didn't give her time to react as he positioned himself and shoved home in one swift thrust.

· · ·

Angeline cried out as he filled her. Without losing a stroke, he slid his hands under her ass and lifted her. She responded automatically, wrapping her legs around his waist, her arms around his neck. The brick wall was hard against her back as he fucked her, each snap of his hips promising bruises. She clung to him, unable to do anything else but ride out the assault on her senses. Her skin was humming, her ears filled with the sound of their flesh slapping together. She could see the dim outline of his face and knew his eyes would be wild, pupils blown wide. The scent of their union filled her nostrils, overriding the dank stench of the alley, and the taste of him was still on her tongue. The pressure was building inside her and she knew she was going to explode, her body unable to handle anything more.

"Scream for me, Ang," Rafael's breath was hot against her cheek.

She whimpered, the sound neither protest nor acknowledgement. Her head fell forward against his shoulder.

"Scream for me," Rafael repeated before sinking his teeth into the flesh of her shoulder, not hard enough to break the skin, but hard enough to leave a mark and send Angeline's body into convulsions.

Her mouth opened, a breathless wail echoing off the brick walls. Her body shook, ever muscle quivering, nerves sending rapid-fire pleasure signals to every cell. She was on overload, limbs twitching as Rafael continued to pound into her, grunting with the force of every thrust. And just when it became too much, when she was nearly sobbing with the intensity of it all, he buried himself deep inside, emptying himself as he called out her name.

When they emerged from the alley a few minutes later, only their self-satisfied smiles indicated that anything had happened. Rafael reached for Angeline's hand, threading his fingers through hers, and they continued down the sidewalk.

"Think we should tell your sister why we're late to her poetry reading?" Angeline asked. Rafael looked down at her. "No, but I think we might need to consider adding the coffee house to our list."

Angeline's pussy gave a throb. She quickened her pace. "Then let's hurry up and maybe we can cross two off the list before the night's over."

CHAPTER 31

I DID NOT KNOW YOU COULD DO THAT WITH ICE CREAM

JENNIFER AND FRANK were a married couple. The only thing that made them stand out was their weird obsession with one another. All of Jennifer's friends were amazed at the fact that they were still very much in love with one another and were still happily married. Karen, her best friend, asked her how things remained fresh and new. Jennifer told her the secret. It was the use of ice cream in the lovemaking. Karen was amazed. Jennifer retold a story to Karen about how the ice cream came into play between her and Frank.

It was a typical day and Jennifer had been working a long week. She came home and decided that she was going to surprise Frank by bringing something new into the bedroom. Jennifer had read some online articles that gave her some creative ideas.

Jennifer made dinner as she usually did. She and Frank sat and discussed each other's day. Jennifer was looking forward to dinner being over. Finally, it came time for desert and Jennifer said she needed to go to the bedroom to get something. Frank was anxious to see what Jennifer had made for desert. Jennifer went into the bedroom and put her plan into place. She had made herself into a banana split. When everything was in place, she called Frank into the bedroom. Frank walked in and his eyes got real big when he saw his surprise. His wife had made herself into an edible dessert. Frank began to undress as he stood and watched his wife lie there and invite him to come over and eat her. She wanted him to come and lick the cream out of her. Frank took the time to walk over and take a taste of the whipped cream that was covering her nipples. Frank went back to the foot of the bed and began to slowly lick his way towards the whipped cream-covered cunt. There was a cherry that had been placed just slightly on the inside of her pussy. The idea was to have Frank take his mouth and gently suck the cherry out of her slit and eat it while still licking her cunt. Frank did just as he was supposed to, then it was up towards her nipples. What Frank was not aware of was that she had placed a scoop of ice cream on each nipple. This was then covered with magic shell and whipped cream. This allowed for her nipples to be hard for when Frank finally got to her nipples and was ready for him to begin to suck on them.

Frank was too busy with the whipped cream that was on her nipples to even discover that there was chocolate underneath the whipped cream. After he had devoured the entire shell on both tits, it was time for the ice cream part of desert. This was quickly eaten and left Jennifer with a couple of rock hard nipples. Frank was now ready to give his wife what it was that she desperately was seeking out and that was a royal fucking. Frank took his hard member and drove it deep into her pussy. The instant that he inserted his cock into her, she let out a wild unbridled moan that had to have been heard by the neighbors. Jennifer did not care. After he finally reached the point of no return, Frank unleashed a torrent of his own cream onto Jennifer's tits. The pure white cum splashed onto her tits and dripped down her areolas. Jennifer finished herself off by working her hole over with a couple of fingers. Finally, all of desert had been taken care of it was time to go and clean up. Jennifer made her way into the shower and started to wash all of the stuff off of her. Frank came in a few minutes later and began to wash her. The attention that he was paying her was focused on her nipples, as he loved sucking and playing with them.

Frank bent her over in the shower. It seemed that he was still worked up from the desert and that his hunger had not been satisfied. Frank took his rod and slid it up against the opening of Jennifer's hole. The sensation of this led Jenifer to know what was next and that was that he was going to have his wife from the rear as well. The sensation of his cock sliding past her hole was painful yet pleasurable as well. Jennifer needed to brace herself, as she did not want to fall. Her body was pressed against the shower door with her tits pressed against the glass. This had been done before and Frank knew how hard he could or could not ride Jennifer to keep from breaking the glass doors. The assault on her ass was almost unrelenting. The rest of the night was spent just being close to one another and being a couple that had discovered a new way to keep the dull and bland from being a reality in their relationship. Jennifer finished telling this story to Karen and all she could say was that she had a desire for ice cream.

CHAPTER 32

I OBJECT

SHE LOOKED THE PART, "BACHELORETTE" sash draped across her skimpy party dress, a tiara with attached veil, the whole tacky garb, but she just wasn't feeling it. She had been completely swept away when he proposed. Who wouldn't be, I mean just look at that ring, but the engagement had sure flown by. Her rowdy bridesmaids had been planning the party for weeks and had the champagne flowing so she would certainly do her duty and fake it. Victoria loved her girlfriends but they had gotten somewhat starstruck by Beverly Hills. They adored Charles. On paper, he was quite the catch, and he did treat her like a princess. Maybe it was just cold feet, she thought, as she plastered on a smile and posed holding up another pair of edible panties. In all honesty, she did need a wild night. They had been few and far between since she'd met Charles, her inner dialogue urged her. So she threw back a shot, stepped out on the dance floor, and introduced California to Tori.

A ruckus erupted the moment he stepped through the door, the crowd parting as he made his way toward her. She did love a man in uniform but his cut-off sleeves were anything but regulation she thought as she spun around shooting Jill an icy stare. Jill threw her hands up in claim of innocence head bobbing the guilt toward Robin. "Robin, really?" she accused. "You're welcome," she replied with a wink. The girls turned to jelly as he approached her from behind. "I've heard you're armed and dangerous ma'am, I'm afraid I'm going to have to frisk you," he said as he slid his hand down her backless dress, its silky finish inviting him to squeeze her curvaceous ass. She gasped both offended and titillated as he cuffed her hands behind her back. The girls poured another shot down her throat as the arresting officer lead his captive to the chair where he'd soon pleasure her. The gentle slope of her back as he lowered her into the chair fascinated him in a way he'd not been charmed in years. As he placed his lips to her earlobe, his whisper was bewitching, her skin dimpling in response. He positioned his body before her as he removed the dark glasses that had obscured his chiseled features. Her heart slammed in her chest as if beating for the first time rendering her breathless and temporarily unable to speak. He vehemently ripped off his pants and she exploded in laughter as they shared the moment of recognition.

"Tori?" he questioned as he stepped out of character and back into her life. "Yes Nick, it's me," she beamed, standing and falling against his bare chest as he pulled her into his arms.

Gazing into her eyes, he ran his fingers through her golden tresses removing the hairpins that had tamed her mane for far too long. Oblivious to her friends and her impending nuptials, she said, "Let's get the hell outta here"

Nick opened the car door and removed the handcuffs allowing Tori to sink comfortably into the soft leather seat, before tossing them into the back. "Are those the same ones?" she asked, a blush tinting her cheek. "Nope, came with the costume" he laughed, adding, "Those toys couldn't hold you down babe," punctuating his claim with a devilish wink. Tori reminisced all the times they'd shared in that '69 Camaro. It still had the same license plate- "cherry" it read. He bought it the night they went to the fair after she'd given him hers. A pulsating warmth crept between her legs as she laid her head against the seat, kicked off her heels, and allowed herself to fully take in his masculine beauty. She didn't even have to ask where he was driving, that stretch of beach had always been their place, and the best part of all, far, far away from the hills. Nick possessed the power to arouse her like no other man ever had. She'd often used his memory to reach orgasm when she had sex with Charles, and now here was the man, flesh, and blood right next to her. Feeling incredibly horny and a little buzzed Tori reached over and ran her hand up his thigh, leaving it there. With Nick showing no objection, she repeated the move, this time increasing the stroke to lightly caress his balls through his soft worn jeans. He slid a bit lower in the seat and opened his legs in approval. His foot slipped off of the gas pedal causing the car to lunge as she groped his growing erection through the obstructive denim. She fumbled with the button and slid down his zipper in pursuit of what her body ached for. He raised his hips allowing her to slide his jeans to his knees. His thick, hard cock stood at her atten- tion as she placed her head into his lap and licked the tiny drop of semen that awaited her famished kiss.

She trailed her tongue the entire length of his shaft as it bobbed with delight before completely taking his turgid manhood into her mouth. He moaned in ecstasy as she sucked his dick with all the passion she'd been missing for so long. He wrapped his fist in her silken hair pulling it back as she struggled to reap her reward. Toying with her only added to his excitement. He then thrust his cock back into her eager mouth grinding against her sex-stained kiss until her suckle overtook his trembling body. As his hot gratification flowed she swallowed appreciatively looking up at him with primal need. "I can't wait to be inside you again," he whispered. Her only response, "mmhmmm."

Tori's heart pounded as he pulled off the main road and onto the beach. The moment she stepped out of the car Nick lifted her up and devoured her mouth with his until they were both breathless. As he sat her bare feet into the sand, he demanded, "Take off your clothes." "Nick, here?" she questioned. His nod was insistent as he slid the satin strap off her sun-kissed shoulder, her dress puddling into the sand. As she stepped out of her damp panties, his eyes explored her voluptuous body illuminated in the moonlight. Nick pulled a blanket from the trunk, "For you my lady," he softly spoke as he placed it against the sand and his love upon it. He pulled off his shirt, her gaze feasting upon the musculature of his broad chest. As she removed his loosened pants, he commanded, "Lay back and close your eyes my beauty." A sly smile spread across her full lips as she complied. She loved the eroticism of not knowing what he was about to do to her. The bit of exhibitionist in her reveled in displaying herself to him, not to mention the danger of possibly being seen. The felt the heat radiate from his body as he raised himself over her. He dragged his tongue from her navel to her breastbone, her skin electrified by his contact. She squirmed into him begging for more. He blew against her chilled flesh, her nipples hardening against his breath before taking the peak into his mouth and sucking feverously. The throbbing within her becoming unbearable and she pleads, "Nick please." He raised his lips to her ear and whispered, "Patience love." Her anxious sigh interrupted by the breathtaking plunge of his tongue into her drenched pussy. Tori thrashed wildly beneath him as he bathed her swollen clit with kisses, drinking every drop of her silken dew until she came hard against his tongue. She hadn't been pleasured like this in years; Charles refused to give her oral sex, although he regularly scheduled it for himself. She quickly put him out of her thoughts as Nick pressed his hardened cock against her opening, sliding up and down her quickened slit. She inhaled deep as he thrust himself inside her, very suddenly recalling his girth. He knew precisely how to pleasure a woman, swaying his hips from side to side, as he literally danced inside her, bringing her to the cusp of orgasm over and over again. He pulled his erection nearly out and slammed it back into her until she begged him for release. He thrived on his control of his lover, dallying with her until he owned her, yet always fulfilling her desire in the end. That he took great pride in. He buried himself to her depth finally allowing her orgasm before claiming his own and pouring his seed into her. As Nick lowered his damp blond tresses against Tori's chest, he confessed that he'd never stopped loving her.

Tori no longer had cold feet about the wedding. She had found the love of her life and daydreamed of walking down the aisle to him as Jill put the finishing touch on her makeup and Robin unrolled the last curl. She slipped on the flowing, sheer gown colored only in sparkles, and stepped barefoot into the sand where their love began, then began again.

CHAPTER 33

JOY IN THE MORNING

KATIE WOKE GRADUALLY, drifting up from the layers of slumber that enveloped her. The dream faded but the erotic sensations still remained. She found that her pussy ached from the visions she'd had of someone licking and sucking her clit. Her nipples were tight, standing up, begging to be tweaked and sucked.

She looked over at her husband, Josh. He was still asleep. She smiled as she contemplated waking him for some morning fun. They hadn't done that in a long, long time, she thought. It was Saturday and they were both off from work, so there was nothing to interfere with some lovemaking.

The sun gently gilded the room with a golden glow and Katie wanted to see Josh's beautiful body in the daylight. She slid her hand down over her stomach until she reached her pussy. She found that she was very wet indeed and that her clit was swollen with desire. She was horny as hell and ready to go.

Moving slowly, Katie uncovered Josh, looking at his rock-hard chest and abs. Then she uncovered his cock and her hormones kicked into overdrive. She was glad to see he had some morning wood going on and was already at half-mast. She scooted down in the bed until she could lightly grasp his cock. She started at the base of it and ran her tongue up its length.

He always tasted great to her and she loved giving him blowjobs. She ran her tongue around the head and Josh stirred a little. Katie smiled and took his cock in her mouth, licking all around the head and then filling her mouth even more. Josh moved again, thrusting his hips a little and letting out a soft moan. Katie sucked harder and pulled off his dick.

She moved faster and Josh moaned again and his eyes opened and focused on her. Now he understood what was going on and smiled.

"Good morning," he said. His voice was a little husky and very sexy.

Katie stopped long enough to say, "Good morning to you, too," and then go back to what she was doing.

Josh reached down to stroke her long dark hair, loving how soft it felt. She was making him rock hard and he loved it. She hadn't woke him up like this in quite a while and it was making him incredibly horny now. She licked and sucked and he throbbed and moaned. Katie knew just when to stop and gave him a last lick.

Josh was on her in a flash, rolling her over and spreading her legs wide. He saw how wet she was and how swollen her clit was and could tell that she needed to cum badly. Josh lightly touched her clit with his fingers and Katie moaned and moved her hips vigorously.

"Baby, please," she said and cupped the back of his head. "You got it, honey," he answered.

He inserted two fingers inside her cunt and Katie

arched her back. He started finger fucking her and then added his tongue. Katie couldn't hold still. Josh's tongue and fingers felt incredible and as his tongue flicked over her clit, she could feel her pussy clench.

"Honey?" she said. "Hmm?" Josh muttered.

"I'm gonna cum for you. Keep licking it just like that. It feels so good. Yeah, lick my clit, baby," she crooned to him.

Josh licked faster urged on by her sex talk. He felt her cunt spasm around his fingers and knew she was almost there. He pressed harder on her clit and moved his tongue faster. Katie felt like she was going to burn up. Her climax built until there was a sharp ache in her cunt. Josh started going up and down and it put her over the brink.

"Josh! Oh! Oh! I'm cumming, baby, I'm cumming! It's so good, so good, don't stop!"

The pleasure seemed to roll on forever and Josh loved knowing that he made her feel that way. She got extremely wet and Josh's fingers were drenched in her pussy juices. Her hips gradually stopped moving and Josh rose up on his knees.

"Rollover, babe. On your knees, girl," he said. Katie said, "Yes sir."

She flipped onto her stomach, put her ass in the air, and propped herself up on her elbows. Josh slapped his cock against each of her ass cheeks and then rubbed it along her pussy a few times before sliding inside of her. Kate moaned as Josh started moving. Josh reveled in the tightness of her cunt and how slick she was.

· · ·

He grabbed her long hair then and pulled it lightly. Katie liked it a little rough sometimes and Josh could tell that she was in the mood for it. He pumped hard, and slapped her ass hard enough to sting.

"I'm gonna fuck that pussy," he said to her. "I'm gonna fuck it hard."

Katie loved the feel of her hair being pulled and said, "Yeah, fuck it hard. Fuck the shit out of it."

Josh responded by getting a harder grip on her hair and slamming into her cunt. Katie moaned every time he thrust inside. Josh let her hair go and started making shorter, faster thrusts and Katie went crazy.

"Yeah, yeah! Yessss!" she said as she came hard.

"God, I love making you cum," Josh said through clenched teeth.

Katie caught her breath for a few moments and then pulled away from Josh. "Your turn. On your back, lover."

Josh rolled over and watched as Katie climbed on top of him facing the opposite direction. She guided his dick into her pussy and started bouncing up and down. She knew the rhythm that excited Josh the most and settled into it quickly. Josh stroked her back as he watched her ass bob up and down. His wife had a fine ass and he always loved watching her from behind.

He reached in front of her, cupped her tits, and played with her nipples. Katie moaned and leaned back further. Josh pulled her all the way back on him and ran his hands up and down her stomach. Then he found her clit and rubbed it as he pumped his hips against Katie. Fire spread rapidly between them and Josh was almost there.

Katie slid into another orgasm and took Josh with her. He felt Katie tighten around his dick and he launched into an intense climax. They called out their mutual joy to each other as the wave of ecstasy crashed over them.

They lay there for several minutes before Katie rolled off Josh and snuggled next to him. Josh kissed her and cupped her face lovingly.

"What a way to start the weekend," he said with a big smile.

CHAPTER 34

JULES AND DAN

AFTER THEIR FIRST DATE, they parted at his front doorstep. She had another appointment and he had arranged to meet a friend. The talk in the car was just chitchat, almost wholly unrelated to the afternoon they had spent making love. They only called it making love because they had returned to the people that they were usually. Two lonely people, usually unassertive.

Later, alone in her flat, she remembered what she had done to him, partly inspired by 50 Shades and partly by a Nancy Friday book she had hidden in her bedroom. The truth was that none of her previous lovers had really satisfied her, never allowed her to experience the sexual fantasies that she wanted. The truth was she had settled for second best and she got it. Perfunctory love-making and dull uninteresting men. When Dan had caught her with the book and started flirting with her, it was her chance to control what she wanted, to make a statement about her sexuality. It didn't take her long to start remembering that afternoon's activities. Reviewing it in her mind, she began to get aroused and she decided to pleasure herself before going to sleep.

Across town, Dan was in a similarly reflective mood. He had been out for a curry and had returned exhausted and lay on his bed thinking of her. He was surprised at how much he enjoyed Jules taking control of their lovemaking. Pretty soon, he was hard again and in his head, she was making him subservient to her sexual desires. He began rubbing his cock and was just about to undress, when a text came through on his cell phone. It just said, "Call me". He quickly called her.

"Jules today was lovely, I was thinking about you and..." He stopped confused, as there was no response.

There seemed no end to the silence and he listened and just heard her moaning. He realised she was playing with herself and understood she was teasing him and that made his cock even stiffer. Her moaning was enticing him and the deliberate strokes of her vibrator made her moans deep and sexual. This turned him on but he knew that he was not allowed to speak. He was transfixed and whilst he was tempted to begin to stroke his cock, he did not want to without her permission. He could hear her breathing heavily as she pushed her toy inside her faster and faster making her moan in tune to her thrusting.

.   .   .

Soon she was screaming his name and when her orgasm came, it made her convulse and the contractions held the toy inside her, giving her another intense orgasm and she almost giggled with delight.

He was transfixed at her voice and when she calmed down she just said to him. "Did that make you hard?" When he answered in the affirmative her only words were, "You have 15 minutes to get here". The click of the phone being switched off was deafening. He got his clothes on and headed for the door

Dan parked his car in a state bordering on frenzy, so keen was he to get to her. In his head, there were warning voices and they all revolved around what the parameters of this relationship should be. Today had been the first date and yet here he was again just about to make love with Jules again. He considered also the power dynamic and wanted to know what that meant, for times when they weren't making love. All of that was mushing around with a bizarre sense of sexual vulnerability and the excitement of tasting her again.

By the time he got to her door, nothing made sense except the thought of having her. The door opened in no time, in response to his knock and she was dressed in a silk dressing gown. He could see that she had lingerie on and that made him hard at the thought. She held out her hand and immediately led him upstairs. At what he presumed was her bedroom door, she stopped and turned to him.

Looking him in the eye she gently said, "Dan I really like you a lot, today has been fantastic and I want it to continue.

" He nodded his approval, and she continued. "The idea of you making love to me, fucking me really at my command, having you serve me is fantastic, and I want to explore that."

He felt like a dullard and just waited until he was asked a direct question. Luckily, she went on, "I want a relationship that is cool and funky and romantic but in the bedroom, I want a wild ride with you as my toy. If you want that then come inside, if not let's go downstairs and talk." There was the tiniest of pauses before he opened the door and said, "After you, Jules"

Smiling, she walked in front of him, and truth be told, except for that little speech she had not much of an idea about what she was going to do. Whatever it was though she knew that she want to be "on top" in the bedroom. It was like a reversal of her life, which up to this point had seen her as a grey little mouse timid and unassertive. Now here in her bedroom, she had a willing partner someone who would inspire her deep sexual fantasy.

Meanwhile, Dan was just standing there, looking to her for instruction almost. Looking at him, she grew authoritative and reaching back to a fantasy she had read about ordered him to kneel. He complied at once, and she took her gown off and exposed her underwear-clad body to him. Her black thong and suspenders were completed by stockings and a plunge bra. He gasped quietly and she dragged the gown over his face. Looking down at him, she circled him trailing the gown over him. Then she sat on by her dressing table, and said, "You must undress to your underwear."

He did so and her command for him to do it slowly made him do it as provocatively as he could, at no time did he speak. When he was down to his pants she told him, "Stop, and come over here"

Walking over he felt a little foolish, but did not smile and his hard-on betrayed his state of mind. She began rubbing it through the fabric of his pants and the pre-come was evident very quickly. Pulling down his pants, she then fingered his cock, moving down the shaft to his balls, which she fondled and gently squeezed until a moan came from him. She stood and told him, "Be quiet and speak when you are spoken to, and always call me Mistress."

He nodded, and quickly said, "Yes, Mistress" Again, she grabbed his cock, "Now what is this?" "My cock Mistress"

Not answering she took a crop that she used to use for riding and lashed him across the ass, making his ass sting. He was going to speak, but she cut him off. "That is my cock for my pleasure. What is it?"

"It's your cock Mistress"

Smiling she just said, "Good."

Pointing at the bed, he sat on the edge and she put a sultry piece of music on and danced around him undressing, dragging the clothes over his naked body and cock. The sexuality of it made his balls ache, but he neither spoke nor reacted to the torment. Down to her pants, she became a true temptress as she writhed around him, gyrating her ass over his cock, forbidding him to move his hands. Then slightly bending, she pulled down her thong and just said to him kneel. Grasping the chair, she positioned herself, bent down, and thrust her ass in his face. He knew what to do and subtly at first began to lick her wet pussy and on her instruction gently stimulates her clit. He was fantastically turned on and his probing reflected his excitement

Jules was trying to hold back her passion but it was too much. This was after all the first time she had done this and she thought that if they had not fucked this afternoon, she would have come ages ago.

His tongue and fingers were working hard on her pussy and he hardly heard her commanding that he stand up. He actually was disappointed that she had not come. He followed her to the bed and she sat down and demanded he fuck her. Dan moved towards her and she lay back and he stood and entered her. Both of them by this time lost in a dark sexual place, oblivious to anything other than the sexual intensity. The thrusting became faster and Dan had to use every trick not to just unload into her. He wanted to be told, be given permission to com. Indeed, it was like a gift he desperately wanted to give to his mistress. He thrust deeper inside her; he could feel her wetness on his balls and again tried hard not to come. Jules was lost to all of that and as soon as she reached a certain point began a stunning spiral of physical sensations that heralded her orgasm. Dan was amazed at the contortions her face was making and he blurted out, "Can I come Mistress?" Her only reply was a strangled "yes" as the orgasm began to overwhelm her, she was only distantly aware of him coming inside her with an amazing level of come considering his performance that afternoon.

Soon they were in bed together, and she whispered, "Are you ok?" It gave her a huge electric thrill when he sleepily said, "Yes Mistress."

CHAPTER 35

JUST A LITTLE BIT DEEPER

HE HAD her mentally as well as physically. It wasn't an obsession, it was possession, and he had her. All through her life, she had used her looks to capture men and used her body to get what she wanted. Then she had invited a friend over to her house and that's when it began.

He was an artist, the partner of her bitchiest friend Donna. He was not a good looker, certainly not wealthy, and completely out of step in their world. She asked her 'why?' and a giggle was the answer. "Listen tonight and you might hear," and off she trotted to drag her man away.

Julia could hear what she meant long after she went to bed alone. The sound of her friend's lovemaking, the slaps, and the screams of pleasure could be heard all around the house. It thrilled her to hear it and her hands caressed her own body as their ecstatic sounds rose to a crescendo. Then she heard her Donna begging him 'please let me come, please.' Then the screams of her coming and the quiet rustling of sheets as they retreated to bed. Her own pussy was wet from the assault and her orgasm had been fantastic but obviously less noisy.

At breakfast the next day they were there smiling and she smiled back. Donna caught her elbow later and said, "See what I mean?" She just nodded back at her. All weekend the lovemaking continued. Julia always accompanied their fucking with masturbation. The climaxes were fabulous and it reminded her of how much she missed sex.

The artist Neil was very articulate and witty, but it was as a lover of Donna that she judged him. Her friend offered her a threesome but she declined, not wanting to partake. As she fingered herself that night in response to their furious fucking, she regretted that decision, thinking that she wanted his hard cock inside her.

Later at breakfast, he offered to paint her portrait and she accepted. The thought that it might lead to a session like she heard last night was a motivator. The orgasm her friend experienced was begged out of him and she heard his slaps on her ass that thrilled her.

So after returning home and a week of finger fucking she found herself in his studio and it didn't take long for her to start flirting, but he was not responding. He focused on the work and despite her low-cut top and hints about how easy it would be for him to have her, he seemed uninterested.

This went on for weeks and she stopped her attentions and just watched him work and then when he unveiled the painting she was shocked at how good it was. A great likeness of her and her thanks were genuine and he offered her a drink, which she drank quickly. Another came and she felt fantastic. Relaxed he started flirting with her. She asked about Donna and was told she was out for the day and she went for it and responded to his attention.

"Did you hear us fucking when you stayed with us?" His question was so direct that she was taken aback. He continued, "I've no time for coyness I'm afraid." Again she stayed mute. He walked over, pulled her head back, and kissed her and she was stunned by the shock of it. The next hour was taken up with a passionate and steamy session while he dominated her. Her last orgasm was on all fours with him thrusting his cock in her ass, pulling her hair back. He unloaded his come on her back after he allowed her to come and when she finished he gave her back her clothes and was aloof with her.

Two days later, he called her back for a re-sit on the portrait to tidy up some details. She was desperate to discuss the fucking he had given her. He was having none of it and by the end she was angry. When he finished she challenged him. "Why did you fuck me and then ignore me?"

He looked coolly at her and said, "You wanted me to fuck you. I fucked you, what do you want?"

It was a surprise, not many men treated her like this.

"I want more," she replied wanly, "I want another fuck."

"Beg me then."

"Please fuck me," she whispered, but he ignored her. He stood up and she repeated her appeal. His look was full of sexual avarice, and he just said, "Kneel"

She was on the floor before she knew it and he said to her, "Repeat after me, I'm a dirty bitch."

She complied and he continued. "Repeat after me, I am to serve my master's cock. I will kiss his cock, I will suck his cock, and I will lick his balls and swallow his come. I am a dirty slut and I am his to command."

He pulled her up, marched her over to his table, and bent her over it. Pulling up her skirt, he pulled down her thong to just below the cheeks of her ass. "Count." He brought his hand down on the cheeks of her ass and she counted out, "One". When he reached 10 her backside was red.

"What do you say bitch?"

She knew instinctively what to do. "Thank you master"

"Good now get down and suck my cock." She responded and licked and sucked his cock with enthusiasm, willing to surrender to his domination of her. He held the back of her head and thrust his cock in her mouth. She sensed him about to come and was excited expecting a hot jet of come in her mouth. However, he stopped and lifting her up again bent her over the table. Sliding his cock inside her, he began to thrust inside her and she could feel him fingering her ass. The feeling of her pleasure was enhanced by him repeating the mantra, "You are my dirty bitch, and don't you forget it."

He demanded she repeat it and all through her fucking. "I'm your dirty bitch," she moaned as his cock slid in and out of her and he continued to probe her asshole. Moaning she began to come, and he pulled her hair and she groaned as that drove his cock further inside her. "You cannot come until I tell you". She answered "yes master" and still holding her hair he went harder into her. It was nearly beyond endurance and she begged him, "Let me come." He refused, and she kept asking and he drove faster into her and ignored her.

"Now you can come, bitch," and he began to ejaculate into her and this was accompanied by her massive gush of orgasm. She felt her knees buckle and his hot sticky spunk running over her ass. He pulled up her thong and said, "Go home and call me as soon as you get there. On no account are you to tell anyone I've fucked you."

Walking out of the house, she felt his spunk inside her mixing with her come. The creamy wetness made her uncomfortable but strangely turned on too. The phone was lifted and so began her surrender to him. It began that day.

Now he will just call and she must attend. There is always the ceremony. "Repeat after me, I am to serve my master's cock. I will kiss his cock, I will suck his cock, and I will lick his balls and swallow his come. I am a dirty slut and I am his to command."

As ever, she repeats it like a mantra, and every time he calls, it is a surprise. Sometimes Donna joins them and fucks her with a strap-on, sometimes a male friend joins them and they fuck each other and her together, or sometimes it's just her. Every time he pulls up her panties and she gets that feeling of filthy wetness of their mixed come as she drives home. Sometime it is with come on her tits or in her mouth, but it's always at her master's pleasure.

CHAPTER 36

LITTLE MAN IN THE BOAT

ONE WARM AND sunny Saturday afternoon my new hubby and I gave the phrase "Little Man in the Boat" a whole new meaning. To most people aware of erotic terms this particular term is talking about a woman's clit. It kind of resembles a little guy sitting in a canoe. I have always found the term erotic and silly all at the same time, but after hubby's and my adventure aboard his new "toy" - his canoe - that day, I didn't have any idea just how hot this term really was. My lips always seemed to resemble a canoe, long and luscious. And when my little man stood up, it was time to rock the boat if you catch my drift.

CHAPTER 37

WHATEVER FLOATS YOUR BOAT

HUBBY and I headed out fairly early that late spring day. The weather in New England was perfect. It wasn't too cold or too hot. The birds were singing, the lilacs were blooming and he and I were inseparable. I had never been in a canoe before so I was rather excited about a brand new adventure with my beloved. I trusted him with my life and he assured me the worst that would happen was that I'd get wet, and boy was he ever right!

We finally got the canoe in the water. I was sitting back watching my hubby get his rod and reel all situated and I couldn't help but think how ruggedly handsome he was. The warmth of the New England sun beating down on me made me feel warm in more ways than one. It made me want to strip completely nude and have my way with my hot and sexy fly fisherman. It made me want to do a little fly fishing of my own if you catch my drift.

Hubby was deep into his fly and things and I was deep into my naughty thoughts and such. He was at his relaxed bed, and I on the other hand was tensing up in all of the right places. I wanted him and I wanted him now. Hell, I always wanted him. He had turned me on immensely ever since we first met. We had a unique chemistry from the word go, and it only seemed to increase over time. I could only imagine how much he would excite me after ten years of being together. We might set off fires across town if this intensity keeps up. It might seem like a tall tale, but the intensity between us reeked of total abandon.

As I pondered the immense sexual attraction between me and my lover, I began to get increasingly wet. I could feel my lips tremble and my clit begin to ache. Then I started to wonder just how much hubby would love me taking my fingers and playing with my pussy right there in his canoe as he fished! The very thought was delicious and I decided I would do it. Why the hell not? I had nothing to lose and everything to gain, and gaining 8" of the hard shaft inside me was worth a few flicks of my stiff clit in the bottom of a canoe.

At first, he didn't seem to notice my own fishing that was going on in the bottom of his canoe. He was a very intense fisherman, but I knew if the wet sounds coming from my folds got any louder, he'd take notice very soon. Any louder and he'd have two rods in his hands, not just the one he was fishing with. I so loved watching his expert technique using his rod.

My assumptions were right and I saw hubby looking over at me by way of his peripheral vision. At first, he tried to act as though he hadn't seen me going after my clit like a savage beast, but I knew he had. I saw him nonchalantly glance over and what was really cute is I saw him reach for his cock and give it a little tug over his camouflage fishing pants. I could see that he was teasing the head of his cock that lay stiffened beneath the fabric.

Knowing he was aroused only increased my desire to

pleasure my cunt in any way that I could. The hardest part was trying to prolong the pleasure. Watching him stiffen his cock with his fingers had always made me want to frantically rub myself until I came hard, but extending the pleasure was always better. I came harder, longer and wetter when I made myself crazy with lust. The more I teased, the hornier I got. I could almost taste his cock in my mouth while I stroked the edges of my drenched cunt lips.

He finally gave into his carnal needs and looked at me straight on with lust in his green eyes. I knew he would give in eventually. It was inevitable. I continued to toy with my horny twat as he licked his lips and finally unzipped his trousers and out popped his cock as hard as a rock. I went down on it like a lead weight sinking to the bottom of the pond.

His cock twitched in my mouth as he fucked and stroked my palate with his dick head. I cupped his balls and gave them a gentle squeeze. I loved his huge balls and even had thought about cramming them into my cunt to fuck them and his cock at the same time, but for now, it was all about his cock in my mouth. I knew that he and I were about to fuck and there wasn't any way 2 people could do it in a floating canoe. I suggested to hubby we take our lust party to the soft grass. He agreed and took my hand and led me to a soft mossy area under a huge oak tree.

My fingers flicked my stiff love bud while my mouth worked his swollen meat to perfection. I could feel his orgasm approaching and suddenly released my lip-lock on his love muscle. Falling onto my back on the soft grass, I drew my legs up beside my ears leaving my drenched cunt wide open for him. He quickly sunk his cock balls deep in my throbbing cunt. The moss felt cool and smooth against my naked ass.

I laid back in extreme anticipation of hubby's first slow and excruciatingly delicious thrust inside of me. He delicately picked one leg up at a time and placed them up by his ears. His hazel eyes glistened with intensity in the morning sun. The smell of our lusty love filled the air of the woods around us. I knew he was about to make slow passionate love to me just as I liked it. I absolutely was on fire with anticipation. The first thrust of his rock-hard meat inside of me sent electric jolts throughout my molten flesh. I was covered in goosebumps from head to toe. It was like a divine impalement each time his dick thrust deeper inside of my needing folds. I felt my reddened and drenched pussy lips wrap around his shaft like a snuggly blanket. When my legs were seductively draped up by my hubby's ears we could both easily see his shaft thrusting and pulling in and out of my drenched cunt. It was a sight that made us burn with extreme desire and hunger. I had a feeling he and I would never tire of one another sexually or intimately.

Our hearts beat as one and our bodies moved as one with amazing passion and naughtiness. As he thrust in and out of me, his mouth kissed me hungrily. I pulled his head into my mouth hard and furious. I had never desired him more than at this very moment we were intertwined together. He turned me on like no other man before. I simply could not quench the sexual thirst he caused in me. My hungry pussy lips grabbed him tighter until I thought he and I might both explode in rapture.

My thoughts were dead on because we were both moments from orgasmic delight like we had never experienced before, not even together! I could feel his massive balls tighten by my ass and his girth stiffen inside of me. He was about to shoot his wads deep inside my folds and it drove me wild knowing it was seconds away. My lips continued to grope and grab as my own orgasm got closer and closer.

I felt the warmth rise from my toes to my head and I knew I was going to gush all over the two of us. As his balls began to unload inside my wanton cunt I began to squirt with power like I had never gushed before. We both rocked in the rhythm of our mutually satisfying orgasm as the sun beat down on our lustful and intimate union there under that oak tree. After out lovemaking we enjoyed the rest of the day canoeing with a satisfied smile on our faces knowing that many canoe trips were to come and maybe we could make each one a bit more exciting than the last. As I thought this, I looked over at my hubby fishing and gave him a seductive look and a wink. He smiled back as if to say, "You think that was hot? Just wait until I get you home."

CHAPTER 38

LONG NIGHT

IT ALL BEGINS with the eyes. With a look. A deep gaze as I tell her, "Trust me. I'll take care of you." I approach her face slowly, our eyes locked, breathing on her lips, my hands on her hips. My breath is the most gentle breeze that could ever grace such a perfectly beautiful face. My fingertips touch her jaw; caress it while I plant another kiss on her cheek, even more gently, even more slowly. I feel her pressing her face against mine. She smells like all the things that remind me of good memories; her breath fills me with warmth and kindness. My hand slips to the back of her neck and I hold her, allow her to rest her head as our tongues touch, barely, just enough for me to show her I love every wet bit of it, want it always. My kisses grow gentler. I approach her neck; allow my tongue to taste her, to meld with her warmness. I wrap my arms around her and embrace her as if it's the last time I'll ever see her. I rest my lips between her breasts. I feel the beating of her heart, soft and rhythmical, and it makes my mind burst to know she is real, with me, next to me, where I can love her and touch her, feel her. For a moment I forget I exist, that there even is a Me. I sit her down on the bed; stroke her face, gently running my fingers over her full lips as she looks up at me, smiling and content. I sit beside her, turn her face to kiss her soft cheek again, whisper in her ear I care for her. I begin to undress her, slow her down with gentle kisses when she begins to rush – just so she knows I'm not going anywhere, that this is exactly where I want to be, where I had always wanted to be.

I remember little of what goes on before we are both naked; it all becomes a blur of emotion, of gentle cuddling, kissing. But what I do remember, what I always remember, is how I feel when I touch her, how much I care that I can, and how my hands seem like they are a part of her, how they tingle, cry out with pleasure. How my lips, my tongue, my hands, my whole body, wants more of her. Always more. The sounds of her breathing and quiet moaning becomes a symphony, one accompanying every note ever conceived, each more beautiful than the last. I feel myself inside her. Every bit of her is smooth and perfect. Her warmness, the love I feel for her, it takes me away from everything. Reality becomes a blend of her and me, nothing else exists. It even feels like, before this, nothing ever truly has. I hold her, look into her eyes; tell her again I live only for her, while my gentle thrusts bring her to a climax. We curl up together. She takes hold of my hands and presses them to her breasts, kisses them, her breathing falling upon my skin. I stand up and open a drawer. She smiles at me as I pull out a black, leather collar. Its sheen is bright in the low lights. She sits up as I step over to her. The collar hugs her tightly as I slowly wrap it around her soft neck. I put my finger through the silver ring in its middle and pull her close to me.

. . .

"You get to be my bitch today," I tell her, and she nods. I pull her even closer, towards my cock, her mouth open and dripping. She wants this, she always wants it. And that's what I love about her. She will never get enough of me, just like I'll never get enough of her. I fuck her mouth. It isn't enough just to love her, to kiss her and make love to her. It will never be enough, and I love that she thinks the same way. Her mouth is dripping, her juices flowing down my tights.

I grab her hair and make her face me. I give her a slap and, pointing a finger at her face say, "You know better."

She did know better, knows exactly what I meant. She swallows it, gags on it, and makes it harder than it has ever been. I put my finger through the ring again and make her lick my feet.

"Lick them clean, slut," I tell her. She nods and moans. "The whole tongue now." She nods again.

There's always a time when good little sluts should get their reward. And after she licks my feet, I tie her hands behind her back; her feet together, place a pillow under her and stand above her. She turns her head to see me jerk off to the sight of her.

"I'm going to fuck you, and you're gonna love it like good little whore you are," I tell her. "Yes, daddy," she says.

I don't waste time. In one thrust, I ram it deep into her pussy. Then again. Then again. Again. This is for me, and she knows it. Her pussy is for me, and she loves it. She puts her ass up, the sight of it making my saliva drip down on her back. I fill her mouth with my fingers as she begins to moan and scream and my other hand on her upper back. I pin her as I fuck that tight little pussy of hers. She grows quiet as she comes, and so do I. But I am not quiet. I want everyone to hear I have just filled my little bitch with all that I had. I lay on her for a while, semen dripping from her pussy as I remove my cock from her swollen clit and leave her there for a while. I come back after I had showered and find her asleep. I untie her and carry her to the bathroom, where I gently lay her in a bath full of warm water.

"The night's not over yet, my dear," I whisper.

CHAPTER 39

MAKING IT FIT (WHEN BIGGER IS BETTER)

THE ROOM SMELLS of spices and chocolate. It's richly decked in gold satins and silks. There are reds and purples too. The bed is sprinkled with petals of many scented blossoms and many roses. The young couple in the room couldn't have dreamed of a more fitting boudoir in which to consummate their marriage. The bride is beautiful, thick black hair frames a perfect face, her body toned and slim, its proportions ideal. Her vagina is covered in the softest black mat of curls, its full lips barely visible. The groom is a slender man, thick black hair, a strong regal Indian face, massive, cut cock. They are perfect. This is going to be perfect.

Gopal approaches his new wife cautiously. They have had some time to get acquainted but this is the first time they've seen each other naked. Sumaya didn't expect the massive cock before her and she trembles now that he is close enough to touch her. She shrinks back as he reaches for her. She isn't ready for this. She is definitely not ready for all that he has brought to the party. He runs his hands over her beautiful body, his dick growing monumentally as he does, amplifying the tension in the room. Sumaya seems genuinely fearful of him. He doesn't understand why, and kisses her as reassurance that he will be a most gentle lover.

"*I'm a virgin*," she whispers before she is too afraid to say it out loud. Gopal looks at his new wife with a mixture of apprehension and gratitude. He lifts her in his arms, kissing her for the short distance between where they stand and the bed. He lays her on the bed and instructs her to be still, to relax and to speak only if he is hurting her. She agrees, almost embarrassed that she is proving to be an inconvenience already. He lies next to her and gives her the deepest, most sensuous kiss she has ever received. His hands move lightly over her entire body. He has her on her back, the only part of him on top of her being his head as his lips make fiery temples of hers.

Gopal's hand is on her breasts, his other hand on her face, caressing it gently as he kisses her. He gives her virgin breasts light squeezes. The mounds tingle under his touch. There is a deep almost itch inside each breast that shoots through her nipples, making her want to pull hard on them. But the nipples harden between Gopal's fingers and he presses them firmly between his fingertips, reading the signs perfectly. He keeps caressing her face as he lifts his mouth from hers and settles his lips, then his tongue on her breasts, sucking on her nipples, giving each one a fair amount of attention. His hand moves down to her crotch, his fingers gently scratching at the soft curls he finds there. She places a hand on his, reflex, but then lets her hands rest on her thighs and then drops them onto the bed.

He continues his gentle scratching, deliberately avoiding her clit. The area starts to tingle as her breasts had, and there is a deep and powerful drum that starts to beat in a steady rhythm somewhere inside and outside her pussy.

She wants to touch herself but needs to trust that he knows what to do with her. Her nerves seem to give way to what can only be described as hunger, for him, and everything he wants to do to her. Her breasts are aflame in his mouth now. Gopal really has an expert touch. Sumaya hasn't even noticed that he has the tip of his index finger on her clit, the tip of his thumb settling comfortably on the entrance to her pussy. Only when he lifts his mouth off of her breasts and his lips are on hers does she register the activity on her lower lips.

His mouth is off hers and their eyes lock. His eyes ask for complete trust. Hers say yes. He takes the green light and digs his thumb gently into her moist cunt. The heat inside it is unexpected and his cock grows immediately to its full 28 centimeters, touching against her leg, startling her and arousing her at the same time. He starts to rub his cock against her leg so that she processes its length. She starts to enjoy the feeling of the heat rod against her skin. His thumb goes into her a little deeper and the finger on her clitoris rubs the flowering bud a little harder. He fucks her for twenty minutes with just his thumb, his cock thrusting gently into her leg, his lips moving from her mouth to her neck, her breasts, her belly, and then back up to her mouth the way they came.

Sumaya holds tightly onto his arm as his thumb brings her to an orgasm. She can't believe that he has managed to make her entire body shake with just his thumb. She wonders if this is sex. But he seems far from done. She is caught in that beautiful place where if that was it, it was enough, but if not, then *thank god!* He pulls his thumb from her and then gives her a loving stare before taking a look at his thumb. It's coated in the contents of her pussy, the same contents that should make the acquisition of her virginity a pleasant one. It is this almost translucent love potion that will facilitate their impending merger. He takes the thumb in his mouth and sucks *her* off it, showing her just how completely acceptable she is.

Suddenly he is between her legs, each leg in each of his arms, his mouth on her pussy. She wants to fly away from him but he has her in a firm hold and is pulling her pussy into his mouth. His sucking now is not like his thumb was. There is nothing gentle about the way he is chewing on her vagina. Then his tongue is inside her. The fire that it sends into her pussy pulls rivers from inside it. These waters do nothing to put out the flame though. Over and over, he sends his thick tongue into her until eventually her cunt gives enough way for him to settle his tongue inside her and lick the interior of her vagina for a long while before it closes back over him and forces him out. He manages to get back inside her a few more times with his tongue though and the fifth time he brings her to a second, more powerful orgasm. She is now sweating tiny drops over the entire surface of her body.

Gopal sits up between her legs. He places each one of his legs over each of hers but keeps her on her back. He starts to hit the surface of her pussy with his heavy, loaded cock. She immediately senses that this is going to be it, that sensation she has been trying to imagine but failed to despite the double orgasm she's just had. She knows that this is not going to be as easygoing, as completely pleasant. But she also knows that lovemaking is beautiful or else people the world over wouldn't be so obsessed with it. So she decides that she is going to just have to get past what-ever it is that constitutes the losing of her virginity, and then get on with the fun part. She closes her eyes and takes herself to the beautiful places she was just at with her very patient husband. Gopal gives her pussy a few more whippings from his cock, making sure that he gives the clit a couple of solid hits.

Then he pushes his cock hard onto her clit, the length of it along the line of her cunt. He starts to rub it back and forth over her cunt, heating her clit as it glides across the surface. He pushes down harder and harder on her pussy as though he expects it to give way. She senses that any second now he is going to be inside her. She doesn't know how to prepare herself for this. She has no idea how to brace herself for it. A strange tingling shoots through both her legs and they go weak, then lame, then all tingly again. There is an absolute sense of exposure that overtakes her cunt, then a feeling that something has suddenly lodged in her stomach. It isn't so much painful as it is awkward. She wants to look but can't, aware only of the backward and forward movement in her pussy. Gopal rubs gently on her belly and then less gently on her thighs as he holds his cock in place, gets on his knees, and then reaches to lay over her.

On top of her now he locks her stare, then kisses her. He thrusts into her from somewhere high above but it still feels like there is too much of him inside her. She wants to ask him to give her a minute but something about the way he is moving in and out of her has her lift up to his mouth and initiate a deep kiss herself. He gives a few more insistent stabs and then returns to his gentle strokes, his kissing consistent. More and more his cock moves deeper and deeper into her; Sumaya not noticing for the distraction of her mouth. Then suddenly she feels as though he has ripped into her and exited through her naval. She gasps and pushes on his chest so that she can throw her eyes in the direction of her cunt. He throws his weight onto her, knowing that he has reached her final barrier. He gives her the deepest, hardest kiss and then drops his entire weight onto her, breaking her virginity at last.

Suddenly the back of her vagina seems to open up. She feels his hips on hers and knows that now he is all the way inside her. Everything she thought was fucking until now wasn't. He was being gentle and patient and preparing her for this. Now he was inside. He had broken through and could now give himself to his wife because he had opened her up for himself. Now the massive cock is everything she had dreamed, and not the cause of anxiety. She is still awkward and doesn't know what to do, but with Gopal now where he wants to be, there seems nothing for her to do but to be the fiery hot punani that her husband is screaming like a girl inside. Each stroke that he makes into her has Gopal whimper like a child tasting chocolate for the first time.

Gopal is in no hurry to cum. He fucks Sumaya in gentle strokes for hours before he eventually shoots a massive load inside her already salivating cunt. She has lost count of her own orgasms. He watches her face as he shoots more and more jizz into her, her eyes closed on her beautiful face. This was the perfect wedding night. His family had found him the perfect wife. He knows that he will enjoy discovering her. He knows that he will keep her satisfied because her innocence inspires him to take care of her in every way. He gives himself two more orgasms and Sumaya a further seven as he introduces her to the pleasure of sex over the next *twelve hours...*

CHAPTER 40

MASTER OF HER DOMAIN

THE HONEYMOON HAD BEEN WONDERFUL. Hawaii had to be the most beautiful place on earth. The ocean was liquid turquoise, and best of all, it never rained like this, she thought as she stared into the gray drab of Seattle. It had been Tori's home all of her life, but that too was about to change. She missed Nick but there was no way he could get more time off upon returning from a two-week vacation. Unfortunately, that left her alone in tying up the loose ends in Washington and moving her things to California. Her mom wasn't thrilled about the move even though it wasn't all that far away. She had been a fan of Charles and the stability that came along with him, flabbergasted that she had dumped him to marry a dancer. Of course, never giving recognition that Nick had gotten his master's and was now a professor at the college he'd once dropped out of. Thank God daddy understands, she thought. All he wanted was her happiness, and he saw how happy Nick made her. Although she had a million things to do, the drive from Ventura had wiped her out, not to mention she had totally bummed herself out by dwelling on the whole yucky weather/bitchy mom thing. So she justified herself a nap.

She missed him as she snuggled into the bed he hadn't slept in for six years. She closed her eyes remembering their college days when they first met and fell in love. They had been in journalism class together. Nick had noticed the statuesque blond right away, everyone had, but he never spoke to her in class fearing she was out of his league. Little did he know she had noticed him too. He was fully immersed in his grunge phase, but Tori saw past the dreadlocks and found his crooked smile and playful sense of humor completely adorable. Luckily, their professor recognized their talents and got them both an internship at the Gazette. That is where their love story began. Forced to cut his hair for the job, Tori complimented his shaggy cut. All of his apprehension melted away with her warmth. She was as sweet as she was beautiful. It didn't take long for their friendship to grow into full-blown lust. Everyone in the office felt it.

There was a constant heat that hovered whenever they were together. Not having a clue why either of them were fighting it Tori asked him over one night under the pretense of a working dinner. Half a pizza and a bottle of wine later they surrendered. That was the first night they'd made love. She replayed every moment of that night as she drifted off to sleep.

She'd purposely worn her favorite sweater; a soft low cut sky blue number. She knew it brought out the color of her eyes, and her large breasts sitting at attention certainly wouldn't hurt. The loft was chilly that night and she had asked Nick to build a fire. Once he had it roaring, they sat in front of it finishing the wine when suddenly his emerald eyes fixed on hers, and for once, she didn't look away. In an instant, they were in one another's arms kissing with all the passion they'd held back. His hands were wildly exploring her body. My God, how she wanted this man. She pulled the sweater over her head and unhooked her bra in one quick shot as he simultaneously removed her slacks. The goddess he had longed for was now naked before him.

He had to take a moment to adore her beautiful body, giving special attention to her amazing breasts. Nipples in the shade of a rose at dusk. A hue so unique that even in his fantasies, he could never have created it. He lightly dragged his tongue over the hardened bud. She sighed with delight leaning into his kiss, causing him to suck it between his teeth, nibbling slightly. He trailed his tongue down her abdomen to her navel. She raised her hips in anticipation. He ran his fingers through her perfectly manicured bush noticing she was already wet with desire. "I want you to lick me all over," she pleads. He flashed the devilish smile she so adored.

He ran his thumb across her engorged clit as he slipped his middle finger inside her. Withdrawing his finger, he seductively glossed her lips with the silky moisture and inserted it into her mouth. She giggled as she sucked his finger in and out a time or two. So turned on by the bad girl he'd set free, he parted her wet folds and ran his tongue from bottom to top as if he was marking her. Her body rocked in response as she opened her legs farther, inviting him into her depth. He took her clit between his teeth just barely raking it as he sucked it fervorously. She violently ran her fingers through his thick curly hair pushing his face into her throbbing pussy causing him to eat her as if he were starving. She begged him to take her but she was too close to orgasm to fuck, she needed to come first. So instead, he fingered her as his mouth made love to her clit, drinking up her moisture until her cream bathed his fingers with hot need. He stood up, took off his t-shirt, and began unbuttoning his low-slung jeans.

Her eyes fixed on the golden-brown line of hair just below his navel leading to what she'd fantasized about for months. As he stepped out of his faded jeans and boxers his hard cock sprang free, and she was not disappointed. She leaned over and pulled a condom from a decorative wooden box on the end table. Approaching him on her knees, she helped herself to the tiny drop of semen at his tip before rolling the condom onto his thick hard shaft. She was a woman in control, but not this night he thought. In his desire to possess her, he said, "Get on your back." Her pleasure. He parted her quivering lips with the head of his cock and entered her with one deep thrust. He was in ecstasy hearing her gasp as her pussy molded to hold him. His strokes were slow and rhythmic instinctively finding her g-spot, every movement bringing her closer and closer to orgasm. He cupped her heaving breasts running his thumb over two rock-hard nipples before lowering his mouth to suckle.

The sensation of his dick caressing her most elusive spot as he nursed her sensitive peak both satisfied and increased the need between her legs. She raked her nails down his back, a clear indication she was enjoying him immensely. His desire to watch his beauty come overpowered both his body and his mind as he began pumping her with no restraint. He felt the wave of climax overtaking her as a convulsion began in her pussy and quickly traveled through her entire body. As her quaking slowed, he watched the primal beauty of her face as she climaxed and it was the most sensual moment he'd ever experienced. Without any hesitation, at all, he loved her exactly as he wanted sharing his own mind-blowing orgasm. She felt his hot load warm her from the inside out as their bodies melted together in complete exhaustion and satisfaction.

Tori awoke tangled in damp sheets and horny for Nick. She snickered as she debated whether to do it or not. "What the hell," she said aloud to the empty room as she hit the send button. She had never sent anyone a nude photo of herself, but she had to admit waiting for his reply felt delectably naughty. Only moments later her cell vibrated. She couldn't wait to read it. "Who is this, really?" she said. Following it immediately was another text, "lol" she read as she waited for the attachment to upload. "Damn," she spoke as if the word were three syllables, practically drooling over the crotch shot of her man with a major hard-on. She dialed him and breathlessly purred, "mmmm." It wasn't as good as the real thing, but his very personal directions got her there. SO inspired by the absence of Nick, Tori called a moving company the next morning to pack and deliver the entire contents of her loft. She locked the door without even looking back. It wasn't home anymore. She belonged with Nick and wherever he was, she would be beside him, 'till death do them part.

CHAPTER 41

MEET ME ON THE STAIRCASE

MY HUBBY and I have been married about 2 years now and we are still hot for each other and passionate, but both of us have been looking for new and exciting ways to spice up our sex life. We liked to explore some of the kinkier things of the sexual realm, and no, I don't mean the typical threesome. We had been there and done that. We were both kind of bored with some vapid situations and the same boring outcomes. We wanted to do something exotic for two people in love to explore the hot and lusty side of marriage.

My hubby and I both were of the opinion that marriage and intimate sex were far too underrated. We were out to prove that theory in many of our latest sexual adventures. We had webcammed each other unbeknownst to the other one and I had also masturbated while my husband peeked through our bedroom window. We both loved the whole hot idea of being caught while in the act of self-pleasure or in the midst of wild and crazy sex. I doubt there was much we wouldn't do given the right situation. Today I had a wickedly hot plan in store for my lover. I was housesitting for a close friend of mine and she had an amazing spiral staircase in her condo. Since last night, I had been fanta-sizing of my husband fucking me hard on the banister and easing our way up the stairs in the grips of unadulterated and heated sex.

I left my hubby a message on his cell phone about an hour before he got off of work and it said this: "I am thinking about you walking in the door, dropping your brief-case, and ripping my clothes off right here in this room, without saying a word. Guess what I want more than anything? I want you IN me. Meet me on the staircase lover."

I giggled to myself seductively because I knew that would drive him crazy. I headed to a hot soapy bubble bath and lingered in the sudsy water for a while. The feeling of the ripples on my skin ignited the flames inside of me. I was beginning to feel warm and tingly in anticipation of my meeting with hubby on the staircase. As the bubbles tickled me between the legs, I squirmed a bit in the tub getting more intensely aroused by the second.

The feeling of hot water on a body that needed sex was almost too much to handle. I couldn't hold back. I knew my fingers would find their way under the bubbles and between my legs. My fingers made their way to my pink and swollen lips. One at a time, I played with them. I loved to tease myself before I knew my hubby was going to bang me hard and bang me good. I was so anxious for him to get home and get inside of me. I needed to be filled up. I loved the feeling of being full of my man's meat. My fingers were going crazy plunging into my depths and feeling the warmth and the wetness. My inner folds felt achy and swollen like one lick would make me gush.

I was almost ready to squirt but thankfully my husband texted me and said this in his text: "My cock aches for your cunt to lap me with your wet lips." I knew that he would be home soon. I looked down at my lips and saw the bubbles hanging off of them precariously, but it looked incredibly hot. The bubbles hid part of my long lips so I could see the edges peeking out from the white froth. It was all I could do not to gently pull a towel tip across them, but I knew it would drive me over the edge, and that was for him. My fingers trembled as I gently dabbed at my swollen lips. I could barely look at them as it only made me crave his cock inside me more.

The more I looked at my rubbery lips the more my mouth watered and I licked my mouth lips wishing it was my pussy I was licking. The agony of holding off, the pure torture of a clit throbbing so hard I could feel my heartbeat through my lips...the need was frantic...

Just a gentle touch to my nipples felt like someone had sucked my clit into their mouth my breath was shallow and gasps that needed to feel the weight of him and to feel his meaty balls nestled in my butt crack. I longed to beg him with my mouth, to kiss him with my lips to feel his hands all over me pulling my flesh into absolute surrender. Where was he? My entire body was calling out to him begging him to take me yearning to be taken and to gaze into his eyes as they clouded over with unyielding passion. Where was he? Where? I could taste him in my mind and feel his breath upon my skin. My heart raced looking forward to my hubby. We had been married a few years but he was still the man who ignited all of the passionate embers inside of me. I find it incredibly hot that we have passion and intimate love. It is far more erotic than most people ever dream it can be.

CHAPTER 42

STAIRWAY TO HEAVEN

I HAD SLIPPED into my crotch-less red leather bodysuit and positioned myself on the bottom of the staircase. I wanted hubby and I to screw our way up not down. My furry muff poked out like a powder puff to greet him as he walked through the French doors. I saw the door latch turn and I knew it was wild and erotic sex time. Without saying a word as I had hinted strongly to him in my text, he walked over, plunged two fingers in my pussy, and kissed me passionately and hungrily. I grabbed his face pulling him to me biting his lower lip as he thrust wet fingers in and out of my throbbing bits. When his finger slipped inside me, I could feel the cool metal of his wedding ring bump across my sensitive pebbled inner flesh. An involuntary spasm racked through my entire body as his fingers pushed and pulled their way in and out of me. Every movement inside me was a three-alarm fire rippling through every inch of my body. I gasped and reached around him with a leg pulling his fingers tightly against my overly sensitized flesh.

He backed me up the staircase kissing me furiously and deeply. Our tongues did the dance of our bodies' movements. His tongue licked the tip end of my tongue mimicking the very motion his 3rd finger was doing on the head of my aching clit. He leaned me over the banister, yanked his cock from his zipper, and buried it deep inside my folds. I reached frantically with my foot to steady myself from the waves of absolute ecstasy ripping through her entire body. When my foot touched the stair, I gasped as he slid his finger deep inside my inner flesh and wiggled the tip against my sensitive g-spot. I lay back on the staircase and spread my legs as wide as I could to show him the full spectral vision of my folds. I tempted him to bury his face in between my throbbing petals. I inched backward until finally he latched onto my pussy and would not let go. I pushed his head hard down towards my aching and demanding flesh.

He looked up at me with a hunger and an erotic fire in his eyes and said, "I want to feel you deep in my mouth. I want you to cover my face and fuck it."

I replied to him with a growl in my voice "I demand it!" and I thrust his head down harder. I humped hard on his face and nearly took his breath away with my force. I squeezed my long thighs around him and demanded he not stop eating until he drank every drop of the juice I was offering to him.

I started to swirl in ecstasy from the tip of my toes to the top of my head and then I unleashed a flood of cream on him. He lifted his head for air but I kept squeezing him down upon my need. We reached the top of the stairs and hubby said to me

"I want you to taste what each stair meant to me." I smiled and did as he asked.

I took my husband's girth in my hands and stroked it tenderly and sweetly before engulfing his swollen handful. I didn't ease off of his throbbing lust until I had swallowed drop after delicious drop of his sweet release. I swallowed and released his aching meat with an audible pop, and I smiled up at my husband with ecstasy-filled eyes as I licked one residual drop of cum from my chin.

I could taste each stair upon my lips for every pleasure they had been. The teasing way he made me tremble, the fevered need he built inside of me, and the amazing explosion of my mind-bending orgasm. Each was another step towards where we both had found heaven in each other's arms. The climb was pure enchantment and the ecstasy so real it still reverberated through my body and my nipples still screamed out for a gentle tongue to swirl them into submission.

CHAPTER 43

MIRROR, MIRROR

EVERY YEAR FOR HER BIRTHDAY, John would take her out to dinner or a club. In the first year of their marriage, he took her to a restaurant in Madrid. He bought her an overpriced, fancy drink with a fancy name and an umbrella, and then he talked, laughed, and danced with her until the place was completely deserted. Afterward, they took a long walk to the hotel, holding hands.

The moment they walked through the door, she shoved him down onto the hotel bed, tore his clothes off, took him inside her, and rode them both into oblivion.

This became their thing. Every year, for her birthday, they would go to a fancy place, and then they would come back to the hotel and fuck as if it was their last day on earth.

But this year, she wasn't feeling up to anything special. The last twelve months were tough on both of them. So John took her out to an Italian restaurant, just a few blocks away from their apartment. Once they got there and ordered a pizza – vegetarian with mushrooms and vegetables – John, as usual, couldn't keep his hands to himself. Emily could feel him, caressing her under the table. His deft fingers sneaked under her black dress. The fact that he wanted her, after all those years of marriage, excited her. It made her warm inside and a bit jittery, it made her heart quicken.

"If you keep doing that, I won't be able to finish the pizza."

John just smiled and started to massage her through the material. Emily bit her lip. He really had skilled hands.

"I'm serious. I can't focus on my food."

John looked at her and raised an eyebrow. His fingers grazed her center, making her shiver a little bit. "Why, is something distracting you, honey?"

She knew John was just toying with her, but right now, she didn't mind. She went with the charade.

"Well, I thought you said you wanted me to eat more, keep my strength up."

"I said that?" His fingers brushed her thighs and then they slipped between the fabric of her panties.

She had to close her eyes to remain calm. She bit her lip so hard, trying not to moan, but it was too late. She ruined the whole thing. He slipped one finger inside her, firm and persistent. Oh God, she missed this. She opened her eyes to see John staring at her with a seductive smile on his face, trying to look innocent. He knew exactly what he was doing to her. Bastard.

Oh, fuck this.

She knocked off her glass, splashing the wine all over the table and their pizza. She felt like a completely different person, the kind of a girl who liked to do it in a locker room or the kind of a girl who took her boyfriend to a restaurant and let him finger her under the table, not caring if the waiter saw it. Not caring if anyone saw it.

She leaned over the table and licked his ear seductively. "Bathroom. Three minutes. Finish your wine."

She stood up and reluctantly made her way to the bathroom, walking away from him and his clever hands. She knew he would come. Still, she looked over her shoulder to send him a seductive glance, and swayed her hips. When she saw the expression on his face, she couldn't help smiling.

Oh, yes. He'll follow her like a puppy.

She closed the door and looked in the mirror. She was flushed, she felt too hot. All she could think right now was his hands inside her. She couldn't wait to finally feel him inside her. She wanted him so badly it almost hurt.

John, of course, didn't listen to her. It wasn't even a minute and she could hear his steps, far too impatient.

He didn't talk when he shut the door behind him. He just grabbed her, pulled her flush against him, and kissed her breathless. Their teeth knocked together, and she briefly wondered if anyone from the restaurant even suspected what they were doing in here, but she didn't care. All Emily wanted to do now was to stay close to him and never let go. She latched onto him and hissed him forcefully.

Without looking, John backed her against the wall and held her firmly against the sink. She moaned against his mouth as she felt his hardness press into her, making her wetter,

making her loose her mind. His hands wandered frantically all around her body, squeezing her through the clothes.

"John," she managed to say. "I need you to fuck me right now."

His hand shot out, reaching blindly for something, and then she heard a click. It took her a second to realize he locked the door, something she completely forgot about. But right now, she was completely lost to him, she forgot about everything else. How could she be reasonable when the whole world was on fire and the only thing she could focus right now was his hardness pressing between her legs.

Another noise escaped her throat when he was frantically fighting with the zipper of her dress. Their ragged breathing and moans echoed in the bathroom. She wanted more, and she wanted it now, so she just sends the buttons of his shirt flying everywhere. Then his hands were at her waist, underneath her dress. His clever fingers searched for the waistband of her panties, and Emily spread her legs to give him better access when he took them off. He shoved her panties into the pocket of his jeans, and then she fumbled with his belt, desperate to free him. Finally, Emily took him in her hand, making him gasp. He was warm, smooth, and deliciously hard.

She smiled as she pumped him teasingly a few times, making him moan.

"Em," he growled. "Want you . . ."

"You can have me," and this was all she could say because the words were lost on her when John lifted her and sat her on the cold marble, sending a shiver down her spine. The cold mingled with hot as he lowered her onto him, so slowly it was almost agonizing. When he filled her entirely, they both cried out in pleasure.

He started thrusting into her in a steady rhythm, until she forgot about everything, about being quiet, about the time, about the whole world. There was just the erratic movement of their hips, their desperate moans, their quickened breathing.

Suddenly, he pulled out and she gasped in protest. But John grabbed her legs and placed her on the floor, then turned her around, grabbed her hips, and entered her from behind, pushing himself in all the way to the hilt. She was beyond words; all she could do was push her hips back onto him to meet his thrusts. She found support on her arms, taking hold of the cold marble beneath her hands. Her face was inches from the mirror, she could see her widened irises and a deep flush that covered her cheeks, she could hear the slap of shin on shin echoing in the bathroom, and feel his hot breath and his cock moving deep inside her.

And then he hit that spot, that one, and this was enough to send her falling from the edge. She clenched around him, clawing at the mirror, as John moved inside her, quickly, erratically, desperately, until finally, he reached his orgasm, filling her with a long, desperate cry.

When he pulled out of her, it was far too soon. Emily turned around, leaned toward him and their lips joined in a long, lazy kiss that seemed to never end.

"Jesus, Em," he murmured into her hair, still breathing heavily. "That was amazing."

"Yeah. We should do this more often, "she rolled down her dress, not caring to put on her pants. She smiled. "You think that we can finish our pizza now?"

He chuckled, pulling her flush against him and looked at her meaningfully. "Not a chance."

CHAPTER 44

MORE THAN FRIENDS

RACHEL AND TOMMY had been friends since high school. Their parents had been close friends and so the two of them had grown up together. They'd both dated other people, but Rachel had always harbored a secret attraction to Tommy. He'd never indicated that he felt the same way, until recently.

Two weeks ago, he'd almost kissed Rachel, but had suddenly pulled away. Rachel hadn't had the guts to bring it up at the time and had acted as if she hadn't noticed. However, it had given her hope that she and Tommy could have a romantic relationship.

Now, she was determined to make that happen and she was going to do it in a big way. She was going to appeal to the base of the male mind: sexual attraction. She planned everything and then set her plan into motion one night.

She'd invited Tommy over for dinner and a movie, something they did a lot. Tommy didn't realize that anything was different. Rachel was a little nervous when she answered her door, but she hid it well.

"Hi," she said with a smile up at Tommy. It struck her

again how good-looking Tommy was. His wheat-blonde hair was a little rumpled and his green eyes smiled down into her dark gaze.

"Hi, yourself," he said and gave her a kiss on the cheek. This wasn't out of the ordinary, either. "Come on in. You're not company. You know what to do."

"Sure do," he said as he shed his leather coat and put it over the back of a kitchen chair.

Rachel poured them some wine and then they settled down to eat the chicken Alfredo she'd made. All through dinner, they laughed and talked just as they always did. The movie was funny and made them laugh hard. When it was over, Rachel excused herself to her bedroom for a moment and stripped down after closing the door.

She lay down on her bed and stroked her hands over her thighs pretending they were Tommy's hands. Playing with her clit, she imagined it was Tommy's fingers. She stopped and got her vibrator from the drawer in her nightstand. She rubbed it against her pussy lips. It felt good and images of Tommy flashed through her mind. Rachel decided that it was time.

"Tommy, can you come in here and help me with something?" she called loudly.

A moment later, she heard his footfalls outside her door. Then the door opened and he came in. Tommy froze in shock at the sight of Rachel naked on the bed rubbing a vibrator over her most private place. His mouth opened and shut without him uttering a sound. His green eyes were wide, much as a child's when they see Santa Claus. Finally, he found his voice.

"Wh-what are you doing?" he said. His voice cracked a little on the last word. Rachel giggled and said, "What does it look like I'm doing, silly?"

"I can see what you're doing, but why? I mean, why while I'm here? Why did you call me in here?" he asked. Tommy was shocked but he couldn't look away. He'd always thought that Rachel was beautiful but seeing her completely naked and her legs spread open was doing things to him despite his shock.

"Tommy, I'm horny and I'm horny for you," she said. She'd decided to be direct and she didn't know what could be more direct than that.

"You're horny for *me*?" he asked.

"Yes. You. See how horny I am?" she said sliding the vibrator inside her pussy. "Don't you wish this was your dick?"

"Yes," he said without thinking. "No! I mean, I don't know!" Tommy still couldn't look away and it seemed that his body was going to react to the affirmative despite his protest.

Rachel said, "Well, I wish it was your dick. I'll bet your dick wishes it was."

Tommy couldn't help but smile at her statement. He felt the blood begin to flow into his non- thinking member and said, "Yeah, I think you're right."

As of late, he'd begun to be sexually attracted to Rachel. It wasn't surprising since she was so beautiful. Her blue eyes and dark hair were a pretty combination and she obviously had a smoking hot body. Now, as he looked at her, Tommy couldn't deny his attraction and from what Rachel was saying, she felt the same way.

"Are you gonna just stand there and watch or are you going to get naked and join me?" she asked playfully.

Tommy made his decision after about five seconds. His clothes came off quickly as Rachel watched on. She practically salivated over every delicious inch he revealed. She'd seen him in swim trunks a lot over the years, but now she could ogle him openly. Plus, she was going to get to see all of him.

His underwear came off and his penis proudly jutted forth. He wasn't totally erect but he wasn't soft either. This was evidence that he was attracted to Rachel and that he desired her. Rachel let her gaze roam over his beautiful body, noting that he worked hard at staying in shape.

Tommy came over to the bed and lay down beside her. He looked into her eyes for long moments and then said, "Are you sure this is what you want?"

She nodded. "I've wanted this for so long, Tommy, but never had the guts to do anything about it until now. I just couldn't stay silent anymore."

"Ok. I just wanted to make sure," Tommy responded.

Then Rachel kissed him and his world seemed to tilt. Everything became clear for him. Passion roared to life within him and he kissed her back without hesitation. Their tongues came together, twisting and teasing each other until they were breathless. Rachel drew back and smiled at him, then slid her hand up Tommy's thigh until she found his cock.

Gently she ran her hands up its hardening length, tickling around the head and running her fingers back down to his ball sac. She played with the two full orbs there, enjoying the softness of his skin. Tommy moaned softly and lay back. Her touch felt so good as she explored his body.

Rachel was in heaven. She pressed Tommy onto his back and trailed her hands over his broad shoulders, well-muscled chest, and arms. She traced the contours of his six-pack abs and oblique muscles. Her hand returned to Tommy's dick and she grasped it and began working it slowly.

Tommy's hips jerked reflexively and he moaned again. Rachel moved her hand faster, loving the way he felt. Then she rose up on her knees and started to lick his cock. He tasted so good. Tommy's breath came out in a hiss as she closed her mouth around the head of his dick and licked all around it.

She took more of him into her mouth and then pulled back, sucking as she went.

Propping himself up on his elbows, Tommy watched as she licked and sucked, marveling at how good she was at giving a blowjob. He thought of all the wasted time between them and then figured that things were happening at the right time. Watching her mouth close over him and draw-back made him even hotter and his loins constricted in response.

His hips hitched and he moaned, as fire seemed to spread through his lower half. "Oh, Rachel, that feels unbe-lievably good," he told her.

Rachel stopped and looked up at him. "I'm glad."

He smiled and said, "You're gonna have to stop that for now or it's all going to be over." She laughed. "I think you're right."

He lay back and said, "Come up here. Put that pretty pussy of yours right in my face."

Rachel scooted up in the bed and then straddled his head. Tommy ran his hands up her body to cup her tits and squeeze her nipples. He rolled them and Rachel grabbed onto the headboard. She whimpered a little as Tommy played with them. He varied his attentions, vasilitating between pinching and rolling to flicking and rubbing.

When Rachel began moving her hips, Tommy trailed his hands over her flat stomach and rubbed her pussy with them, grazing her clit. She made a sound of need and

Tommy used his thumbs to spread open her pussy lips. He ran his tongue from her entrance to her clit, familiarizing himself with her taste and feel. She was delicious and felt like wet silk. Tommy began flitting his tongue over Rachel's clit, drawing a moan from her.

Rachel was so horny and Tommy was even more talented with his tongue than she'd imagined. He alternated his speed and direction, teasing her until she thought she would die. Then Tommy stayed on target and her breathing became ragged and then a loud cry erupted from her as she came in a glorious release.

Her grip on the headboard tightened and her hips undulated as the spasms diminished. "Oh, damn, Tommy. That was incredible," she said breathlessly.

Tommy gave her several licks before she shimmied her way down his body and sucked on one of his nipples. Tommy laughed and playfully swatted her ass, then squeezed it. He felt Rachel's hand on his cock again and it throbbed harder as she manipulated and stroked it. Then she positioned it at the right place and sat down. His cock slid easily into her pussy because she was so wet.

Tommy marveled at how warm she was inside and that she was nice and tight. The sensation was exquisite and he growled as she took more and more of him inside. Rachel was so excited and Tommy felt so good inside her. She'd waited a long time for this day and she was going to enjoy every second of it.

Reaching up, Tommy grabbed one of Rachel's breasts and took a pink tip into his mouth. He sucked and Rachel gasped. Her pussy spasmed and she began to move. Tommy loved how wonton she was, how hungry she was for him. Rachel began riding Tommy fiercely, reaching toward the ultimate goal.

"Yeah, baby. Ride my cock," Tommy urged her.

The whimpers she made and the expression of joy on her face told Tommy how good she was feeling. Every time she moved, intense feelings of pleasure ran through Tommy. Sweat soon glistened on their bodies as they thrust and ground against one another.

Rachel's clit kept hitting Tommy's lower abdomen and that combined with his dick sliding over her G-spot launched her into a shattering orgasm.

"Tommy! Tommy! I'm cumming. Oh, shit! It's so good, so good!" she cried out.

Tommy's mouth opened and he threw his head back as he began to cum. "Yeah, Rachel! Fuck, it's unbelievable!"

Their words faded as they rode the undulating pleasure to its completion. They whimpered and groaned, not being able to form coherent sentences. Gradually Rachel's moans died down and she slowly lay down on top of Tommy. Both of their breathing was harsh in their chests from the exertion.

Rachel felt Tommy kiss the top of her head and turned her face to his. He was smiling even as he still panted.

"Rach, that was incredible," he said. "I never imagined it would be this way between us. I didn't know that you felt this way."

She smiled back at him. "I didn't know how to tell you and I was afraid of ruining our friendship, but I needed to know if there was any hope that you felt something more than friendship for me."

"Well, I obviously do," he said.

"I would say so," Rachel agreed. "So where do we go from here?"

"Let's just take it one day at a time. We don't need to

rush. We have to get used to this change in our relationship, so let's take it slow," Tommy said.

Rachel nodded. "That makes sense."

They kissed slowly, enjoying their new connection, both happy with the turn of events and committed to following things no matter where they led.

CHAPTER 45

MORNING YOGA

DREW LEANED over leisurely into a yogic forward bend, wrapping her long fingers around her ankles and feeling the burn in her hamstrings. Her shoulder-length orange curls fell one at a time to hang toward the floor in front of her face. She could see the sprinkle of gray hairs in them, but it brought a smile to her face. She was becoming a wise older woman, and it didn't seem so bad right now.

Sliding her hands slowly up her strong calves, she appreciated the smooth, silky feeling of the full-body leotard she wore for her daily yoga practice as she rose back to standing. She planted her bare feet firmly into the carpeted floor and wiggled her toes.

Drew stretched her arms to the ceiling and then moved them out by her sides, exhaling. She drew her hands together into a silent "Namaste" and bowed her head. She could hear the peaceful chirping of the early birds outside her window.

Rolling her head around in circles to self-massage her neck, Drew could feel immense relief in her usually sore, stiff joints. She had been practicing yoga off and on for over two years but had really increased her efforts in the past few months. Drew was in her mid-forties, but she often felt much older because of early-onset arthritis. Since she had begun a daily yoga routine, however, she had been feeling much better, physically and mentally.

The door opened. Her husband Greg peeked his head in around the doorframe. "Hey Drew, I'm not interrupting am I?" Greg whispered.

"No, not at all," she beamed at him. "I actually just finished right before you came in.

Do you need something?"

Drew and Greg had been married for over twenty years, and she had always been a very caring, generous woman who took good care of her husband. In return, he had always provided for their family and offered her protection and comfort. They had a loving relationship that was the envy of their friends and neighbors.

The couple had two children early on in their marriage, and Greg and Drew were rather happy to have the house to themselves after years of being full-time parents. Their kids had moved out in the past year, affording them more time to devote to rekindling the fire with which their relationship had begun.

"Well, there is one thing," Greg said thoughtfully.

Greg opened the door a little farther and set a foot inside the room. He had thick, graying hair with a receding hairline, but was still a very handsome man. Drew felt like his hair made him look sophisticated, but he didn't see it.

"What is it, dear?" Drew stooped to pick up the cork block she used to aid her in some of the more difficult yogic poses. She walked lightly across the room and stood on her tiptoes to put it on the closet shelf.

Greg quickly moved to stand behind Drew and ran his

hands over her shoulders, squeezing lightly where he knew she was always sore. His touch gave her goose bumps on her arms and relaxed her muscles. He continued to rub his hands down her arms. From there he moved them to her hips and lightly stroked up her sides.

"Mmm," Drew sighed. "That feels amazing." Greg smiled. "I'm glad. I love you, Drew."

Drew turned around to meet his gaze. "Well, I love you too, Greg."

"Now how about showing me how much flexibility you've been developing with your yoga," he suggested with a glimmer in his eyes.

Drew laughed and took Greg's hands in her own. "If you can figure out how to get me out of this leotard."

"Oh, I'll find a way," Greg replied, looking her over from head to toe for a zipper or buttons. There were none.

Greg took the shoulder straps and stretched them down over Drew's freckled arms. She lifted them one at a time as he freed them from the stretchy fabric, holding them over her head gracefully. He rolled the bodice of the leotard down to her waist, leaving her breasts unclothed. Her smell was so comforting, so unique.

As Drew lowered her arms, Greg lightly stroked her breasts, admiring their pointy shape and spatter of light freckles. Even though it had been a while since the couple had been intimate, there were familiar sights and smells that neither would forget no matter how long it had been.

Greg bent down to his knees and slid the leotard fabric down over Drew's hips and thighs. She lifted a foot and he removed the clothing, then she kicked the one piece to the floor with the other foot.

Greg touched Drew's toes and wrapped his hand around her ankles. He slid his hands up her legs, and she closed her eyes to increase the sense of touch. He continued up to her thighs and then around her hips, squeezing lightly when he reached the cheeks of her bottom on his journey to explore her body.

The birds still chirping outside in the morning sun, Greg kissed Drew's belly and ran his tongue up the line from her belly button to her chest.

"That feels amazing," Drew encouraged, Greg. She touched his face lovingly.

Greg stood back up. He took one of Drew's hands and placed his other at the base of her back. He leaned her back as far as they could go, as though he was dipping her in a dance.

Drew's hair fell over her shoulder to hang behind her, and she smiled up at him. "I can see a dramatic improvement in your flexibility," Greg complimented.

Drew blushed as images of her husband penetrating her while she held yoga positions crossed her mind.

Greg pulled Drew to the carpet.

"Show me one of your poses, you beautiful thing," he instructed.

Drew put her hand on Greg's chest and guided him to lie on the floor on his back. She straddled him, hovering above him as she knelt. She leaned back, her chin pointing toward the ceiling, and rested her hands on her ankles behind her.

"This is the full camel pose," Drew said, "modified to include you underneath me." The couple laughed as she came back to face him.

"That was beautiful," Greg said.

Drew noticed that his penis had begun pressing into his pants, unfolding and trying to find a way out. She unzipped his pants and began pulling them down from his hips.

Very gracefully, Drew pressed up into the Downward-facing Dog position, still bent over but with legs and back straight. Her butt was pointing toward the ceiling. Walking her hands back, she peeled Greg's pants off him and slowly rose to standing.

Greg watched enthusiastically, enamored of his wife. Drew stood over him and he could see a teasing hint of her vulva through the short, neatly groomed orange pubic hair his wife always sported.

Drew put her arms out and swooped her top half down until her face was close enough to Greg's to give him a sweet kiss. Then she lowered her bottom half down to let the soft skin of her inner thighs make him tremble with its caress.

Greg kissed the pointed tips of Drew's pink nipples and licked around the outer edges of her small, bumpy areolas. She shivered and moved them closer to his face. Greg buried his face in them as she squeezed them from the outside, increasing the lush cleavage on either side of his face.

Reaching beneath them, Drew guided the hard, familiar penis of her lover into the crevice between her legs. There was a slight resistance, but Drew used her new breathing techniques to consciously relax her muscles and flesh, and her yoni opened wide to accept him.

Husband and wife both moaned as their bodies moved together. Drew rode Greg passionately, her legs spread wide and her torso folded down over him like a flower folding its petals. They rocked slowly, working together to pump his penis in and out.

Drew raised her chest and moved her legs to a yogic squat over Greg. She bounced up and down, using the strength of her legs to achieve the desired rhythm. The pressure of her sitting and rising drove him deep, and they both felt the change in intensity.

As the couple's breathing mounted into a slow, heavy cadence, the power of the sexual energy that flowed through them increased. Drew felt Greg's hot breath on her neck and ears as she leaned her face close to his.

Drew paused and turned her body around without taking Greg's dick completely out of her. Now with her back facing him, she let her legs stretch out toward his head and leaned forward into a position similar to one of her favorites in yoga, the Cobra Pose. With her back arched and chin turned up, she rocked forward and back to methodically bring them both to climax.

Greg's breathing faltered in its pattern, and he grabbed Drew's hips firmly as he rose to the peak of his pleasure. He plunged further in, his penis throbbing. Drew tilted her head back more, bending her back more as she felt Greg exploding.

Drew raised herself off of her husband and turned around to face him. "I'm so close," she moaned.

Greg moved his hand down to Drew's crotch and inserted three fingers, using his thumb to rub her clitoris. Drew loved the way it felt, and began to vocalize her pleasure with sweet little noises. Her husband always knew exactly how to touch her.

In no time at all, Drew was twitching with ecstasy and pressing against Greg's able hand with her pelvic bone. She shuddered at the waves of sexual rapture that coursed through her and felt the numbing effect on her brain trickle down through the rest of her body.

Lying side by side on the floor, the lovers exchanged a wordless communication of their love. Drew was amazed at how wonderful she felt, and wondered if her regular yoga had improved her self-esteem as well as the condition of her body. Greg was elated to have shared an intimate moment with his wife after so long without.

They looked at each other and smiled simultaneously. Looking into each other's eyes seemed to complete the experience.

"I guess I should make this a regular part of my yoga routine," Drew said jokingly, stroking Greg's limp hand softly.

"Well shoot, Drew," he replied, "I'll even start doing yoga if this is what it's like."

CHAPTER 46

MR. AND MRS

GRACE WAS twenty-seven when she married her childhood sweetheart, Oliver Morgans. From the day they had met one another at the sweet age of sixteen, it was meant to be.

"You two really make the perfect couple," their friends told them, all secretly jealous of Grace and Olly's perfect match. They even looked great together. Grace was a slender brunette with big green eyes and a wide smile, Olly, equally dark at six feet. They'd both graduated from the same university with good enough degrees to get them jobs in the city.

Marriage seemed inevitable, as did the house, the car, and somewhere down the road, children.

"I can't wait to call you Mrs. Morgans," Olly whispered to his beloved, a few weeks before their wedding day.

"I can't wait to *be* Mrs. Morgans," Grace replied, excitedly. It was true; they were both optimistic and positive about their future together.

Besides, not everyone is lucky enough to meet their perfect match at sixteen. But Olly felt that something was missing: they had only ever known each other- they knew each other inside out, back to front and upside down.Olly knew how Grace liked her eggs in the morning, and Grace could tell when Olly was vexed, because his mouth twitched, oh so slightly. For Olly, his urge to know a different woman's body was strong, but he loved Grace, he wouldn't compromise his relationship with this wonderful woman for a quick fuck with somebody else.

Would a lifetime of familiarity satisfy both of them? Their lovemaking, good enough for a couple who had known each other's bodies for ten years. They knew what worked and what didn't. It was comfortable, like scratching an annoying itch in exactly the right place. Would marriage change that? Would it dull? Olly didn't dare to admit his fears to Grace, so he went ahead with the wedding, all smiles. On the outside, nobody could tell that anybody had doubts. It was strange though, how neither of them could foresee the excitement that the boundaries of marriage would inject into their relationship, it was as if two completely different people had come together.

Their wedding gift from their families had been two sun glorious weeks in the Dominican Republic in a private villa for their honeymoon. On their first night together, they clinked champagne glasses and toasted their future together beneath the stars on the veranda.

"To Mr. and Mrs. Morgans," he said, proudly.

"To us!" Grace beamed, fingering the wedding band on her finger, still unfamiliar and new.

"You know, sweetheart, we should celebrate with some

you-know-what" "You want us to play, Mr. Morgans?" Grace teased, a lock of dark hair falling in front of her face."

"I like it when you call me Mr. Morgans," Olly mused, narrowing his eyes at his new wife.

"Oh, you do?" Grace replied, quizzically. "Well, I'll keep doing it," she said, looking at her new husband beneath those big, green eyes that had an endearing innocence about them.

"How would you feel if, we, er, tried something new?" Olly asked, tentatively.

"Anything for you, Mr. Morgans."

"Alright, you said it," replied Olly, deeply. He scooped up his new wife into his strong arms and carried her into the bedroom. When they got to the honeymoon suite, Olly threw her onto the bed.

"I want to put this over your eyes," Olly instructed, handing her the silk tie he had worn at their wedding ceremony.

"Wh....why?" Said Grace, who had sat up, surprised.

"I want unexpected, I want a surprise, and I want danger," Said Olly, suddenly understanding what he needed from Grace and what had been missing in their relationship. "We know each other so god damned well, I need more, Mrs. Morgans." Grace was taken aback by her husband's outburst, but she couldn't deny that she was incredibly turned on by his assertion and newfound domi-nance over their lovemaking. She silently obliged, tying a hard knot behind her head. She was plunged into darkness.

"Now strip," Olly told his wife. Grace let the zipper fall on her black dress, revealing herself in just a silk black camisole that she had bought specially for the wedding night. She'd had no idea that it would turn out like this.

"Very nice. Now get on all fours so I can see you from behind"

"Yes Mr. Morgans," Grace said meekly, she felt her breasts swell with each harsh instruction. Who was this new, sexy man she had married? Olly pulled his wife's panties down slowly, relishing her wetness. "Why Mrs. Morgans, you're absolutely soaking," he said, as he pushed two fingers into his new wife, and massaged the front wall of her vagina. Grace let out a small cry and then began to groan.

"Mr. Morgans, what are you going to do to me next?" Grace asked, panting as he continued to finger her.

"I'm afraid I can't tell you that," said her husband. But I promise I won't hurt you; if it gets too much, just tell me, ok?"

"Ok." Olly pulled his hand out and Grace gasped.

"I want more, Mr. Morgans, where are you going?" Olly looked around the room for something to tie his wife's feet together, another tie-that would do it.

"I'm going to tie you up, ok?"

"Do it," Grace said, succumbing to the dark pleasure that was enveloping her. She felt silk fabric tracing itself down her thighs and then tightening around her ankles. She wanted to spread her legs and open herself for her husband, but the resistance from the knot made it difficult, instead, she presented her buttocks to him in half thrusting motions, aching for the next touch. Just then she felt a thwack across her backside that stunned her, completely unexpected. She cried out half in pleasure, half in pain. "Unexpected, like I said, Mrs. Morgans." Olly had spanked Grace with the flat of his hand, with his other hand he pulled at his shaft that was hard as a rock.

"I wish I could see you, Mr. Morgans," Grace said

through gasps, as each thwack made her tingle with plea-sure and a satisfying sting across the backside.

"I'm fucking myself and watching you squeal, Mrs. Morgans," said Olly as he continued to rub his cock at the sight of his wife's bare, reddening backside; her opening dripping with wetness and aching to be fucked. "When are you going to fill me? Mr. Morgans?"

"Just when you least expect it." Olly slapped Grace's backside one last time and then pushed his cock into her dripping pussy. "God, you're so tight!" He declared as he pumped her, her tied ankles causing the just the right resis-tance in her. He leaned over her and rubbed her clitoris with the heel of his hand, and grabbed her buttocks with the other, digging his nails into her flesh so she gasped. She came quickly, around him in violent bucking motions that she couldn't control, and finally he came inside his wife, filling her deeply.

When they had both caught their breath, he untied his wife, gently, tenderly.

"Darling, are you ok?" He asked.

"That was incredible," Grace said, looking deep into her husband's eyes, as if for the very first time.

The next morning they woke to the sunshine streaming through the blinds on the first day of their married life together. Olly turned to Grace and cupped her face in his hands. "What would you like to do today, Mrs.

Morgans?"

"Anything you desire, Mr. Morgans."

CHAPTER 47

NEW MEANING TO THE TERM SEX ON THE BEACH

JESSICA WAS FURIOUS. Her husband Dan was late. This time it was almost inexcusable. It was their anniversary and Dan had promised that he would not be late. Jessica was really mad because there was not even the courtesy of a phone call letting her know what was going on. She could only think that one of two things was going on. Either he was having an affair with another woman or he was the most insensitive husband on the planet. Either way, Jessica was ready to tear his head off.

Dan finally came home three hours late. When he walked into the door, he was met with a blanket and pillow lying on the couch, which told him, "You know what to do with these." Dan knew he had screwed up but did not know how to tell his wife he was sorry. Dan had to do something that would make up for his lack of thoughtfulness. He came up with the idea of taking Jessica on vacation to one of the beaches on the West Coast. This, he figured, along with a nice vacation would help to repair some of the damage that he had done.

Dan made all of the arrangements. All Jessica had to do was get on the plane and let the airlines take her away. When they checked into the room, Jessica was still a little mad about what had happened with the anniversary. Dan reassured her that this was the make-up for the lack of an actual anniversary celebration. Jessica was still doubtful but willing to give Dan a chance to make things up to her. Dan arranged for the two of them to go to one of the top restaurants in the San Francisco area. Dan had to pull some strings just to make sure that he had a reservation. During dinner, Dan got on one knee and asked Jessica if she would be his wife again. Jessica was surprised and speechless. Of course, she said yes and gave her new husband again a giant hug.

After dinner, she and Dan went for a walk onto the beach. The moon was out and the waves were hitting the shore making a very romantic setting. Dan saw that the next part of his plan was going to be easy to implement. Dan stopped Jessica and asked her to have a seat beside him on the beach.

"What about my clothes? I am going to have sand all over them. Can't we just stand and you say or do what you need to?"

"Jessica, you won't be wearing those clothes very long. I have some special plans for us. "

. . .

Jessica reluctantly sat down beside Dan on the sand. She was still trying to wrap her head around the fact that her husband had asked her to marry him again. Dan sat there and slowly slipped his hand over to Jessica who was nervous sitting on the beach.

"Dan stop, we are in a public place. What if someone sees us? The cops could get called. Do you want to spend our vacation in Jail?"

"Jessica, you need to settle down and not freak out so much. This was part of my plan. I want us to do something that we never have done before. If we are seen, then they can just watch. If the cops are called then I will just have to do you in the jail cell. How would you like, to have sex in a jail? We could have people watching as I bend you over and plow you. You have to let your hair down and allow yourself to have a little fun. We have forgotten what it was like to be fun and free."

Jessica began to remove her top including her bra. Her DD breasts fell free for Dan to do whatever he wanted with them. Dan scooted closer and began to fondle her nipples. Jessica had surprised Dan when he was off sightseeing a couple of hours before they went to dinner. Jessica had found a place to go and have her nipples pierced that was for the most part cheap. Dan was incredibly interested in the fact that his wife now had two rings attached to her nipples. Dan gently nursed on them and stimulated Jessica to the point that she began to masturbate with a couple of fingers shoved into her tight hole.

. . .

Jessica laid Dan on his back and opened his pants up. She straddled his hard cock. Pulling her panties to the side, Jessica mounted onto her husband's reverse cowgirl and began to go up and down on the rigid member. Jessica was not paying attention to what was going on around her, as neither was Dan. The sensation of having sex in public was exciting and daring. She had never been in this position before and she was certainly excited that her husband was just as into this as she was. The motions were becoming more and more intense. Jessica had tossed care to the side and was simply looking to get the screwing that she so desperately in needed. Jessica realized that she and Dan were still young enough that she could still have a child. Jessica was determined that she was going to have Dan shoot off inside of her.

Jessica never even saw the crowd that had gathered let alone the cops that had made their way to the beach. The cops were at least nice enough to allow them to finish up before approaching. Jessica was so embarrassed but she also felt a rush of excitement that shot through her at the thought that she had been caught by the cops having sex with her husband on the beach in plain view of everyone. Dan was right. This did make up for his screw up and actually brought them closer.

CHAPTER 48

PARALLEL PARKING

WATCHING her drop the two bags she carried from inside the mall in the trunk of his sports car is quite a remarkable sight. Shelly has the perfect Latina ass, and Alistair, her Latino husband, has the perfect cock for her ass. He gives the butt a firm squeeze with both hands and then pushes his cock against her, checking to see if anyone is watching. They both wear track pants and t-shirts, appropriate for Saturday morning shopping. Unfortunately, they also both have underwear on.

Alistair continues to suggestively fuck his wife's ass through their clothes and very quickly succeeds in turning them both on.

He closes the trunk before Shelly can put her purse in it and moves her to the side of the car between the vehicle and the wall. He throws his hands in the air as if they are arguing and then drops one hand low, sending it down her pants, under her panties. Alistair rubs on her vagina hard and then searches for her hole with his thickest finger. Finding it, he enters her slightly and then, once sure of the direction, moves his finger deep into her. He watches her face and then checks for movement close to them. When he sees none, he moves the finger around inside her and then pushes it in deeper. Shelly holds on to the side of the car while he searches her cunt.

With his eyes fixed on the patrons moving in and out of the entrance to the mall, he pulls his finger from her and puts it in his mouth. He sucks every bit of her off of it. She laughs at his madness and is quickly silenced as the finger again finds the inside of her pussy. Again, he moves around in her for a bit and then pulls it out and sends it straight to his mouth. Alistair does this a couple of times, watching for an audience. Nobody seems to have caught on that he has now turned his wife's pussy into a fondue, and so he gives the cunt a few more dips and his finger a couple more licks.

Shelly opens her purse and fumbles around in it, pretending that what is happening isn't. Alistair unlocks her door and moves her aside slightly so that he can open it. After reminding her of his tinted glass windows her drops her pants and panties to her knees and smiles as he throws his eyes in every direction. He gets down low and turns her so that she faces him while he sits on the car seat with his legs on the concrete. She puts the bag on the roof of the vehicle and continues her pretend search while watching for potential spotters. Alistair proceeds to give her cunt a delicious sucking.

She parts her legs and makes room for him to further explore her cunt. His fingers are dipping into it now, the contents of her pussy spread over his tongue. He sucks hard on her cunt while she continues her imaginary search, almost dropping her bag off the roof of the vehicle a couple of times. Alistair slides out of the car and stays low as he gets behind her. He parts her ass cheeks and gives her hole a solid lashing. He sends his tongue into her asshole and fingers her pussy at the same time, solidifying his cock and also her arousal.

Shelly leans on the roof of the car now, looking frustrated at not being able to find what she is looking for. A minute later, she resumes her digging, Alistair still determinedly digging around inside her. He frees his cock and then slowly makes his way up. He checks through the dark window and pauses before standing straight. By the time he straightens up completely his dick is already inside her. He reaches over into her bag and pretends to help her while moving all the way in and then some of the way out of her vagina. Her pussy is elated.

He continues to fuck her while they both start to remove the contents of her bag and place the items in a straight line on the roof of the car. They laugh at how systematic they are about pretending not to be fucking. His cock practically glides in and out of her now as he leans into her and onto the car. Shelly pushes back into him, but not too much so that she is not at an awkward angle for what she wants to have everyone think she is doing. She moves a lipstick around and then loses it as it rolls off the car and onto the cement. Again, they are in stitches.

Before anything else is lost to the floor, they start to replace the bag's contents. Alistair doesn't stop fucking her as one by one her stuff is put back into the leather accessory. They both feign frustration at not finding what they are looking for. Still, Alistair's fourteen inches of curved cock are exactly where they want to be. He gives her a few harder thrusts, deliberately unsettling her as a group of four walks towards them and gets dangerously close. She smacks the side of his ass, unable to get to the meat of his behind. He gives her another quick thrust.

Alistair pulls her back and bends her into the car. Her

bag remains on the roof now but Shelly is for all intents and purposes out of sight. Her hands are on the seat with her cunt suspended on her husband's cock. He fucks her hard now while he pretends in vain to appear to be looking for something in her bag. He can't focus on the leather and instead leaves it where it is and takes Shelly's hips in hand. He fucks her in long strokes so that the bend in his cock pulls her towards him and then pushes her further into the car. He keeps a firm hold of her throughout and watches as a few people figure out what is going on. The women drive off quickly but some of the guys give him a Bluetooth high-five. Without too much concern for the small audience, he brings his wife to what can only be described as a perfect orgasm!

He pulls his cock from her cunt and immediately points it towards her ass. He dips it into her asshole and pushes himself into her. She helps by sticking her butt up as high as she can and raising her one leg into the car. Shelly steadies herself on the seat as he fucks her tight asshole hard, watching some more eyes fall knowingly on him. He starts to thrust now so that he is performing for the audience, and Shelly, oblivious to his acting, feeds more of herself to him as his strokes get deep down into her spot. She loves being fucked in the ass even more than she enjoys being fucked in her vagina. Pussy fucking is after all a standard.

A security guard approaches them and he tells Shelly not to move. Alistair busies himself in her bag again as he moves slowly off her ass and removes his cock. Shelly falls forward into the car and gets into the seat. Alistair throws his hands in the air in an 'I give up' gesture and drops Shelly's bag on her lap. She takes out a lemon-scented wipe and starts to clean her man's cock in anticipation of a wrap-up and go. But the guard turns the other way about four cars from theirs and Alistair bangs hard on the roof of the car. Shelly takes his balls into her mouth and then sucks on the now lemon-flavored cock, undeterred.

She gets him as close as she can with her mouth before resuming her position in the car with her ass extended out towards him. He wastes no time getting back in there. She hopes that with the oral aid she provided he's going to be quick about wrapping up this bit of mischief. He is determined to make it good though and so he again sends his curve into her in long strokes. His fucking seems to slow down as the parking lot gets busier, much to Shelly's frustration. But she does know how he likes to show off and so she lets him have his fun, watching through the tinted glass to make sure that while he gets carried away, this morning doesn't end badly.

A couple is getting into their car just two spots away from them but Alistair keeps fucking. He fucks her despite another couple spotting them and staring at him about three bays away. There is no stopping him now as he gets into the end-zone, past the point of no return. He glides steadily in and out of her now as Shelly also starts to feel his cock begin to throb as it approaches explosion. Alistair pulls her onto him repeatedly and sends himself into her without skipping a single beat. The sounds around them become louder and Alistair decides that it is perhaps time to make for the finish line. Before he does though, he gives her a dozen more slow strokes.

His explosion into her ass is amazing! His cock pulsates for every load, every drop that escapes into her hot ass. He fills her so much that even after he has stopped ejaculating he can feel his heat on his cock, his meat swimming in its own sauce. He thrusts deep into her to ensure that once he has removed his penis she won't be dripping his love juice all over the place. He really shoots an impressive load. Slowly he removes his hands from her hips and gives her a few thrusts, moving just his waist. His dick is still super solid and seems to have no desire to be anything else. Even Shelly moves her ass back and forth on the solid meat, wondering why it's still so hard but not complaining that it is. If they were anywhere but here, she would be the one initiating a mind-blowing encore. But there is ice cream in the trunk that needs the freezer; and also, families have started to arrive and the last thing they need is a five-year-old with questions!

He pulls himself from her and pretends to adjust the mirror. Shelly gets into the car without straightening up and Alistair closes the door for her. He moves to his side still carrying her purse and jumps in as though nothing had just happened. After adjusting his dick in his pants, his erection refusing to subside despite the fact that he quite literally emptied his cock's contents into his wife, he drives off. They haven't even left the parking and Shelly is already freeing his dick again and taking the head into her mouth...

CHAPTER 49

PARK PLEASURE

THE FEELING of his cock stretching on the inside of his tight running pants surprises him. Bevan had cum twice already just this morning courtesy of his wife's sweet pussy, and now as they jog through Central Park, the last thing on his mind is fucking, despite the tight running clothes stuck to her every curve making her appear rather fuckable. He tries to ignore it, running another hundred meters or so before he has to stop to inspect the happenings between his legs. The tight pants he has on means that his cock has to strain towards the ground against his inner thigh. This is not the most comfortable place for any cock.

His thick eleven inches juts out in front of him, pitching a massive teepee in the stretch fabric as he tries to adjust it. Rowena bursts into laughter as they both stare at his humungous dick. The boner really is surprising, not just in that it is there, but also the fact that is seems to be larger than Bevan's regular erections. He jumps around for a bit trying to get his mind off it and also to try to get his blood moving to other parts of his body. It doesn't work; instead, his cock grows another inch.

Rowena pulls him behind a tree and starts rubbing it over his tights. She pulls the black material covering her husband's dick forward so that his penis can project skywards and therefore be a little more comfortable. The elastic is back against his waist, but his massive tool sticks out of it at the brim. She runs her hand up and down the impressive shaft and dances her fingers around over its head while checking to see that they are not being watched. While rubbing on the meat through the tights she bends to take the exposed tip in her mouth, sucking on it in the hope that he'll just shoot a quick load onto her hot tongue and they can get on with their jog.

The penis begins to throb in her mouth, the head swelling with every movement her tongue makes over it. She giggles to herself and secretly wishes that they were home. The cock in her mouth is a massive mess that her cunt immediately acknowledges and desires. She gets further down the shaft, sucking harder, hoping for an eruption. But even after she has pulled his tights below his balls and is pulling on his nuts while sucking his cock, all she gets is a loud groan and a "don't worry there's nobody around". She takes this to mean keep sucking, baby, PLEASE!

Rowena's fingers are in the inside of her own pants now, the cock in her mouth having started a fire in her cunt. She feeds her pussy the tip of her index and then uses just this bit to dig and stir hard in the entrance to her Eden. With her own arousal now peaking, she gets the bulk of Bevan's cock into her mouth. It's impossible for her teeth not to make contact with the thick dick but Bevan seems blissfully oblivious to the biting. He forgets for brief moments to watch for eyes as his wife deals rather effectively with this unexpected menace.

It becomes clear to him quickly that Rowena's mouth

simply doesn't have the scope to deal with this new cock; at least not in the time and circumstance, they find themselves in. He brings her to her feet. Trying as best as he can to pull his pants up above is now aching erection, he uses his wife to hide the bulk in case somebody passes. He drops his face to hers and kisses her while his hand replaces hers on the inside of her pants. He doesn't look around now, hoping that any passersby will see nothing more than a couple kissing by the tree. His index is double the size of Rowena's and he feeds her the massive tip and half the finger.

It's Rowena now who scopes the scene as the rest of Bevan's index finds the inside of her cunt. After adding his middle finger he pulls the two digits apart and then back together inside her so as to stretch her pussy open quickly. His fingers fill her for about five inches pushing into her forcefully. She holds onto him to steady herself and pushes against him so that he himself is against the tree. Her eyes are closed now as Bevan gets her cunt wet and he himself resumes guard duty.

He knows that her pussy isn't wet enough yet for his cock but the park is starting to fill. He manages some spit on his dick and then asks her to check her own supply, the nerves having dried his mouth completely. She coats the tip of his cock while he fingers her cunt a little more. He manages a bit more of his own spit but instead of putting it on his cock, he coats the outside of her cunt and then sends his fingers back in. He stirs her vagina open for a little longer and then kisses her again just as soon as she has taken the last wetness from her mouth and transferred it to his dick.

His eyes on the new pockets of life around them Bevan pulls her pants just low enough for his cock to make direct contact with the entrance to her vagina. He lets the elastic go and moves his dick forward, into her. The strain of the erection is upwards and so the entire tool shoots into her in the direction of her belly, filling her vagina. Bevan turns them now so that it is Rowena with her back against the tree. He holds her against the bark and immediately begins to fuck her hard. The massive meat inside her has her instinctively push against him in an attempt for relief she knows will not come.

Bevan has never had as massive an erection. They both wonder silently how it is possible for a person to suddenly gain five inches of solid penis in the middle of an open park at five in the morning. But whatever the explanation, right now, this monster needed to be dealt with. Bevan thrusts his almost eight-inch girth into his wife whose back brushes hard against the bark of the tree so that she pushes him harder away from her. She wants him off her, not out. Bevan responds by pulling her pussy towards him so that he is only fucking this part of her and the rest of her is simply relaxing against the supportive oak.

The surroundings are forgotten now and Bevan is savagely fucking Rowena in an attempt to empty and there-fore deflate his cock. Her cunt is enthusiastically absorbing the full shock of his attack and even she is no longer checking to see who sees. She grabs onto the sides of the tree now as Bevan intensifies his assault. There is hope between them that the climax that will relieve Bevan of his frustration will come soon. He can finish her up at home. Rowena parts her legs a little more so that Bevan can dig as deep as he needs to get to where he wants to.

The livelier the park becomes the livelier his fucking. Faster and faster he moves himself in and out of her. Pulling her to him and then pushing her into the tree, Bevan tries to find an angle from which to approach this orgasm. Everything he tries is both awkward and uncomfortable, or it gives their activity away completely. Eventually, they are back at the original position with Rowena's back against the tree and Bevan ramming her into the bark. She foregoes the discomfort, knowing that they have minutes now before the first of the morning rush pushes through the park.

Bevan practically impales her now to the tree. His own hands are on the bark as he hugs the oak as though it was the tree he is fucking. Rowena holds onto him and pushes herself off the wood so that her back isn't ripped raw. This forces Bevan's cock deep inside her and so she maintains her hold on him in order for every part of his cock to capitalize on every square inch of her cunt. She hopes that this helps him because quite frankly there is nothing else that she can do. It's up to him now to get his rocks off. All hope for her own climax is abandoned as she is so completely focused on him.

Despite not expecting it though Rowena's cunt gives way and she has a magnificent orgasm. As her pussy beats through the climax it swallows the last four inches of Bevan that it had been struggling with. This final absorption into her is just the trigger necessary for him to finally gain sight of the shore. He swims for home. Every thick inch of him ravages Rowena, tearing the insides of pussy into a million pleasure-colored ribbons. He loses his desperation to cum because now he knows that he is about to. Over and over, he sends all of the cock he has gained this morning into her and over and over she receives it in its entirety.

He fucks her harder and harder as the sound of dogs being walked and hotdog stands being set up overrides the sounds escaping the two of them. His hands are again on her and hers remain on him as he ploughs into her repeatedly, getting closer and closer to climax. She responds to his request for him to pull on his balls by doing just that and his thrusting slows down. He gets his cock all the way inside her with each slow stroke but there is no rush now so that her hands can stay working on his nuts. She pulls harder and harder on his massive balls at his request but his fucking maintains a steady pace.

She cums again with her hands on his sack and pulls harder as her orgasm processes. Bevan picks up the pace only slightly now as he begins to shoot his seed into his wife. Every inch of his cock throbs as he cums, sending pulses through Rowena's pussy that mimic her own orgasm and make her want to get her husband home fast. He is slow about removing his cock from her and careful not to make her dressing conspicuous. With his cock back to its manageable flaccid size he simply lifts his tights back over it. They find a fountain and splash some water over themselves before taking a few sips. The jog is over for the pair now and they make the most of the shortest walking route home.

CHAPTER 50

PRE-WEDDING SECRETS

THEY HAD CALLED A PRE-WEDDING MEETING, as both of them were having doubts. They loved each other and they wanted to get this out of the way. They had been engaged for six months and both of them had a secret to keep. Felix had tried really hard to deal with it but knew he couldn't and Stephanie was the same. They both knew that somehow, despite being in almost every way compatible they couldn't get around this. It was torture for them both.

They knew that the wedding was off if this wasn't sorted out. Neither one of them wanted that. They had agreed to meet in their new house, the one that they were going to live in after they were married. It only had a table and chairs in it but that didn't really matter.

The truth was that they were bad in bed. In the beginning, like most couples, they had fucked like rabbits but after quite a short time he began to lose interest, and on the rare occasions that they could raise the enthusiasm she didn't come. He also had made a point of telling her in the early days not to fake an orgasm, so she hadn't felt that need to booster his ego. Now with two weeks to go before the big day, both of them needed this dealt with. They both loved sex and they wanted their lives together to be perfect. Separately they had come to the conclusion that needed to tell the secret that they believed was at the heart of the issue. Each of them had a secret and because it was at the heart of their sexual issues, it was vital for their future together.

The stakes were high as they sat across the room from each other, and the wine was open. Both of them felt the need to have a glass or two before they could confess. Both of them were very experienced, but they had met in the polite society of the office. They had courted each other in the full glare of a busy lawyer's office and both felt that the other needn't know about the sexual desires that had driven them before.

Felix finished his third glass and after all the small talk and nonsense had been exhausted, he decided to open another bottle and just start talking. It was the only way this was to be sorted. "Stephanie, I love you with all my heart but I think you know that we have a problem with sex." She nodded but was reluctant to continue, so he carried on. "I am so in love with you that I think that we ought to try and sort it before we get married, that way we can start our lives together openly and honestly"

. . .

This was exactly how she was feeling but she was afraid that he would either blame her or blame himself for not satisfying her. She decided to say something at this point. "Darling I really love you too but...this is so hard."

He had decided that whatever happened he needed to find out why she didn't come and why he seemed uninterested, but he didn't know how to proceed. He had thought about a plan that might work and he tried it out. "Listen I have an idea. Let's spin a coin. We have to get to the bottom of this. Let's spin a coin - the loser goes first. They have to tell the other one what they want sexually from the other person that way we can see if this can work, see if there's room for compromise." Stephanie thought about this for a while and she said, "OK spin the coin"

Felix flicked into the air and as the coin turned in an arc, she called "Heads!" Catching it, he revealed the answer to her and she groaned as it came up Tails. It was a time for a stiffer drink than wine and she went to the kitchen and got a vodka and coke from the stash that they were hoarding for their wedding.

The drink lasted only a few seconds after she sat down and she knew she had to spill it. "The truth is...err...I want you to...OH, FUCK IT! You are too fucking polite. I am going to tell you a fantasy of mine and it doesn't mean I want you to do it; this is just what turns me on. OK?" He nodded and she bumbled on. "OK in my fantasy, I am a sexually charged but very submissive woman, I'm turned on by a powerful man with powerful sexual urges who possesses me and treats me like a whore. He doesn't make love to me he fucks me. He talks dirty to me and he dresses me like a tart. If I fail to please him, he spanks me and he does it often. I want to ride his cock and I want him to treat me like his dirty sexual slave."

There was silence as he tried to take in her confession, which had been delivered like a verbal machine gun. He tried to smile, but she was really upset he could see that. "Do you mind if I ask you a few questions before I tell you mine?" It was a nervous nod she gave him, she wanted reassurance very quickly. He sensed that, and gave her a smile, and said, "Darling, I love you, please don't worry I just want to know a few things, ok?" Again she nodded; his protestation of love calmed her a little. He started his questions, "You say you want to talk dirty?" She nodded and he continued, "So if I said that you were, for instance, a bad girl would that do it or do you need something harder?"

She thought a little a little but this was not the moment to compromise. "Harder, I think." Impassive, he looked at her and carried on his questioning. "So it would have to be something like, 'You're a dirty little bitch' would it?" Even if he couldn't do it at lest he understood, she thought and nodded to show him he was on the right track.

He smiled at her and then said, "So you want to be my dirty whore?" There was a change in his voice, a masterly quality that replaced his usual politeness. "Yes," she mumbled in reply. Again he continued, "So you are saying that you want me to treat you like a whore?" There was no waiting for a reply. "You want me to fuck you, make you beg to come as I ram my hard cock into your dirty whore cunt?" Her feelings were mixed. She didn't know if he was angry or trying to turn her on and she was excited never the less. Her nipples showing through her blouse were showing her aroused state and he stood up and stood in front of her. "You want me to command you onto your knees and force my hard cock into your mouth you dirty little bitch?" It was a whimper more than a real reply, as her pussy was throbbing as his jeans clearly showed the bulge of his cock. He unzipped his jeans and slowly pulled out his cock, which was hard and she slipped on her knees ready to take like he wanted. However, he had other ideas. "Who told you to do that?" There was an audible gasp as he pulled her hair and forced her to bend over the table. "You need to learn obedience!" Her pussy was soaking and she gasped as he pulled up her skirt to expose her panties. With a savage tug, he pulled then down over her ass and spanked her. "What do you need to learn?" Her whispered "obedience" was answered with another spank, which had her whimpering with exquisite pleasure. "You forgot to call me sir you dirty little bitch," and he spanked her again. Eventually she called him 'sir'

There was sexual tension in the room and he wanted to run with it. "Now get up," he said, and she stood up. There was a command for her to get upstairs and wait for him. Unlike the downstairs, the new house was furnished upstairs.

He took the wine and walked slowly upstairs. He wanted her to be turned on by the control. It was after all her fantasy and he wanted to make it good for her. Walking in the bedroom, he saw her on all fours on the bed naked except for panties. The spanking he gave her was unbelievable for her and then he slid his cock into her pussy and asked her. "Do you want me to fuck your dirty cunt?" There was a moan before she replied, "Yes master." Then slowly he began the thrusts that she craved as his cock explored deep inside her, driving her wild. He reached out and pulled her hair, "Are you my dirty whore?" There were almost tears as she replied, "Yes Master." His cock was grinding into her and occasionally he would slap her arse with a sting that mixed the pleasurable with the painful. It was an exquisite torture for her and soon his frantic thrusting indicated he was ready. The two of them were lost now as she reached a pitch of frenzy as his come unloaded into her and her orgasm convulsed her body driving her and him fucking crazy.

They kissed and he joked with her, "Is that better?" There was a smile and both of them knew the wedding was on and happiness beckoned. "Darling," she wanted to please him now, "Tell me what your fantasies are, I want to please you." The smile he gave her was full of satisfaction. "Darling my fantasy has just been fulfilled. I really think we will be very happy together." They burst out laughing which didn't stop for a very long time.

CHAPTER 51

QUIET, MY WIFE MAY BE HOME (MARRIED – LONGTIME SPICING UP MARRIAGE)

ASHLEY WILLIAMS and her husband Mike had been married so long that they knew each other's routine. Mike would be home at a certain time. She knew that he would walk in grab a beer, take his shirt off and then flop down in his favorite chair. This was the scene on most nights except for bowling night, and then the routine was altered when Mike would change clothes and head out to go bowling with the guys. Ashley had become accustomed to this routine and did not let it bother her most of the time. On the rare occasion that she was upset, her husband seemed to not want anything to do with her. Ashley had talked to a number of people in an effort to get some sort of insight into what she could do to get the spice back into the marriage. Ashley then had a great idea.

She made it a point that she was not going to be waiting by the door with the beer in her hand. If she were nowhere to be seen, he would have to search for her. She would be in the bedroom dressed up as a French Maid. When he discovered her, Mike could not believe what he was seeing. Ashley could sense that he was staring at her ass. She wanted to see how far was this going to go, so she continued cleaning the room.

Mike walked over and gave Ashley a hearty slap on the ass. It was one of the high points of their relationship in the last few months. Ashley stood up and looked squarely at Mike. He had that fire in his eyes that he used to have for her when they were first married. Mike reached up and began to caress her breasts.

Ashley lowered herself to her knees and unzipped his jeans over her. Ashley took the cock out of the Jockstrap that he was wearing. Ashley had never seen her husband as erect as he was at the moment. She could tell that what she was doing was getting him aroused and working him up into frenzy. Ashley too the knob of his cock into her mouth and began to gently suck on it causing him to become very relaxed. Mike took Ashley's head and began to give it a gentle in and out motion. Ashley was working her cunt over with a couple of fingers. She did not want Mike to see her doing this just yet. Ashley continued this for a while before getting up off her knees and making her way to the bed. Stripping, Ashley stood naked in front of her husband and waited to see what his next move was going to be. He walked over and began to fondle her large breasts and play with her nipples. He then turned her around and bent her over the bed. Mike took his cock and placed it slightly against the opening of her asshole. Ashley had not been penetrated in a long time like this and she was slightly nervous about what was about to happen. Mike leaned down and whispered into her ear to be quiet as his wife may come home at any time. Mike had taken to the role-play quite well and wanted to be a part of it as well as Ashley.

Mike took a little spit and used that as his lube to drive deep into her ass. With one swift movement, Mike drove in deep. She let out a little of a yelp as the sensation of the large cock drove deep into her virgin asshole. Mike took one hand and placed it on her shoulder to help and steady him while he was plowing her ass like a new oil field. Ashley had never had a cock this close to her hole and had never even let Mike into the sacred hole. This was, however, a chance to begin things anew and to release old habits that had allowed the relationship to become boring. Ashley had made this plan and Mike was going along almost too well. It did not bother her since she wanted this to open new doors to drive a new level of their relationship.

Mike kept driving in and out with a rapid pace not wanting to let up at all. This made Ashley want it even more as she was desperate to be used and abused and to show her husband that if he went outside of his comfort zone things could be better. The pounding became more paced and Mike reached around and grabbed one of her breasts to use to keep his balance. Mike was determined that he was going to come inside the ass of this French Maid. His hips tightened and before long, Mike was unleashing a torrent of cum into her virgin hole. Mike fell onto the bed leaving Ashley with a mess that was dripping out of her hole. Grabbing a towel, Ashley stood naked looking at her husband. This was the first time that she had seen her husband with a smile on his face. Ashley knew that there was going to be a new beginning in their love life and that she and Mike were going to be happy for a very long time in the near future. Ashley got dressed and suggested they go out to grab a bite to eat. It was after all a special time in their relationship as the flame that gone out had been reignited.

CHAPTER 52

SEX IN CELL BLOCK C

JADE AND JAMES SMITH were having some serious marital issues. They were simply looking to let off some built-up sexual energy. They were in an empty parking garage. Most of the cars were gone. It was 3AM and Jade did not think that there would have been a problem. They had been out at a club trying some experiments. The night was a complete bust. They just wanted to get the night over with. Jade had an idea that before they went home, to have one good screw in the back seat of the car. It had been a long time since they had done anything like this. James was a little concerned about being caught but thought that nothing would happen this late at night. Jade had gotten into the back seat and was fully naked when James joined her. James sat in the seat beside Jade and leaned over to at first suck on her nipples then went south. He began to lick her cunt in circles that allowed his tongue to hit her cunt lips. James was getting wetter and wetter. Then she decided to repay the favor to James and went down on him. Jade was working her cunt over and James had his head back enjoying the blow job when there was a knock on the window of the car.

James opened his eyes to see a police officer standing there. The next thing he knew; he was ordering them both out of the car. Jade had enough time to put her bra on before the cop pulled her. Both jade and James were being arrested for lewd acts and indecent exposure. James saw his job going up in flames, as he would never be able to explain this at the office. James just hopes that he could keep it a secret. Jade was still worked up at the thought that she had been caught for the first time giving head to a man in a car. At first, she was mistaken for a hooker until the truth that she and James was the husband and wife came out. James was thinking about who he could call to bail them out of jail. He had to call someone who wouldn't make a big deal about this. When they arrived at the detention center, they were separated. There was a crowding issue so they decided to house them together Jade and James were placed into the holding cell to wait and see if they were going to get bailed out or not.

James went and just sat down in the corner of the cell. There were several other men in the cell that all looked mean and aggressive. Jade was busy making the rounds seeing just how many phone numbers she could get. The thing that she did next that took James, the other inmates, and the officers working all by surprise. Jade walked over to James and took her clothes off. Getting down on her knees, she went back to the task that had got them arrested in the first place. Even her playing with herself was picked up where she left off in the car. The other inmates as well as the officers all stood around and watched as this woman went to town on the swollen member. James finally had to get into the action and let loose. He figured the damage was already done. Finally, James told Jade to get on her back on the bench that he was sitting on. She did as she was told and spread her legs. James took his cock and slid it into her wet hole. Jade began to moan immediately. Jade began to moan even louder and James knew that part of this was for the entertainment factor of the people watching his wife having her brains fucked out. James made it a point that he kept going in harder and deeper with each motion. Jade was getting hammered so hard that her tits were bouncing up and down. James was not focusing on the people watching or anything else. All he was worried about was to give his wife the screwing that she so desperately needed.

"Harder, James, fuck me harder. I want to feel your cock abusing me and making me your little whore. I need you to remind me that you take what you want when you want. "James kept going in and out with more of a deliberate motion. He was getting to the point that he was going to cum. He wanted to give the people a real show. James took his cock out of her and aimed for her tits. There were several globs that hit her. James was certain they had given all of the people gathered one of the most intense sex shows that they had seen in a long time. Jade and James had an incredible sexual experience that had all of the other men on the verge of shooting off.

While they were sitting there getting them back together, one of the officers came into the cell and told Jade and James that they were free to leave. It appeared that the officer that arrested them had forgotten to file some paperwork and they were not able to process them because of the error. This lead to them being able to simply just walk out the door. Jade and James were almost unable to understand what they were being told. It was true that sometimes the best sex was that which was not expected especially in places that you had never thought of doing it.

Jade and James were perfect examples of this

CHAPTER 53

SHOWER ME WITH YOUR LOVE

THE OUTLINE of her body in the shower is a perfect pear.
A mix of Greek and Italian heritage, Giotta has very good
genes. Leo is sure to be as quiet as possible, already having
taken his clothes off in the bedroom. He creeps towards the
shower with nothing but his necktie in hand, hoping that his
new wife of a few weeks doesn't get that *'somebody's
watching me'* feeling that will see her turn around and ruin
his surprise. The shower doesn't have a door, just clever
paneling of glass and steel that obscures the view of your
genitalia if you're the right height.

Leo is in the shower with his tie around Giotta's neck
just as the smell of him gives his presence away. The silk tie
wraps around her tiny neck twice, the ends in each of Leo's
hands. He pulls them down so that he can tie each end to
each of his wife's wrists and then together. He moves in
close to her and whispers *shhh* in her ear. She obliges the
thought of what is now possible, sending streams of heat to
her pussy. She wants to both part her legs and pull them
tightly together, unsure and excited all at once. She does
both in turn until Leo's large hand between her legs keeps

them from closing. The other hand is on her breasts, pulling hard on them, just the way she likes it.

The hand between her legs hugs her pussy, palm up. Leo rubs hard, forwards and backward, forwards and backward until Giotta starts to groan. He enjoys this sound and so he keeps rubbing. Leo takes his time about leaving the warm cunt, moving over it with as much care and attention as he knows his wife to lavish on his cock. He wants to get her pink between his teeth but can't resist sending a finger into her first, just for a reaction. He gets the reaction he wants, Giotta letting out a very soulful moan. It is her reactions that make Leo so excited about surprising his wife with steamy sex as often as possible. The more surprised she is, the more her responses turn him on.

Leo's index finger moves back and forth in his wife's hole, and also in and out. The up/down motion of his thick appendage increases steadily in intensity and depth. He has to push his wife up against the tiled wall to keep her from falling over. With her hands tied tightly behind her back, she loses her balance easily, so that even with her legs parted, the finger darting into her aching pussy is enough to unsettle her center. Leo loves the control he has over her. As does she.

With her legs apart and her feet firmly on the floor, Leo pushes against the back of her thighs to keep her steady. He's on his knees now, finding her center with his face. The smell of her has his cock strain towards the sky, swaying from side to side. Leo stops himself from charging her with it by sending his tongue into her and sucking on her deliciousness hard. Drawing from inside her a flow of love juice, he uses the fingers on one hand to open her vagina. This allows him to lick the inner walls, tasting not just the syrup, but also the fleshy fruit producing it. His tongue manages to go deep into Giotta, the strength of it able to fuck her to her first orgasm. She exhales rapidly as her vagina folds into itself and then yawns.

A long middle finger is inside her as Leo gets to his feet. The finger stirs her gently so that her climax, still in full swing, comes to a dreamy close. Another finger joins this one, then another. At four fingers, Giotta's cunt is stretched wide. He stops moving around and lets her bob up and down on his hand, his arm creating an upward tension that allows her to move around freely. She relaxes her cunt enough for it to make the adjustment, and then start a steady ascent almost immediately to a second orgasm. This one will take a little longer she knows, so does he. But Leo has always managed to get her pussy to do the most incredible things in the shortest amount of time.

He pulls on the tie so that her breasts graze the wall of the arch of her back. With this, he pushes his fingers deeper into her and then wiggles them slightly apart. Immediately she feels the stretch, almost as though her pussy is about to be ripped open. Then his fingers wriggle back together, forming an upside-down funnel as his thumb manages to meet them somewhere just beyond the entrance. All five fingers touch at the tips, making a steady entry to the base knuckles. Giotta is ecstatic, audibly so. Again the fingers wriggle apart, an opening lotus, widening her cunt again, so close to ripping it apart that she can't help a mini-orgasm. She screams loudly. The sound of her has Leo's other hand give his cock a few strokes. Its patience will be rewarded, but not yet.

The lotus formed by his fingers opens and closes repeatedly. Each time Giotta is pushed over the edge, her ecstasy amplified. Also, with each opening, he pulls his fingers somewhat out of her.

With each closing, he makes more and more headway into her. Over and over he opens and closes his five-finger flower in her cunt, tense and tight against the fingers now for all the mini- climaxes. Eventually, his entire hand is inside her, Giotta gasping as she realizes that her pussy lips have wrapped around Leo's wrist. Then, slowly, very, very slowly, Leo closes the flower into a very tight fist, lodging his hand inside the cunt that has now sealed quite tightly over his thick wrist. Giotta needs to find his mouth, the assurance of his lips essential now. He assures her.

Slowly his fist moves in a half circle to the right. Then he returns it to its original position before making a slow half circle to the left. He repeats this gentle motion until Giotta and her vagina make peace with its presence. This takes several kisses, and several half circles. In an almost breathing motion, the fist opens, as slowly as it had pivoted on Leo's wrist, until each of the fingers sticks to the walls of Giotta's cunt individually. Each of the fingers slithers up and down the vaginal walls as Leo teases her with the possibility of exiting. He doesn't though, instead returning his fingers to their original fist and then easing the fist in a left/right pivot deeper into his wife. His patience is rewarded with a generous amount of cunt as another couple of inches of his forearm disappear up the extremely elastic cunt.

Now that Giotta wants his fisting as much as he does, he sends himself into her further and then pulls himself along with her pussy towards the outside world. Leo's fist eases back into her, replacing the parts of her he had pulled out, at least in their imaginations. The fist moves easier in and out of her with each insertion, never losing the pivoting action. Giotta's cunt sweats over the hand and further facilitates the fisting. She rises to her toes and squeezes her pussy over him and has the umpteenth orgasm, much to the delight of her husband, who now eases his slippery hand slowly out of her. Along with her climax, his hand has pulled the most erotic scents from inside her, these aromas filling the shower and sending power to his cock.

Pulling on her hair he turns her around and then places a firm hand on her head, pushing her to the ground. On her knees, he sends his cock into her mouth. She opens wide so that he gets as much of his dick into her mouth before she lets her lips settle on the circumference of the aching cock. His hand still on her head, he fucks her mouth in the longest strokes, belying the urgent need to shoot that has his dick in knots. Giotta has a way of sucking Leo's cock that makes him forget whatever his own plans for her mouth were. Pretty soon he can do nothing but surrender his dick to her. Even without her hands, she has such a solid grip on Leo that his own hands rest on the wall behind her, the only thing he can do is thrust steadily into her mouth.

Leo is close now; close enough for him to render more determined thrusts into Giotta's mouth. Her sucking also gets harder. His hands find his heavy balls, pulling down as hard on the sack. She knows what this means. Taking deep breaths, making sure that her throat is clear, she sucks even harder, taking him deeper into her as he thrusts down harder. He's fucking her now as though his cock was in her pussy, as though the back of her mouth opened into cunt. But she can take it. He knows she can. Harder and harder, deeper and deeper, closer to the edge he brings himself. Moments later he is shooting massive amounts of cum into Giotta's mouth. She starts swallowing immediately to avoid choking or wasting a single drop. He pulls her to her feet once she has licked stray shots from the side of her lip.

On her feet, he sends his cock straight into her. His dick

spits some final drops into her and throbs momentarily, adjusting to her hot cunt. Slow thrusts ensure that what should now be a flaccid cock is in fact maintaining its solid stature. His cock gets all the way up inside her and settles his thrusting for the most part unimposing. He lets himself breathe just until his orgasm is forgotten and then starts ramming her with renewed prowess. Leo has always fucked hard; the only gentle strokes managed post cum. The reason for this is that he has an incredibly fat cock. The thick meat needs hard strokes for the pleasure to reach its center, and so he fucks fucking hard. Over and over he shoots his rod into the back of Giotta's cunt, filling her and stretching her. In minutes he is already sensing a second orgasm. He fucks even harder.

He picks her up onto himself and holds her on his cock, pushing her against the wall without forgetting that her hands are still behind her back. He doesn't fuck her so much in the direction of the wall as he does up towards the ceiling. Leo is pushing her onto his cock while shooting his dick up into her and it isn't long before he has her in another orgasm. His dick swells too now and he shoots harder and harder into her, his head thick and sweating inside her as it too starts to spew jizz into her cunt. This climax is so intense that Giotta shoots her legs straight behind Leo and sits with all her weight on his cock as he shoots liquid fire into her. She almost swallows his tongue as he thanks her for an amazing fuck with a series of passionate kisses.

CHAPTER 54

SCHOOLED

IT APPEARED that she was listening to the lecture, but nothing could've been further from the truth. All she could think about was how the obscure lighting of her bedroom would play off his hazel eyes. Something about the richness of his voice and the calculated mess of his long dark rock star hair drove her thoughts straight to sex every time. She wasn't a slut, she didn't really even sleep around, but for him, she'd make an exception. Something had grown between them the first semester when she took his English class. It had been a requirement for her major.

However, the following series of creative writing courses, although her passion, had nothing to do with the pursuit of a nursing degree. The chemistry between them forced her to make him her extra credit. He got her. She had never shared her poetry with anyone, for fear that it wasn't any good, but he validated her gift, and that's when he went from just another hot professor and morphed into a demi-God.

He appeared to be focused on the strict outlet of the assignment, but his mouth was just going through the motions of his lesson plan. His mind, cock, and a piece of his heart were focused on his star pupil. She purposely sat in the front row every Tuesday and Thursday pressing her breasts together in a display of her perfect V-neck cleavage, large rock-hard nipples poking through the tight t-shirt she'd selected just for him. The power position of being a professor often got him hit on, but she was different. Sure, the lusty tone of her voice flirting with him bi- weekly, not to mention her huge tits gave him an instant hard-on, but there was substance to this girl. She was a Barbie doll, but one with a brain, and a hell of a lot of souls. Through her writing, he glimpsed into the pain and insecurity of the woman hidden inside a perfect exterior, and that's when she went from another bimbo to his goddess.

She had to come up with some lame excuse to stay after class, something she didn't understand. That was often her modus operandi. He knew it, but he played along, hell, they both knew what was happening between them, but it was a chance to be physically close to her, and he never flinched from her close proximity.

He pulled a chair close to his desk as he explained the formula of writing the perfect sestina. The lengths of the stanzas and importance of the last word placement of each sentence. He even wrote little notes in her margins with his trembling hand. The heat between them was palpable, it felt like they were both holding their breath each and every time they were this physically close. Lately all of her writing had been about him, and every time he proofread her pieces, he wondered if he was the lover her words ached for. She tossed her long copper colored curl over her shoulder as the exotic fruity aroma seduced his olfactory. The sexual tension was becoming unbearable. How much longer can I continue this charade he wondered? When suddenly that same curl dropped from her shoulder casting a shadow over the work they both pretended to be focused on. His hand, without thought swept it back against her neck, lightly grazing her collarbone. She gasped unintentionally and caught his fading resistance off guard. "You're so damn sexy Anastasia," he confessed completely devoid of any thought of repercussions. "Oh Robert, you have no idea how much I want you," she replied reaching down and gripping his growing erection through his faded jeans. His gingered vixen locked his office door removing the low-cut tee as she sauntered back to him. She wrapped her hands around his neck and ran her fingers through his hair wildly as he brought his mouth to hers. Her lips opening willingly as his tongue danced beautifully with hers. Their kiss was passionate and filled with need long suppressed. "I probably shouldn't have done that," he truthfully stated. "I can't stop now," she moaned adding, "I need you inside me."

Her sex-starved words burned down any remaining wall of resistance as he cleared his desk and sat his beauty upon it. He unclasped her bra freeing the tits she'd used to tempt him. They were amazing. So soft and beautiful with big brownish-pink nipples that begged to be sucked. She jiggled them as he sucked their bouncy sway intoxicating. "I can't wait to fuck you," he said with no intent of going back now. He was going to fuck her properly, she needed a good fuck, and so did he. Moisture soaked her panties as each draw on her nipple shot straight to her pussy. Her trembling hand removed his belt, tossing it across the small office. She unbuttoned his jeans and slid his zipper down watching as they hit the floor freeing his massive dick from the confines of his clothes. She slid off the desk and turned her back to him as she stepped out of her jeans revealing a thong tucked into her perfectly rounded ass. He grabbed both cheeks as she bent over modeling the string of a garment. She seductively lay back on his desk spreading the shapely legs he longed to be between. "You're gorgeous Stasia," he said his eyes feasting on the rosy folds soaked in her desire for him.

"You're the sexiest man alive," she replied dragging her red fingernail down his chiseled abs. The fragrance of her drove him insane, somehow making his cock even harder. He consumed her pussy from opening to opening in one long lick as her body shivered in response. Her cream coating his tongue as he flicked her engorged clit. "Yes baby," she moaned in approval. Robert slid a finger into her wet opening moving it in and out of her and she thumbed her swollen bud. "Come for me, baby," he urged as he again lapped the juices from her as she arched her mound against his mouth. The light sucking of her clit took her over the edge as her body shuddered with orgasm. "Damn baby, you know how to eat pussy," she purred as she licked the glisten from his lips adding, "I knew you would."

"Sit," she demanded pushing him into his chair, his cock bobbing in anticipation. She fell to her knees and licked the pre-come from his tip before lowering her mouth onto his throbbing erection taking him in a little more with each stroke. She raised and lower her suckle bathing his dick in her deep kiss until she felt his balls quiver with impending climax. "Oh no you don't," she said adding, "I want you feel you come inside me." She hurriedly sprawled atop his desk and pleaded, "Robert, fuck me now." He said nothing as he slammed his cock into her cunt up to his balls. She moaned a guttural cry as her body stretched to accommodate him. "Stacy you're so tight," he whispered trying not to come. "Harder baby," she pleaded as he pounded her soaked opening attempting to knock out its bottom. "I love the way you fuck," she cooed with satisfaction. Her praise along with a heat and tightness he'd never felt pushed him too far as he fucked her cunt with animal need driving his cock to her complete depth before her body convulsed in a mind-numbing full-bodied orgasm. Her eyes rolled back into her head as if she were possessed as his dick poured complete satisfaction into her.

She bathed in the afterglow, as he got dressed. Both of them knowing they could never sit in that classroom again without replaying the scene. "What'cha doing next Tuesday and Thursday?" she said playfully as he fisted her auburn curls. "You," he replied. "What you doing next Monday, Wednesday, and Friday?" she purred batting her emerald eyes. "You," he replied opening the door and exiting the office without looking back.

CHAPTER 55

SHOWER SEX

I MET Ed in a nightclub in London just over two years ago. From the second our eyes locked, I knew he was the one for me. He isn't classically good looking. Ed was a rugby player and had the physique to match. The man is made of pure muscle. My name is Anna. I'm an average blonde. I'm big in the bust and big in the hips; I'm not every guy's type but I'm Ed's and that's all that matters. The night we met we danced for three hours straight, our hips grinding to the sexy music that pumped out of the speakers. It was like we were part of some kind of dance marathon, checking out how much stamina we both had. Lucky him, I love tennis, and very fit.

I went home with Ed that night, sweaty, and hungry for more of this delightful hunk of a man I'd just met. I don't usually go home with guys on the first night of meeting them, but this felt different, it felt natural. "Anna, how about a shower first?" Ed asked me, his T-shirt soaked with sweat. I couldn't wait to see him out of it.

"First? Before what?" I replied, trying to be coy.

Coyness just wasn't my thing though. He laughed an easy, low chuckle that brought these adorable dimples to his face. He pulled me into his big chest and kissed me hard on the mouth,

"Before I fuck your brains out," he said, into the nape of my neck, grabbing my behind and letting his hand wander between my legs. "Hmm, not sure I can wait until then," I replied. Then he led me to his bathroom, by the time we got there we were both naked, our clothes leaving a frenzied trail across the apartment. He led me to the shower cubicle and pushed me gently back against the cold tiles and leaned over me with one arm protectively above my head. I felt his erection between us. From somewhere he produced a condom, which he put on one handed that's when he hoisted me up so that I was sitting above him. He was so strong and I felt light as a feather in his arms.

"Do you like it hot or cold?" He said to me.

"The shower?" I said, feigning innocence. He slammed it on and jets of hard, hot water engulfed us. At the same time, he pushed himself inside me- we both came in a few short minutes with the water gushing around us, steam rising.

Well, that was our first shower. In the two years since we've been dating, finding the best shower to fuck in has been our mission. To date, it was at the Lady Grey hotel in Islington, the one with nice flower arrangements in the lobby and the painting of austere Victorians on the wall.We stayed there on our two-year anniversary. It comes highly recommended.

. . .

On the evening of our anniversary, Ed picked me up in his battered Toyota. We had dinner in a little Indian restaurant around the corner from our hotel and exchanged silly little gifts: he gave me a rubber duck; I gave him a ridiculous blue shower cap. To any onlookers, we looked like a couple stupidly in love. After we'd finished eating, Ed took my hand and looked into my eyes and smiled at me- he looked so good I could eat him. "You look absolutely filthy, Anna," he told me, grinning stupidly. "You need a shower."

"Same to you too," I replied, batting my eyelashes. "I've got something extra-special lined up for tonight" "I should hope so, I am *exceptionally* dirty tonight"

Back at the hotel, Ed had prepared the room and showed me the large walk in shower. "It's got two shower-heads," he said proudly. I looked at him quizzically.

"Anna, you have *no* imagination," he said.

I stripped, stepped into the shower and Ed followed. He already had a hard on. I was looking forward to this. He kissed me hard on the mouth and then pushed my head downwards. I knew what to do. He slammed on the hot water and I took him in my mouth, the water and his cock half choking me but just enough space to get my breath whilst I sucked on his cock I fingered myself, using my slipperiness to flick my clitoris until I thought I might come.

"You are fucking filthy, Anna, I love it".

"Are you nearly there?" I asked him, above the sound of gushing water and in between the thrusts of his cock. I could feel the tightness in him filling my mouth and my legs began to shake in that delirious, pre-orgasm way. Ed didn't have time to reply because he came hard and full into my mouth, gripping the back of my head and pulling at my wet hair.

But just as I thought I was going to come, Ed pulled away from me and pushed me back to the other end of the cubicle.

"*This* is what two showerheads are for," He said as he slammed on the second shower, dousing me in hot, delicious gushes. I was panting hard for him, aching to be finished off. Ed had switched off the first shower and had brought the showerhead forward. "I'm going to fuck you with this, ok?" He said. I nodded - I'd never actually fucked the shower-head before. This was a new game. I spread my legs for him; he squeezed shower gel over my naked body and my breasts. Despite the heat and the steam, my nipples were rock hard and Ed leaned in and bit down on one of them, pulling and biting hungrily.

"Ed, please, for the love of god, give me some release!" I cried above the steam. He pulled the other shower head down and turned the pressure up and directed it at my clitoris, the hard jets tantalizing me. He pushed the second showerhead into me and massaged the delicious spot that finally made me come, hard, shattering- it felt like steam was coming out of every pore of my skin.

Finally, we sank back against the tiles, sitting next to one another. "Funny how we end up more dirty when we get *in* the shower" Ed mused, slinging an arm around my shoulders. I leaned in and rested my head on his big chest, and listened to his heart beating hot blood around his body. It was then that I noticed the broken tile.

"Ed! We broke the shower!"

"Oops..." He replied slowly, suddenly realizing the damage we'd done to hotel property. The cable had been pulled from the wall, and the showerhead dangled forlornly on the cubicle floor. "Oh well," he concluded, "That's why there are two showerheads in this bathroom." He slammed on the shower again, ready for round two.

CHAPTER 56

SILK RESTRAINT

THE ROOM WAS DARK, lit only by the candles. She shuddered, tugging at the blue silk that bound her wrists over her head. She was lying on the bed, her body even more appealing like this, spread wide for his enjoyment. Jon licked his lips, savoring the deep flush that covered her delicate skin, before gently brushing the bamboo rod he was holding over her hip. Amy moaned at the contact. She was so beautiful, especially like this, with the red marks from kisses on her skin, seen even in the dim candlelight. They wanted to do this for a while and finally, Amy, a bit reluctant at first, complied with his request. But she was so gorgeous, bound and vulnerable like this. If only she knew.

Jon brushed the rod around her navel, making patterns and circles on her belly, around her breasts, on her thighs. He licked her wrists, her toes, and her throat. He kissed her behind the ears.

The faint cry that met his ears was like music, and Amy's hips moved forward. She tilted her head, exposing her long throat. He grazed the rod under her bare breasts, teasing her pink nipples, making her moan once again, this time louder.

"Look at me," he commanded, tilting her chin towards him and gazing into those blue eyes burning with fire. "What do you want?" He received only a shallow exhale in reply. "Tell me."

Taking a step forward, Jon ignored the way Amy arched towards him, yearning for contact, and slipped the wood between her legs, adding pressure against her entrance. She whimpered loudly, biting her lip, and she thrust back, wanting more. "Is this what you want?" Jon repeated, voice low and husky, his own erection throbbing almost painfully.

Amy looked almost as if she'd forgotten how to speak, swallowing hard. "P-please" She swallowed again. "More. Give me more."

He pressed the rod more firmly into her, and Amy whimpered again.

"How?" She made a quiet, frustrated noise and shook her head. She was still very shy about it, maybe because it made her feel so dirty. "How?" he said once more, persistent. He wanted to hear her say it.

"Jonathan," she whispered, quietly, so quietly it was almost impossible to hear between her ragged breaths. Amy, for some ridiculous reason, loved to use his full name. "Please."

"Please what, Amy?" asked Jon, smirking. He wanted to make her beg.

"Please. Touch me." She could feel the goose bumps all over her skin. She groaned, trying to break her hands free, to touch herself, to pleasure herself, to do something, but the silk was too tight. Blood was pounding in her ears; her heart was fluttering wildly in her chest. She didn't think she'd ever felt this wet before. The rod was so hot against her entrance it was almost painful.

"How, Amy?"

Not waiting for her reply, Jon's shifted and proceeded to kiss and lick Amy all over the chest, down to her thighs and lower. And then, without any warning, she heard something rustle, and her thighs were lifted by strong, muscled arms. She was spread wide. Amy felt herself flush thinking how she must look right now, naked and open and bare, but she didn't care. She just wanted more.

"Please," she whispered again. "Jonathan."

"You want me to touch you?" said Jon, ghosting the rod over her stomach. "You want me to lick you? To suck you? To fuck you?" And the rod broke the air with a sharp smack. "Say it."

She couldn't breathe.

He licked her down there, around the bamboo rod, mercilessly. She couldn't think. Both of them were breathing heavily as if there wasn't enough air in the room. It was too much, the scents of sex lingering in the air, the ache in her arms, sweat trickling down her body, the wetness between her legs. She felt herself twitch madly down there. She wanted to be filled with something, anything, right now.

"Jonathan, just..." wailed Amy, pulling at the silken bindings, feeling the muscles protest at being held in one position for so long. "P-please... Come on, please..."

His tongue darted inside her, teasingly. Her toes curled in sheer pleasure, her vision started to blur. "Please what?" he stopped licking, and oh God, now she felt so empty, she wanted his skillful tongue inside her again.

"Please," she said, surprised her voice still worked. "Just

fuck me," she murmured voice quiet and wavering. "Fuck me."

"Finally."

Jon dropped the rod on the floor with a thump, touching, really touching Amy for the first time since he had tied her up. Amy melted into the touch, her feverish body arching against him. His hands roamed over her body, over her ribs, ghosting over her stomach, stopping to tease her breasts.

She writhed and whimpered and begged, now without any restraint or shame. He smiled to himself as he kissed her stomach lightly. He bit into the skin and caressed her breast, while the other hand touched her core. She was impossibly wet and he could barely keep himself still. Quickly, without any more delay, he lifted one creamy white thigh and thrust sharply into his fiancé.

Amy cried out loudly. Her whole body convulsed in pleasure, and she yanked hard on the binds, but with no effect. Jon growled, sucking on the skin beneath his lips, marking her as his. She clamped around him like a vice, so hot and impossible and wet he thought he would explode right there and then. He pressed again between her legs, deep into her center and she whimpered. And when he kissed her on the lips for the first time, she gasped in surprise.

Their tongues met and Jon lost all control. His hips sank to meet hers, again and again, pulling them both apart. His hands gripped her hips, slamming them down to meet each of his thrusts.

Jon lifted those beautiful legs around his waist and Amy complied in an instant, locking her ankles together, rolling her hips down in pure, raw need. Jon drove deeper into her, hitting that spot he knew would make her see stars.

"Oh my God, Jon, don't stop. Fuck me, please, fuck me!" she wailed. "Jonathan!"

Jon was so close, they both were, and he knew he wouldn't last much longer. Not when Amy was saying his name over and over again.

He drew back, pulling out almost entirely out of her, and thrust roughly inside again. They fell into a quick, hungry rhythm. And then, when he knew she was close, he freed her, tearing at the silk in one, smooth movement. Amy howled, and clung to him, bucking her hips. "Yes, yes" her voice was shaking, urgent, and Jon couldn't have stopped even if he wanted to. "Jonathan, oh God, please," she gasped, and then she was beyond words as he thrust his fingers inside her, quickening his movements as her breath grew harsh and desperate. "Fuck me."

He knew Amy was right on the edge. It was the way her heels dug into his back, the way she contracted around him. It was the low moan that marked the beginning of her orgasm. "Fuck me," she pleaded again, her hips moving erratically. He felt her orgasm then, her muscles clasping around him tightly and this sends him into oblivion. With one last quick thrust, he came, groaning with relief.

He pulled back, completely spent and so tired, to look at her. She was flushed, her chest was heaving, and there were faint, red marks on her wrists.

"God," she whispered, lying back down against him, nestling her face against the hard muscle of his chest. "Oh my God." She met his eyes and brushed her hair back from her face.

"Are you ok?" "Yeah," she smiled.

"You were brilliant," he said as he slipped his arms around her and placed a soft kiss on her cheek. "Completely amazing. I love you so much," he breathed, kissing his fiancé again. "And I think I'm addicted to you."

"Good," she said with a mischievous grin. She kissed him back and they laughed. "Because next time, it's my turn."

CHAPTER 57

SIX DATE RULE

THE SIX-DATE RULE was something I'd always stuck to. Giving in just wasn't an option. My group of girlfriends were the first to chastise one another if any of us broke the: *don't sleep with him until at least the seventh date* decree absolute. It would only end in tears if you gave in too soon, however delectable, charming, or *genuine* he seemed. Besides, seven seemed like a good number- you work your ass off for six dates, by the seventh you've more than earned it.

"I just don't understand what's wrong with me!" Beth wailed after Sam didn't call her back. "He was, so, gentle." I had to admit, that Sam did seem like the real deal, kind, generous, on time.

"You gave out too soon, lady!" I consoled her, half scolding my beautiful but weak-willed friend who couldn't stop sobbing into the ice cream I kept in our refrigerator for these kinds of emergencies. But somehow, the rules changed when I met Steve, a waiter who, when giving me the bill, had also slipped in his phone number.

"He's definitely hot," Beth said admirably, almost fully recovered from Sam-gate.

"I might call him, I might not," I replied, all cool and aloof, but unable to take my eyes of the lean arms and tight ass that glided through the busy restaurant. He turned his head and caught me checking him out - sending a dazzling, wolfish grin my way. "Ah hell, it's happening," I said, half to myself and half to Beth.

"Remember, lucky number seven!" She warned, only half jokingly. I was going to have a tough time keeping a lid on it this time around.

On our first date, I met Steve outside the restaurant. He'd showered, and was wearing a white shirt with the collar undone and nice fitting jeans. I opted for a low neck-line black chiffon number and jeans- you know, the ones that fit really tight around the ass.

"Looking good!" He said, as he slung an arm over my shoulder, confidently. I had to admit, I like the attention and his cockiness. *He must have a lot to be confident about* I said to myself. We spent the evening at the cinema sitting way too close to one another, letting the sexual tension build between us, our fingers touching in the popcorn bucket. I was convinced he was going to try it on that night, instead, he left me hanging at the door to my apartment, the lightest of kisses traced onto my mouth.

Our second date happened the following Thursday. "Do you like food?" he asked me over the phone.

"Uh, yeah, what weirdo doesn't?" I replied.

"Great, then I am taking you out for dinner," He was so self-assured, and I loved it.

That night we sat opposite one another in my favorite restaurant downtown. I have to admit, I kind of lost my appetite, watching him slowly spoon ice cream into that gorgeous mouth of his. *Seven whole dates?* I thought, panicking. That night, he kissed me longer, pressing his hand into the small of my back. When I got inside I went straight to my bedroom and made myself come, hard and quick, with thoughts of Steve's mouth all over my body. Oh boy. I was in trouble.

Date number three was kind of a non-date. We met on a Saturday during the day and agreed to go for a run together. We had to do something with this sexual tension. By the end of it he was drenched in sweat, his gray singlet showing off his wide chest and those strong, lean arms that I wanted all over me. *Oh Lord, why are you torturing me?* I'd have to rethink the rules. I'd asked Beth to define them once again. "You know the boundaries!" She cried, "Keep your underwear *on* and definitely *no penetration of any kind.*"

You really have no imagination, do you, Beth. I thought to myself.

On date number four we agreed to meet after our respective work shifts - late. "How about a nightcap?"

"Sure thing" I replied, all casual. We spent the time kissing in a booth of a late night coffee shop, under the dim light. He held my head back whilst he worked his way around my mouth with his tongue; I held those lean biceps with my hands while he worked me harder. I'd reached down to find himself hardening against me, I gripped it. He groaned. *No penetration.* I could hear Beth's words already scolding me.

"Touch yourself," Steve said through his hot breath. "What, here?"

"No one can see us, your hands are under the table" He said, but he was already moving my other hand inside my jeans, that had, miraculously, come undone. I took his cock out with his other hand and ran my fingers up the shaft. "Do it" he instructed. "And do *you* at the same time" There, right under the table in the dim café light, Steve came into my hand whilst I stifled my own groans; his hot breath on the nape of my neck making me tingle and my nipples harden. Thank god the café was empty, but it wouldn't have mattered anyway if it hadn't been.

We tidied ourselves and left the café, stepping out into the hot night. "Soon?" He said to me when he dropped me home.

"Soon," I replied, definitely. I had a plan.

I made a deliberate plan to bump into Steve on his way home from work. We walked together for about three blocks. Fifteen minutes. That definitely counts as a date, I told myself.

"Could you drive me to work?" I asked Steve, two days later. "My car won't start." Lies. A car journey definitely counts as date number six. We arranged sate number seven on the way to work.

· · ·

"Does tomorrow night work?""Yep, it works," I said, super casual.

"Meet me from work? I have to lock up at the end of the night," he said. "I'll be there" We locked eyes for a moment as I jumped out of the car. We both knew it.

Date number seven: I thought I'd surprise Steve. As he was turning the key in the lock, I placed a hand on his. "Inside," I whispered. He grinned at me and both went into the now dark restaurant where we had first met. He switched on a light and I let my knee-length coat fall to the ground for him, revealing just a pair of knee-high boots and panties.

"Good God, you are beautiful," he declared, gulping. I ran a finger down his front and opened each button, running my hands over his smooth chest.

"What can we use from the kitchen?" I asked him, playfully.

"Wait here," he instructed. He came back with a tub of whipping cream and a bowl of fruit. "Will this do for starters?" He swept a table clear with one swipe of his long, lean arm and pushed me gently onto it. I opened my legs up for him and offered up my bare breasts, on which he slowly trailed cream between them.

"Eat me," I told him. Steve straddled over me and took one of my breasts in his hands, cupping it hard. He sucked on my nipple, and then the other, letting out small groans of pleasure, which I returned. His other hand pulled my underwear down, yanking it right off so the elastic cut my thigh. He poured the remaining cream onto the place that was aching for pleasure the most, and then went down with his mouth, working my clitoris into a frenzy. I came into his face within a minute.

. . .

"On your back," I told him, after I'd got my breath back. He complied, grinning hungrily at me. He laid his beautiful long body onto the table and let me admire his hard, red erection that was just aching to fill me. I took the cream and dribbled it onto his taught stomach, licking the trail it made down to his cock. I took him in my mouth and sucked and licked the hard shaft that I'd been waiting so long for. Finally, I lowered myself onto him, gasping at his large size as he filled me.

"Now fuck me like you've never fucked before," he said to me.

"My pleasure," I panted, and proceeded to grind myself into his hips, and his into mine- the tension of our six encounters climaxing into another orgasm I thought would split me in half.

"So...how was it!?" Beth teased when I returned home the next day. "Oh, you know, worth the wait I guess,"

CHAPTER 58

STUCK

ANDREA SLAMMED her fist into the elevator button in a fury. Not today. This was not happening today. If she didn't get into the meeting in 47 seconds, she will probably get fired. No, scratch that. She would definitely get fired. And then she will kill herself.

"Hey, relax. They're going to get us out," said Charles from IT. Charles was the most annoying guy in the whole building. Charles would always talk to her when she wanted to be left alone, and brought her muffins or coffee at the wrong moment, and had the most irritating smile in the world. Charles, with whom she has been secretly in love since the second day she started to work for the company.

Somewhere above them, an actual alarm bell started to ring. Andrea jabbed her finger at the ground floor button. The alarm stopped and was replaced by dead silence. But the elevator still wouldn't move. It just wobbled in place.

"Fuck."

. . .

There was another wobble and the ceiling lights in the elevator flickered and the fan died. The dim emergency lights turned on. It was like a scene from a horror movie. And they were stuck on the 44th floor.

"Well, that's just brilliant. This is the end of the world. We're going to die."

"No, we won't," said Charles and watched her sink onto the floor. "It's probably an electrical fault." He took off his phone, tapped something in and got almost an immediate reply. "Yup. The technicians are on their way. But it'll take a while. Nothing to do but wait."

Andrea made a noncommittal sound. And then she really tried not to panic. Because it wasn't just the fact that she was going to get fired, she was also claustrophobic. And the whole building knew about it. Including Charles.

"Don't say anything," she raised her finger at him to prevent him from speaking. He raised his hands in a gesture of mock surrender.

"I wasn't going to say anything." The silence between was deafening.

"But you know, the lift won't fall down. It's highly unlikely. And why are you so annoyed?"

Andrea rolled her eyes. "Maybe it has something to do that I'm stuck in the elevator on the 44th floor with the most insufferable guy in the whole building?"

"No, that's not it," he licked his lips and tilted his head. "I know you like me." She glared at him. "And I know you're claustrophobic."

"Oh yes, great! So what, do you have a cure for it? Or

are you just going to laugh and leave me here to suffocate and die?" she exclaimed, knowing she was blushing. The bastard. She will never speak to him again when they get out of there. She will kill him with a stapler and get her revenge.

"Actually, there is a cure for claustrophobia," said Charles with a smug, self-satisfied smile. Andrea banged her head against the wall in despair. "Yeah, and what would that be? Magic?" "Sex."

Andrea stared at him, completely dumbfounded. "What are you, twelve? Besides, I don't even..."

"Like me, yes, I know," and he was on her a second later. Andrea gasped in shock. This wasn't happening. This was Charles. He was annoying and she hated him, and Charles was kissing her, his tongue inside her mouth and oh God, that felt so good.

"Do you like that?" he broke the kiss to look at her. Andrea stared back. "Did I tell you to stop?"

This was invitation enough.

Charles was on her and then it got serious. He was a really good kisser, but he apparently wasn't going to be gentle with her. Andrea liked it and slammed her fists into the wall when he nipped at her bottom lip. There wasn't anything a little violence couldn't solve.

Charles dug a hand into her long, brown hair and shifted his attention to her neck. He used his tongue and teeth, biting her hard enough to leave marks and elicit little moans from her throat. She gripped him and held his head in place and Charles caught on pretty quick. He bit her harder. That will probably leave a mark later. Andrea knew Charles was a quick learner and has excellent observation skills. He was also cheeky, annoying, geeky, compulsive, and obsessive.

But he was also apparently a damn good kisser.

Her thoughts got a bit derailed when Charles lifted her skirt. Andrea shifted her legs to give him better access. He wasted no time in getting his hands where he wanted, pushing her panties aside to touch her flesh. He slid his finger deep inside her, into the wetness, and Andrea moaned. His fingers were in all the right places, moving fast, exploring, and it was so good Andrea slammed her fists into his shirt. Then he bit her again, hard and she knew she was close.

With one hand, she reached for his trousers, palming the bulge in front of his pants. He moaned but kept moving his fingers inside her. She undid his belt and shoved his pants open. He tugged at his pants, forcefully, and finally, Andrea took him in hand.

Charles withdrew his fingers from her, took hold of her legs, locked them around his waist, and pushed her to the wall with a grunt. Andrea made an annoyed noise.

"What are you waiting for? Charles..." she rocked against him or tried to, given the fact that she was sandwiched between him and the wall.

"Always so impatient." He pulled back from her and finally entered her. Andrea dug her heels into the backs of his thighs.

"You want it fast and hard? Is that it?" and he gave it to her. He drove into her, giving her no time for breathing or thinking, there was no finesse or delicacy in his movements. She was overwhelmed by the power of his hips, slamming into her, driving her against the wall. He knew what he was doing when he kissed her again. "You're going to come for me, hard and fast, baby." He punctuated every word with a slam of his hips, his cock rubbing inside her perfectly.

He moved his hands down to cup her buttocks, hoisting her up, changing the angle, and driving into her even deeper.

"Oh fuck!" she exclaimed. Charles watched her as her eyes rolled into her skull in pleasure. Andrea frantically held onto him and wrapped her legs around him tighter, urging him to fuck her deeper. She was gasping and bucking beneath him, so he began to thrust quickly. Their lips crashed again, tongues fighting for dominance.

An electric feeling started to rise up inside her. When he hit the spot, the one, she cried out and almost lost her consciousness. He followed close behind her. He tensed, his hips were still inside her and then he came inside her, the wave of his orgasm almost swept her from her feet.

They rolled onto the floor, a mess of tangled limbs and clothing. "Well," Andrea panted. "Why the fuck didn't we do this earlier?" "I don't know. Maybe because you were being obnoxious."

Andrea rolled her eyes and smiled at Charles. "You're being obnoxious right now. Stop it," she kissed him sweetly on the lips.

"I cured you from claustrophobia, you should be thankful."

She smacked him. "Now you've ruined it. Again. I really hate you," she replied teasingly. "You will have to cure me again; I'm starting to feel dizzy."

"Well, that can be arranged," his husky voice sent a delicious shiver down her spine.

CHAPTER 59

TAKING CHANCES TO TRY NEW THINGS (BDSM)

FRANK AND GLORIA were not people that shied away from new and exciting things. They fully believed that variety was in fact the spice of life. They had tried having sex in public places and had even tried swinging. The one thing that they had not tried was BDSM. This was a part of their life that had not yet been explored or given a chance to blossom. Frank and Gloria had talked about it over a number of times.

Gloria decided that a little BDSM role play was in store. It had been a long week and their one-year anniversary was coming up. She decided to surprise Frank with an early gift. Gloria got off from work early. She went to the house to get her surprise ready for Frank. Gloria had figured out a way to tie herself up and make herself unable to fight when Frank got home and was ready to ravish her. Frank was about to be home so Gloria had to get naked and tied up in a hurry. Sure enough, as expected, Frank came home and went looking for Gloria when he saw her car in the driveway. Frank found his wife tied to the bed wearing nothing more than a smile.

"Well, well what do we have here? A woman in my bed all naked and unable to fight off my advances? I wonder what I can do to the woman that will allow me the chance to get my thrills with her, I know I can make her my little submissive. I bet you would like that wouldn't you?"

Gloria was able to get a weak acknowledgment out through the gag that was placed into her mouth. Gloria knew that the sight of this was making her husband harder than anything else she had done Juices were leaking out and causing a glistening effect on her pubic mound.

Frank went over and untied her and had her come over and get on her knees in front of him. Gloria was worked up at the fact that she was about to be used by her husband for his BDSM fantasy. Frank reached over into the dresser and got out the riding crop that he had bought to surprise her. Gloria's eyes lit up at the sight of the riding crop and knew at once what was about to happen. Frank took the item and at first gently spanked Gloria with it. Then it was increased a little more as he watched her reaction the entire time. He wanted to make sure that he was ready in case she said stop of the safe word that they had established. Gloria went ahead and continued with the scene that was playing out in front of her. She took the entire length of Frank's pole down her throat. While she was bobbing up and down on his member, Gloria was being smacked with the riding crop. Gloria had to wonder if her surprise was not in fact Frank's surprise as well. Frank grabbed Gloria and hoisted her up onto her feet. He then took her and pushed her onto the bed making sure that she landed on her back. Frank took her legs and tied them to the bed. She lay spread eagle onto the bed. Frank smiled, and then drove down between her legs. Frank began to eat Gloria's pussy. Gloria hated to have her cunt licked unless it was her idea. Gloria had to lay there while Frank took his turn. While she did not want to admit it; the sensation of Frank eating her out was getting her sexually aroused. At one point, she grabbed the back of his head and shoved it down there so he could get deeper into her wet, aching cunt with his tongue. Frank came up off her cunt with no warning and then proceeded to tie Gloria back up. Frank was now 100% back in control and he knew that what he wanted to do was going to be the biggest surprise of all.

Frank knew Gloria's cycle pretty good and had been making notes of it. He had a surprise that she was not expecting. He took his rigid member and drove it into the cunt of Gloria without a rubber. Gloria was at first confused as to what was Frank doing as every time near her cycle he had always had sex with her while wearing a condom.

Tonight he was going at it bareback. Gloria was ready to explode. As all of this had been ten times better than what she had planned. He was going to show his wife that he too could be a kinky when it was needed. Frank continued to pump in and out of Gloria as hard as he could. The moment arrived that he was going to give Gloria the surprise that he had been planning. He took his cock and placed it between Gloria's large tits. Frank decided to give Gloria something that he had never given. After about a half hour, Frank let loose and sprayed her face and her swollen tits.

CHAPTER 60

TEACHER BLUES

"JOE, WHAT WERE YOU THINKING?" Caroline asked, an expression of incredulity taking over the delicate features of her face.

"I don't know, Mrs. Dawkins," Joe replied. He looked down at his big, awkward feet, trying to appear apologetic despite his inherently mischievous freckled face.

Caroline sighed and picked up the papers that loomed on the desk before her. She grabbed her stapler from the neat assortment of tools and objects arranged on her oak desk, and with a loud click that echoed in the empty classroom, she attached them.

"You've left me no choice but to file another disciplinary action report," Caroline explained to her troublesome student. "I think this may put you at your limit."

Joe looked up, startled. He scratched his head nervously and tugged at the frayed edge of his dirt-stained T-shirt.

"What does that mean?" Joe asked.

Faint sounds of the other kids yelling and playing as they started to head to their homes drifted through the open window of the classroom

Caroline picked up her ink pen and, shaking her head of short dark curls, she began signing the paperwork. She flipped and scanned through the pages and made sure everything was filled out properly.

Caroline stood from her desk, and her chair screeched against the tile floor. She walked around the desk and presented Joe with a loose paper from the stack.

"Your parents will have to sign here," Caroline explained, pointing to the blank space at the bottom of the page. "And no forging. I'll know because I'm also calling them to come in for a conference with the principal."

"Mrs. Dawkins, please don't do this!" Joe begged. He took the papers from her hands and looked at them deject-edly. "My Dad'll kill me."

"Joe, you've left me no choice. You're probably going to get kicked out of school." "What? No, that can't happen. Mrs. Dawkins," Joe pleaded. His eyes began to tear up.

Caroline put a hand to her temple. She felt a headache coming on strong. She couldn't wait for the day to be over. It had been a particularly trying one.

"Sorry Joe," she said, "but there's nothing I can do. Your behavior is unacceptable, and your grades are suffering because of it. Now let's just go home."

Caroline quickly gathered her books and purse. She ushered her student silently out the door of the classroom, locking it behind her. She walked at a fast pace to her car in the parking lot, anxious to get home, kick off her shoes, and sprawl out on her soft, inviting couch to unwind.

Driving home, Caroline listened to some light jazz in an attempt to clear her mind. The soft tunes did little to relax her though, as her thoughts were racing about all the things she had to deal with as a sixth grade teacher. She hated disciplining her students. It was her least favorite part of an otherwise rewarding job.

Caroline walked through the door of her house. Her husband Matt was home early it seemed, as his car had been parked in the driveway already when she pulled in.

"Matt?" she called, closing the door behind her with a click that seemed loud in the stillness of the house. "Matt, you home?"

Caroline let her bag of school books slide off her arm and collapse onto the floor. She kicked off her shoes, and one of them hit the wall next to the door. She ruffled her curly black hair as she made her way toward the large, over-stuffed suede couch that had been calling her name all day.

Just as she plopped down and tossed her legs up over the arm, Matt walked into the living room. He was completely naked, his penis partially erect.

Caroline laughed. "Well, hello to you too," she said.

Matt smiled and moved closer to where she lay on the couch. His green eyes glowed roguishly as he looked down at his wife, his tall muscular body towering over her.

Caroline looked up at him, a soft smile on her pale face. "I had a rough day," she told him. "I don't know if I'm really in the mood."

Matt's smile faltered a little. "You're just going to leave me hanging like this?"

"Leave you hanging?" Caroline giggled. "That thing does not look like it's 'hanging' right now." She glanced at his hard penis, which was at her eye level, close to her face.

"Damn right," Matt said. "Come on, baby, it'll help you forget about your day."

"I don't know." Caroline rolled over slightly and looked at the painting that hung over the couch. "I just had to write up that kid Joe I'm always telling you about, and I feel terrible for doing it because now he's probably going to be expelled."

Caroline let out a long sigh. She looked back toward Matt, trying to avoid looking at the details of his cock, close enough for her to see each vein. "It just always puts me in such a downer mood to discipline my students."

Matt crossed his thick, tan arms over his bare chest. "I know what you need."

"What's that?" Caroline asked half-heartedly, crossing one leg over the other and looking for the TV's remote control. She saw it between the cushions and reached for it.

Matt dove to grab the remote just as her fingers were about to close around it. He snatched it out of her grasp and threw it aside.

"Ugh, Matt," she groaned.

"I don't think so, little lady," he said sternly. "You're grounded."

Caroline giggled and said, "I haven't been grounded in fifteen years. I don't think so."

Matt flopped down on the couch beside Caroline and grabbed her around the waist. He pulled her over his lap, laying her roughly over his legs facedown.

"What are you doing?" she demanded, still giggling.

"Disciplining you," Matt stated matter-of-factly. "You teach all day, every day.

Someone's got to teach you a thing or two."

Matt pulled Caroline's plain gray skirt up over her plump, soft butt cheeks, revealing the backs of her lush thighs and black panties. She squirmed to sit up, but Matt's hold on her firmly.

. . .

"What has gotten into you?" Caroline asked as she strained to turn over. "The question is, what's about to get into you."

Caroline caught her breath as it became clear that Matt would not accept her answers of refusal.

Matt slid his hand under the elastic waist of Caroline's panties and began to pull them down. He left them around her, just under the crease where her thighs met her bum, and he admired the smooth, milky white, round form of his wife's ample rear end.

Matt smacked Caroline lightly on the butt. She jumped, surprised.

"You've been a bad girl," he explained, "and now you have to get the punishment you deserve."

Matt reared back his hand a little more and slapped Caroline's other cheek, harder this time. The sound was worse than the impact, but it stung her a little. She winced, but with a slight smile on her rosy lips and a hint of a blush rising in her face.

Without warning, Matt spanked Caroline harder, several times in a row. His hand felt the impacts now as they jiggled the flesh of her butt, sending waves of pleasurable vibrations through the tops of her plump thighs and through her lower back.

Caroline quivered a little as she realized her clitoris was beginning to tingle with desire unexpectedly. Her crotch was getting warmer, and she could feel a bit of wetness slowly seeping out of her vagina.

"Now are you sorry for what you've done?" Matt asked playfully, letting his sturdy grip on Caroline relax.

"No," she nearly shouted. "No, and I never will be."

Matt was taken aback by her answer. He had expected

her to squirm free, change into sweatpants, and go pick the remote up off the floor.

"You better just keep disciplining me before I do something else naughty," Caroline teased. She lifted her head and turned to give her husband a taunting smile.

Matt laughed, admiring the beauty of her face as they held eye contact. Caroline turned back around, and then he spanked her some more.

Matt licked his right finger to moisten it. He slid it between her butt cheeks and down into the warmth of her womanly slit. Caroline gasped as she felt it enter her, gliding in smoothly from the immense wetness that had secreted as she was caught up in the excitement.

With his left hand, Matt slapped her rump again, then again, in a slow, steady rhythm that accented the rhythm of his finger as it pulsed in and out of her inner lips. He leaned over and ran his tongue down her lower back, and the peach fuzz hairs that made Caroline so soft to the touch stood on end.

Caroline couldn't believe how wonderful it felt to be held down over Matt's lap and spanked as he fingered her. She had been fingered hundreds of times in her life, but never had the sensation been quite like this. She closed her eyes and felt an involuntary moan escape her lips.

Matt suddenly flipped her over and began tugging her blouse over her head. As soon as her arms came out of it, he threw it aside. It landed in the fireplace. Caroline had already unfastened her bra before Matt had a chance to get his arms around her.

Her voluptuous breasts, soft and round with large areolas and nipples, tumbled out of the cups of her black bra. Matt's penis stiffened more at the sight, veins purple and pulsing under the skin. He reached out and squeezed them roughly, then moved down to put her brown nipples in his mouth.

Caroline shuddered as Matt's lips closed softly around her areola. His tongue flickered against the nipple, sending little shockwaves through her nerves. She arched her back, pushing her plump breasts deeper into his face.

Matt pulled his face away and lightly slapped her breasts from side to side, watching them bounce and sway. He pushed Caroline down onto her back and moved over her, his knees on either side of her. He lowered down until his rock solid cock was pressing into her cleavage.

Caroline moved down and slid his penis into her mouth, letting her saliva drip all over it.

Matt closed his eyes and sighed with pleasure as she sucked lightly on his member. She let it slip out of her mouth, pausing to look up at Matt seductively with her large, moist green eyes.

She moved back up to let his penis rest on her tits, then grabbed it confidently and stuffed it between them. Caroline rocked her body up and down to make Matt's dick slide in and out of the crease between her breasts. Matt began moving his hips forward and back, matching her rhythm and massaging his ready-to-burst penis.

Just as Matt was about to come, Caroline sensed the moment was right and leaped out from under him. She got on her hands and knees in front of him and looked over her shoulder, inviting him to enter her doggy-style.

Matt stroked his dick a couple times and then pressed it into her hole. It wouldn't slide right in. He softly pushed the head against her lips, pushing a little harder with each pulse until the head would enter.

Caroline threw her head back, thrusting her waist toward the couch and her butt into the

air.

"Just put it in," she demanded.

Matt responded instantly, ramming the swollen head of his dick into the sweet wet

crevice. It split Caroline in two and made her smile with the rough bliss of the feeling. Her head swayed each time Matt drove his dick into her and hit her bottom with his pelvis. Over and over he pounded, his hands grasping her hips so hard it was leaving pink marks in her flesh.

"I told you you needed discipline," Matt grunted, and he smacked her cheek hard.

Caroline let out a little shriek of surprise and lowered her head down into the cushion of the couch, her ass still high.

Matt continued spanking her, turning her cheek rosy in the shape of his hand, until suddenly he felt himself about to come harder than he had in ages. Caroline was right there with them, a feeling similar to panic overtaking her as the extreme intensity of orgasm began to flood over her. It started in her clitoris and bled all the way to her toes and her fingertips.

Matt's penis pulsed with orgasm inside her, intensifying her own. They rode the wave of pleasure all the way through together, and collapsed onto the couch in a heap of skin and sweat.

"Oh my God," Caroline gasped, her chest heaving. "That was amazing." Matt smiled, breathing just as heavily. "Yeah, it was."

They lay on the couch gradually cooling down and returning their respiration rate to normal. The room was quiet now except for the relaxing rhythm of their own breathing.

Caroline felt the slimy warmth of Matt's come dripping back out of her and onto her inner legs. She rolled over and put her arm over his smooth chest, and, smiling wickedly, she said, "Now it's your turn to get a little discipline.

CHAPTER 61

THE BREAK-IN (MIDNIGHT TIE-UP)

THE CURTAINS BLOW lightly in the breeze coming through the open window. The problem is that the window shouldn't be open. Lisa had made sure every door and window was locked shut, especially since Bruce had already been away a few days and was only due back after the weekend. The sound of a drawer opening startles her enough for her to gasp, whereupon she realizes that she can't open her mouth. She breathes hard through her nose as she tries to figure out what the tight obstruction on her mouth is, tied around and knotted at the back. Instinctively she wants to sit up, to get up and get out. But her hands are bound above her head and so she can only flail her legs wildly, something she knows from all their discussions about security she shouldn't be doing. But since she's already tied up she knows that the intruder expected that she would wake up at some stage during the robbery.

She watches in the dark as drawers are tossed and the dark-clothed man scratches around in their things. She hates that a stranger is going through their stuff and anger fills her so that she is flailing again, making as much noise as she can with her mouth bound. After exhausting herself she starts to make the observations she knows she should be focusing on. Height, build, ethnicity if possible, is he going to come close enough for her to see his eyes...Oh shit, he is. He's walking towards her. He's on the floor next to her, holding her face so that she has to look at his ski-mask-covered face. She checks his eyes. Even in the dark she knows these eyes. She looks harder, straining for a memory. Then the aftershave blows into her nose, her augmented sense of smell making the association immediately. She checks his hand. He forgot to remove his wedding ring, or wear black gloves as they had discussed when they planned this charade. But who gave a fuck. She didn't even care why he was home and not in San Francisco. For now *Bruce* is an intruder about to violate her. That's all she needs to know!

Her legs are crossed now as she resists the hand already between her thighs. The hands force her onto her back and pull her legs apart. She tries now to get into character quickly, needing to believe that the man wanting to spread her apart isn't her husband. But it is. And even now that Bruce has remembered to remove his wedding ring it is difficult for her to get him out of her head. As much as she feigns resistance, her body knows his hands, and her cunt knows that he is the owner of at least fourteen and a half inches of dick. Already she is warming up and wetting up in the places her perpetrator is trying to get to.

Suddenly her legs are open, one hanging off the side of the bed, its foot on the floor. Bruce kneels gently on it to keep it where it is. He moves the other leg further on the bed away from him, his hand high up on her thigh but not touching her pussy, which now sweats in the moonlit room.

There is nowhere for her cunt to hide now as Bruce stares at it, taking in the sight of the perfect pussy just waiting for him to make his next move. Lisa squeezes all the muscles of her pussy tightly together both in mock resistance to him and also because doing so gives her a deep and intense pleasure in anticipation of the real thing. Her arousal is augmented by the fact that she has absolutely no fucking idea what Bruce has in store for her.

Then he gives her cunt a hard lick. He gives her aching pussy another lick, then another. He continues licking the fat vagina, the mound seeming to grow towards his mouth as it becomes more and more aroused. Lisa cannot remember being so totally fucking turned on before. And never before has she appreciated what many have often thought of as Bruce's abnormally large cock. It is going to be most welcome when he eventually lets her have it. For now, she wonders what beautiful tortures he has in store for her. He gives her cunt a couple more licks and then he is staring at it again as if he expects it to give him feedback on his tongue's performance.

Using his thumb and index he pushes open the entrance to her pussy. He keeps it wide open for a minute before letting it close again. Seconds later he presses the entrance open again, and gives the inside of Lisa's cunt a long look. He lets his fingers come together a little and then pushes them as far apart as they will go, turning the pussy into a gaping, yawning crevice. The index on his other hand dips its tip into the wide opening and plays around in the space. Then Bruce lets the pussy close over the fingertip just as he sends the rest of the finger into it. Lisa now parts her own legs and pushes her cunt up so that the finger finds her depths faster. Bruce waits for her to circle his finger for a bit, her movements up and around while his is just a firm thrust of the thick appendage down into the cunt. Then he watches as she reaches for the sky with her cunt as he slowly pulls his finger from inside her.

Her frustration is evidenced by the way she rubs her legs together, especially at the thighs. She is almost flailing around on the bed now, proving that she is anything but a victim of a crime.

Bruce needs to bring her back into the game. But how, since she has already been so completely turned on by just the suggestion of the game. He presses down hard on her belly and sends his index back into her, along with his middle-finger this time. This time he isn't watching the proceedings on her cunt, but watching the expression on her face as he forces his fingers deep inside her, pulls them out, and then sends them back into her. Bruce repeatedly extracts his fingers from inside her completely before forcing them back inside her. This new roughness satisfies Lisa's pussy but also reminds her of the dynamic of the game. She immediately forces her legs shut, crossing her leg as far over her pussy as it will go, given that Bruce is still half-kneeling on the other one. This renewed resistance stretches his cock to a maximum, fifteen solid inches of Caucasian cock.

He can't focus on fingering and freeing his cock at the same time and so he removes his fingers from Lisa. The strain on his dick against the hard denim of the black jeans he wears is unbearable now and he uses both his hands to loosen his belt and then the jeans, pulling them and his briefs to just below his balls. With his cock free he can breathe again, and focus on the matter at hand. Lisa forgets that her hands are bound and she reaches for the cock peeping at her over the side of the bed. Frustrated she accepts that this isn't her show. Bruce returns his fingers to her pussy, this time using his other hand to stroke the full length of his dick. His hot palm on his cock has him so aroused that he digs harder into Lisa, squeezing tighter on his cock as well. Soon his has three, and then four fingers inside her, digging around in her pussy wildly as his penis throbs, oozing precum. He lets go of his dick before he ends the game too soon.

Realizing that four of his thick fingers are moving easily in and out of Lisa Bruce can't resist pushing the envelope just a little. He holds her down, his large hand palm-down on her stomach. He pulls his fingers from her and then replaces the four with just his thumb. Then he lets his index and thumb dance together around the entrance. The middle finger turns the couple into a threesome. He follows with his ring finger and then the pinky, all his fingertips joined together as he feeds Lisa his entire hand. Again the idea of what he has just done sends the elasticity of her cunt to a whole new level and soon Lisa is again arching towards the sky, wanting more of Bruce inside her. She gets just that as his hand disappears into her, all the way to the wrist.

He slides his other hand underneath her and after a brief search, his middle finger finds the entrance to her ass. He manages to get three of his fingers into her ass without any lubrication, aided only by the stream flowing from her pussy and coating the outside of her asshole. He gives her ass a good dig, slow and deep as he turns his fingers in her fanny into a very large fist. With the fingers in her ass and the fist in her cunt Lisa is filled just about as much as is possible for her. Bruce takes her pussy and her butt for the best ride they've ever been on, and it takes him mere minutes. Lisa feels very close to an orgasm now, without having had her man's cock inside her once. But instead of an orgasm, Bruce pulls all his fingers from her almost one at a time.

He manages to rid her of all her clothes quickly. He takes her breasts into his mouth and then fondles them with both hands. Then he leaves one hand to work on her breasts as he returns his entire fist, finger by finger into her cunt. The fingers become a fist again and while he feels over the entire surface of her chest he pivots his fist around in her cunt while moving it back and forth at the same time. Again she is so close to cumming that she moves her cunt high up and around. Bruce knows that there is no other time but the present and he brings her system to a shocking pause by yanking his fist from her. It feels like he's left her vagina with all its contents. He is on the bed quickly, on top of her and staring her in her eyes, watching every response as the massive eight-inch girth of his cockhead finds her pussy and then guides the rest of his shaft inside her.

He immediately fucks her like a rabbit, his cock having been neglected too long.

He's in deep, all the way. His strokes are fast, but with fifteen inches of dick they seem deliciously slow. It takes less than fifteen strokes of his fifteen inches for him to draw what seems like liters from Lisa's cunt. Her body writhes underneath him and he keeps going. She cums for a good few minutes, soaking the bed underneath them, but still Bruce doesn't let up his fucking. He can't bring himself to pull his cock from inside her. But he also can't seem to bring himself to a climax. It feels, for both of them, as if he could fuck her forever. He could. With the massive amounts of lubrication he pulled from her pussy there isn't enough traction even for his mammoth cock to head in the direction of anything that even vaguely resembles an orgasm. But this doesn't mask the fact that he needs to fucking cum. He knows what he needs to do.

He lifts her leg that's on the ground onto the bed and turns her onto her stomach. He digs into her pussy and then uses the wetness he finds there to send his fingers into her ass. After giving her a few digs, a couple of stretching pushes and pulls, he mounts her and sends his cock into her. The space is tight and hot. He thrusts hard and fast, not going as deep as he was in her cunt though. It takes him minutes before he too is shooting into her hole massive amounts of his own heat. With his meat still in her ass, he reaches under her for her pussy again, digging his fingers into her again just as she expects a reprieve. He keeps thrusting slowly in and out of her ass until, again after only a few minutes, they are both in the throes of an orgasm, this time together. He brings her to a third orgasm before untying her and carrying her to the bathroom to get them both cleaned up for a night of more husband and wife type lovemaking.

CHAPTER 62

THE BUBBLE-BLOWER

THE SOUND of the water raining down on Evan is her cue to move. Rachel knows that she has about ten minutes before he's going to be out of the shower and drying himself. She turns on the taps in the sunken bath in the center of their elaborate bathroom and pours the vanilla-scented bubble bath directly under the rapidly running water. It takes five minutes for the bath to be half filled with water but all the way filled with bubbles. By the time she gets to the frosted glass shower door, she has already left a trail of clothing behind her. Naked, she slides the door open.

Evan turns around mid-lather and has to let the water run over his face so that he can open his eyes fully without burning. Rachel puts a finger to her lips and he says nothing. She takes the sponge from his hand and runs it over his hairy chest, then on his neck before working it back down to his balls. She lingers at his balls and then gets him to turn so that she can give his back and ass a good clean. Again she gets to his sack from the back and lets the sponge linger. When he turns to face her again he finds her already on her knees.

She runs the soapy sponge over her husband's thick legs. By the time she's cleaned his feet, the water has sent the soap onto the mosaic floor and down the drain. Discarding the sponge, Rachel thwarts her husband's attempt to turn the water off by tugging at his balls with just her fingertips. Every finger on every hand makes direct and intimate contact with Evan's big balls, hardening his dick. She ignores the growing cock and keeps her fingers on his sack. Instinct, or habit, has Evan take his penis into his palm and work a few solid strokes up and down his shaft. Rachel lets him have a go at his cock for a minute and then removes his hand from his dick.

Her hands move over his dick and this makes the tool quiver excitedly. Evan looks down at his wife as she works his dick good, making it a menacing, heat-seeking torpedo. Her tongue settles on the tip, his foreskin pulled back so that the delicate head is exposed. Rachel licks the tip of her man's cock as though it was an ice-cream cone. Very quickly he braces himself for one of her super-sucks. She gives one killer blowjob, and she usually has him shooting off into her mouth in minutes. This is perfect foreplay because it's always his second load that takes enough time for her to have a decent enough orgasm courtesy of his cock inside her. So her efforts on his dick are as much for her as they are for him. But then, just as he settles into her licking and prepares mentally for her taking his dick into her mouth, she stops and turns on all fours, walking, no crawling out of the cubicle. She looks like a jaguar or a panther.

Evan isn't letting her get away so easily. He follows her out of the cubicle and is greeted immediately with the smell of vanilla. His eyes fall on the bubble bath and he shakes his head. Evan hates baths. The bath is somewhat sunken but has an above-the-ground rim that Rachel can lean over, raising her ass in an enticing attempt at an invitation. His cock points straight ahead of him, solid enough for it to protrude out of his foreskin. He wants it to be dealt with; something he thought would happen in the shower. After all, he hadn't even thought of sex until Rachel came in and dangled promises of it in front of him. So now he wants sex...*badly!*

He reaches her and runs his cock between her ass cheeks. The heat he finds there draws him in. Rachel allows him a moment between her perfect cheeks and then stands up straight. She pushes back against him, rubs against his cock, and then steps away and into the bath. Evan screams, a perk of the size of their home and the fact that they live all by themselves, domestic helpers intruding but once a week. His eyes look to where his towel waits, warming on the heated rail.

He wants to be dry and dressed and reading the Sunday papers with a cup of coffee in the sunroom. But looking down at the massive erection pointing in the direction of the bubbles, he knows he's going to have to suffer the torture of bubbles and bath if he is to find the hot pussy he knows lies beneath.

It takes longer than it should, but Evan is eventually in the water, settling down in front of his wife. Rachel's hands are moving up and down his legs under the water instantly. Then her fingers are all on his cock again. Evan settles back, lifts his legs out to either side of the bath, his head on the carved rest behind him. In the warm water, Rachel's fingers are slippery, sliding around on Evan's cock, and all over the surface of his huge balls. His eyes are closed, the fact that he's actually reclining in the tub suddenly acceptable. Rachel move over and onto him, one hand on the outer rim of the bath, the other dancing over Evan's cock and sac. She bites into her man's neck, and then into his bottom lip. Evan and Rachel kiss as though they've never tasted each other before.

Thanks to the size of their tub, a luxurious Turkish design, Rachel straddles her athletic lover, wasting no time working his cock into her cunt. The heat inside her is intense, the cock filling her familiar, but deeply satisfying. She knows this cock; *she loves this cock!* With no resistance from the man under her, she eases her cunt over his dick, completely. Rachel swallows Evan's cock as he swallows her tongue. She squeezes the excess moisture from his cock using her powerful pussy and Evan is unable to keep his legs in their relaxed position. Immediately they shoot out straight and then are in the bath pushing against the marble. He also pushes himself up into Rachel, who lifts almost completely out of the water.

With both of them back in the water, Evan's cock is again completely inside Rachel. Their lips are locked in as much heat as they exchange between them under the water. The bubbles, somewhat cooler, send little tremors through the parts of both of them that are in contact with the white. The contrast expands Evan's cock while at the same time contracting Rachel's pussy.

They rise and fall in seamless unison in the water, almost as though they are in a small boat on a vast ocean. The motion lulls them both into fluid fucking so that they forget momentarily where they are. Rachel pulls Evan's tongue into her mouth now and while riding his cock, sucks as much moisture from his mouth as his tongue can deliver. A few final squeezes of her pussy and his mouth is dry, his cock only starting to drip.

It takes no effort to slide in the bath so that Rachel is underneath him. What had started out as her show is now his. She got him into the bath, which itself is a great feat. But her mouth on his cock earlier got him in *fast-fuck/fast-blow* mode and so now, before he can adequately take care of her, he needs to take care of himself. The beauty of being married is that you learn how to read your partner. Rachel brings her legs to her chest and hooks her feet in the carved iron handles on the sides of the bath. She pushes down on the wrought iron and as such pushes her pussy onto her husband's cock. Evan counter pushes, creating incredible drag, pleasing both cock and cunt absolutely.

He grabs the bath in a white-knuckled grip to either side of Rachel's head. His legs are practically straight out behind him as he fucks her hard. His leverage comes from the soles of his feet digging into the marble behind him, helping him to counter the slipperiness of the environment in which he finds himself. He pushes completely into her, digging in hard as he pushes against the bath. Rachel unhooks her feet, needing some relief from the pounding. She knows it won't be too long, this first round. So she takes it in her signature stride, Evan absent except for his cock. A loud scream, and the immediate feeling of warmth in her cunt and belly, and Evan slumps onto her, satisfied.

It's her turn to be satisfied now, and she has no doubt of this. Rachel pulls the plug with her toe, and the water draining quickly. The bath is now half filled with bubbles, thick and luxurious.

Another slip and Evan is on his back. Rachel scoops the bubbles from off of his cock. As much soap off as possible, her tongue is again on the tip of his dick, seconds before her mouth swallows the entire shaft. Sucking on Evan's cock is another of her favorite things. She is thrilled as his hard cock moves around in her mouth, lifting her ass high behind her. Evan reaches over and flattens the white peaks on her ass. He pulls her olive ass apart and lets his long fingers find her hole. As he enters her with a thick fingertip, she goes down completely on his cock.

His cock rock hard, Rachel is off it and facing the opposite direction, her hands on the bath's edge, and her knees in the marble. Evan gets on his knees too, moving in behind her. Being tall, having a long dick, and fingers as lanky as serpents', and as thick, Evan can treat his wife to more of her favorites. He sends his cock into her pussy, leaning back slightly so that he can send a soapy finger into her ass. Filling her ass and her cunt, Evan hits both holes hard. Rachel braces herself against the bath and pushes into him, wanting all of him. He gives her everything she wants. Digging into her holes he gets her screaming in ecstasy immediately. He fucks her with determined focus, getting the fingers in her ass to three while her cunt takes beautiful pressure from his cock as it digs into her and pushes up inside her because of his leaning.

It takes longer for Rachel to cum, and by the time she flows from her vagina they've already been at it for an hour. Evan has a massive second orgasm. He stays inside her as he eases down onto his back. Rachel's back on his chest. He lifts her up so that his cock slips from her cunt.

Easing her back down, his cock shoots into her ass. Moving her gently up and down, he brings himself to a third orgasm, doing the same for Rachel as all his fingers attack her cunt. The plug is replaced and they relax into each other as the bath fills again and they clean themselves up in preparation for what now looks to be a full day of fucking.

CHAPTER 63

THE CAR WASH!

THE CYCLE SAID TWENTY MINUTES. As the car moves into the slot, under the massive jet-spray and brushes, Theo turns the music up a little, mouthing *twenty minutes* to his wife. She gives him a *don't you dare* stare. But no sooner is the back of the car covered in soap and Theo reclines her seat. She knows that it's pointless fighting him. *She doesn't want to!* Just the *thought* of him inside her moistens her pussy from deep within.

Theo is glad they both wore shorts. His fingers make quick work of their buttons. The zippers give way easily and in seconds he holds Savannah's shorts in his hand. A second later he is chewing on her G-string, pulling his own shorts and underwear to his ankles and then off completely. She laughs hysterically at his madness. It is moments like this that remind her why she fell in love with him in the first place. He reclines his own chair and grips his cock at the base, whipping it from side to side.

Savannah descends on the fat, fleshy muscle as though *she* had initiated this event. She enjoys getting Theo into her mouth soft. The taste of his cock, the feel of it filling her mouth warms her pussy, always and without fail. She loves it as his shaft responds to her tongue and thickens, lengthening towards the back of her mouth without forcing itself into her throat. Because of its good behavior, it is very seldom that she doesn't extend it an invitation deep into her mouth.

Even now already the massive head blocks her airway so that the only passage for oxygen in her nose. Theo is rock hard.

He encourages his wife onto his face. This is managed without moving her mouth from its position on his dick. He parts her cunt-lips with his fingers, wide enough for his own lips to drop a few kisses on the inside of her vagina. He follows these kisses up with a few licks, and then some more kisses before his tongue starts to dance in and out of her pussy. Theo digs into her with his index finger, sending it into her cunt along with his tongue. Then his left index joins his right index, the tongue dead-center. Savannah drops a flow on the thick pink tongue in response to this. Hungrily, Theo parts her pussy further so that he can reach in deeper for more juice. His quest is met with enough fluid to quench his thirst, temporarily.

There is a strange vibrating sensation, the whole car buzzing gently with all the movement against it from the outside. This vibration moves through both of them and adds to the sensations transmitted to their genitals. Their arousal peaks. Theo sucks harder on Savannah's cunt in response to the tremors being transmitted to his dick. Savannah sucks harder on his cock, taking more of it into her mouth the more intense her own arousal. They both drip slightly into each other's mouths as they start to lean towards orgasm.

Theo lifts Savannah off his mouth, slightly. He *needs* to see her pussy. The view is magnificent! He takes every finger on his right hand and parts her punani to the right. He sends his left index into her *slowly*; the sight that greets him is the inside of her cunt as it folds inwards in the direction of his finger. Raising his head slightly, he is able to give her clit a few good licks. She moans over his cock as he digs repeatedly into her, the licking becoming digging occasionally and then becoming licking again.

When he pulls his finger from her pussy it draws white love juice with it. Theo enjoys the sight so much that his extraction of his finger is slower even than his insertion was. The pussy above him sweats such thick drops onto his face that he stretches his tongue to find them. The taste of his wife hardens his cock in her mouth so that he thrusts into her as she sucks down on him, drawing a few drops from his shaft as well. A sudden jolt of the vehicle reminds them that they are not at home and that the cycle has progressed. Their time on the belt is almost up, and the vehicle now in the rinse part of the cycle!

A few more insertions of his finger and Theo lifts Savannah off him. She's face down on the passenger seat again, legs parted in preparation for what she knows is coming. There's less than fifteen minutes for them to finish what they've started and so they up the ante. Savannah raises her ass high enough for her pussy to be visible from Theo's seat once her legs part just a little bit more. Theo is immediately on it. His cock is inside her quickly, his weight pushing his dick into her far, and fast. His thick dick has her part her legs a little more and grab onto the seat's headrest, his cock's entry facilitated further. She all but hugs the seat now as Theo fills her beautifully.

His cock doesn't move in and out of her. It moves

around inside her instead, the brushes spinning on the glass panels of the car inspiring this motion. He stirs Savannah's now sweaty, slippery pussy almost severely, Savannah enjoying the fact that she can make a considerable amount of noise without worrying too much that anybody outside of the car can hear her. Round and round Theo moves inside her, going all the way down and then wide, circling her depths.

She squeezes as hard onto the chair as her pussy does on her husband's cock and he strains against her pressure, enjoying it thoroughly. He mixes things up in her cunt so completely that she has no need to do anything else but take it!

The thing about fucking her from the back like this is that he can get all the way inside her without too much strain on her pussy. He can ram as hard as he likes, as hard as he needs to, and get as far into her as his dick desires. But he loves kissing her too, and feeling her breasts against his chest. So he gives a few more deep thrusts and then lifts himself out of her. Theo turns Savannah over so that she is on her back, her cunt visible, wet. He kisses her and then sucks her thick nipples while sending two fingers into her pussy and drawing circles inside it repeatedly.

She lifts her cunt up into his hand and his fingers are deep inside her. They both give her cunt a satisfied stare.

His lips don't move from hers as he removes his fingers and positions himself on top of her. His cock slides into her as she sucks his tongue into her mouth. The sound on the outside of the vehicle changes, and for a moment they both lookup. The car is being polished now. They need not be done in less than five minutes or risk a very embarrassing scenario. Theo moves deep into her, his hand sliding between them so that his fingers can find her clit. He rams into her deep and hard while gently, then roughly playing with her clit. The multiple sensations pull her climax from her quickly and she starts to beat a mean rhythm over the cock moving around inside her.

Savannah's clit leads the procession. It becomes the nerve center of her climax and her entire vagina sends every single one of its nerve endings to congregate there for a mass congress, the tabled agenda being an epic orgasm. The chairman of this conference is undeniably Theo's throbbing torpedo, making its power and presence obvious. It very quickly carries the meeting to a signature finish and Savannah has every tip of every finger on both her hands digging into her husband's biceps. Her climax syncs with the tremors coming through them from outside the vehicle as the last of the buffers work over the vehicle. She doesn't move, knowing that any sudden change would only further delay Theo's eruption.

He places his head next to hers and makes a conscious effort to ignore everything outside of the vehicle. The added pressure just won't do the rushed job needed now any good. His wife has the hottest, juiciest, tightest pussy and so it seems a waste to rush through it. But the situation demands it, and at least he's satisfied her. So the half orgasm he knows is all he's going to get under the circumstance is okay. He starts to make a determined dash for this semi-climax.

Savannah's only involvement now are her arms wrapped tightly around her husband's neck as he thrusts his dick in and out of her.

The heat between her thighs that transmits through his massive sack is enough to shoot the required impetus through his shaft for him to blow. Almost prematurely, given the circumstance, he starts to fill Savannah with substantial amounts of semen. He has such a massive load, the bulk thick and hot, that she starts to move against his cock now as he finalizes his climax. He whimpers silently into her neck as he sends himself into her over and over, but a little slower the emptier his sack. Eventually, he just hangs around inside her as she uses her cunt to absorb the last of his load. They are about as satisfied as the time and location would have allowed even on a good day.

Even after withdrawing his cock from her he hovers over her for a minute, looking around the vehicle as the brushes rotate in every direction at once against the glass. She squeezes her cunt tight, the feeling that its contents will rush out an almost uncomfortable one given the context. They share a final kiss on the lips before Theo runs a sweaty brow over his wife's neck. He takes her nipples between his lips just as the brushes start to slow down. Sucking on them as long as he can he dismounts, finding his own seat with the bulk of his body. His eyes hit the roof of the car as he finally lands completely on the seat, and then they find Savannah, whose eyes are glued to her mischievous man. Theo gives his flaccid cock a few congratulatory strokes before taking his wife's hand in his own.

Both of them are flat on their backs as the sun shines into their spotless windshield. They work their pants up, minus their underwear, and then work the seats back into the upright position before attending to zippers and buttons. Theo had already rolled down his window before realizing that he isn't wearing his T-shirt. Savannah winds her window down and makes a dry comment about the heat just as the attendant leans in to get a signature and payment. They opt *out* of the full valet, unsure where exactly their underwear is at the moment, and both of their crotches needing a valet of their own. The drive home is filled with a pleasant fondling that results in both of them having a second orgasm by the time the car is parked outside their building. A series of further orgasms follow once the couple is in the privacy of their home...

CHAPTER 64

THE THINGS YOU CAN DO WITH COOL WHIP

LISA AND MARK were in a little bit of a rut. They had been married for twelve years. Mark was a contractor, which was a fancy way of saying that he was not around that much. Lisa had become accustomed to her husband being absent husband and had become accustomed to taking care of her own needs. Lisa was determined that this weekend she was going to get the issue addressed in one manner or another. Lisa had discovered that with Mark being gone, she was not as dependent on him as she thought that she was. Lisa was determined that if this weekend did not go the way that she had planned it would, that she was going to file for divorce and get on with her life. This was a very drastic step to take, but she needed to ensure that she was going to be happy. Lisa had made arrangements for them to spend a weekend at a couple's retreat. It was a new alternative method place that she saw online. She figured that they needed a vacation and this would be a great chance for them to experiment and let loose. The main approach to the place was a self-discovery approach.

Couples were allowed and even encouraged to let their sexual journey go wherever it took them.

Mark was not into it at first. He wanted to know what this place could offer that they could not just do at home where he would be able to deal with a client if an issue arose. Lisa couldn't believe that she was hearing her husband say this; he was openly admitting that his clients were more important than his own wife. Lisa had a feeling that after this weekend she was going to be going to her attorney to file divorce papers. Mark finally agreed to come along with Lisa in an attempt to save their marriage. They made their way to the retreat with Mark checking his email every five seconds.

"Mark, this is supposed to be about us. We need to detach ourselves from the world that has allowed us to be in the position that we are in at the moment. I arranged for this weekend as one last way to save our relationship. I have made the decision that if we are not able to get things worked out, that I am ready to file for divorce and move on. I don't want to do that, but I have to look out for me and my needs. I know that you can understand as you are good, you have your career and that is to be commended, I have nothing except you, and here lately that has become less reliable."

Mark took the threat of divorce seriously. Mark put the smartphone away and did not bring it out again the rest of the way up there. Once at the retreat, they were shown to their room. It was a standard hotel room except it had various items that could be used in the course of sexual play. The room had a mini fridge that was stocked with various syrups and whipped creams. Lisa looked around and was in awe of all of the various things that were included in the room. Mark took a liking to one of the sets of handcuffs that were in the room. Lisa went into the bathroom and changed into one of her outfits that she had brought along. She did not want to waste a minute of their time. Lisa made the decision to come out naked. She grabbed the whipped cream on the way to the bed and was looking to use it quickly. She took and covered the entire length of Mark's cock with the whipped cream until it was a nice white fuck stick. Lisa then lay on the bed and had him straddle her to where she could lay there and nurse on his cock. This was going to be the first act of a long list that Lisa was planning on performing over the course of the next few days. Mark began to rock back and forth. Lisa continued to go in and out up and down any motion that was bringing him an immense amount of pleasure. Mark told Lisa that he did not want to shoot inside her mouth as he had a better idea. He took the whipped cream and placed a glob onto her nipples. He then began to masturbate his cock using the wetness that began to drip from the cunt of Lisa, the next actions were what surprised Lisa, and Mark finally shot and placed the load on the tits of his wife.

The next couple of requests were a little out of the ordinary for Mark. He had Lisa lick the whipped topping and cum off of her tits while he jerked on his cock again. Lisa did as she was asked and did not hesitate as she took this as a sign that things might be on the road to recovery. This was a scene that was repeated a number of times over the course of the weekend. Mark and Lisa took turns in performing some of the wildest and most erotic sex that they had ever had. Even when they first married, the sex was not this good. Lisa had found a way to make the marriage work.

CHAPTER 65

THE SECRET ADMIRER

VANESSA CLICKED AWAY on the keyboard of her computer, engrossed in the screen before her. She had a deadline for a writing assignment and could not afford to lose focus for anything. She was completely absorbed in her task.

The bedroom was dim with almost no light finding its way through the slats of the tightly closed blinds. She was reclined against the headboard of her unmade bed, amidst a jumble of blue sheets and pillows. The monotonous clicks of her typing were punctuated only by the occasional passing late-night car in the road outside her window.

Vanessa's unkempt blonde hair had been pulled loosely into a lopsided bun atop her head, and her long, toned legs stretched out uncovered before her. She lived alone, so had little regard for her appearance on a night like this.

The bedroom door creaked a little. The clicking stopped, Vanessa's fingers hovering expectantly just over the computer's keys.

"Hello? Someone there?" she called out.

She slapped her laptop closed, and her breasts fell free

from her unbuttoned shirt. She pulled the shirt's sides together to cover them.

"Who's there?" she asked the door with slightly less confidence than before.

Vanessa stood up from the bed. Her lazy-day shirt barely covered her bottom, showing the purple lace thong and firm, round cheeks underneath.

Vanessa looked around her immediate area for something to use as a weapon if the need arose. The lamp perhaps? Her hands fumbled, breaking the silence by knocking the lampshade askew against the wall.

"Who are you?" she repeated her fear mounting.

As Vanessa grabbed onto the neck of her bedside lamp, poised to hurl it, the door pushed open all the way and a young man nearly exploded into the room.

"Vanessa!" he exclaimed, turning toward the bed where she cowered.

A lungful of air she had been holding in burst forth from her pale lips. She pried her fingers off the lamp as the color returned to her face.

"Dylan, what are you doing?" Vanessa demanded. "I almost attacked you! Why are you in my house?" Her fear began to morph into anger.

Dylan blinked his emerald green eyes, mouth opening, and closing without words. His hair seemed to stand on end from some inner electricity.

Vanessa began quickly buttoning her loose shirt. Dylan had been a close friend for years, but he had never seen her in this state of undress. His eyes seemed to undress her as quickly as she could button her shirt back up.

As she buttoned the third button, Dylan swept across the room toward her in one fluid motion, his eyes glowing. He grabbed the shirt and ripped it off of her body, exposing her ample round breasts and lace thong. Buttons rolled across the floor.

"Dylan!" Vanessa gasped. Her hands instinctively moved to cover her pink nipples, but Dylan swatted her hands away and wrapped an arm tightly around her waist.

Vanessa's breath caught in her throat and her heart raced. His strong hands holding her against him felt surprisingly incredible.

"Vanessa, I have wanted you for so long. This is the only way I know to tell you that."

He pressed his lips, red from the blood coursing hotly through him, against hers. Vanessa melted into the moment, her anger dissipating into unexpected passion as their tongues began exploring one another. Their heavy breathing was the only sound.

Dylan pulled back from the kiss and tossed Vanessa aside onto the messy bed. Her breasts bounced with the impact.

Pulling his shirt over his head to reveal a tight muscular build, Dylan knelt on the bed. Vanessa bit her lush pink lower lip, admiring Dylan's physique. Sweat droplets ran down his chest, finding pathways through the patch of light curly hair.

Leaning down to completely envelope Vanessa in his presence, Dylan kissed her lightly on her neck and chest. He breathed lightly across her nipples, and they stood erect from the sensation. He smiled up at her mischievously, knowing that his plan to get her in a position she couldn't turn down had been a success.

Vanessa's rich chocolate eyes locked onto Dylan's fierce green ones. She reached out and grabbed the warm bulge in his jeans, massaging and rubbing firmly without losing eye contact.

Her sloppy bun fell free, and her long blonde hair cascaded over her shoulders and breasts.

Dylan kissed her deeply, making her toes curl as he pressed down on top of her. Vanessa began unbuttoning his pants, but he pushed her hand away, teasing her. She gasped for air between kisses, overwhelmed by the sexual ferocity she had never known he had.

Vanessa arched her back as Dylan's hands ran deftly down her sides and over her breasts.

He pinched her nipples just enough to make her squeal softly and smiled at the little shivers of pleasure he could sense coming over her in waves.

"Dylan, I..."

"Shhh." He cut her off. "Not now."

Dylan slid a finger under the elastic waist of her purple thong and popped it against her
skin.

"I don't want you to be able to say a word," he whispered into her belly button. The hairs
on her neck stood. She had never had someone take such control of her desires.

Dylan pushed Vanessa back to a lying position and moved down toward her long, graceful legs. Spreading her soft thighs apart, he moved the thong to one side of her silky pussy and moved his face closer to the warm wetness. He looked up at her over the landscape of her quivering stomach and breasts and smiled, melting her deeper into the bedsheets.

Vanessa's eyes rolled back and her back arched uncontrollably as Dylan began to lick her inner thighs lightly, moving closer and closer to her lips with each subsequent lick. Finally he made it all the way there and began tickling it with rapid licks like a lizard.

She moaned softly. No one had ever made her moan out loud. What had she been missing out on all this time? All she could see was the ceiling of her bedroom and her hands moving through Dylan's hair as his head bobbed up and down between her legs.

Just when the sensations of pleasure became almost overwhelming, Dylan stopped and moved a little farther down Vanessa's body. She wriggled as she recomposed herself during the brief relief from ecstasy.

Dylan grabbed her foot and rubbed the sole expertly. Vanessa could not believe how amazing it felt to have her feet stimulated as her clit ached and throbbed with the desire to feel more. He put his mouth on one of her toes and sucked softly, then moved to the next.

Vanessa sighed deeply as Dylan ran his warm, wet tongue from the tip of her toe, down the back of her calf, through the sensitive crease behind her knee, and back to the wet center of her torso that he had left anticipating more. He began again to lick in slow, deliberate motions that made Vanessa's pelvis lift and tilt from side to side.

Vanessa grabbed at her own hair and pulled as Dylan brought her quickly to the brink of satisfaction. She twisted away, then closer, moving her hips in a rhythm that matched that of his tongue.

Just as Vanessa was about to plummet over the edge of a powerful orgasm, Dylan shoved two of his large fingers deep inside her, pulsing in and out and intuitively pressing on the G spot she never knew she had.

Shivers of pure energy coursed through Vanessa from the crown of her head all the way to her stiffened toes. Every vein in her body seemed to pulse with it. She had no idea if her eyes were open or closed because all she could see was brilliant stars.

As she regained her vision, Vanessa realized she was alone on the bed and the touch of a man had subsided. Dylan was standing next to the bed, running a hand through his tousled hair. He had just finished pulling his shirt back onto his sweating torso and glanced in the mirror that hung over her dresser.

"Dylan, you..."

"Shhh," he interrupted, turning toward her with his piercing green gaze. "Next time I'll take what I want. Tonight was just for you."

Dylan walked out the door.

Vanessa was still catching her breath. She could not believe what had just transpired.

She doubted their friendship could ever be the same after that experience.

Vanessa let her head drop back over the edge of the bed and stared at the upside-down wall, longing for him to walk back through her bedroom door.

CHAPTER 66

THINGS THAT HAPPEN IN A PRIUS (NEWLYWEDS)

GLORIA AND FRANK were still newlyweds. The newness of their marriage had not worn off yet. All of their friends told them that the sensation would eventually end. The two newlyweds felt that as long as things remained interesting that they could never get tired of being married.

Gloria and Frank had been invited to another one of their friends' weddings and while neither one of them wanted to go, they felt that not going was not an option. Gloria suggested that they find a way to not be bored at the wedding. Frank tried to make a joke about having sex in the middle of the wedding but Gloria was not amused. The day came for the wedding and they piled into their Prius and headed to the event that they both knew was not going to last as both of these people were not right for each other. Gloria felt that this was a case of two people getting married just for the fact that they wanted to have sex on a regular basis. Frank thought it had to do with the fact that the man was a well-off doctor and that the woman was looking for a sugar daddy that would take care of her while she sat at home all day long.

Frank and Gloria got to the wedding almost an hour earlier than they had expected. They had a great parking spot so leaving to go somewhere was out of the question. Gloria suggested that they could pass the time by having sex in the car. Frank had a puzzled look on his face, as he had never even thought about this. He only one time had any kind of experience like this. Frank was all for it. Frank pushed his seat back as far as it would go and Gloria leaned over and unzipped his pants. Taking his prick out of his boxers, Gloria began to suck. Frank had a tendency to produce a lot of precum so when Gloria began to suck him; he began to pour precum out of his shaft. Gloria was used to this and just licked it all up as best as she could. Gloria went a little farther down on his shaft. While she did this, Frank took the time to occupy his hands by playing with her nipples. Gloria had a ring in one of her nipples and Frank loved to tug on it and get her worked up. The pink panties that she was wearing had a wet spot that was forming where her cunt was flowing like a river. The sight of seeing her dripping wet got Frank even more worked up.

Frank took his right hand and moved into a position that he was able to reach more of Gloria. He wanted to give her the one thing that she loved more than anything; a nice slow finger fuck. Gloria got off more with a finger fuck than any other. Frank wanted to give Gloria a second surprise that she had never had. , he wanted to take his fingers and let Gloria taste her own juices. He withdrew his fingers and brought them up to Gloria's mouth for her to taste her own essence. Gloria had never done this and had never even tasted another woman.

"Frank I want you to fuck me in the car, I want you to mount on top of me and to take that rigid cock of yours and to pound me like a prisoner on a three-day pass. I want you to fuck me hard and to make me understand that I am yours and I want to service you."

Frank mounted up onto Gloria and took his time to get into the right position. His cock was moving up and down and was teasing her cunt that it was going to slide in and fill her hole up. Gloria undid the top of her dress and allowed her tits to fall free from her dress and bra. Frank loved the appearance of his wife's tits. They were the perfect shade of white with a hint of darkness where she had been careful as to tan them just enough. Her milk chocolate areolas gave a sharp contrast and her pink nipples looked new and tender. Most times when her top was off, Gloria's nipples were standing up looking for attention. Frank loved to suck on them and to give them a gentle bite from time to time.

Frank finally found a place to park his cock and slid in and out of the now quivering cunt. Frank knew that at this point it was just a matter of time before he was going to be coming inside of her. Gloria was at her peak of horniness and was not going to settle for anything less than a heart-pounding mind-blowing screw. Frank began to pound Gloria harder as she lay there and barked at him to fuck her deep and hard. Frank was getting ready to give is newlywed wife yet another gift when she told him to pull out and to spray her tits. Frank withdrew and pointed his firehouse at his wife's perky flesh mounds and let loose. The streams of cum came fast and plentiful. Gloria had jizz covering all of her tits and it was even dripping down her side as she lay there and let Frank finish up with what he was doing. Frank went and fell back into the driver's seat. It was then that he noticed the crowd of people that had gathered to watch the show that these two had just put on. Gloria and Frank had a feeling that the talk of today was not going to be how well the bride was or how lovely of a couple that the two were. It was going to be the show that Gloria and Frank had put on for all in attendance.

CHAPTER 67

TIE ME UP TIE ME DOWN

SAMANTHA AND RODGER had been dating since the early days of their High School years. These two were destined to be married. They worked hard to plan the wedding and had placed a considerable amount of effort into the honeymoon. Both of them had taken a vow that they would not have sex until they were married; they wanted the event to be special and to have real meaning. Rodger wanted to be with Samantha. He had dreamed of the day when he finally got to get inside her tight unbroken hole. It was so important that he had even planned a special role-play situation out to make it even more interesting for them. This was going to be the perfect night. All of this had been planned by him and no one else.

The wedding was perfect. There was not a flaw to be seen. The reception was nearly perfect as well. The only real blemish was that of Samantha's drunk father gave a speech that half the people could not understand.

. . .

When all of the guests had left and the final arrangements had been made, Rodger and Samantha got on board a plane and headed to Jamaica. This was the best part of the whole thing in Rodger's eyes, not because he could finally dive into Samantha's love box, but because this was an opportunity to show his new wife that he too was able to plan things and to surprise her. What Rodger had planned, he was certain no one else had ever thought of.

Samantha and Rodger got checked into their room. Sam wanted to grab a hot shower and just relax for a while. It had been a crazy last few weeks and the wedding was almost as insane. Rodger thought that since Samantha was sleeping; it was a great time to put the first part of his plan into action.

Rodger took some ropes and tied Samantha up to the bed. Rodger was planning that when Samantha woke up she was going to be fighting trying to get free from the ropes. This was the first part of the plan. Samantha had always said that she had a fantasy of being in a sexual encounter with a superhero. Rodger had taken note of this and had bought a superhero costume for use between him and Samantha. Samantha was a huge Batman fan so he saw this as the perfect opportunity to use this as inspiration for his fantasy. Samantha woke up and discovered that she was tied up. At first, she was quite upset with this and was not the least bit happy. Then when Batman entered the room, she quickly calmed down and realized that this was part of her fantasy that she had told Rodger about.

Samantha was completely vulnerable; she was in nothing but a bra and a pair of panties. These were eventu-ally going to be ripped off of her and disposed of. Samantha tried to fight but she was not able to fend off the superhero that was sworn to protect people taking advantage of a helpless woman. Rodger came to the end of the bed and pulled off her panties and placed them up to his nose to get a deep breath of the essence that leaked from her. Rodger loved the scent of his wife and often would sneak around when Samantha was not around and sniff them to get his thrill. Samantha was begging to not have her bra removed. Rodger came over, cut the garment away from her, and discarded it into the pile of clothes on the floor. Samantha was now completely naked and at his mercy. He went down on her wet cunt and teased her. This was sending chills up her spine as her dream was finally coming true in front of her eyes. She was going to be ravished by a superhero. This also meant that if he came inside of her without a rubber that she was going to be carrying the baby of a superhero. The thought of this got her nipples all erect and ready. She was overtaken by an immense amount of passion that was going through her body. Rodger could tell that this was the first time that his wife had experienced this. He had seen this done on pornos before and had a decent idea as to how this was done. He was apparently doing it right as Samantha began to squirm and toss about on the bed.

"Oh gods yes deeper, get that tongue deep into me..." Rodger was amazed at the fact that the woman that he knew to be quiet and meek was this unleashed animal in the bedroom. Rodger maintained what he was doing. Rodger wanted to stop this before his wife became completely unglued. Rodger moved into position and then began the slow and rhythmic motions of screwing his wife deep into her hole.

This was the one thing that she was eager to have happen and Rodger knew that this was going to have her climbing the walls. The experience was well more than what he had expected. Samantha was climbing the walls a lot more intensely than what he had even thought she would and when the entire thing was over, Samantha sat there looking at her husband with a smile from ear to ear. She knew then and there that she had made the right choice and she also knew that the Batman costume was going to get a lot more use over the course of their relationship. She dreamed of the day that she and Rodger are celebrating their 50th wedding anniversary. She hoped that Rodger would still be able to fit into it.

It was well worth the wait. Her first time was as magical as she had hoped and then some. She also learned that her husband was excellent at the art of making plans and keeping her or anyone from knowing the. She never knew a thing or even suspected something was going on.

CHAPTER 68

TOUCH IS A MOVE

THE SOUND IS unfamiliar and so he is immediately awake. Ron is a firefighter and so it is unbelievable to him that he wakes up to find that he is cuffed to his bed. He usually has super senses and is immediately awake at the sound of the cracking whip. He catches the unmistakable outline of his wife in the shadows as she cracks the whip on the wooden floor. Again and again, the whip hits the wood until Ron is fully awake, his arms cuffed to the bed above his head, his legs free, and his entire body naked.

There is no confusion about what Dana has in mind as she approaches her husband on the bed. The catsuit has been altered so that her breasts are on the outside of the otherwise leather suit. Perfect circles form the windows through which her perfect breasts and their attached nipples protrude. Her clit is clearly visible through a purposely built slit between her legs. There is also easy access through this same window for her cunt to be accessed. The heels on her feet add ten inches to her height, and much to her husband's surprise, she is extremely comfortable in the stilettos, moving like a lioness towards him, whipping the air to either side of her.

Dana runs the soft leather of the whip over Ron's body. She whips his legs lightly so that his cock jerks in response. The strands land harder across his chest, but still his cock jerks excitedly. The excitement is visible on his face. He wants her badly. But he is willing to go through her torture because he knows that it can only end exceptionally well. Softer lashes fall across his cock and balls, burning lightly. He thrusts up towards the heavens, which is exactly where his dick seems to be headed, herded there by Dana's skill with the whip. She is in no hurry to get anywhere in partic-ular, the clock by the bed reading just after 4 AM.

The heel of her left stiletto is on his thigh. The point digs in as Dana runs the whip over his face and he wishes that he could reach for her cunt and dip his finger into it. He wishes he could get his head close enough to breathe it in, the scent of her pussy lightly gracing the general vicinity of his nose. Dana takes the handle of the whip and puts it in her mouth after running it along her lips. She moves the rubber deeper and deeper into her mouth, mimicking a blowjob so that Ron is begging her to touch his dick. She removes the handle slowly and then runs the strands over his cock and balls again, doing very little to placate his penis. Ron thrusts wildly at the air, groaning loudly in agonizing frustration.

Moving closer to Ron's face with her pussy, she holds the handle against her exposed cunt. While he watches, she inserts it into her cunt slowly, ensuring that nothing about the penetration is hidden from her bound husband. Six inches vanish inside her vagina. She moves in even closer to him, lifting her one leg over him so that her pussy is directly above his face. The whip is held in place by the handle lodged in her pussy. She drops her cunt low and Ron takes the whip's leather between his teeth and pulls on it gently. He watches excitedly as the handle makes a slow exit from his wife. Dana takes the handle in hand and runs it under his nose so that gets a whiff of her cunt.

She places the base of the handle between his teeth and sets her stilettos down on either side of him so that her pussy now hangs directly above him. He bites down hard as he reads the situation, Dana bringing her cunt towards his mouth. She sits directly on the handle and again it is gone up deep inside her snatch. With it inside her, she allows Ron a few licks of her inner thigh and also her clit. Then she is up, pulling the handle with her. Her hands on the base she fucks herself slowly with the thick rubber while Ron can but stare and salivate. The rubber handle is thick, black, and ribbed, and Dana appears to be deriving the most immense pleasure from it. Ron wants nothing but to be the one giving her this pleasure.

Ron is finally put out of his misery when Dana turns her ass to him and bends over his body. She moves back so that he can again grab the whip between his teeth. As he pulls on the leather she sinks down on his dick and wets it completely while lodging it in her mouth. She sucks on it while he slowly removes the handle from her pussy. The rubber is no match for his own cock but the thought that anything but he is satisfying Dana's pussy is too much for the virile firefighter. He lets the whip drop to the bed, then the floor, and blows sharply onto her cunt from the back. Dana moves slightly off his cock and plants her pussy in his mouth so that he can get another preview. She tastes every bit as good in his mouth as she feels on his cock.

His preview doesn't last long. Dana is off him and holding the whip again in a bit. She coils it around his neck and then releases his right hand from its cuff. His large grip is on her thigh quickly and he pulls her to him. She pulls on the coil and chokes him gently into submission. She is on the bed, on her back, with her heels running over his body. She positions herself so that she is able to pull him to her with the whip and push him off her with her heels. She feeds him the ten inches and Ron instinctively licks the red points. This arouses her so much that she pulls him to her and feeds him her punani. He laps it up hungrily. Dana fights to push him off but can't bring herself to because Ron is just so fucking good at eating out her cunt.

She underestimates his desire for her, and Ron, who is unable to revert back into submission, pushes her legs wide open and keeps the heels away from him. He sucks hard on her vagina even when she pulls on the whip and cuts off his air supply. He makes a quick adjustment of the leather around his neck and is inside her cunt with his tongue again. Biting into her clit he brings it to full bloom and then sends two of his right fingers into her. He fucks her with his thick fingers while licking her pussy, and watches as her cunt starts to cry tears of joy. There is no escaping her readiness to be fucked by him now, or his desire to fuck the shit out of her.

Ron pulls his fingers out of her and uses the same hand, his only free hand, to pull her pussy into range of his cock. His thick dick has been dripping for a while now and is in need of the inside of his wife. Dana doesn't resist the reversal of roles and is underneath her husband willingly. Ron gives her a *thanks for the effort* look and drives every last inch of his Italian cock into her. She takes it, all of it, into her in one move. Dana relinquishes control of the whip and it just hangs around Ron's neck now as he starts to fuck her. Her hands are in the sheets, pulling on the linen, taking each thrust completely.

It's clear that the show is now Ron's. He gets her to hand over the key and he frees his left hand. He takes hold of the heels of her shoes, the left in his left, the right in his right. He pushes her legs apart and back and descends into her cunt with his dick. With her pussy pushed up, his cock falls all the way down inside it. Thanks to the leverage provided by the stilettos her cunt squeezes closed so that Ron's cock creates incredible friction inside it. He pushes her legs apart and pulls them together to relieve her of the drag occasionally but her vagina is thoroughly enjoying this rigorous rinsing.

He lets her legs drop to the bed and goes for her mouth. He kisses her while driving his dick into her in a deep frenzy. There is no escaping his cock and it feels now like she is the one cuffed to the bed. The stilettos rest on Ron's back as she wraps her legs around him, the beginnings of an orgasm stirring inside her. Ron stops thrusting and exits her so that he can suck on her breasts. It is her turn to be frustrated. Generously though he digs his fingers into her pussy while licking her nipples. He sucks harder on her breasts the more audible her reactions. So Dana practically screams at his touch. The fingers in her fanny also go deeper.

She starts to blow, his fingers wet and sticky inside her vagina as it tightens and tenses. He reinserts his cock and thrusts hard. He fucks her furiously so that her orgasm is massive. She screams, grabbing everything but her husband as she wants him to stay focused on fucking her. He pulls every last drop of her climax out of her with nothing but his dick. He rams her in broad strokes as his own climax rocks up. He blows his load inside her and still the fucking doesn't let up. He keeps fucking her to her second orgasm, his cock soft and then hard and then rock fucking solid. She pulls her knees up and lets him have her. He takes all of her, totally!

The catsuit doesn't last for the third round, and neither do the stilettos. Ron has Dana completely naked and under him soon after he shoots his second load. His third fucking is ferocious. He digs her pussy into a deep pit and pulls every atom of pleasure she hides inside it. It takes him two hours for solid pussy plundering for him to get a third load from her, and himself. They cum together and then embrace for the rest of the morning as it becomes clear to both of them that there just might be some novelty to the idea of playing dress up. Ron pulls the whip back to him and gives the handle a last look. He gives his cock a long stare and shakes his head, tapping Dana's pussy with his finger as if to confirm for it who the boss really is!

CHAPTER 69

"UP AGAINST THE WALL"

I HAVE BEEN DATING my fiancée for about a year now and I must say we always had the most incredible sex ever. I didn't think we needed to improve on it much, but still, I was always looking for ways to please my fiancée. If I kept him pleased now he'd never lose interest in me.

It seemed to me a lot of people these days were into fucking against the wall as they call it or I even have heard some couples talk about nailing the woman to the wall as a sexual thrilling kind of behavior. I thought it sounded pretty damn hot myself. I go wild at the mere thought of my man screwing me hard against the wall. The thought of him grabbing my leg and pulling it close to his body while his cock was hammering away at my pussy drove me absolutely insane. It was definitely at the top of my list as one of the hottest ways to make love that I could think of.

It was just animalistic enough to be hot yet sexy enough to be amazingly human. I knew that when my fiancée got home from work I was going to take him like never before. I was going to do things to him that he had only ever dreamed of. I intended on making him lust as vehemently for me as I for him and it would all take place up against the wall.

The thought of taking him in my mouth made me throb below. I so badly wanted to trace my fingers deep into my ache, but I held back. I wanted to be turned on as much as possible when he did get home. I finally heard my lover drive up into the driveway. I was completely nude. I didn't have time for lingerie to get in between our flesh tonight.

With a deep breathy sigh, I shuddered just thinking of the sex I was about to have with my fiancée. As he stepped inside the door his smoldering brown eyes met my sparkling blue ones. He whispered sexily in my ear "You are very wet. Have you been touching this pussy while daddy was working?" as he fingered my gushing cunt with two hot fingers.

"Mmmm yes I have been fingering the fuck out of this horny pussy baby waiting for you to come home and fuck me to the wall," I replied in a sexy voice. I whispered hot words of seduction in his ears knowing it would make him like steel in his zippered compartment. Without even looking down but looking him square in the eyes with my smoldering blue eyes, I yanked his manhood out of his jeans. It felt firm as a rock in my palms and within my grasp.

He relentlessly stared into my eyes as he pushed my body into the sheetrock so hard I thought it would leave my impression behind. My hands moved up and down his stiff heat and he groaned grabbing me by the neck forward and pulling me in for a deep, wet kiss. His hands roamed my hips and ass as he securely gripped my hot flesh and at the same time thrust his hard heat into my depths. His thumb rubbed and caressed my clit while he rhythmically pulled slowly out and then pushed inch by inch back inside my folds.

As his thumb pushed my button and his cock impaled

me he began backing me up towards the hallway. As we fucked our way to the hall we landed hard against the wall enclosed in the tight space. I could almost see the sexual energy run down the paint on the walls just as his cum ran down my legs after he banged me. The walls were penetrated by our musky sexual evidence.

As I stood horny as hell and dizzy against that wall he ducked down and dropped to his knees and he replaced his thumb with his hungry tongue as he flicked furiously away at my hardened clit tip.

"Yes, baby keep fucking me. Keep it up. Fuck me harder." I said with a raspy and needy voice.

As quickly as he dropped to his knees in pussy worship to eat my slippery slit, he stood back up and ran his cockhead tip across my throbbing clit head. I frantically clutched the closet door handle behind me to steady my balance from the fierce cocking I was getting against the molten wall. As my hand clutched the door knob my snapper clutched his rod and refused to let go not even a centimeter.

My fiancée looked like a bobbing flotation device on the lake as he came up to fuck me and went down to make my pussy his gourmet dinner. I groped his wavy hair and pushed his head deep into my groin. I stood up so having gravity on my side I took advantage of the leverage and worked my pussy on his face the way I desired.

He stood up again and grabbed the back of my hair wrapping it tightly around his hand and he kissed me hard. I tasted my own scent all over his mouth and the smell of me infiltrated the hallway. My fiancée turned me around and I was pressed into the wall my face plastered to the paint. He took my passionate pussy from behind and his hands were all over the hair on my girly bits, and he traced his fingers in circles up and down my tummy very seductively. He knew my tummy was a direct link to my inner depths and it added to my climax that was nearing closer at warp speed. Each trace of his fingertips sent gushes and waves of pleasure from my head to my curled toes.

In fact, I knew my orgasm wasn't far as I felt my body become tense and be engulfed with heated rapture. I felt the inside of my pelvis clench and then tease me by unclenching. It was just daring to lock into one long and excruciatingly intense contraction of orgasmic fire. His dick became rigid as if it might break in two inside my luscious folds.

I looked down and saw my clit angry rubbing through his cock hair and knew what was going to happen. He had no idea how drenched his cock and balls were about to become. I could feel it bubbling inside me and knew only a few more strokes of his twisting cock inside me and I would gush all over him.

His fingers dug into my ass and I knew he was getting close. I leaned forward and sucked his nipple hard, turning the tables on him. He groaned as his cock went rigid beyond description inside me. I could feel his head stiffening and could almost picture it turning bright red inside me. His ass slammed me against the wall with each violent thrust. His pounding was not only relentless but furious as his balls swayed beneath his hard cock slapping me in the ass.

He began to rise on his toes and I knew what was going to happen as if we had done it a thousand times. My lips quivered and then I had shocks of spasms as his first shot of thick hot cream drenched my insides. The gush was amazing as I looked down to see it bubbling against the shaft of his twitching cock.

. . .

I could hear it as the stream of cream coated his incredible cock with every demand I had dreamed of all wrapped up in his arms. His deep grunt turned into a growl as his cock pumped spurt after spurt of thick hot love juice into my drenched depths. My pussy was on fire. His cock felt like a branding iron inside me and from the feeling burning inside of me it was not going to go away.

All I could feel was my g-spot rubbing against the shaft of his cock as his thrusts slowed to a sensuous crawl. The feeling was the most erotic place my mind could imagine. The smell of our juices mixing was like nothing I could have ever imagined. Finally, I let my legs slip slowly to the floor and stood up, still weak in the knees. His cock was hanging lewdly down with strings of our pearly white cum dangling from it.

I knelt in front of him and took the length of his still swollen cock in my mouth and drew back on it sucking every drop of our cum down my throat. He twitched when my lips dragged across his cock rim. His hands went to my head and eased me standing up.

Taking my face gently in his hands his mouth closed upon mine. That kiss, the passion and the pleasure it brought me shall never drift from my satisfied mind. It truly was a wall that could not be breached.

CHAPTER 70

WAX ON (FOR BETTER, FOR WORSE)

THE BODIES on the large bed are beautiful. Hubert and Tamsin are locked in the kind of embrace one would expect from two people whose wedding reception clothes lay strewn on the hotel room floor. The kisses are as passionate as they were when they met two years ago. The heat passed between them as hot! In the luxurious room, the recently married pair is poised for a night of lovemaking.

Hubert is on his back. With her legs on either side of him Tamsin sits on his belly, his erect cock less than an inch from her ass. She leans forward and plants a deep kiss on his mouth, running her fingers over his arms and then locking her fingers in his. Then her hands are past his and she is breast to chest with him. A second later she is tying a silk scarf around his wrist rather tightly. She extends the silk to the wrought iron headboard behind him and in a slick movement she has him bound by the wrist to the bed. Tamsin smiles with her eyes as his register panic and she works a string of kisses down to his cock where she takes her time sucking on his delicious, full head.

She is almost serpentine as she slithers back up to his

face, her body back on its original perch half an inch from his cock. Her mouth on his, her hands over his arms and then locked in his, she gives his fingers a solid squeeze before moving past them and finding the second scarf under the pillow. His only resistance again is in his eyes, but he lets Tamsin tie his second hand to the wrought iron, between what looks like a goat and a rather large bunch of grapes. His panicked eyes watch her slither back down, past his cock, and settle her tongue on his bulging balls. She licks and sucks the sack all at once, and Hubert is caught between wanting her to continue and wondering what comes next.

He doesn't have to wonder long. With an almost sinister look in her eyes, a look softened only by the beauty of her face, Tamsin ties Hubert's legs to either of the base posts. She sticks to the same silk scarves, soft against his skin, but the knots are solid. With her man bound now, Tamsin pulls some oil from the side of the bed, and pours it over his chest and legs. The liquid is warm, unexpectedly. She works it over his body and then proceeds to give him the deepest, most sensual full frontal massage. She doesn't avoid his cock, giving his nine inches special attention. She also enjoys the new slippery feel of his massive sack. Her fingers work into him, loosening up all the recently created tension so that Hubert no longer feels compelled to query her plans for him on this their wedding night.

With her man relaxed, Tamsin is off him again. She lights the thick scented candles on the bureau and places them next to the bed. The lights are then dimmed to very low and she again perches herself on Hubert, this time sitting directly on his cock, sandwiching it between her pussy and his groin. Her breasts are on his chest as she gives him deep, tongued kisses. Tamsin has just her mouth on his, her one hand rubbing the side of his face as the other one reaches for the side of the bed. Upon rising, she has one of the candles in her hand. Immediately the panic is back in his eyes, and on the rest of his face. Tamsin runs the base of the candle over his chest, Hubert straining to see how close the wax is to spilling over, and onto him!

Tamsin plants the candle in the center of Hubert's chest and gets off him slowly. He breathes very slowly so as not to upset the candle that could pour quite a load of hot, melted wax on him and then roll onto the bed and set the whole thing on fire. She finds a tub in her bag and takes very slow steps towards Hubert who is begging her with his eyes to take the candle off of him. She grabs hold of the candle without moving it, sucking on his cock instead so that he knows that this is going to be very good for him. Only once her lips release his dick and she climbs back on top of him does she take the candle off his chest. One hand layers his chest with the cream from the tub, a waxy white that smells like chocolate and *musk?!*

Moving her pussy up and down the length of his shaft, Tamsin sends pleasure sensations through every part of his body quickly. Despite his understanding now what is about to happen, the fear is overridden by the pulses feeding into his cock from her punani and being transmitted to his fingertips. She moves forwards and backward on his dick and then around and around. Hubert enjoys the heat coming from her but still wishes that his cock was inside her. He needs to get it inside her. But there is no control that he has over the proceedings so he hopes that this is part of the plan at some point. He smiles at the wicked glint in her eyes, wondering why this *vixen* had been hidden until now. Before he can say what's on his mind though hot wax falls across his chest and onto his nipples. He exhales as loud as he can without screaming.

Mouths join so as to silence Hubert. The wax on his chest cools and hardens quickly but he doesn't even notice with the fire moving through his cock. Tamsin is up again and teases the sides of his torso with the flame. Her fingers are behind her and on his balls, pulling hard on them and them feathering them. As soon as he starts to moan with pleasure she lets the wax fall on his chest again, over the first layers so that the *burn* is less intense. She avoids the areas of him that are covered in hair as she teases his skin with the flame again. Hubert is moaning, groaning, giggling, and whimpering throughout this assault. It's new, it's unexpected, it's a little scary, *and he loves it!*

Candle in hand she works herself between his legs. The flame is aglow now dangerously close to his cock as she holds the candle against his balls. He laughs loudly to mask his true feelings. She tells him all she needs to reassure him and then drops a line of wax just below the head of his cock. The hot white runs down his cock fast and over his balls. It hardens before it has a chance to fall off and onto the bed. Over and over she coats his cock in the wax and pretty soon Hubert is keenly anticipating the heat. He wants more and more of it as the fire becomes a warm hug and then a tight squeeze as the wax dries. It takes a minute, but soon every part of his cock except its tip is waxed white. She bites into his thigh as he mouths requests for her cunt.

Satisfied that the wax is dry, she takes his cock in hand and gives it a gentle squeeze. The coating crumbles easily off his cock and then off his balls as they too find themselves between her fingers. Hubert's tool is slightly redder than usual but no worse for wear. She takes it into her mouth and gives it a serious sucking that proves even hotter than the wax. He thrusts into her mouth and again makes a more audible request for her pussy. She can't keep him waiting much longer. He is her husband and shouldn't have to ask twice. Tamsin straddles his cock, facing away from him towards his feet, and starts to fuck him hard.

She continues to fuck him, ignoring his giggles and screams as she rains wax over his legs. With both his legs very well coated she pivots on his dick so that she is facing him now and continues to fuck him, riding him in long strides that drag on his cock quite extensively. She has his cock tucked tight inside her and she is willing it, and the rest of him to do whatever she wants. The wax on his chest runs off the older crusts to find new skin and again there are ecstatic screams. The flame melts some of the wax as Tamsin lets it linger longer on his skin. The wax in the candle is soon all on Hubert's chest, so while she waits for some more to melt, she rides her man's cock in a million *thank you* strokes from her fanny.

Reaching for the second candle she holds them both in her hands. Hubert is thrusting into her carefully so as not to upset her balance and have the wax on him prematurely. Tamsin gives him a final frustration by placing both candles on his chest and reaching back for his sack. She pulls hard on his balls while he uses only his cock to fuck her. Tugging on his balls arouses Hubert so much that he forgets that he has burning candles on his chest and he fucks Tamsin harder. He starts to fuck her so hard that she has to make a quick grab for the candles or risk losing the wax. She gives them a quick inspection and sees that there is a considerable amount of wax now in both candles ready to be poured.

Gentle gyrations bring her to her own orgasm. As she starts to cum she leans forward and lets some wax fall onto Hubert, who immediately starts fucking her towards the ceiling now that he knows that the wax has come into play. Her cunt beats over his pulsating cock and soon he too is in the throes of a climax. The wax is left to fall where it will now and the candles are soon dry, extinguished, and tossed. Tamsin's pussy milks his cock while the wax dries on his chest, and they both reach the apex of their orgasms. Hubert screams a thousand proclamations of love at the completeness of his orgasm and Tamsin is pleased that this other side of her is acceptable to her husband.

They had said for better or worse, and Tamsin proved to be the *worst* kind of dominatrix. She took Hubert on a trip that opened up their sex lives for the rest of their lives. He is exhausted now, a mass on the bed beside his wife who looks at him with love and appreciation, glad that he can handle her punishment. She knows it won't be on the regular, Hubert being the old-fashioned lovemaking kind of guy. But at least she knows that he is open to the occasional session. In fact, he is excited by this new facet so quickly introduced into their marriage. Even as he sleeps he dreams fondly of silk bonds, biting and burning wax...

CHAPTER 71

WOULD YOU LIKE FRIES WITH THAT (IN THE MOMENT – PUBLIC)

GINGER LANCASTER and her husband were the average couple that loved to try new and exciting places to have sex. They actually went around looking for places that they felt would be perfect for having an encounter in public. One of their most recent was on top of a roof during the office party at Ginger's company. The cold temperatures caused Ginger's nipples to be erect for a long time and made the experience a lot more interesting and intense. They would have got away with it had one of the employees not seen them and went to tell management. It was lucky for Ginger that her boss was an open-minded guy. He managed to just laugh off the situation.

Ginger and Kirk had stopped at a local fast food restaurant and decided to grab some lunch before heading back home with all of the stuff that they had bought. All was going well with lunch when Ginger got a wicked idea in her head. She began to sit there and play with Kirk's crotch under the table with her foot. Ginger knew how to get the attention of her husband and get him interested in sex without a moment's notice. She knew that doing this was the button that once pushed was going to drive him over the edge. Ginger looked at Kirk and told him to meet her in the men's bathroom in five minutes.

Kirk knew that this was going to lead to a wild sexual encounter. Ginger never had sex in a restaurant public bathroom. She had sex in the employee bathroom when she was a server but she and Kirk had never had the chance to do it in the view of restaurant patrons.

Ginger made her way to the bathroom and got ready for her husband to appear and to ravish her. She had taken her top off and had tossed her bra over the door of the bathroom to let Kirk know what stall she was in. As expected; Kirk came in and opened the door to see his wife naked and sitting on the toilet fingering herself and playing with her clit. Kirk loved to watch Ginger get into the act of masturbating with herself. It was a sure fire thing that if Ginger was wanting Kirk to get hard and fully erect, that all she had to do was begin to play with her pussy and he was putty in her hands. Kirk walked into the stall and took his hand and placed a couple of fingers into her slit and began to tease her clit and drive her mad with the actions that he was performing. The cunt of his wife was so wet and tight. Kirk took time to make sure that he was careful with how he did things and did not want to make too much of a ruckus. She was getting worked up in hopes that a crowd would gather on the outside of the stall and watch as her husband took and plowed her tight hole with his large fuck stick.

Kirk walked up and took his member and teased putting it in by placing the tip of it right against her hole and seeing what type of reaction that he was able to get from her. Kirk looked at his wife and began to throb at the sight of her cunt lips quivering in hopes that he was soon going to be raiding her hole and making her scream. A couple of men came into the restroom and were trying to not pay any attention to the show. The crowd began to grow as a couple of men walked over and saw what was going on and became interested.

Kirk's cock was awesome and filled her hole just the right amount. Kirk felt the sides of her cunt grab onto his cock and began to pulse in helping him with the effort of fucking his wife. Ginger began her low moans at first, Kirk knew that before long the low moans were going to grow into a much louder moan and that before long people in the waiting line would hear her screaming out in pleasure. Kirk reached down and began to play with her nipples. Ginger was encouraging this, as she wanted him to pound her rough and to not be gentle about it. Today it was about down and dirty sex. All that was important was that Ginger got the screwing that she was seeking out and that she had a large crowd watching

The screwing became more intense and so did the sounds that were coming from Ginger. She was not doing this on purpose, it was truly just how loud she got when it came to having sex. Ginger was a very loud woman. All she cared about was that she got what she wanted when she wanted it. Finally, Kirk was finished and had given the men that were all gathered their reward for staying there and watching the show. Kirk pulled out of his wife and placed a couple of large loads on the tits of his wife. Ginger finished off by licking off all of the jizz that had been planted on her erect nipples. After this, Kirk and Ginger were banned from the restaurant. Ginger learned that way and that the Golden Arches were a little more golden for her.

CHAPTER 72

YOU HAVE THE RIGHT TO REMAIN SILENT

TODD AND SARAH JACKSON were an average married couple. They both allowed their lives to get in the way of their marriage. Todd was an investment banker and Sarah was a therapist. Between the two of them, if they said five words a day, it was considered to be a long conversation. Deep down both of them loved one another. It was just that their jobs were always in the way

Sarah saw that things were going downhill. She tried on a number of occasions to talk to Todd and got the usual half-hearted response that he gave while he was focused on his computer. Sarah knew that if things kept going the way that they were, that they would wind up like all the other couples that they knew and would file for divorce. Sarah also knew that if she got divorced that her parents would never let her hear the end of it.

. . .

Sarah finally had enough. She was determined to take matters into her own hands and get through to Todd one way or another. She had devised a plan. She was going to spice things up if even for one night. She had a friend that ran a costume shop and she needed to borrow one of the costumes that he had. This was certain to be the thing that kick started a fire in their relationship.

Sarah decided that she was going to give Todd a surprise that he would never forget. She had cancelled all her appointments and went and rented a cop uniform. Sarah called Todd and asked him to come home, as there appeared to have been a break in at the house. Sarah knew that he would not pass on the opportunity to head home and make sure that the house was nice and secure. Todd loved that house and the things in it. Sarah actually thought that he loved the house more than he did her. Sarah got off the phone with Todd and set the other part of the plan into motion.

Sarah was dressed up in the cop's uniform and waited for Todd to come rushing into the house. That would be when the fun began. Sarah had taken great lengths to disguise herself. The idea was to seduce him and have him fuck the female officer not knowing it was his wife. Todd came home almost immediately and came into the house frantic about the report that his home had been broken into.

Todd came through the door and saw the female cop standing there writing down some stuff on a notepad.

"Excuse me officer, I got a call from my wife that my

house was broken into. Is everything okay?" Todd asked in a very concerned voice

"Sir you need to just settle down everything is fine, it appears that the alarm scared them off, however, my partner had to go pick someone up for questioning and left me here. I am awfully sweaty, is there a shower I can use to clean up so I can finish my shift?"

"Yeah right down the hall, my wife is at work so it should be okay. If I can help in any way please let me know. I am going to go and make sure that everything is okay in the house. Take your time I have towels in the closet inside the bathroom."

"Excuse me, sir, could you come in here and help me, I seem to be having difficulty in getting my bra unhooked." Todd came into the bathroom to help her. He undid the last hook when the officer turned around and allowed the bra to fall to the floor exposing her breasts. Todd was standing there taking in the sight of the young officer's perky tits. He had to admit that he was tempted to go over there and get a feel of them. Finally, Todd was not able to withstand it any longer, ran over to the officer, and grabbed a handful of her tits. What Sarah had not told Todd was that she had gone and had breast implants about a year earlier. Todd had never noticed as most nights Sarah was asleep by the time he got in and she always wore loose-fitting T-shirts.

Todd took advantage of the fact that the young officer's nipples were standing at attention. He went over and began to suck on them and twisting them to try to get the officer aroused and ready. She lowered her pants exposing her thong underwear. Pulling them to the side she began to finger her cunt. Finally, she walked into the running shower and began to frig herself with her back turned away from Todd. This gave Todd the chance to come over and undress and walk up behind her. He inserted his cock into her pussy. She gave a little gasp, as Todd reached around and grabbed a handful of her right breast. The officer began to work her fingers more and more. Todd no longer cared if Sarah came home or not. It had been a long time since he had such a mind-blowing sexual encounter. He loved his wife; he had just forgotten what it was like to be a man to her. He had decided that he was not going to tell Sarah about this but was also going to remember to take some time and tell her every day what she really meant to him and make more time for him and her to be a couple. Sarah was getting to the point that she was about to let loose all over the shower wall. Todd was about ready to pop. He thought about it and realized that he loved his wife too much and was about to pull out and tell the cop that he could not finish as it was not right to cheat on his wife.

Just as he was about to pull out, the cop pulled Todd close to her and whispered into his ear, "I love you sweetie and I will always be your little pumpkin seed." Todd was almost beside himself, it took a couple of minutes, but he realized that the woman in the shower was none other than his wife. Sarah and Todd from that moment realized that their jobs were not important enough to go and keep ignoring one another. They were determined to make the most out of every day.

ABOUT THE AUTHOR

Kellie Granier is an emerging erotica author of many erotica kinks and sub-genres. Be sure to check out other books and leave a review if this story got you hot!

Visit my blog at Kellie Granier Blog

Join my newsletter for exclusive Kellie Granier Newsletter

Sign up for Free Stories from Xplicit Press Authors

Xplicit Press Author Updates

Like Xplicit Press on Facebook

Follow Xplicit Press on Twitter

Readers: I want to expand a few of the stories to see where the characters can be explored further. If there are any of the stories that you would like to read more about again, I'd love to hear from you!

Keep In Touch
Kellie Granier
info@kelliegranier.com

www.ingramcontent.com/pod-product-compliance
Lightning Source LLC
Chambersburg PA
CBHW030624250626
47154CB00006B/1914